CSI:

CRIME SCENE INVESTIGATION™

SNAKE EYES
a novel

Max Allan Collins

Based on the hit CBS series "CSI: Crime Scene
Investigation" produced by CBS PRODUCTIONS, a
business unit of CBS Broadcasting Inc., and ALLIANCE
ATLANTIS PRODUCTIONS, INC.

Executive Producers: Jerry Bruckheimer, Carol
Mendelsohn, Anthony E. Zuiker, Ann Donahue, Naren
Shankar, Cynthia Chvatal, William Petersen, Danny
Cannon, Jonathan Littman

Series created by: Anthony E. Zuiker

POCKET
BOOKS

LONDON • SYDNEY • NEW YORK • TORONTO

An *Original* Publication of POCKET BOOKS

POCKET BOOKS, a division of Simon & Schuster, Ltd.
Africa House, 64–78 Kingsway,
London WC2B 6AH

ISBN-13: 978-1-4165-1134-2
ISBN-10: 1-4165-1134-2

This Pocket Books paperback edition September 2006

10 9 8 7 6 5 4 3 2 1

POCKET BOOKS and colophon are registered
trademarks of Simon & Schuster, Ltd.

Printed and bound in Great Britain by
Cox & Wyman Ltd, Reading, Berks

A CIP catalogue record for this boook
is available from the British Library.

AUTHOR'S NOTE

From the beginning, as an author of novels based on *CSI: Crime Scene Investigation*, I have followed the lead of the gifted creative team behind the show. As such, these novels have tended to lag behind the continuity of the television series.

This story takes place some time after the previous novel, *Killing Game* (2005), during the period when the CSI team had been split into two shifts . . . and just prior to the dramatic events that would bring this family of investigators back together.

I would also like to acknowledge my assistant on this work, forensics researcher/co-plotter **Matthew V. Clemens.**

Further acknowledgments appear at the conclusion of this novel.

M.A.C.

For the real CSIs of the LVMPD—
who sparked the idea of this novel

"It is completely unimportant.
That is why it is so interesting."

—Agatha Christie's HERCULE POIROT

"There is nothing like
first-hand evidence."

—Sir Arthur Conan Doyle's SHERLOCK HOLMES

"I knew it was a fight for life,
and I drew in defense of my brothers
and Doc Holliday."

—Wyatt Earp at the OK Corral inquest

THE MYTH OF THE GOLD RUSH has captivated the world since America's first post–Lewis and Clark westward move—when mountain men, prospectors, settlers, and gunfighters set out to explore a vast, unknown landscape in search of vast, unknown treasure.

Over the passage of time, that concept has changed only slightly: the gold rush rushes on, but the destinations have shifted—instead of Sutter's Mill or Deadwood or Tombstone, names like Romanov, The Sphere, or Platinum King await fortune-seekers.

Yes, the rush is still on, and those who wish to strike it rich—as always—find a way to make their journeys. No longer do wagon trains bump and bounce over the Oregon Trail, nor do horses sprint over the Great Plains; modern-day prospectors arrive at McCarran by way of airlines. In the wilds of Vegas, riders on mustangs have been replaced by those in Mustangs—not to mention Cherokee and Wrangler Jeeps, Eldorado Caddies, and Dodge Durangos, today's west echoing yesterday's.

Little has changed, however, about what the hopeful expect to find upon arriving in Las Vegas. Sin City—at least in the imaginations of travelers—still has more in common with the Old West towns of Deadwood and Tombstone than the chamber of commerce might care to admit. In their day, those wild and wooly boomtowns were regarded as wide open in a manner not unlike today's Las Vegas. Sex, gambling, booze, and the day's top entertainers could be found in both the notorious South Dakota mining camp and that infamous silver-mining boomtown in Arizona. And, no matter how family-friendly the chamber might paint it, a similar naughty playground awaits tourists in the Nevada desert . . . and not just in Vegas.

Fifty miles down Highway 95, south of Las Vegas (but still in Clark County), planted in Piute Valley, rests Boot Hill, Nevada—a hamlet of 5,654 (prior to the event at the Four Kings Hotel & Casino, that is) with even more in common with the wild boomtowns of the Old West.

Where Deadwood had Wild Bill Hickock and Tombstone boasted Wyatt Earp and Doc Holliday, Boot Hill traded on being the only western town in America to which all three of these gunfighters had, at one time or another, individually found their way. None stayed as long as six months, all traveling on to bigger and wilder adventures; but this bump in the desert road held a rare historical honor as the only place where every one of these Wild West superstars had stopped and stayed for a time and, before leaving the dusty gold camp, taken the trouble of reducing the population of Boot Hill while adding to the population of boot hill.

Perhaps not the greatest thing to build a town's reputation on—three famous gunfighters killing three unknown miscreants—but it had worked. Over the years, tourists had found their way to the off-the-beaten-path hamlet with its dubious place in the history of the Old West—guidebooks, unkindly if accurately, often referred to Boot Hill as "the poor man's Tombstone."

In the late '80s—1980s, that is—the tourist business had dried up, and Boot Hill found itself slinking toward a fate it had once narrowly avoided: becoming that commonplace historical footnote of the Old West, the ghost town. Boot Hill was shrinking by the day—at its peak, over ten thousand residents had made livings from the tourist and gambling trade. By 1991, the town's six casinos had dwindled to two; the only businesses to survive: one grocery, two gas stations, a bank, three restaurants, and a lightbulb factory.

Then the town invested municipal funds in the dot-com boom of the later '90s, and things started to turn around. The city fathers took that money and reinvested it in drawing tourists back—a museum; monthly reenactments of their famous gunfights; statues of Earp, Holliday, and Hickock in the park; even a strip mall—creating a small oasis on the road to that mirage of wealth, Las Vegas.

No one can yet say whether the incident at the Four Kings will prove a boon or deterrent to the future of Boot Hill, though certainly the poor man's Tombstone has finally found its OK Corral gunfight. The crime scene investigators of the LVPD, however, are neither sociologists nor prognosticators, and the only history that interests them most is the recent history inherent in a crime scene.

In Boot Hill, at the Four Kings, after the living are sorted from the dead, the CSIs' job was to sift the sands of evidence not for gilt, but the guilty. . . .

1

HERE IT WAS APRIL FOOL'S DAY, and Vanessa Delware was still in Boot Hill—some joke.

The petite, pretty brunette barely seemed old enough to enter the Four Kings Hotel & Casino, let alone be a seasoned dealer. Even with her shoulder-length hair tucked up in a businesslike bun, and black plastic-rimmed glasses that made her large blue eyes look even bigger, she might have been a high school kid, though she was in fact twenty-one, her tightly packed little body swimming in the white frilly shirt with red bow tie, and black tuxedo slacks.

At least dealers didn't have to wear the skimpy outfits the barmaids did, not that that stopped drunks from grabbing at her and making salacious remarks. If this were Vegas, that sort of thing wouldn't have been tolerated. And anyway, Vegas promised a better class of groper.

Yet, here she still was in Boot Hill, working second shift, just as she had been for most of the last year. But Vanessa had vowed long ago that she would get out of Boot Hill—growing up in a little bump in the road had been bad enough and contributed to the poor decision she'd made, putting out for a cute boy whose body piercings were many but whose prospects had been zero.

Pregnant at twenty, local girl Vanessa had found herself abandoned by her boyfriend—*ex*-boyfriend, the loser—and barely tolerated by her mother, who'd had enough trouble making her own ends meet since divorcing *her* loser husband when Vanessa was fifteen. Cody Jacks, a family friend who worked part-time at the Four Kings, had pulled some strings and helped Vanessa get the job. The casino was glad to train her—a pretty young dealer was a nice draw (nicer draw than most card players otherwise got).

She'd taken this small opportunity to heart and vowed to make her life as a single mother succeed.

The plan had been formulated in the hospital. She and Cyndi, her infant daughter, would be in Vegas by next Thanksgiving . . . which became next Christmas, then Valentine's Day, and now here it was April *Fool's* Day and she was still tossing cards in Boot Hill, not in a glitzy casino along the Strip.

Of course, working here, sort of apprenticing here, had been part of the plan (even a cute girl couldn't walk in off the street and get hired in a top casino without credentials, without skills). But *staying* this long *hadn't* been.

Oh, she made decent money, really good tips some nights, but always there were bills and more bills (babies were *expensive*), and she just could not seem to get enough saved for her and Cyndi to make that mere fifty-mile move up the highway.

She hated her situation; she felt stranded in the midst of her own life. Vegas was the promised land, so very close and yet always just out of reach. . . .

Usually around this time of day, the casino was empty, most tourists either having an early dinner or in their rooms resting before the night's attack on the gaming tables. Around her blackjack station, bells tinkled, whistles blew, and the slots made their various obnoxious noises over the piped-in country-western music, the whoosh of the air-conditioning, and the chatter of the gamblers who were scattered around the casino's convention center–size floor. The cacophony barely registered with Vanessa, who had long ago learned to tune it out. She concentrated on the cards . . . and the people.

Unlike on most days at a slow time like this, Vanessa found herself with three gamblers seated at every other chair of the seven places at her table. To her left, a fortyish fat man in denim shorts and a souvenir T-shirt ("Go to Boot Hill and Live!") constantly had to be reminded about the hand signals used in the game to aid security cameras in following the action. At center sat a younger guy, mid-thirties with a nice build and an okay face; beyond him, a busty middle-aged woman with weary features and dyed blond hair was clad in a beige sweater and tan skirt.

All three were losing—only the guy in the center seemed to have any idea how to play—and they were all chain-smoking. Vanessa knew she shouldn't be annoyed by that—heavy smokers were an occupational hazard—but why couldn't they have plopped down across the aisle at Laura's table? Laura smoked even more than *they* did!

No, they had to gather around Vanessa's table, constantly belching fumes in her direction; and what with the way they were losing, she had absolutely *no* tip to look forward to.

Even if she was the dealer, Vanessa felt like the *real* loser, on a day like this. . . .

"Hit me," the guy on the left said, hands on the table's edge.

"Sir . . . your hand signal?" she reminded him for what felt like the hundredth time (though the guy had been playing barely ten minutes).

The guy gave her a "sorry" shrug, made the proper gesture, and she hit his fifteen with a queen and busted him out of another five dollars, which she swept away as if it had never existed.

The younger center-seated guy offered up a sympathetic smile and tapped the table for a hit on his thirteen. She fed him a three, his smile got broader, then he tapped the table again and she busted his sixteen with a seven. His smile quickly disappeared, his body not far behind as he spun off the stool and stalked off.

The weary woman down at the end took a drag on her cigarette and decided to stand on her fifteen after watching what had happened to her compatriots. Flipping her hand, Vanessa showed a seventeen and sucked up the chips from the woman, just as she had with the other two.

Scanning the room slowly, she mindlessly dealt another round to the two losers. Even though she gave them an empty smile with each card, she was paying them only the barest attention now as her eyes caught a group across the casino, a regiment of leather-clad bikers emptying from the three elevators—the Predators.

Here for the annual Boot Hill Biker Blowout, the Predators had been spending one week a year in town for as far back as Vanessa could remember. Many retailers had ceased to see the advantage of having several-hundred-plus rowdy bikers around, even if they *were* pumping money into the local economy. She'd on more than one occasion overheard some merchants bitching that the Biker Blowout was turning their "fair city" into Boot Hell.

Hypocritical jerks, Vanessa thought. The city fathers gladly accepted the bikers' money, only to constantly complain about the gangs and the sort of trouble they brought with them.

"'Nother card, honey?" the bottle blonde asked, sighing smoke in Vanessa's direction.

"Sorry," Vanessa said, and managed a smile and a card for each: the heavyset T-shirt guy a seven to go with his nine, the woman mumbling an obscenity as Vanessa dealt her a five to go with her eight.

T-shirt Guy studied his hand for a long moment, said, "Stay," then at the last minute remembered to wave his hand for the benefit of the camera.

As she dropped the last card on the bottle blonde's hand, Vanessa saw the group of maybe twenty Predators moving across the casino floor in her general direction. After a moment, the woman motioned for a hit and Vanessa dropped a queen on her hand and busted the woman out.

The bottle blonde seemed just about to say something when the Predators started fanning out around the table. She and T-shirt Guy seemed to suddenly have somewhere else to be, and gathered up what was left of their chips and scurried away.

With proprietary swaggers, the four Predators sat down at Vanessa's table. The two in the middle she recognized as Nick Valpo—the Predator leader himself—and his second-in-command, Jake Hanson.

Vanessa had known guys like these all her life— hell, her baby's father would have fit in with the Predators. And she didn't mind them—really. One at a time, they could be fine. They could be nice.

In groups, however, they could be . . . a handful. Particularly when they had eyes glistening with the dullness of drink.

Of the half-dozen security men in the casino at this hour—late afternoon, fairly light security staffing, a few more in the video room—the only one Vanessa's eyes sought out was Cody.

A Boot Hill police officer, Cody Jacks moonlighted at the Four Kings, as did virtually every cop on the force. Cody was a big, tough, dependable bruiser whom she could count on to keep the peace.

Finally, she spotted him over near the slots, his eyes glued to her table, even though he was mostly out of sight. He wore the silly red sport coat of the male floor employees—black slacks, white shirt with a black string tie. Already she felt comforted, knowing he was looking out for her.

Tall, with lupine gray eyes, Jacks may not have been the hardbody he was twenty years ago (why hadn't her mother married *him*?), but he still provided an imposing figure. Sure, his hair had grayed at the temples, and his waistband hung farther south than it used to.

But Cody Jacks could still lay down the law; and that feeling calmed Vanessa.

Not that she was really worried about Valpo, Hanson, or any of the other Predators, for that matter. All the years the Blowout had been going down, the motorcycle gang had never started any *real* trouble in either of Boot Hill's casinos or any of its several saloons.

Oh, yeah, of course, some fights here, some drunken partying there, a couple of broken slot machines; but stuff like that happened in a gambling town whether a motorcycle gang was around or not.

Her concern—and no doubt Cody's, too—was the Rusty Spokes, another motorcycle gang that had been regularly attending the Biker Blowout for the last couple of years.

A Phoenix outfit that seemed to go out of its way not to get along with the Predators, the Spokes had infringed a little more on the Predators' turf all week, at every turn.

Tensions were running high.

The Predators were staying at the Four Kings, technically, but not really—their rooms were strictly for partying; the gang kept its HQ at a campground on the south edge of town.

The Spokes, meanwhile, had taken up residence at the Gold Vault, the casino motel directly across the street from the Four Kings. A certain antagonism between the two casinos underscored the rivalry between the motorcycle crews.

Fistfights and worse had been going on all week. Around the casino, rumor had it that the Rusty Spokes planned to force a showdown with the

Predators and had designated Boot Hill to host the action.

While Vanessa would have liked to dismiss the rumor as paranoid b.s., she knew it made a sick sort of sense. After all, Phoenix had too big a police force to risk a showdown, and the Predators seemed to have no fixed home, bouncing between dozens of small towns in California, Nevada, and Arizona. Both groups knew that Police Chief Jorge Lopez had only a small force in Boot Hill, and that the nearest Highway Patrol substations in Jean (to the northwest) and Laughlin (to the southeast) were both over thirty miles away.

The only real police force of any size was the Las Vegas Police Department, the nation's ninth largest . . . but that, as Vanessa knew only too well, was a world away, fifty miles from Boot Hill.

Two nights ago (and this was no rumor) Chief Lopez and three of his officers had broken up what appeared about to turn into a nasty knife fight between the two factions (her coworker Laura had said, "It's a real powder keg, I tell ya, Vannie . . . and it's *lit*!").

She'd talked to Cody about it just before her shift started.

"Should be cool," the older man said. "Jorge put the fear of God in 'em. Past twenty-four hours, Spokes and Predators been avoidin' each other like the plague."

"Really?"

Cody nodded. "Tomorrow, Blowout's over, and these fellas'll be on the road back home. Like the song says, 'head out on the highway, lookin' for adventure.'"

And, across the room, Cody was giving Vanessa a reassuring smile. She gave him a little nod, then turned her attention to the Predators at the table.

The first one on the left, long brown hair swept straight back, wore worn jeans, a white T-shirt under an Army shirt with the sleeves ripped off, and that same smart-ass smirk that Vanessa had seen on a hundred bullies. Though thinner and younger, he reminded her of that weird-hair guy from *The Sopranos,* the one in Springsteen's band.

On his left sat the head Predator, Nick Valpo. Nearly fifty, the shirtless Valpo sported a black cotton vest, his skin frog-belly white, belying how much time he spent on his hog tearing across the desert. Two tattoos nestled in the hairy thatch on his chest— over the right breast, a dagger pierced a heart, blood drops trailing down his torso (allegedly one for every man he had killed), and center-chest a caricature of himself with the words "Ride Or Die" emblazoned beneath it peered from between dark curls.

Like his underling, Valpo wore his hair combed straight back, which emphasized his widow's peak, showing shiny skull where some balding betrayed his age. A black goatee, three or four inches long, looked like an odd sponge hanging from the leader's chin—a clownish effect that was nonetheless intimidating, perhaps due to Valpo's seemingly black, burning eyes.

To Vanessa, the Predator leader looked like Charles Manson on crank; on the other hand, during the several times he'd sat at her table this week, he'd been nice, even sweet to her, and not in a coming-on-to-her way.

Next to Valpo, his chief lieutenant, Jake Hanson, provided a contrast to his buddies, his jeans relatively new, white T-shirt cleaner, and an unbuttoned blue-and-white short-sleeved shirt, not a ratty vest. Hanson had soft blue eyes that reminded Vanessa of a mountain stream. The others were definitely bikers, but Jake Hanson might have been a rock star.

The final Predator of the quartet wore his dark greasy hair parted crookedly near the middle and had a skinny black beard and mustache, possibly intended to make him look older, though the effect was the opposite. He might have been a high school thespian who'd glued on a beard for a role. Vanessa probably should have carded the kid, but why push it with this bunch? Like Cody said, tomorrow they'd be going, going, gone.

"What're you waitin' for?" the bearded kid asked irritably. "Deal, bitch!"

Valpo shook his head, eyes narrowed, and gave her a warm, apologetic smile. "Vanessa, he's young. Be patient with his young ass. . . . Dicky, shut the hell up and treat her like the lady she so obviously is."

Vanessa nodded her nervous thanks to Valpo and dealt. The first guy busted and Valpo got a blackjack.

"Surprise, surprise," Dicky said from the far end.

Holding his breath for a long moment, Valpo seemed to be concentrating on something somewhere in the distance; then his eyes found Dicky's and held them, snake and mouse.

"Dicky, I swear to Christ, if you don't shut it, I'm gonna take you outside and beat the ever-livin' piss out of you myself till your manners improve."

"Ah, come on, dude—"

"Dude. I don't care if your mom's my cousin or not. Be nice to the dealer. Try to remember you're indoors."

Hanson held on nineteen and Dicky managed to start out with nine and still find a way to bust.

"Daaaamn!" Dicky yelped.

Vanessa turned over an eighteen. "Paying a blackjack and a winner." Her eyes caught the blue-eyed Hanson's, and when she passed over his winnings their hands brushed for an instant.

God, he is cute, she thought. *Who does he remind me of?*

"I can't believe this crap," Dicky groused. "Is there any other kinda luck but bad luck in this town?"

Valpo shot him a glare and Dicky went silent. "Here's a thought, sunshine—don't hit on seventeen and maybe you won't lose every damn time."

"You think I don't know how to play cards?" Dicky challenged. "I know how to play cards."

Laughing, Valpo said, "I *know* you *can't* play cards. You can barely play with yourself . . . Dicky bird."

Dicky reddened, but Hanson and the other guy joined Valpo's laughter and nothing was left but for Dicky to take it: he was the kid, Valpo the man.

Vanessa was working not to join in the laughter when she looked toward the front door and beheld an unsettling sight.

Twenty or so Rusty Spokes were rolling into the casino like a bad wind.

That put a chill up Vanessa's spine, and her eyes immediately darted around looking for Cody, for *any* security guy. . . .

She caught Cody, already moving toward the door. But as she turned to see what the Spokes were going to do, guns—as if from nowhere—seemed to appear in all of the intruders' hands. Revolvers, shotguns, rifles . . . was that a *machine* gun? Jesus!

The first shot was fired before Vanessa could utter a sound.

Her mind managed to form the thought, *What about the damn metal detectors?*

But that was as far as she got before Jake Hanson leapt over the table and swept her into his arms. They rolled to the floor and Vanessa looked up just as bullets from the machine gun ripped into her table, tossing splinters like a dealer flipping cards.

Instinctively, she turned her head away and found herself staring into the blue eyes of Jake Hanson, who still held her. His face seemed peaceful even as hell exploded around them.

Mouth to her ear, as if kissing it, he yelled, "Are you okay?"

That's what it took for her to hear the words over the din of the gunfire.

She nodded. He released her from his grip, and the fear hit her harder—she had felt safe, somehow, cocooned in his arms. He flashed a smile, winked, rolled away, rose to a crouch, and moved off.

The smell of shooting filled the air, making her choke. Gun smoke and stirred dust and wood fragments clouded the room and, cowering behind and flush against the bullet-riddled blackjack table, Vanessa felt like this might go on forever—already it seemed like forever since she had turned to see the Rusty Spokes entering the casino and those guns materializing and yet still the guns clattered, some of the Predators now returning fire.

How in God's name had this many guns made it past the metal detectors?

Around her, other patrons, the ones on the floor in fear, those not part of either gang, still had the wherewithal to gather up chips spilled around them by the battle. Nothing could kill greed.

Or anyway, nothing as inconsequential as a firefight in the middle of a casino.

She did not avert her eyes, much as she wanted to—she was not ready to shut the world out and just wait and hope and pray she would open her eyes without a bullet finding her first. The violence, the carnage, the destruction had the same hypnotic effect as being in a car crash and having the world go into slow motion. The heavyset guy in the Boot Hill T-shirt took a bullet in the chest and scarlet showered from the ripped logo as he keeled over backward, smacking his head on the corner of a slot machine as he went, which made Vanessa wince even though she knew the man might be dead before his head came anywhere near the machine. . . .

To her right came an explosive sound—*a grenade?*—and her eyes shot in that direction of their own volition. On the floor, in an aisle, a man twitched and danced, blood spurting from a hole in his right pants leg where his limb had been severed by the blast—shotgun, not grenade. He was screaming, but she could not hear him, or anyway discern distinctly the screaming out of the overall din. But she could tell he was bleeding to death, and she averted her eyes, finally taking control of them.

She could feel the wet warmth of tears on her cheeks and wondered, as if from a distance, why she was crying when she was not among the injured, one of the lucky ones in this unlucky casino.

Farther to her right, Jake Hanson was ducking behind a craps table, jamming a fresh clip into a huge black pistol. He then rose and fired several rounds in the direction of the Spokes and ducked down again.

To her left, maybe twenty feet away, the Predators' leader knelt behind a video poker machine. Every few seconds, he would peek out, squeeze off a couple shots, then dodge back behind the machine. When he turned toward her, he saw her watching him and flashed her a grin as if he was having a great time.

The insanity in that smile gave Vanessa an urge to jump up and run screaming from the room; but survival instinct overrode that. She kept her head down and did not move. As for Valpo, he still had that maniacal grin pasted on, though his wide eyes spoke of hysteria and fear.

Valpo leaned out from behind his cover, raised his pistol, and a crimson flower bloomed in his right shoulder, the gun springing from his grasp and bouncing out of reach under a table across an aisle where bullets zinged and pinged.

As Valpo fell sideways, back behind the poker machine, Vanessa finally picked out a sound other than general gunfire—*sirens*.

Whether they were near or far she could not tell, but help was clearly coming, the wailing getting louder by the second.

As if wanting to strike back before the local law arrived to stop their fun, Valpo scrabbled after the pistol, shots chewing up the carpeting and shaking machines till their coins rattled, bullets all around him as he dove for the weapon.

Just as Valpo got to the pistol, a ghostly figure moved through the smoke and dust and running people and came up behind the Predator leader, aiming a handgun at the back of the man's head. . . .

Vanessa saw the flash from the barrel more than she actually heard the sound.

She jumped, a full-body twitch, just as Valpo's body did much the same, the pistol dropping from his dead hand.

Vanessa felt herself screaming, but could not hear it. The shooter now turned to face her, lowered the gun toward her. The scream died in her throat and she followed the line of the gun barrel to the mad-man's eyes burning through her.

Her mouth dry now, she struggled to cry out, but no sound would come.

Vanessa suddenly felt that distanced, slow-motion sensation again. Almost serene, she prayed in the church of her mind that someone would take care of her daughter.

She knew she would not live through the next minute, let alone her shift. The house always wins, they say, but this time a dealer could lose.

Then, just as suddenly, the killer lowered the pistol and gave Vanessa a smile so gentle and sad that she knew she'd been reprieved, she knew she would see Cyndi again, after all.

"I'll never tell," she said, and averted her gaze, but guns were still firing, and no one heard her, not even herself.

Something slammed into her.

The breath left Vanessa's body and she felt herself toppling to one side—it was as if she'd been struck a blow.

But she had, indeed, been shot.

Her eyes went back to the killer, who turned away now, not meeting her wide-eyed amazement at his having reneged on the reprieve, shooting her after all, and she tried to inhale, but a rope must have been constricting her neck. The more she struggled, the less oxygen she seemed able to gulp down. Her side ached like she had a really bad bruise, but beyond that, all through her body, flowed a red hotness like swallowing a whiskey shot too fast . . . only the burning ran horizontally through her and warmed much more intensely.

Each breath was a greater struggle now.

Surprisingly, no real pain—the broken leg she got when she fell off a garage roof at twelve hurt a lot worse than this, way worse. Okay, she'd been shot, but wasn't sure it was so bad. You can recover from gunshot wounds—her ex-boyfriend had. Her baby's father. Her baby . . .

If only she could breathe. She was sure that would help. Somebody must have hit the air conditioner with a stray bullet, because it seemed to be running full tilt now, getting colder by the second. For a moment she caught the killer walking away and wondered if she'd have kept her promise, if it had been heard, if she'd been allowed to live.

Oh hell, she thought, *I hope it's not Mom who raises Cyndi,* and then even the coldness was gone.

2

Friday, April 1, 2005, 4:28 P.M.

CATHERINE WILLOWS WOULD HAVE RATHER kept a dental appointment than go to this meeting.

Maybe that's why she was cutting it so close—the 4:30 was at the other end of CSI headquarters, and she'd have to hustle to make it. She jogged up the hallway, her red hair trailing behind her trim dancer's frame.

Assistant Lab Director Conrad Ecklie, her boss, was a stickler about punctuality, beyond which this was not just *any* appointment: Ecklie, Sheriff Burdick, and graveyard-shift supervisor Gil Grissom were having a rare staff meeting to discuss inter-shift cooperation.

Everyone even remotely associated with the Vegas Crime Lab knew of the animosity between Ecklie and Grissom—which was remarkable in and of itself, because rarely had either man spoken a cross word to the other. Professionalism was something both men valued, as was public decorum, though Catherine considered the two to share the social skills of a dill pickle.

And, of course, she had worked the night shift herself for several years and had been Grissom's right hand until her promotion to supervisor of swing.

So she had a history with and loyalty for Gil; but Ecklie was the one who'd promoted her and for whom she worked on a daily basis—so those ties weighed on her, as well. She was not anxious to become the net in a tennis match between two strong-willed, passive-aggressive men.

And it wasn't like she didn't have anything *else* to do! Her shift was already shorthanded, due to Warrick taking a vacation day, plus two investigators with court dates and another investigator calling in sick. Basically, she had Nick Stokes, Sofia Curtis (borrowed from Grissom's shift), and herself. Oh yes, and a great big city called Las Vegas cooking up all sorts of crimes to solve. . . .

As she approached the glass-enclosed conference room, Catherine could see the others already inside.

A tight-eyed Ecklie—slender; balding; with alert hawkish features; his gray suit, white shirt, and blue tie immaculate (a sure sign his time in an actual lab was limited)—had taken the chair at the head of the table and left the corridor blinds open. A placid Grissom sat to Ecklie's right, facing her as she slowed to a walk near the door. At the other end of the table, a quietly unreadable Sheriff Burdick sat, a cup of coffee in one hand, his forehead in the other.

Allowing herself one deep breath, Catherine slipped into the conference room.

Ecklie glanced at his watch and then at her, but to his credit said nothing. A manila folder lay on the table in front of him like a restaurant place mat. She did not dislike this man, though in her night-shift "days" he had been the object of much coworker griping; now her personal experience indicated Ecklie to be fair and smart.

But his blind spot was Grissom, much as Grissom's was Ecklie—a classic crime-lab case of bureaucrat versus scientist. If she had a dollar for every conflict like this in every crime lab in the nation, she could retire tomorrow. . . .

Sheriff Burdick, his own suit almost as perfect as Ecklie's, gave Catherine a polite smile as she sat. Thinning brown hair clipped short, the sheriff had a quietly rugged way about him, with a certain gentleness in his calm brown eyes that drew voters' confidence, especially (the pollsters said) the female voters.

Catherine had long since proved immune to those eyes, but she respected this man, who backed the crime lab all the way. He seemed less prone to the politics of his recent predecessors.

Across from her, Grissom looked haggard—tiredness was a given for CSIs, and for a driven workaholic like Gil, a constant. But this was different. His hair, especially his beard, seemed grayer than she remembered, and his eyes looked puffy, like he hadn't been getting his usual, already limited hours of sleep.

Despite this, a tiny, barely perceptible smile lurked on his lips. Dressed in his customary black shirt and slacks, Gil Grissom, weary or not, somehow seemed in better spirits than either of the other men.

"Catherine," he said as she pulled her chair up. "Thanks for joining us."

Catherine said nothing, smiling, nodding, then waiting for Ecklie to start the meeting.

Only she soon realized it had already started, and the sheriff was driving the bus. . . .

Burdick's gaze focused on Grissom. "I just have one more thing to get off my chest. Gil, you don't make Conrad's job—or anyone else's, for that matter—any easier by pushing the political and public-relations ramifications of a case to the side."

Grissom could only nod.

"Just because you have the ability to remain objective, don't mistake the world for sharing it. Understood?"

"Yes, sir," Grissom said.

"And Conrad, you'll make an effort to treat Grissom in a fair and impartial manner. Understood?"

"Understood, Sheriff."

"You're two of the best. If you ever got on the same page, do you have any idea how much we could accomplish?"

Catherine supressed a smile. These two strong men—the scientist and the bureaucrat—were sitting with their heads slightly lowered, like two kids a principal had put in their respective places.

"All right. Let's move on." Burdick turned to Catherine. "Can't *you* make these two get along?"

She smiled and shrugged. "How would you say I'm doing so far, sir?"

After a chuckle and shake of his head, Burdick was about to move forward on the meeting agenda, when Nick Stokes burst into the room.

"Yes?" the sheriff said, surprised at the intrusion.

"Sorry," Nick said. "I know I'm interrupting, and I apologize—but we have a big one. Real trouble."

A buff former Texas A&M football player with close-cropped dark hair, piercing dark eyes, and a heroic jaw, Nick was normally the epitome of cool—he did *not* excite easily. But right now, as he approached Grissom, planting himself between Gil and Conrad, the broad-shouldered CSI seemed pretty worked up.

That worried Catherine.

"What kind of trouble?" Burdick asked, resuming his position at the table.

"We got a major shoot-out between two motorcycle gangs, the Predators and the Spokes—that annual Biker Blowout at Boot Hill?"

"Damn," Catherine said.

"You haven't heard the really good part—it went down *inside* the Four Kings Casino."

Burdick put a hand to his head as if checking for a fever.

"Dead?" Grissom asked. "Wounded?"

Nick said, "I don't have all the facts yet, this is straight from Dispatch; but, yes, Gris, there are dead and there are wounded. Not just bikers but civilians—casino employees, tourists . . . sounds like they pretty much trashed the place. D-Day indoors."

"And that's our crime scene," Ecklie said gravely.

"All right," Burdick said, heading for the exit. When he got there, he turned and issued orders. "I'm going to call the governor—he's probably a heartbeat away from sending in the National Guard. Conrad, you get the crime scene team organized and on its way."

"Right now," Ecklie said, nodding.

Catherine stepped forward. "We need the media kept out for at least twenty-four hours. We'll have an extensive crime scene and a volatile situation with those two biker gangs."

"We can handle our end of that," Burdick said, "and I'll talk to the Highway Patrol . . . but anything you can do to encourage the local people to keep the lid on will tell the tale."

Burdick left and the others turned to Ecklie.

"If it'll help," Grissom said to Ecklie, "I'll go—Catherine's shift is shorthanded."

"Good idea, Gil," Ecklie said.

The graciousness seemed strained, Catherine thought, but at least Ecklie was trying.

"This is a unique situation," Ecklie was saying. "Possible mass injuries and deaths to rival a plane crash. And as Catherine says, a high-profile case that'll attract media attention. I need my best people, so I appreciate your offer, Gil. You'll go."

"Good," Grissom said.

"I want Stokes, Sofia, and Catherine there, too," Ecklie said. "Gil, call in Sidle from your shift."

"No problem."

"Catherine, you'll be in charge."

She sneaked a glance at Grissom, but he seemed to accept this as a matter of whose shift was on duty and not an Ecklie put-down.

Ecklie was saying, "Catherine, call Brown in for me, would you? His vacation day is canceled. Gil, better get Sanders in here early, too."

Grissom frowned. "Conrad, I don't think we need him. Somebody has to hold down the fort."

"I agree. My intention is that Sanders will work with Brown, here in the city. Better divide up the calls—Gil, I'll ring Sidle for you."

Warrick Brown, Sara Sidle, and Greg Sanders were fellow LVPD crime scene investigators—Warrick on

Catherine's team, Sara and Greg from Grissom's shift.

They all started moving at once, cell phones coming out, speed dialers in play, and gravitated to different corners of the room so they could hear themselves, leaving Nick standing alone by the door, the messenger who'd started all this having nothing to do at the moment.

Five minutes later, the little group huddled around Nick again.

"Sara will be here in twenty minutes," Ecklie said.

Grissom added, "Greg's on his way, too."

"Warrick will be here in ten," Catherine said. "Nick, get the trucks loaded. Gil, you want to collect Sofia?"

Nodding, Grissom went out the door in search of his team member. Nick followed him out, leaving Catherine alone in the conference room with Ecklie.

The assistant lab director put a hand on her shoulder. "Wrap this up quick, Catherine. This could be a real problem."

"Sounds like it already *is* a problem," she said, finding the remark odd.

His eyes narrowed. "Aside from any injuries and loss of life, the potential for disaster here is imminent. If CNN gets a story about a gunfight in a casino—with motorcycle gangs!—the public won't care whether it's Boot Hill or Fremont Street. Once they hear *Nevada,* the tourists will stay away in droves."

Catherine was glad Grissom hadn't heard that. She had a tolerance for political views like this one, where the lives of human beings seemed secondary in importance to tourism concerns, but the goodwill the politician and scientist had shared in the wake of the sheriff's reprimand would likely have been short-lived had Gil been privy to that PR speech.

Twenty minutes later, two dark, sleek SUVs pulled out of the CSI parking lot, dashboard-mounted emergency lights flashing as they made their way east on Charleston Boulevard to Decatur Boulevard, then north to Highway 95 and the long looping trip south to Boot Hill.

Nick drove one SUV with Catherine in the passenger seat. Sara Sidle—the striking brunette's hair tucked up under a CSI ballcap—was at the wheel of the other, Grissom in the passenger seat and blond Sofia Curtis in the back.

On the highway, Nick barreled along but could have made better time if people got out of the way. Not particularly wanting to die prematurely of a heart attack, Catherine had, over the course of her years on the job, trained herself not to yell at motorists who refused to pull over when they saw the alternating red and blue flashing lights.

Drivers always seemed to move over for ambulances and fire trucks, but most went brain-dead when it came time to pull over for the cops. Why that was, she had no idea; but it was one of the little-known truths of the job.

They were maybe halfway into the forty-five-minute trip when they got a radio call from Burdick.

"*Jorge Lopez is the police chief out there,*" Burdick's voice told them. "*A good man. You shouldn't have any problem with him cooperating.*"

"What about the Guard?" Catherine asked.

"*I don't have to tell you about the shortage of personnel,*" the sheriff said.

Sixty percent of the Nevada National Guard was deployed overseas.

"*By the time the governor gets you any help,*" Burdick was saying over the radio, "*you probably won't need it. Half a dozen state troopers are there or en route, but you know they're scattered to hell and gone, too.*"

"What about our people?"

"*We're spread too thin, too,*" Burdick said. "*It's mostly going to be you guys and the locals. But, as I say, Chief Lopez is terrific, and he has strong people. We'll maintain media blackout as long as possible. Good luck.*"

The sheriff signed off.

Nick flicked a glance at Catherine. "Yeah—good luck to us."

The two black vehicles rocketed down the highway, Nick barely keeping the speedometer below one hundred. Once away from the metropolitan area, traffic thinned, though the highway was not deserted: they passed eighteen-wheelers, a few cars, and at one point, just south of Searchlight, both SUVs slid to the right lane to let a Nevada Highway Patrol car buzz by.

The state cop was definitely not holding his speed under a hundred. . . .

"Nice to know the Patrol'll beat us there."

Nick grinned. "Not by much."

"From Primm Substation, Jean Substation, maybe."

Nick said, "You'd think a bunch of the Highway Patrol guys from Laughlin'll make it over there quickly."

"If not," Catherine said, "no telling *what's* going on in Boot Hill. Those two gangs might still be going hot and heavy."

"Instead of a crime scene, we could be driving into a battlefield."

"D-Day, you said before. Maybe you were right, Nicky."

He grimaced. "Yeah, well in this case, I don't particularly hope to be. . . ."

They passed the wide spot in the road known as Cal Nev Ari—little more than a casino and a stop sign. The latter Nick blew through.

Catherine was on the radio now, trying to get a sit. report from Dispatch.

"*Lots of cross traffic on the Highway Patrol channel,*" the dispatcher said. "*Sounds like things have calmed down a little, but hard to tell.*"

"Thanks," Catherine said. "That's better news than it could've been. 3CSI out."

She replaced the microphone in its holder and sat back. "Gonna be a *looooong* shift, Nick."

"Think the bikers've all split town?" Nick asked.

She shrugged. "We'll know soon enough, but the cops are most likely way outnumbered by bikers. Be hard to round them all up."

"And *keep* them rounded up. Normally, the perps would head for the hills."

"Normally, Nicky? Based on all the other biker gang shoot-outs in casinos we've worked?"

He laughed at that.

But neither one of them really saw anything funny about what they were heading into. . . .

About halfway between Cal Nev Ari and the intersection with Highway 163 that led to Laughlin, Nick took a right onto a two-lane blacktop road.

The desert world this far outside Vegas looked more like a moonscape than Earth—rocks, sand, and the

at odd angles, one car blocking the street, its driv-
or standing wide open. Also on the street were
mbulances, their back doors open, their gurneys
ll of the vehicles had their light bars going. The
and EMTs, though, were nowhere in sight.

casinos, neither big enough to displace the
t Vegas Strip hotel, squatted on opposite sides of
eet, two broad-shouldered gunfighters getting
to shoot it out. The Gold Vault occupied the east
st south of a two-story building with a sign pro-
ng it THE OLD WEST MUSEUM & GIFT EMPORIUM. Six
with a parking garage to the south, the Gold
ppeared to be doing well enough.

oss the street, the Four Kings seemed to be faring
etter. Eight stories and taking up twice its rival's
the Four Kings could damn near have made the
n downtown Vegas.

y piled out of the Denalis and unloaded their
ven though it was early spring, in the shadow of
untains with a purple dusk settling, the town
at like a skillet. Whether it was the temperature
weather or the different kind of heat that gener-
l this violence, Catherine could not hazard a
he only knew that for this time of year, Nevada
naturally hot.

Hill, Nevada, anyway.

ive Vegas CSIs joined up behind Catherine and
ehicle. They were red in the blush of a big neon
a fanned-out poker hand revealing four kings
obscured kicker. Underneath, smaller signs ad-
an all-you-can-eat buffet and this week's enter-
t, a one-hit wonder band from the early '70s
be had one original member.

occasional plucky green plant doing its best to hang on in this harsh environment, where the summer temperature would regularly reach 120 or higher, at which point even the snakes looked to cop some shade. With all the hills and valleys out here, Boot Hill wasn't readily visible from Highway 95; but before long, going down the two-lane, the outlines of the town's buildings could be made out in the distance against the background of the mountains to the west and south.

Driving in from the east, still a couple of miles away, the onset of twilight began to give the poor man's Tombstone a surrealistic cast—from here, the place looked to Catherine like a miniature movie set from a Godzilla movie, maybe.

Nearing the town, Boot Hill gained scale, of course, but the movie-set feeling would not let Catherine go. Blue Highway Patrol cars, red lights flashing, sat at angles blocking the road; no one was being allowed in or out of town. Well, they never were in a science-fiction film, right?

Nick slowed as he neared the roadblock and a Highway Patrolman with a shotgun at his side waved for Nick to stop. Catherine counted three more Highway Patrolmen on the scene: two were on the opposite side of the road, one on either side of their car, preventing anyone from leaving to the east. As the shotgun-toting Patrolman came toward the Denalis, his partner remained on the other side of the vehicle, which would provide cover should anything go wrong at the checkpoint.

Normally, the flashing lights would have gotten the CSIs a wave-through. But with two motorcycle gangs shooting up a casino, "normal" was not an operative term, and Catherine didn't blame these guys for being cautious.

The Patrolman nearing Nick's window was a burly guy whose frame had probably been plenty muscular twenty years ago (maybe even ten); but now, the man had gone soft around the middle. His face, however, hadn't gone soft at all; under a sand-colored crewcut, he had on seriously dark sunglasses and a surly frown.

"Las Vegas Crime Lab," Nick said, showing the Patrolman his ID.

"We need all the help we can get," the officer said, his voice friendly though the frown remained.

Leaning toward the driver's side, Catherine asked, "How bad?"

The Patrolman seemed to notice her for the first time; he bent down a little more. "Shooting seems to be over, at least for now. But everybody within ten miles of here is pretty edgy."

"Town under control?"

"Good guys in charge," the Patrolman said. "For now, anyway."

"Possible it could go the other way?"

A tiny shrug from the big officer. "Lots of tension . . . and there's nowhere big enough to lock up everybody on both sides. We're way outnumbered. Chief Lopez has the town locked down."

"How many officers does he have?"

The Patrolman said, "Counting his detectives, eight . . . ten, when two more off-duty guys are rounded up."

"And you state boys?"

"Four of us here. Four more at the west end of town,

even though that blacktop peters mountains."

Nick said, "Well, there's five of

For the first time, a glimmer of trolman's face. "You Vegas CSIs p

"We do," Catherine said, and N

"Good to hear. Every little bit h

Nick asked, "Where's the casin

The Patrolman pointed. "Ther across the street from each other. into town, go two blocks, then l casinos are in the first block."

Catherine said, "Thanks, Office

"No problem." He backed av dow and waved to his partner, car and backed it out of the w car was on the shoulder, the the SUVs through and they r Boot Hill.

The town seemed to have fina ghost town. Deserted streets ga the whole population had gone ally a venetian blind or curtai only sign that the inhabitants ha doors. The Denalis moved west edge of town. As they passed th looked down the corridor of bu The only movement was a down, slowly rolling in their di

"Cue the tumbleweed," Nick

Allen Street, the next block Here three squad cars and a Bl words POLICE CHIEF stenciled

"No police in sight," Grissom said. "You know what that means."

Catherine nodded and frowned. "They're tromping through our crime scene."

"*Your* crime scene," Grissom reminded her, and his tiny smile held not one hint of condescension. "How do you want to play this?"

"Let's see our cards first, and then decide."

"That's a good policy."

Crime scene kits in hand, they strode toward the row of six glass doors at the Four Kings. Catherine could hear more sirens in the distance.

One of the six front doors had shattered, glass scattered across the sidewalk like broken, punched-out teeth. The team picked the door farthest from that and entered. The air-conditioning hit them like a refreshing breeze.

What they beheld was anything but refreshing.

"God in heaven," Sofia said softly, shaking her head.

"This wasn't a gunfight," Nick said, wincing. "This was a goddamn war zone."

Around them only the five remaining glass doors looked like they were part of a casino. The rest of the huge room was like nothing Catherine had ever seen. She'd worked her share of shoot-outs in the past—gang violence was not unknown on her Vegas beat—but none of those had amassed anything remotely like this sort of destruction.

The stench of cordite permeated the air, as did dust motes, and bodies were cast about the floor like discarded refuse among the knocked-over and broken, bullet-riddled slot machines; chips, glass shards, and bloodstains mingled on the patterned carpet.

Four EMTs from the two ambulances were scattered

around the room, each attending to his or her own patient. Professionally soothing conversation and occasional moans and cries pierced an otherwise ominous silence, the eerie aftermath of tragedy in which Catherine could almost hear the echo of gunfire. Three Boot Hill police officers were providing first aid for a trio of victims, and a wide berth was given to two bodies, obviously dead.

In a snack bar off to the right—where cartoony cut-out images of cowboys, Indians, and gunfighters jovially rode the walls—four more uniformed officers and two detectives were taking statements from a shell-shocked group . . . probably patrons of the casino during the shoot-out.

Near the entrance to the snack bar stood three men: a beefy guy, about fifty, wearing black slacks, a white shirt, and a red suit jacket with the Four Kings logo over the left breast; a fortyish fellow wearing a charcoal suit that accentuated a pasty complexion; and a tall, thin Hispanic man with slicked-back black hair and a hawk nose, police badge on a chain around his neck over a blue button-down shirt tucked into worn jeans.

When the three saw the CSI team, the Hispanic man headed over and the other two followed his lead. Catherine and Grissom were in front, colleagues fanned out behind. Catherine watched the leader trying to figure out which of them was in charge—but at least times had changed enough that the assumption that the man was the boss wasn't made . . . at least, not out loud.

Unable to make up his mind, the cop took a spot in front of and between Catherine and Grissom.

He extended a hand in their general direction. "I'm Police Chief Jorge Lopez."

Grissom's hand started to come up automatically, but Catherine took a slight step forward and accepted the chief's clasp. "Catherine Willows, Las Vegas Crime Lab. We've heard nothing but good things about you, Chief. This is Gil Grissom, Sara Sidle, Nick Stokes, and Sofia Curtis."

They all nodded in turn and Lopez gave them a group nod.

Finally letting go of Catherine's hand, he asked, "You're the supervisor, I take it."

She nodded. "Supervisor in charge. Dr. Grissom here is also a supervisor—we've combined elements of two shifts in anticipation of a big job."

An eyebrow rose. "You anticipated right, Ms. Willows." He turned slightly so she had a better view of the two men behind him. "This is Sergeant Cody Jacks— one of mine, also works part-time here, like a lot of my fellas. He saw this thing go down. And this is Henry Cippolina, chief of security and floor manager of the casino."

She shook hands with both men.

"Looks like Custer's last stand," Grissom said grimly.

Lopez's dark eyes, behind wire-frame glasses, were hooded, his expression grave. "Twenty-three years on the job, never seen anything could touch this. Thank God, only two deaths so far . . ."

"Small miracle in and of itself," Grissom said.

". . . but three more are critical, and five others are going to need serious medical attention. There's also quite a few with splinters, glass cuts, assorted bumps, bruises."

Grissom said, "When panic sets in, people run blindly."

Catherine said, "Which means even the luckiest survivors'll have at least superficial injuries. . . . How many shot?"

Lopez's sigh bore the weight of the world. "Ten we know of . . . Christ knows how many others. Both gangs cleared out and, except for the one dead Predator"—he pointed toward a male lying facedown on the floor, the back of the man's head very bloody—"they took their wounded with them, if there were any."

"We're going to need to clear the people from this room," Catherine said, "the living ones, that is. We're limited in what we can do till then."

Lopez held his hands out. "We're treating the wounded as fast as we can, and our officers are getting statements in the snack bar—really the only part of the casino that took little or no damage—to avoid having the witnesses traipsing through your crime scene."

Cippolina then spoke for the first time, his voice a shade higher and louder than it should have been, his hands trembling at his sides. "How long do you think we'll be shut down?"

Grissom blinked. "What? You plan to reopen?"

"No, no, no—I mean . . . before we can start cleaning up that mess."

"That's not a 'mess' out there, Mr. Cippolina. That's evidence."

Catherine slipped gently between Grissom and the casino man. "This is going to take quite some time, Mr. Cippolina," she said. "It's a huge scene and we won't finish until we're satisfied that we have collected every scrap that might matter."

"Which means?"

From the corner of her eye, she saw Grissom tense; but he said nothing.

"We'll work as fast as we can, Mr. Cippolina, but this is not fast work. We'll do our best not to have your casino shut down one more minute than it has to be."

The casino's floor manager still frowned, but he said nothing more. The unspoken tension between him and Grissom was not lost on Catherine, however, nor did she think it was lost on Lopez, who seemed not to miss much of anything.

The chief put a hand on the shoulder of the man beside him. "Sergeant Jacks is the lead detective on this case—I'd appreciate it if you'd keep him apprised of your findings."

"Mr. Jacks, aren't you a witness?" Grissom asked.

Jacks's voice was deep and resonant. "I was here—saw a lot of what happened, but not all of it. Gave my statement to Adam Bell. I can stand down, if you think I should."

"Dr. Grissom, we're lucky Cody was on the scene," Lopez said. "He's got the detective slot right now."

"Detective 'slot'?"

"We have three sergeants who rotate on a six-month basis in the one detective post on the force. Adam Bell, another one of our sergeants, for example, is interviewing witnesses right now. We're a small department—only have one detective going at a time."

Catherine looked toward the uniformed officers in the snack bar. One had sergeant's stripes on his sleeve. He and a plainclothes officer were in the midst of interviews on the far side of the restaurant. "If you only have one detective slot going at a time"—Catherine gestured with her head toward the snack bar—"how can you have two detectives interviewing over there?"

Giving her a tiny smile, Lopez said, "The bald guy is Troy Hamilton."

Catherine studied the man from a distance. Forties, paunchy, and so darkly tan he might have spent every waking moment outdoors, Hamilton was talking to an African-American woman of maybe twenty-five.

Lopez said, "Troy retired a year ago—bad back. But because of the size and nature of this crime, I called him to come help with interviews."

"Good thinking on your part," she said. "And generous of him."

Looking at Cody Jacks, Grissom said, "Speaking of seeing what happened, is there video?"

Cippolina was the one to answer, though. "Too much."

Grissom almost smiled. "My kind of problem."

Catherine took Sofia aside. "Collect all the videotapes and take them back to the lab. We can get by with one truck here, and our own facility will be better suited to the task."

Sofia nodded. "I'll pick up some Visine and get right on it."

Turning to Cippolina, Sofia asked, "Could you show me to Video Surveillance?"

"This way," he said, and led her to the left and up a corridor.

Sheriff Lopez said, "We can't lose sight that there were crimes committed here besides murder—attempted murder, assault with a deadly weapon, rioting, destruction of property, and on and on."

"Our evidence processing will cover all that," Grissom replied. "Video tapes alone—"

"I appreciate that," Lopez interrupted, "but my handful of men and my five jail cells won't cut it."

Catherine said, "Well, we can have the state police handle that—their investigation division can come in and grill our gangs."

Then Catherine surveyed the ravaged casino. The other CSIs gathered around her and did the same as if viewing a battlefield after the fray.

"Let's each take a quarter," Catherine said, pointing, "and work from the outside in. Take lots of pictures—don't be shy; we don't know what might be important later."

Grissom took the quarter with the biker body, and Nick and Sara got the two far quarters, while Catherine assigned herself the nearest quarter with the other corpse.

Getting out her camera, Catherine moved slowly through the detritus of the crime, careful not to disturb anything.

She bent over the body.

The woman was young, early twenties, brunette—a dealer, judging by her clothing. A name tag introduced Catherine to Vanessa Delware.

Lining the woman's body up in the viewfinder, Catherine wondered idly what her story was.

3

WARRICK BROWN WAS PISSED OFF.

This was not a common state of mind for the tall African-American with the piercing green eyes. Not that shades of inner anger from disgust to rage were uncommon on the emotional rainbow of this man, whose demeanor was generally so low-key. But "pissed off" was something Warrick rarely got.

Today was different.

Warrick Brown was a dedicated professional, a CSI devoted to his work, who routinely went above and beyond the call of duty and had logged more overtime hours than anybody in the department. Couldn't he even have one goddamn solitary day (and night) for himself?

He hadn't shared this feeling with anyone else in the office, but as he sat in the locker room in one of his best ensembles—brown cashmere sweater, brown jeans, and brand-new sneakers—he was genuinely, definitely, decidedly, well and truly *pissed off*.

I'm supposed to be having dinner tonight, he told his sympathetic inner self, *with the most beautiful woman in town—and the* town *is* Vegas! How could Catherine do this to him?

The woman in question, a nurse with only one day off a week, had finally acquiesced to Warrick's appeals and agreed to go out with him—tonight.

He'd been halfway out his door for the evening when Catherine summoned him. After calling and getting an understanding but clearly disappointed response from his date, he'd gone straight to HQ, since he kept a spare set of clothes in his locker and could change there. But now, sitting on a bench staring at the interior of his locker, he was realizing that he did not have a spare pair of shoes here, which meant the brand-new sneakers would be going out into the field with him tonight. And who knew *what* kinds of crime scenes awaited?

Case in point—Frank the Perv, a deviant so far off the path that Warrick refused to ever use the guy's real last name, even in the privacy of his own brain. When called upon to investigate Frank the Perv as a sex offender, Warrick had entered the man's house to discover that Frank kept an extensive collection of jars of his own feces, urine, and semen. ("Everybody needs a hobby," Grissom had remarked.) The shoes worn into that house for that investigation had ended up in a Dumpster when Warrick refused to wear them again after wandering through Frank the Perv's love nest.

Warrick had changed pants and was just pulling on a tan T-shirt when Greg Sanders came into the locker room.

"Looks like it's you and me tonight, 'Rick," Greg said.

Shorter than Warrick but similarly lanky, Greg had finally tamed the unruly thatch of brown hair, blond-highlighted within an inch of its life, and—since moving out of the DNA lab into the field as a CSI—dressed more professionally now, or at least conservatively (tonight, blue polo shirt and black Levi's).

"Who called you in? Catherine?"

"Yeah."

"She tell you what's up?"

"No—just said we were shorthanded and I was needed. Man, I almost didn't answer my cell. This is supposed to be a vacation day for me—the night I had planned, aw . . . don't even wanna talk about it."

"Bummer," Greg said, and filled him in on the Boot Hill shoot-out.

As the realities of his job came into focus through the young CSI's words, Warrick felt a twinge of shame for having been petty about the broken date. Hell yes, he deserved his day off and this date; damn right, he wanted it right now more than a new car or a raise. But with something this serious, not some bureaucratic screwup, a genuine emergency?

After all, somebody had to hold down the fort.

And suddenly he really didn't mind at all.

Gears shifted within him, and he was cool and ready to work.

"We've got a call," Greg said, holding up a sheet of paper with an address scribbled on it. "Apparent suicide."

"Where?"

"Sweeney Avenue." Greg rattled off the house number.

"Let's roll." Warrick shut his locker and they were moving. "Where exactly is that on Sweeney?"

"Just west of Maryland Parkway."

They went out to their SUV, Warrick climbing into the driver's seat, Greg dutifully walking around to the passenger side.

As he drove west on Charleston, Warrick hit the flashing lights.

He glanced at his young partner. Before the night-shift team had been split up, Warrick had mentored the young CSI, and falling back into that role felt natural.

Warrick asked, "So . . . what do we know?"

Greg got out his small notebook but didn't refer to it in the dark SUV. "The vic, Kelly Ames, apparently locked herself in the garage with the car running. A friend thought it was weird when Kelly didn't show up for work, then weirder still when she didn't answer her phone. So the friend called nine-one-one. Officer found the body and called the vic's husband, Charles Ames, to come home from work."

Turning off Charleston onto Park Paseo, Warrick asked, "Officer on the scene?"

"Weber," Greg answered.

Warrick jogged left on Eighth Street, which would intersect with Sweeney. Jackson Weber, a swing-shift beat cop for most of his twenty years, was a good man with solid instincts.

Taking a left on Sweeney, Warrick didn't need to check the number on the house because emergency vehicles out front, their light bars flashing, identified it. A squad car, an unmarked vehicle, and a coroner's wagon lined the street in front as well.

A one-story stucco with a two-car garage tacked onto the left, the house was decades old but well tended. After pulling to a stop facing the squad car, Warrick jerked the gearshift into park and climbed out. As he did, Greg seemed to sprint to the rear; he already had the doors open and was pulling out his crime scene case when Warrick arrived back there.

"Moving fast is good," Warrick said.

Greg eyed him. "But . . . ?"

"Haste makes waste at a crime scene."

They were just getting ready to walk up the driveway when Captain Jim Brass emerged onto the front porch, then wandered down to meet them. A dogged detective with a world-weary mien and eyes that somehow seemed sad and sharp at once, Brass—in a crisp powder-blue suit with a dark blue tie snugly in place—was the one detective that Warrick always wanted at his side, whether at a crime scene or heading down a dark alley.

"Aren't these vacation days relaxing?" Brass said with a faint, knowing smile. "Think she'll give you a second chance?"

"They reelected Bush, didn't they?" Warrick said. "What have we got?"

Brass, like Greg, had a small notebook in hand; and, like Greg, he did not refer to it. "Kelly Ames. Twenty-four, suicide. Still in the garage."

Frowning, Warrick noted, "Garage door's open."

Brass shook his head. "Officer Weber said she was definitely dead when he arrived, and there was no reason to disturb the scene with attempts to revive the vic . . . but he opened the overhead door to clear the garage of carbon monoxide. Hard for you fellas to do your thing, otherwise."

"What else's been done?" Warrick asked.

"That's it," Brass said with a shrug. "Scene's undisturbed."

"Where's Weber?"

Brass gestured with a head nod. "In the house with Mr. Ames."

Warrick led the three of them up the driveway, where a navy blue Toyota Rav4 was parked. The left side of the garage was empty; on the other side beckoned the rear end of a gray Honda Accord, maybe seven years old.

When they got to the garage door, Warrick and Greg both set their crime scene cases down as Brass looked on. As they got down to business, Warrick noticed that the Accord was a four-door, no kid's seat. No kids' toys in the garage either.

"A childless couple?" Warrick asked.

Brass said, "Yeah—husband I haven't really interviewed in depth. He's reeling. Typical reaction—can't believe she'd do this, happily married, no problems. Met at UNLV. Both graduates. I'll get more."

Brass headed off to do that.

"Greg," Warrick said, "camera."

But then Warrick noticed that Greg was already on one knee, opening the case that held his thirty-five-millimeter camera with flash attachment.

A lot of police departments were going digital, but Vegas had not completely turned that corner yet.

Though digital was unquestionably faster and cheaper, with no need to develop hundreds of rolls of film, digital photos still were not admissible in court in some venues, viewed as too easy to doctor.

While Warrick went up the driver's side, Greg took the passenger's. Before either touched anything, Greg took several photos of the vehicle from every angle. The car windows were down, the engine turned off, probably by Weber when he showed up. Through the driver's window, Warrick saw the young woman leaning forward in her seat, her forehead resting against the steering wheel. Long brown hair hung down, obscuring her face from view. She wore an orange T-shirt and—when he looked in through the open window—Warrick noted purple shorts and white tennis shoes.

Something about the color combination of the shirt and shorts struck him as odd; but then, suicide always struck him as odd. He understood how things could pile up on you so much that you'd consider killing yourself—he'd been there, till he licked his gambling jones, anyway—but some of the methods chosen over the years by perp/vics had made him realize that this was one "crime" he could never entirely understand. After all, he had once been called to a suicide where the man had not only killed himself but shot his pet ferret and taken a ball-peen hammer to his cat.

Some suicides were ritualized, some were simple, some included a note, some didn't. In this case, a white business-size envelope waited on the dashboard.

Warrick wished Catherine were here—he would have liked to have asked her about that odd combination of clothes. He tried to think of a time when he'd seen a reasonably attractive woman wearing purple and orange. Most didn't wear such a jarring color combo, he decided.

Of course, most women didn't kill themselves, either. Maybe they were the first two pieces of clothing she grabbed; maybe the explanation was just that simple. Perhaps the combination of colors meant something significant to her or her husband (school colors? wedding?); no way to immediately tell.

"Did you get a picture of that envelope?" Warrick asked.

"I got *four* pictures of it," Greg said.

Wearing latex gloves, Warrick picked the envelope off the dashboard.

Unsealed. Flap merely tucked inside.

He carefully extracted the flap and found a tri-folded piece of paper inside, which he also removed. When he had the note unfolded, he held the sheet flat on the hood of the car while Greg photographed it, then he read the typed note.

Charlie,
I'm so sorry but I just can't take it anymore. The pain was too much to bear. I hope you can understand and forgive me. I will always love you,
   Kelly

In the movies, on TV, the typewritten suicide note is always a sure sign that someone is trying to cover up a murder. In real life, Warrick knew, this was not always the case. Some people just did not write out their suicide notes by hand. Often such notes these days were typed on computers, and the suicide just grabbed the paper out of the printer (or left it there) and didn't bother signing it.

Hell, only a little more than half of all suicides even bothered to *write* a note. . . .

Carefully, he bagged the sheet of paper.

This one still felt odd, though—peak ages for women to commit suicide were between forty-five and fifty-four, with another large at-risk group over seventy-five.

Kelly Ames appeared to be in her mid-twenties.

Although women attempted suicide twice as often as men, their male counterparts were successful four times more often. High school graduates and those with some college were more likely than high school dropouts to kill themselves, but Kelly had graduated from UNLV. Warrick also knew suicide was more common among women who were single, recently separated, divorced, or widowed. Kelly Ames was happily married—supposedly, anyway.

Although poisoning, including drug overdose, had long been the leading method of suicide among women, guns now held the top spot, in fact used in sixty percent of all suicides.

For this case, the statistics were all against Kelly Ames committing suicide.

What did all that mean?

At this point, nothing. Statistics were numbers, and victims like Kelly were human beings. But Warrick knew he would be watching this one carefully, making sure that nobody was just going through the motions. That this suicide was not by the numbers did not make it murder; it meant the investigators needed to *not* work by the numbers and to be painstakingly thorough.

"What next?" Greg asked.

"Check the backseat—I'll take the front, starting with the passenger side."

"You got it."

"Then we'll process the body together."

Greg jumped to work, going over the backseat with care. Warrick did the same with the passenger seat in front, and when they were done, all they had were two cigarette butts from the ashtray in the front and a gum wrapper that Greg had dug out from under the driver's seat.

Nonetheless, Warrick was pleased with Greg's processing—that the body was keeping them company did not seem to bother the young CSI, neither spooking nor intimidating him. For a former lab rat like Greg, this was no small accomplishment.

"All right," Warrick said. "Let's do the vic. Who's here from the coroner?"

"David."

"Find him and get him over here."

"On it," Greg said, and disappeared.

Rigor had set in, so Warrick had to be careful prying the dead woman's fingers from the steering wheel.

By the time Warrick had managed that, Greg was back with assistant coroner David Phillips in tow. His dark, curly hair receding, the boyish Phillips took a position on the driver's side, next to Warrick. He pushed his black, wire-frame glasses up on his nose, then jammed both hands into the pockets of his dark blue lab coat. Normally Phillips had a wide, easygoing smile, but not when he was working.

"Where shall I start?" Phillips asked Warrick.

"Time of death?"

"Judging from the progression of rigor—midday. Maybe noon or so."

"Where was the husband then?"

"According to Brass, Mr. Ames says he was on his way to work. Brass called him at his job; guy's a second-shift supervisor."

Leaning the victim back in the seat, Warrick examined the woman's face. Her eyes were closed, her face was peaceful. High cheekbones; small, sharp chin; full, pink lips; no lipstick. What she did not have was the extremely red skin that comes with carbon monoxide poisoning.

"Pretty lady," Warrick said to no one in particular. "Something's not right about this."

"She *is* awfully young," Greg said, not seeing what Warrick had seen.

Warrick cut to the chase. "David, why isn't her skin red?"

Phillips shrugged. "That doesn't happen one hundred percent of the time with carbon monoxide death."

Warrick thought he saw a shadow under the tousled brown hair and he pulled out his mini Maglite and examined the victim's neck. . . .

A dark spot about the size of a dime.

But whether this was a bruise or even dirt or possibly makeup, he could not tell. Before he took it to the next step, he asked the coroner's assistant, "Is that a bruise?"

Phillips leaned in through the back driver's-side door, moving Warrick's hand slightly to get more light on the darkness on the woman's throat.

"Could be," Phillips said. "Can't tell for sure . . . yet."

Warrick grabbed a breath, told himself not to push. "The autopsy will tell us about that, and the lack of redness. Got anything else for us, Dave?"

Phillips shook his head. "No. Check with me later, at the lab."

Moving the light farther around the throat of the vic, Warrick could not find any more marks, bruises or otherwise; but when he got to the back of the woman's neck, he said, "Hey, guys! Have a look at this."

Phillips leaned in closer and Greg came in through the passenger-side rear door, camera at the ready.

"What?" Greg asked.

Warrick used his flashlight to highlight the tag on the back of Kelly Ames's shirt.

"It's on inside out," he announced.

Greg snapped a picture.

"It could mean," Warrick said, "she didn't dress herself."

"Or it could mean," Greg offered, "she just threw the first thing on because she was distracted and distraught—what kind of state of mind would she be in if the top of her priority list was coming out here to start the car and take one last ride with the garage door shut?"

"That's a well-reasoned possibility," Warrick admitted. "Okay, David, your guys can take her out of here."

Phillips was handling that when Greg asked Warrick what was next.

"I need to talk to the husband. Let's clear up some questions of evidence. Come on."

Entering the house through the attached garage door, Warrick found himself in a tiny mudroom with a washer and dryer. Beyond that lay a galley kitchen and then a small dining area with a round table and four chairs, two of which were now occupied, one by Brass and the other by, presumably, Charles Ames.

A scrawny guy with blond hair, big blue eyes, and a wispy beard, a hollow-eyed Ames sat across the table from Brass. In the living room, near the front door, Sergeant Jackson Weber stood tall, his blond crewcut and matching mustache perfect down to each hair. His face was impassive, his gray eyes unreadable, his presence comforting for investigators, intimidating for anybody else.

"We're sorry for your loss, Mr. Ames," Warrick said as he and Greg moved through the small dining area and took up positions, standing on either side of Brass.

Ames said, "Thank you," but there was no inflection to the words at all.

Warrick introduced himself and Greg, and Ames said, "Call me Charlie."

"We were just getting ready to start the interview," Brass said.

Warrick nodded and, as procedure and courtesy dictated, let the detective carry the ball.

"Some of these questions will make you uncomfortable," Brass said. "But in situations like this, Mr. Ames, they have to be asked. And sooner is better than later."

Ames nodded, saying nothing.

"Have you and Kelly been having any trouble lately?"

Ames shook his head.

"Has she been despondent about anything?"

"Not that I can think of. Everything's been pretty good between us, always."

"Mr. Ames," Brass said, "taking one's own life is always done for a reason—it may not seem logical or even sane to the survivors, but there's always a reason."

"I know, I know," Ames said, a little agitated. "But I can't *give* you a reason. I didn't see this coming at all!"

"Nothing going on in your marriage," Brass gently probed, "that you want to get in front of . . . and tell us about? Just so we don't get the wrong idea, later."

"No!" Ames said. "What do you mean, wrong idea?"

Brass said nothing.

"I told you, Captain—told you, we were happy. She was my best friend . . . I loved her. . . ."

The man's head lowered, chin to his chest. Warrick looked for tears. Didn't spot any.

Brass was asking, "Any friends she might have confided in, Mr. Ames?"

"Maybe Megan—Megan Voetberg. Her best friend. They work together." He frowned. "Didn't you tell me she was the one who called you people?"

"Yes," Brass said. "Any others?"

"Hell, I don't know," Ames said, and shook his head. "Megan could give you a better idea than me, if there are other girlfriends of Kelly's who she might've opened up to. But honestly, we didn't keep secrets, we talked to each other, not like some

couples. . . . Captain, I understand this is important,
but . . . but . . . I'm not really doing very well right
now. Can we wrap this up?"

The tremble in the voice, the pain in the face. But
still no tears.

Warrick said, "Just a couple more questions, Mr.
Ames."

The man nodded wearily. The color had drained
from his face and his lank blond hair lay limp against
his forehead. Dry eyes or not, Charlie Ames looked
so depressed, he might not have been far from following his wife's example.

"Did your wife use a computer at her job?"

Ames winced, trying to make sense of the question. "Yes, I'm sure she did—she's a postal worker.
Yes, sure. She keys in zip codes and stuff, over at the
encoding station. She worked nights."

"Did that put a strain on your marriage, working
different shifts?"

The husband shook his head. "No—I mean, I can
see how you'd think that, but she just got the job. It
was like a . . . probationary deal. If Kelly worked
out, they'd give her a raise after six months and
eventually a chance to go to days."

"When would that have come?"

"Another month."

Warrick had one more question. "Is there a computer in the house?"

"Yeah. Why?"

"We'll need to take it with us."

"Take it with . . . Why in hell?"

"It's evidence, sir."

"Evidence?" Ames asked incredulously. "Kelly

dies in our garage, and our *computer* is evidence?"

Warrick said, "Technically, a suicide is a homicide, Mr. Ames—and we investigate that as thoroughly as we would a murder."

Suddenly Ames seemed a little unsteady. "Guys— I need that PC for my job."

"What do you do?" Brass asked, even though Weber had probably already told him, from when the Patrolman had called Ames at work.

Returning his attention to Brass, obviously relieved not to be responding to Warrick, Ames said, "I'm second-shift production supervisor for Cactus Plastics."

"What does your home computer have to do with that?"

"Sometimes I type up production reports and the like. Almost everybody works partly out of their homes these days, Captain."

Warrick said, "We'll get it back to you as fast as possible, sir. We have no desire to inconvenience you."

Ames's frown dug deep lines in his forehead. "I still don't get it—why do you *need* it? I mean, I want to cooperate, but—"

"Your wife's suicide note seems to have been written on a computer. We'll need your printer, too. Knowing whether she wrote that note on her work computer, or here at home, might be instructive as to her state of mind."

Greg gave Warrick a sideways look, knowing that Warrick was, like any magician, using misdirection.

Ames thought about it. "It's in the spare bedroom. First door on the left . . . but I better get it back from you people! You gotta sign for it!"

Brass said, "We wouldn't have it any other way."

While Weber and Brass stayed with Ames, Warrick and Greg checked out the spare bedroom: single bed coming out from the wall on the right; long, low bookshelves filled with paperbacks running below the window on the wall opposite the door; and a student desk on the left wall with a monitor, two speakers, mouse with pad, and a keyboard on a pull-out shelf under the desktop. The computer tower itself sat on the floor against the right side; on a separate stand perched an inkjet printer.

Greg took pictures of the whole setup, then he and Warrick tore the machine down, taking the tower and the printer with them, leaving the rest. When they had everything loaded in the SUV, they came back into the house.

"Again, Mr. Ames," Brass said. "We're very sorry for your loss."

Ames said nothing and did not rise as the detective and CSIs filed out.

On the front stoop, Officer Weber asked, "You fellas need anything else?"

Brass shook his head. "Nice job, by the way."

"Yeah," Warrick added. "I appreciate your not disturbing the crime scene."

"I got reamed by your buddy Grissom, once, a hundred years ago," Weber said with a grin, "and I've been real damn particular ever since."

Weber headed to his cruiser, climbed in, and rolled off. David, his guys, and the body were gone already, too.

Turning to Warrick, Brass asked, "What was all

that stuff in the house about taking the computer and finding out why Mrs. Ames killed herself?"

"It's about," Warrick said, glancing toward the house, "Kelly Ames not killing herself."

"This is a murder?"

"I can't go there . . . yet. Signs are it might be."

"Share with the class," Brass said, crossing his arms.

Warrick took only a few moments to collect his thoughts, then went into full oral report mode.

"Okay," Brass said. "Where does that take us next?"

"To the post office."

Brass closed his eyes. He seemed just about ready to drift into a nap when he said, "You really think the U.S. government mail service is going to let us take one of their computers without a court order?"

"Hell no," Warrick said with a shake of his head and a wide smile. "But we *will* be able to talk to Megan Voetberg. Then if there's nothing on the home computer, maybe we can find something on the work computer."

"Something," Brass said. "I hate these damn fishing expeditions."

"Hey, like I said to the husband—Kelly had to write her suicide note somewhere. Or should I say, somebody had to write it, somewhere."

Brass managed a rumpled grin. "Good point. Let's go to the post office and talk to this Megan Voetberg."

"Greg," Warrick said. "You drive—I have a phone call to make."

As they wove through the city after dark, Warrick withdrew his cell phone and made a quick call to a freelance computer expert, Tomas Nuñez, who had helped the CSIs on numerous cases in recent years.

"*Hola,*" Nuñez said, his voice seeming to come from some very deep place inside.

"Tomas, Warrick Brown. Busy?"

"Never too busy for my friends."

Greg was puttering through the light traffic. Greg's excessive caution unnerved Warrick, much as Warrick's own loose yet speed-of-light way behind the wheel unnerved everybody else at CSI.

"Tomas, I've got a computer that may have some vital material on it."

"Where and when?"

"Crime lab. Say an hour?"

"No problem."

Warrick looked through the windshield; Greg was stopping for a light that had just turned yellow. "Better make it an hour-fifteen, Tomas."

Nuñez said, "Sure thing, Warrick. *Adios.*"

They broke the connection and when Warrick looked up, Greg was frowning at him. "Should I have run that yellow? Say it—you think I drive like a schoolgirl!"

"High school girls in this town," Warrick responded dryly, "get seventy-three percent of the speeding tickets in their age group."

Greg was still parsing Warrick's remark when they got to the postal encoding station, where Brass was leaning against his car.

"You two take the scenic route?" he asked.

Greg's chin came up, just a little. "I drove the speed limit and obeyed the traffic signals."

"Imagine how impressed I am," Brass said. He made a sweeping "after you" hand gesture. "Shall we?"

Unlike a normal post office, no customer business was conducted within—this was strictly a glorified sorting house. A low brick building with a parking lot out front, the encoding station sat in a strip mall on the aptly named Industrial Way. Maybe fifteen cars filled the slots of the lot, the lights of the station the only ones on in the entire area.

"You been inside yet?" Warrick asked, as they headed toward the facility.

Brass nodded.

"Did you mention the computer?"

"No, but I did talk to Megan Voetberg. She's got a break coming up . . ."—Brass tilted his watch toward one of the lights that illuminated the parking area— ". . . in about two minutes . . . and she'll be out to talk to us then."

Warrick smiled at Greg and said, "Hey, bro—nice timing."

Greg grinned and said, "Shut up."

Exactly two minutes later, as if she had been using a stopwatch, a young, thin, dark-complected woman with straight black hair and exotic brown eyes swivelled through the door and came out to join them. She wore hip-hugging jeans and a tight white T-shirt emblazoned with a Chinese take-out container smiling and playing guitar. Above the crazy little caricature were the words THANK YOU and below it WEEZER.

Three coworkers trailed out behind the woman, moving to a picnic table at the far end of the building.

"Captain Brass?" she asked tentatively, walking up. She had a soft, almost soothing voice.

"Megan Voetberg," Brass said, "this is Warrick Brown and Greg Sanders from the crime lab."

She nodded and glanced toward the table of coworkers.

Taking the hint, Brass said, "Maybe we should move around the corner?"

Again, she nodded. Even in the dim light, Warrick could tell the woman was trembling.

"I thought you people only did crime scenes and lab stuff," she said as they walked.

Warrick, falling in next to her, said, "Not all evidence of a crime is at the scene of that crime. Your friend, Kelly, working at this station, for example, brings us here."

They eased around the corner between the building and its twin, fifty feet down the parking lot. The light was even dimmer here, the flick of her lighter causing a tiny flashfire as she lit a cigarette.

As an afterthought, she said, "Hey, do you mind?"

They all shook their heads.

"We're sorry for your loss," Warrick said.

"Thanks," she said. She took a deep drag, shaking more as she exhaled. "I can't believe . . . believe Kelly's dead, really dead."

They said nothing.

She frowned as if something smelled bad. "*Suicide?*"

"That's what we're trying to determine," Brass said.

She scuffed a shoe at an invisible piece of dirt. "Guys—Kelly did *not* kill herself."

"Why do you say that?" Warrick asked.

Megan shrugged. "Not the suicidal type. All there is to it."

Brass asked, "Then she wasn't depressed, or despondent?"

The young woman considered that for a long moment. "Depressed, probably. Who isn't sometimes? . . . Despondent? What *is* that, really?"

"Depressed," Greg said, "is being in low spirits. Despondency is the same thing, only worse—no hope."

They all gave him a long look.

Greg stared back. "Sorry. But they are different."

Megan said, "Then she *definitely* wasn't despondent . . . even though she was a little depressed. You wanna know mostly what Kelly was? Mostly Kelly was pissed."

"About what?" Brass asked. He nodded toward the postal building. "Her job?"

"No! No. Hell, no. What do you think? Her stupid husband! She wasn't going postal pissed; but, maaaan, she was getting there."

Brass's eyes tensed. "Why was she unhappy with Charlie?"

Megan's look was incredulous. "Duh. What's the usual reason? Because the jerk was having an *affair*."

Warrick exchanged glances with Brass.

"She knew that for sure?" Brass asked. "She had proof?"

Taking a long drag on her smoke, Megan considered that momentarily. "Not smoking-dick-type proof, no. But she was pretty goddamn sure . . . Kelly was *convinced* she knew who it was."

"Who?"

"She didn't tell me. Not the name, anyway." She dropped her cigarette and snuffed it out under her shoe. "Just some slut Charlie worked with. Hey, my break is over, you mind? . . . You guys can call me at home if you want more—not that I have anything."

They took her contact info, then thanked her and watched as she and her coworkers went back inside at the end of their break.

"So Kelly did have a reason to commit suicide," Brass said when the three of them were alone.

Warrick nodded. "Right, and maybe she hated her cheating hubby so much she set him up to take the fall for her 'murder.'"

"Yeah," Brass said with a sardonic laugh. "That could happen. You been doing this how long?"

"Twelve years."

"You ever see that happen before?"

"Couple of times . . ."

Brass frowned at Warrick, as if to say, *Say what?*

". . . on TV."

Letting out a single laugh, Brass said, "Then you *don't* think that's what happened here."

"No way."

"Then why even go there?"

Warrick shrugged. "Because Grissom taught me to never overlook any possibility—no matter how crazy it seems."

Brass frowned. "Then what *do* you think happened here?"

"I think Charlie Ames killed his wife," Warrick said. "And you know what else I think?"

Greg asked, "That we're going to prove it?"

"Damn straight," Warrick said, grinning.

He held out his open hand, and Greg seemed confused as to whether to shake it, or give him a high-five, or . . .

"Car keys, Greg."

Greg handed them over.

4

FIRST THEY'D USED UP ALL THEIR PLASTIC A-frame evidence markers.

Then, following Grissom's advice, they'd fashioned more, using two decks of cards—turning the numbers outward—and even that had not been enough.

Finally, they resorted to masking tape and a black marker.

And when they were done, over one hundred and fifty bullet holes had been marked and photographed inside the Four Kings Casino.

Sara Sidle didn't know if they had brought enough bullet trajectory rods to mark the scene. She guessed she would soon find out.

With Nick's help, Sara set up the DeltaSphere-3000 3D Scene Scanner. One of the newest tools in law enforcement's crime-fighting arsenal, the 3D scanner had been secured by Ecklie for the lab, on loan from the device's manufacturer, 3rdTech. The

DeltaSphere was like a yacht: if you had to ask how much it cost, you couldn't afford it. But 3rdTech had provided it in hopes of a sale, and Ecklie hoped they would "donate" it to the LVPD in exchange for a glowing recommendation from the ninth largest police force in the United States.

Sara figured that by the end of the trial, both sides would leave disappointed. In the meantime, she and Nick would have a pricey new toy to play with.

Sitting atop a tripod stronger but no larger than a photographer's, the DeltaSphere looked like a silver briefcase with a four-inch black square in its top border that housed the scanner's lens and laser. Weighing in at a shade over twenty pounds, the device would give them a 3D color scan of the crime scene in less than fifteen minutes.

When finished, the scan would be loaded into a computer and give the team a 3D rendering of the crime scene with as much detail as a drawing that would have taken hours to complete. As Sara watched the machine cast its laser around the room, the red, pencil-thin beam slithering over every centimeter of the crime scene, she couldn't help but think how much time this machine would save them if it was just half as good as advertised. She had seen Nick use it at another crime scene and knew that the DeltaSphere was everything it claimed to be, and a bag of chips.

Once the scanner had done its thing, they had marked and photographed over one hundred shell casings, then bagged and tagged those casings (the bullets they could find), and hundreds of other things that might or might not be important evidence. They had shot so many rolls of film that the casino had donated three money bags just to hold them. And Sofia had loaded close to one hundred videotapes into several boxes that were now on a two-wheel cart near the door, along with the film and other evidence.

The wounded had been rushed to hospitals in Laughlin. The *seriously* wounded—those who could make the flight—rode the medevac chopper to Vegas.

To Sara Sidle's surprise, the investigators still only had two deaths on their hands—one male, one female. Henry Cippolina, the Four Kings's floor manager, had identified the female as Vanessa Delware, a twenty-one-year-old dealer and single mom. Both Chief Lopez and Sergeant Jacks had ID'd the male casualty as Predators leader Nick Valpo, the kind of corpse that could spark not just more trouble but grow the past battle into a future war.

Though a couple of the injured hailed from one gang or the other, the largest percentage of wounded were your garden-variety innocent bystanders— staff, tourists, casino regulars, even one poor schlub who'd wandered in off the street for a drink, all simply in the wrong place at the wrong time.

Grissom approached Sara with a tiny thoughtful frown. He said, "Something odd."

"Odd?"

"After all," Grissom said, "everything here seems pretty straightforward."

She arched an eyebrow. "*Riiiiight*—for a biker fire-fight that broke out in a casino."

He did not acknowledge her sarcasm, still frown-ing thoughtfully, looking out on the torn-up landscape of the casino. "Everybody that got hit was shot from a distance, right?"

Unable to figure out where Grissom was going with this, Sara took the ride. "That seems to be the consensus."

"Shot from the front," Grissom said, gesturing to himself, "or side."

"Right. That was the line of fire."

"Mostly hit with nine-millimeter rounds, correct?"

"Mostly, or something bigger. From the shell casings and bullets we've harvested, I think a couple of the shooters had three-fifty-sevens."

Nodding, Grissom said, "So, if we begin with everybody shot with nine mils or larger, and from a distance . . . how do we explain Nick Valpo being shot up close and personal . . . from *behind* . . . and with a small-caliber weapon?"

Now she frowned in thought. "Somebody took advantage of the melee . . . and committed a murder in the middle of a gunfight?"

"Yes," Grissom said, pleased with her. "But not a murder, exactly."

"No?"

His eyes tensed. "An execution."

Sara considered that for a moment. "Small-caliber, you say—what kind of gun?"

"We may have the shell casing among all those we gathered. But we won't know for sure until we see the autopsy results. Judging by the wound, though . . . something small—a twenty-two or maybe twenty-five."

Sara blinked. "That's a purse gun. What self-respecting biker carries a twenty-two?"

Grissom shrugged. "A gun that size would make a good backup piece. In a boot, maybe. . . . Come with me."

She followed Grissom to Nick Valpo's body. Near a large bullet-scarred column, one of many scattered about the room, Valpo lay facedown on the floor, left hand on a pile of glass from a shattered slot machine, right hand reaching into an aisle for his Glock, just out of reach.

Sara knelt over him.

The entrance wound in the back of Valpo's head was just a small, round hole with gunshot residue making a dark targetlike circle around it. Another larger dark blossom opened from the right shoulder of Valpo's black vest—an exit wound.

"He got hit," Sara said, "went down, then someone came up behind him and finished the job."

"Yes," Grissom said.

"Videotapes should tell us the story on that one." She looked across the aisle at the deceased dealer lying on the floor, the dead woman's eyes staring at nothing but locked in Sara's direction. "If she wasn't already dead, the dealer saw the whole thing. . . . She won't be taking the witness stand now, though."

Grissom's eyes narrowed. "No—but if she was shot because of what she saw, the caliber of the bullet inside her *will* testify."

He led Sara over to the woman's body and they had a look at an entrance wound similar to the one on the Predator's remains.

"No powder burns," Sara said. "Shot from a distance. But that doesn't look large enough to've been made by a nine mil—though too big to've been made by a 357."

"I'd agree," Grissom said. "This will be a key autopsy."

They stood back and watched in respectful silence as the paramedics put a sheet over the dealer's body and loaded it onto a gurney. Catherine came over to join them.

"A young one," Catherine said quietly.

Sara said, "With a baby. Single mom."

"Not young," Grissom said flatly. "You don't get older than deceased."

The two women looked at him, wondering at the seeming coldness of the comment; but Grissom's grave expression belied that.

The gurney rolled out, and Chief Lopez edged around it, coming in. Sara had not seen him leave, but for a crime scene that should be secured, people were sure wandering in and out, almost as if the casino was open for business.

Lopez crossed to them, looking like he'd aged a year for every hour the CSI team had spent in Boot Hill.

"Nice kid," the chief said sorrowfully.

"You knew her?" Grissom asked.

"Boot Hill isn't a very big town. You get to know a lot of people. At least she has a mom who can look after the baby."

Catherine asked, "How's it going, getting control of the town?"

"It's about to get harder," Lopez said with a sigh, thumbs in belt loops. "One of the biker casualties just became a fatality—a Spokes member died from his wounds before he even made it to the hospital."

A few ominous moments of silence followed, or at least near silence—omnipresent was the sound of glass crunching underfoot.

"'Revenge is a kind of wild justice,'" Grissom said, "'which the more man's nature runs to, the more ought law to weed it out.'"

Sara said, "Shakespeare?"

"Francis Bacon. Chief, were you able to line up any more help?"

"The governor sent us two dozen more Highway Patrolmen," Lopez said, with a that's-something-anyway shrug. "Got ten of 'em tryin' to keep the Rusty Spokes rustled up in the Gold Vault, across the street."

"And the rest?"

"Tryin' to round up the Predators and keep them from laying *siege* to the Gold Vault."

Catherine blew out a breath, as if trying to put out candles on a birthday cake. "This doesn't sound promising."

"Sure it does," Grissom said. "We just don't like what it promises."

Lopez said, "I've got a police force of twelve plus me, two dozen Highway Patrolmen, and then there's you folks."

Patting the holstered weapon at her hip, Catherine said, "If you need us to walk away from the crime scene and lend support, you give us the word. We're all law enforcement here."

Sara gave Grissom a sideways look to see how he liked the sound of that; apparently he liked it fine.

Lopez was saying, "That gives us a little over forty

on the home team, and those motorcycle gangs have closer to a hundred members—each."

Grissom asked, "Prognosis?"

Lopez's eyebrows hiked. "I think we can probably handle one or the other of the gangs . . . but I see three ways for this to go down. First, they all decide to go to their separate homes and lick their wounds— most of these bikers have lives outside of the gang: families, day jobs, what have you. And we all walk away from this with our skin still on."

"How likely is that scenario?" Catharine asked.

"About like hitting a million-dollar jackpot on one of these slots. The *likeliest* scenario is both gangs decide to go at it, and Boot Hill's the playing field, and we're stuck in the middle, refereeing."

"Chief," Sara said, "you said you saw *three* ways this could go. . . ."

But it was Grissom who replied: "They bury the hatchet . . ."

"Well, that *does* sound promising," Sara said.

". . . in us," Grissom finished.

"I don't get it," Sara said.

But Catherine did.

She said, "The gangs realize that together, they outnumber law enforcement five to one. They join forces, table any interpersonal disputes, and come after us. Secure the battlefield, or the playground, depending on how you look at it."

"Do I have to look at it?" Sara asked, upper lip curling.

Catherine's eyes were hard. "With forty or fifty cops out of the way, the combined bikers could do a lot of harm to this town, and each other, before any cavalry got here."

Grissom said cheerfully, "That's probably a record number of mixed metaphors, but I think we have the situation well analyzed, at least."

A sick feeling washed through Sara's stomach.

Nick came up. "Anybody got anything? I feel like I'm putting together one of those thousand-piece jig-saw puzzles that's mostly blue sky."

"Not much blue sky here," Sara said, and gestured toward Valpo's corpse on the floor.

"What'd I miss?" Nick asked.

"Execution-style slaying," Grissom said as Nick knelt to look at the two wounds in the Predators' leader.

"An orderly kill in the midst of chaos," Nick said quietly, then shook his head and stood.

"The Predators will want revenge for Valpo," Catherine said to Nick, but for everyone's benefit.

Lopez nodded. "And the Spokes for their loss. That's why we're trying to keep the two gangs sepa-rated. Hell, maybe they'll cool off."

Irritated and frankly a little afraid, Sara asked, "Make up your mind, Chief—first it's they'll combine and come at us, then it's they'll fight each other. . . . Either way, why haven't you just *arrested* them all?"

Grissom, gesturing around them, said, "Not every gang member was part of this."

An insistent Sara said, "But they're all suspects—why not round them up, using that as an excuse? Then thin them out, based on the video surveillance cameras."

"Only a police state rounds suspects up on an ex-cuse," Grissom said.

Catherine said, "With murder only one of the

crimes committed here, questioning all concerned is called for—and the state police investigators will swell our ranks soon enough, and help on that score."

Flashing a sad grin, Lopez said, "Afraid the point is moot, friends. We've got five, count them, *five* two-person cells. There are in excess of two hundred biker guests in Boot Hill right now." He waved vaguely in the direction of the street. "If we can keep the Rusty Spokes holed up in the Gold Vault, we're halfway home. We're trying to keep the Predators' camp under control, too, of course; but they're not confined to a building, so that proposition is a little trickier."

"Let me ask the key, as-yet-unasked question," Grissom said.

They all turned to him.

Grissom's eyes were slits. "Doesn't the Four Kings have metal detectors at the door?"

Running a hand over his face as if that would wipe away the exhaustion, Lopez said, "Yeah. Of course. I don't have to tell you that's standard nowadays."

Now Grissom's head tilted to one side, eyes still narrow, and he said, "That raises the obvious question then, doesn't it? How did so much hardware wind up inside the casino?"

The chief gave a huge sigh and shook his head. "I frankly just don't know the answer to that one. We're looking into it, and it's important now, Dr. Grissom, no question. But understand that for the last few hours, we've all been more concerned about the *aftermath* of guns getting in than *how* guns got in."

Grissom nodded. "That's fair."

Cody Jacks, his red jacket still showing spots of dried blood and small pieces of glass that glinted when the light hit them right, joined the ever-growing group. His tie was loosened and the top two buttons of his white shirt were undone.

"Guess this is one time you guys aren't exactly short on evidence," he said.

Catherine said, "There's enough that it'll take days to sort it all out."

Nick said, "So, Mr. Jacks—you were here when all the fun went down, we understand."

"Make it 'Cody,' and yeah, I was." Jacks pointed to some shot-up slot machines not far away. "Right over there."

"Dangerous place to find yourself," Grissom said.

"No shit. I hit the deck and started crawling like a baby—tryin' to find somewhere where I could return fire."

Grissom asked, "You had a gun?"

Jacks nodded and pulled back the red jacket to reveal a Glock 19, a nine-millimeter pistol with a fifteen-round magazine. "I work floor security—we're *supposed* to have the only guns in the casino."

"How many rounds did you get off?" asked Nick.

"I'm not proud of this, but . . . not a one. By the time I felt safe enough to pop my head up, the shooting had stopped. And to tell you the truth, it would've been risky in any case, with all the chaos, patrons and staff running around."

"Makes sense, I guess," Nick said.

But Jacks seemed to take Nick's innocent remark wrong, puffing up to his full height.

"You weren't here, son," he said, ears reddening.

"Me, I saw combat in Desert Storm, and lemme tell ya—that was small change compared to this, forty or more guys all firing at the same time, none any too worried about taking aim or even which way their weapons were pointed."

Nick held up his hands in surrender. "I wasn't questioning your bravery, Sergeant."

"If I could have fired, I would have. I had friends in here I would give my life to've helped—that little girl, that blackjack dealer? I got her her job."

Nick flicked a look at Catherine as if to say, *What's this guy's problem, anyway?*

But Sara thought she knew: survivor's guilt.

Jacks was going on, "Truth is, I figured most of the people in the joint would be dead. It's a good thing none of those assholes can shoot straight or this would have been a goddamn slaughterhouse."

"You're right, Sergeant," Grissom said. "Many of the people here were luckier than anybody in a casino has any right to be—at least one hundred and fifty rounds were fired."

Jacks shook his head. "Felt like forever, Dr. Grissom, that's for damn sure. But I'll bet you both my jobs that when you look at the time stamp on the video, whole shooting match didn't last a minute."

"Neither did the OK Corral shoot-out," Grissom replied.

Catherine said, "Why don't you give Chief Lopez's guys a hand, Nicky, and see if you can figure out what's up with the Case of the Mysteriously Malfunctioning Metal Detectors?"

Nick nodded and moved off toward the front of the casino.

"For that matter," Grissom said, "why didn't those metal detectors go off when *we* came in?"

Again they all turned to him.

Grissom had made a good, obvious point that no one had previously commented upon.

"I hadn't really thought about it," Lopez said, "but you're *right*, Doc."

Both Catherine and Sara exchanged glances and stifled smiles: nobody had ever called Grissom "Doc" before.

But Grissom didn't seem to mind. After all, this was Boot Hill, wasn't it?

Lopez was saying, "Those damn detectors should have been howling all night."

Catherine said, "We'll figure it out."

Lopez ran his hand over his face again. "This is going to give Byron Ivers and the rest of that crowd all the ammo they're gonna need."

Sara considered the bullet-riddled casino around them and wondered about Lopez's choice of the word *ammo*.

"And who is Byron Ivers?" Catherine asked.

Jacks said, "He's one of the assholes . . ."

Lopez shot the sergeant a withering look.

". . . I'm sorry . . . *concerned citizens*," Jacks continued, "who bitch about the Biker Blowout every year."

Lopez said, "It's a constant argument here—the merchants who consider the event bad for the town's reputation, and others who appreciate the business the Blowout brings in."

"The anti-Blowout group," Grissom said, "would seem to have a pretty good case now."

The chief said, "Maybe, but nothing remotely like this has ever happened before, Doc. Generally, the bikers were rowdy but behaved. A good segment of the population here thinks it's important that the town continue to host the event, since basically it supports some businesses for the next six months."

"Sounds like a real love-hate relationship," Sara said.

Lopez nodded. "Not a lot has changed here since the days of the Old West. Same thing happened back in Tombstone."

"Tombstone?" Catherine asked.

"Yes," Grissom said, jumping in. "The city fathers there had the same problem. The cowboys who spent their paychecks in town supplied a large part of the economy, but those same cowboys, including the Clantons, McLowerys, Frank Stillwell, and the others, were the very ones that were tearing down Tombstone, making it impossible for the city fathers to lure families in and build a respectable community."

Cody Jacks said, "One family came—the Earps."

"True," Grissom said with a small smile. "They came to represent the town and eventually it got to the point where they had to make a stand . . . and the cowboys lost."

Suddenly Sara understood why Grissom had the history of Tombstone on his mind.

Sofia came up, planting herself in front of Catherine. "I'm heading back to Vegas," she said. "Anything else we need to take?"

"I think that's everything," Catherine said, eyes narrow with thought. "For now, anyway. I'm sure we'll be collecting more evidence throughout the night."

"I'll take the stuff to the lab," Sofia said, "then I'll get to work with Archie sorting through the videotapes."

Catherine gave her a quick nod. "Let us know as soon as you have something."

They said goodbyes and all watched Sofia pick her way through the mess on the floor and go out the door even as the paramedics came in with another gurney—this one for Nick Valpo. The group moved to one side as the paramedics loaded the body and hauled it away.

The next thing Sara knew, Grissom was hovering over where the body had been, his eyes scouring the floor amid the broken glass, scattered chips, shredded gaming tables, and other flotsam left over from the battle.

"Grissom," she asked, "now what?"

He froze, his eyes coming up to meet hers. "Valpo was right there," he said, pointing to the spot where the body had been.

"Yeah, so?"

"That means the killer had to be right about where I'm standing."

She glanced at where the body had lain, her memory going back to the near contact wound of the head shot that had killed Valpo.

Grissom's eyes met Sara's and a reconstruction played in the theaters of both their minds.

The killer is in the casino. He or she is watching Valpo, waiting for their chance, or waiting for the Rusty Spokes to start the gun battle, depending on whether this is all part of a plan or just a lucky break for a murderer.

The firefight erupts.

Bullets fly, everywhere. The killer is either already close or gets close to Valpo. He or she wants this badly enough to be at personal risk in order to assassinate the gang leader—both in public view and in the line of fire.

Valpo takes a hit to the shoulder and goes down. His killer senses the opportunity and moves even closer, the small pistol seeming to fly to the back of the Predator's head, the trigger practically pulling itself. A flash of light from the muzzle, and half a second later, a sharp crack barely makes a dent in the cacophony of the gunfight going on around it.

Flopping once, Valpo goes still. The deed is done and the killer relishes the exquisite feeling of accomplishment, an electric jolt of victory—Nick Valpo is dead.

"Okay," Sara sighed. "You're standing in the right place."

"If I shot Valpo with an automatic," Grissom said, "the shell casing should be around here somewhere. I looked for it when the body was here but came up empty. A second try can't hurt."

Being careful to avoid standing in Grissom's light, Sara joined the search, combing the floor for a metal casing little bigger than a fingernail.

In the meantime, Catherine moved off to search a slightly wider area, in case the thing might have been kicked or knocked away somehow. She also checked where the female dealer had died, since a similar casing might have been produced if the vics had shared a killer.

Lopez and Jacks seemed just about to walk away when Nick hustled up.

"Not rocket science," he said with a crooked grin,

"figuring out why those metal detectors didn't work."

Sliding back a few steps to the group, Catherine asked, "Why's that?"

"Batteries are dead."

They all looked at each other, dumbfounded.

"Batteries?" Chief Lopez asked incredulously.

"The Four Kings, it seems, did *not* spend top dollar on their security equipment," Nick said. "After all, from a management point of view, how often is there going to be a shoot-out in your casino, anyway?"

Lopez was shaking his head in disbelief. "Dead batteries made this possible?"

"As a police chief," Nick said, "this shouldn't surprise you. What industry spends the least on video surveillance equipment?"

The chief did not hesitate. "Banking."

"Same theory here," Nick said. "Don't spend too much money on what you'll never really need. There's nothing wrong with the detector itself—it's a model I'm familiar with. Battery life, on a normal day? Upwards of nine or ten hours. Somebody needs to regularly change the batteries, which is no big deal—except in this instance, they didn't do it."

Without moving his feet, Grissom asked, "How does every metal detector in a casino have its batteries go dead at the same time?"

Nick said, "Who's to say they did? Who knows how long they've been dead? Anyway, if they did have one staffer in charge of the whole perimeter, and changing all the batteries at once, all of 'em going dead at about the same time is possible."

Lopez snapped into action. "Cody, find Henry, now. Tell him to get his ass over here now."

"What if he doesn't—"

"What part of *now* don't you get, Cody?"

Looking a little wounded, Jacks lumbered off in search of the casino's security chief.

While they waited, Grissom and Sara resumed the search for a possible shell casing.

"A lot of places have battery-operated metal detectors," Nick said to Lopez. "For one thing, during a power outage, they'll still work."

Lopez nodded, but obviously still seethed.

Nick went on: "I would've expected them to stagger the times more between each individual detector, just to avoid this very thing. You have six detectors, like the front doors here? Then you have three that have their batteries switched from midnight to noon, and the other three that get changed between noon and midnight, so you've always got at least three working."

Grissom looked up long enough to say, "This is sounding more like conspiracy than simple bad planning."

"You think?" Lopez asked, with no trace of sarcasm.

Shrugging, Grissom said, "If not conspiracy, how did both gangs know that the metal detectors would be out at this precise time?"

"Or worse yet," Catherine said, "that they've been off all *week*?"

Sara was shining her flashlight on a spot near Grissom's right foot.

"Right *there*," she said.

Grissom bent down and picked up a small brass shell casing that had been obscured not only by the shadow of Valpo's pant leg, but by a small pile of chips that had provided the casing a small cave to hide in.

"Nice eye, Sara," Grissom said. "A twenty-two."

He plopped it into an evidence bag and sealed it.

Catherine said, "Too bad we couldn't have found it before Sofia left."

"At least we've got it," Grissom said, and put the bag in his pocket. "Chief, you know anybody who carries a twenty-two automatic?"

"Pretty common piece," Lopez said. "Could be townie, tourist, or biker."

"Nonetheless," Grissom said, undaunted, "it's a start."

Sara began working the area where the dealer had died, and soon said, "Bingo!"

And Grissom bagged a second twenty-two shell, saying, "So the execution was witnessed, and the witness was executed."

Cody Jacks sauntered up, Henry Cippolina at his side.

"Henry," Lopez said with a terrible smile, reaching out to put his arm around the security chief's shoulder. "Who's in charge of changing the batteries in the metal detectors?"

Cippolina looked confused. "Maintenance department, Chief—why?"

"Because all the batteries, in the metal detectors?"

"Yeah?"

"Are dead."

The already pasty Cippolina somehow went a shade whiter. "Oh, shit."

"Can I quote you on that, Henry? . . . Now, whose job would it be to make sure the maintenance department has actually changed the batteries?"

"I usually have one of my security guys check them," Cippolina said.

"And who would have had that responsibility tonight?"

Cippolina rubbed the fingers of his left hand across his forehead, as if he might squeeze the information out. After a moment he said, "Tom Price."

"Where's Tom now?"

Cippolina and Cody Jacks were both craning their necks around to look for the security guard.

"Well," Cippolina said, "he *should* be here."

"Snack bar?" Catherine offered.

They all turned in that direction.

"Maybe," Jacks said, "but he should have been among the first to give statements, so he could get back out here and help keep order."

Grissom asked, "Remember seeing him, Sergeant?"

"Hey, I'm not in charge of him. Right now I feel lucky to know where my *own* ass is."

The group headed over to the snack bar, Cippolina and Jacks slowly scanning the place for their lost security guard. The snack bar was full, probably far more crowded than during its busiest rush, people filling every seat—counter, tables, booths.

Everybody looked exhausted, sweaty, and scared. A few had broken down and ordered something to eat, but most just nursed half-full cups of cold coffee, the only waitress now leaning against the counter, her trailing mascara an obvious sign she had been crying. The smell of cordite had been replaced by the familiar if pungent aroma of fried fish, french fries, burgers, stale sweat, cigarette smoke, and fear.

An older woman touched Lopez's hand as they passed. "Chief Lopez, are those terrible bikers going to come back?"

Lopez patted the woman's hand and shook his head. "No, Mrs. Hill, they're not coming back."

As they moved on, Lopez told them, "Mrs. Hill is a regular. Lives over on the west side."

Catherine asked, "You spotted this fella Price yet?"

"No," Jacks answered.

Cippolina added, "I don't know where in hell he coulda got to."

Sara was right behind Lopez when the chief called over his two investigators, Adam Bell and Troy Hamilton. Bell, blond and in his mid-thirties, sported tiny laugh lines around light blue eyes; he wore a Boot Hill PD windbreaker over a white shirt and jeans. Hamilton's outfit was the same, except his shirt was blue; he weighed maybe fifty pounds more than Bell, was about ten years older, and his hair had gone gunmetal gray.

"Either of you boys seen Tom Price?" Lopez asked.

Bell and Hamilton looked at each other, then shook their heads in unison.

"Was he even *working* today?" Bell asked.

Scratching his neck, Jacks said, "I do remember seeing him around three, come to think of it . . . beginning of shift?"

Lopez heaved another of his trademark heavy sighs. "Nobody's seen him *since* then?"

Bell shrugged, Hamilton shook his head.

As the local cops spoke, Sara noticed a man in a

cheap tuxedo, possibly a pit boss, rising at the far end of the snack bar and making his way toward the far exit.

"Sir," she called to him, but he either pretended not to hear her or actually had not.

"*Sir,*" she called, loudly this time, the group around her all snapping their heads in his direction.

The guy looked back and now seemed to be deciding whether to stop or make a run for it.

"Keith!" Cippolina said.

The guy froze.

"Mr. Draper," Jacks shouted in his cop voice, "get your ass back over here. Pronto."

But Draper hesitated.

Jacks took an ominous step in the man's direction, the others starting to fan out, a practically instinctive move, making themselves less of a cluster target.

Finally, Keith Draper started back toward the group of law enforcement. He had short black hair, a neatly trimmed salt-and-pepper beard, and sharp dark blue eyes. The tux looked like he had been wearing it a while, and the black dress shoes had not seen polish since the Clinton administration.

Draper had taken only two steps toward them when his right hand went into his jacket pocket and their hands all went to their pistols.

"*Freeze,* Keith!" Jacks ordered, his pistol in hand.

Draper took another step.

Jacks's gun barrel leveled at Draper.

"Whoa," Draper said, the hand moving away from the pocket, fingers splayed to indicate that hand was still empty, "Cody! Easy!"

"Then don't move, Keith," Jacks said.

Lopez and Bell each had their pistols drawn now and had fanned out so each had a clean, clear shot. As Jacks kept Draper covered, Lopez and Bell moved in from the sides. While Bell got the man's right hand and swung it behind him, Lopez dipped into the jacket pocket and pulled out a small blue pistol.

"Gun!" the chief said.

Frightened murmurs filled the snack bar.

Bell wasted no time forcing Draper down. "Spread 'em, Keith," he said, his voice high, tense. "You know the drill. . . ."

Draper started to say something, but Sara couldn't make it out.

"*Do* it," Lopez interrupted.

Draper complied, and Bell cuffed him and patted him down.

"Clean," Bell said, helping Draper back to his feet.

"Keith," Lopez said as he holstered his own pistol, "what the hell are you doing with this piece?"

Draper whined, "I *always* carry it."

"Why in the hell did you reach into your goddamn pocket? You got a death wish?"

Draper shrugged. "I . . . I was going to give it to you."

"Oh?"

"The *gun*! Hand over the gun. . . ."

Jacks was shaking his head. "Goddamn . . . you fired it during the gunfight, didn't you, Keith?"

"Well . . . they were all shooting!" Draper pouted. "I was trying to protect the customers, is all."

"Then why were you sneaking out just now?"

No response.

"You were going to ditch the pistol, right?"

Draper said nothing.

Grissom stepped forward and Lopez dropped the pistol into an evidence bag the CSI held out.

"Smith & Wesson 2214," Grissom said. "Quite possibly the same caliber that killed Nick Valpo. And possibly Vanessa Delware, as well."

Every eye in the snack bar had turned to Keith Draper. He was crying now, shaking his head.

"I didn't think I *hit* anyone. . . ."

"Oooh, Keith," Lopez said, "you're in a lotta trouble. You wouldn't have any idea where Tom Price is, would ya?"

Draper shook his head and kept sniffling.

The police chief shook his head. He glanced at his CSI guests, and his gaze settled on Grissom. "I tell you, Doc, sometimes I don't know what's worse— the bikers or the casino employees."

5

WARRICK HAD DEPOSITED TOMAS NUÑEZ at a workstation in a lab office, with the Ames computer hooked up to a flat screen.

Nuñez had a room-filling personality. He was shorter than most people perceived, and older, though the thinning hair should have been a giveaway. The charismatic computer guru projected a bandito vibe in his faded jeans and black T-shirt (emblazoned with the spiked wheel logo of Colombian singer Juanes), and his shoulder-length black hair (slicked back and ponytailed) bore modest, almost stylish streaks of gray; his black mustache seemed more droopy than usual, but late-in-the-day CSI calls like this one weren't SOP.

"You want to know all you can, naturally," Nuñez said.

"Naturally," Warrick said.

"But these things can take time. Fast track or slow?"

"Fast would be cool."

Nuñez said, "I can give you both—from what you've told me, I have a few ideas about where to look. That'll get you *on* track, fast; then I can go through in-depth, so when you go to court, every digital 'i' and 't' will be dotted and crossed."

"No wonder Catherine adores you, man."

"From your lips to her ears. . . . Check back in an hour, *amigo*."

"Office is yours."

A throat cleared and Warrick glanced over at Greg, in the doorway, paperwork in hand.

Warrick slipped out into the corridor with the young CSI. "Got something already?"

"Couple of prints off the note, couple more off the envelope."

"Good start."

Greg gestured with a head nod down the hall. "David told me that Dr. Robbins is ready to go over the autopsy with us—can you get away?"

"Your timing and the doc's are perfect. Tomas says he may have an idea or two about the suicide note in an hour or so."

"Cool."

Warrick stuck his head back into the office and told the computer expert he was heading over to Doc Robbins's domain.

"If you get something before I'm back," Warrick said, "call my cell."

"You really want to wrap this one up quick, don't you, *jefe*?"

"If it's a straight suicide, I want to get out of the bereaved husband's life. But if he's a murderer, I'd like to do his late wife a favor and not have him sleeping in their double bed, enjoying the extra room."

"I hear you," Nuñez said, and turned back to the screen.

Warrick and Greg walked briskly to the coroner's wing, got into blue scrubs, and joined Dr. Albert Robbins in the autopsy room, a sterile chamber, cold in several senses of the word, with tiled walls and floor and metal doors—not Warrick's favorite place to be, but always a vital stop to make on the journey to justice.

The body of Kelly Ames lay nude on the metal table; Dr. Robbins stood on the opposite side as the two CSIs joined him. Graying, with short hair and a full beard, Doc Robbins had warm, crinkly eyes that seemed at odds with these surroundings, not to mention his profession. Warrick had known Doc Robbins for some time now and had never once seen the man lose his professional cool or his personal compassion. The coroner possessed one of the sharpest minds in the department.

"David said you have doubts this is a suicide," Robbins said blandly, leaning over the body, his metal crutch occupying its usual place in the corner while he worked.

Warrick shrugged. "Let's say I've got issues."

"That's good to have, issues," Robbins said. "Because there's no doubt Kelly Ames was murdered."

Greg's eyes tightened. "You know that because her skin isn't red?"

"It was a good indicator," Robbins said, switching to teacher mode now. "Do you know why?"

"Well, I don't claim I knew this before Warrick told me."

"And what did he tell you?"

"That people exposed to lethal doses of carbon monoxide turn that shade."

Smiling gravely, Robbins said, "That's one of the symptoms. If, as in Kelly's case, her skin *hasn't* turned color, what would be the next step?"

Greg knew he was being quizzed, but from what Warrick saw, the kid seemed to be thriving on it.

"I'd come knocking on your door and ask you to do a blood test . . . to tell us if there's CO in Kelly's lungs."

"Good. But you don't have to knock, I can tell you right now—no carbon monoxide in her lungs at all. Which tells us . . . ?"

Greg didn't hesitate at all. "She was dead when somebody put her in that car and staged a suicide."

Warrick said, "Which is likely why she had on the odd combination of colors and a T-shirt on inside out."

Nodding, Greg said, "Someone else dressed her."

Warrick asked the coroner, "What about time of death?"

Robbins also didn't hesitate. "Sometime around noon."

"Which is when Kelly's husband said he was on his way to work." Warrick studied the somber, pretty face belonging to the corpse on the slab. "Did you find anything else?"

"Cotton fibers in her nose and lungs. She was suffocated with a pillow, most likely."

Greg said, "So she was in bed, in pajamas or lingerie or undies or whatever, and the murderer smothered her and then got her into some clothes and into the garage and the car."

"That's a reasonable reconstruction," Warrick said. To Robbins, he said, "Thanks, Doc."

"Sure. Warrick?"

"Yeah?"

Robbins, his face blank and yet infinitely sad, nodded toward his patient. "Let's see if we can't do right by her."

"That's gonna happen," Warrick said with quiet confidence.

He and Greg left the autopsy room, got out of the scrubs, and—in the corridor—Warrick said, "So far, we've got two suspects, the husband and the friend."

"Why the friend?" Greg asked.

"You know the rule, Greg—first on the scene, first suspect. Who called nine-one-one?"

Glumly, Greg said, "The friend."

"That makes you unhappy?"

"Yeah, well, I liked her. She was nice."

"You mean she was a hottie."

Greg frowned. "Hey. That's not fair. I'd just hate to think she's a killer, is all."

Warrick shook his head. "Do you want chapter and verse on how many hotties have torn up chicken coops since I started this job? I don't care if she lives at the Playboy Mansion or she's some little old lady offering us cookies—this is business. Stay objective, and let's check out both the friend and the husband."

"Good idea," Greg said. ". . . I'll take the friend."

Warrick sighed, then laughed. "Oh-kay. Just remember what I said, and meet me where Nuñez is working, in an hour."

They parted ways and Warrick found himself a quiet office where he could try to corroborate Charlie Ames's story.

Tonight's return to graveyard provided him a reminder of why he preferred swing shift. Here he sat in an office just after one A.M., with no one he could call at Cactus Plastics to find out what time Charlie Ames had come into work and no one to question about Megan Voetberg's assertion that Ames was having an affair with a coworker, and that his wife knew about it.

Most of the questions Warrick really wanted answered would have to wait until sunup, toward the tail end of the shift. This was an old pattern, a constant night-shift problem, that he hadn't missed at all. In the meantime, he settled for doing background on Charlie and Kelly Ames, tapping the many data banks, local and national, that didn't care what time it was.

High school sweethearts who went to college together at UNLV, the Ames couple had been married a little over two years. After college, Kelly had worked briefly for an insurance company before taking the job at the postal encoding station that allowed them to work roughly the same hours. Charlie, who had spent college summer internships at Cactus Plastics, had graduated to a decent job there. If something had gone south with their marriage, their online story didn't reveal it.

An hour later, Warrick knew little more than that and was running late to meet Greg. After shutting down his computer, Warrick trotted off and found Greg sitting with Nuñez, both of them wearing headsets, bouncing to two different rhythms, the pair having traded iPods.

"I like this," Nuñez said, too loud. "What is it?"

"The last Garbage CD," Greg said, his voice also rising to where he could hear it over the headphone volume. "Great, isn't it? . . . This is pretty tight, too."

Nuñez said, "That's Molotov. Latin punk."

Normally, this musical detente across cultures and even generations (Nuñez being at least twenty years older than Greg) would have given the music-loving Warrick a warm glow. Tonight, the only glow in him came from a burning desire to capture whoever murdered Kelly Ames.

Greg looked up, saw Warrick, then grinned and jerked the buds out. "You gotta hear this stuff. Tomas, what's this band again?"

"Molotov," Nuñez repeated.

"Molotov," Greg said, slipping the buds back on. "This *rocks*."

Warrick shook his head and Greg grinned sheepishly; the buds came out again.

"Sorry," Greg said.

Warrick tried to soften the blow: "I'll have a listen after we close the case."

But it came out harshly, and the mood in the room changed as abruptly as if Grissom had just walked in and found them using a Bunsen burner to warm up pizza.

While Greg looked chagrined, Nuñez only smiled.

All professionalism now, Greg said, "Megan Voetberg checks out. She's the real deal."

"You already *had* that opinion," Warrick said.

"Hey," Greg said, hurt or pretending to be. "She may be hot, but work is work . . . and her story checked out, and nothing suspicious turned up."

"What about prints from the note and envelope?"

"Just one set," Greg said. "And here's the fun part—they *don't* match Kelly Ames."

Warrick thought about that. "We'll run them through AFIS and—"

"Hey, *amigo,* you want a killer," Nuñez said, his grin growing wider, "I got a killer for you."

"That sounds definitive," Warrick said, and pulled up a chair.

"Your guy Ames is not an idiot," Nuñez said. "He's even kind of smart . . . just not—"

"Smart enough," Warrick said.

"Had enough on the ball to figure out somebody might go poking around in his computer." Nuñez pulled out a printout and handed it to Warrick, keeping a duplicate in hand for himself. "Hubby wrote the suicide note *after* Kelly was gone."

Warrick digested that for a moment, then asked, "How could you know that?"

"Here's how smart Kelly's husband was—smart enough to change the clock, move the file, delete the original, then change the clock back. To the naked eye—the untrained naked eye, anyway—it looked like Kelly typed the suicide note within an hour of her time of death."

"And we know she didn't how?"

"'Cause of the metadata."

"The meta what?" Warrick asked.

"Metadata," Nuñez said. "That's where our smart killer turns very, very dumb."

"Well," Greg admitted, "I never heard of meta-data, either."

"Yes," the computer guru said, "but you aren't a

murdering husband faking his wife's suicide. . . . See, metadata is basically data *about* data. It's embedded in every Word document, Excel spreadsheet, and PowerPoint presentation. Tells when the original file was created . . . and the metadata for the suicide note? Over an hour *after* Kelly's TOD."

"Whoa," Warrick said. "Never mind Catherine, Tomas. *I* love your ass."

"Well, I do have my moments," Nuñez grinned. "But be prepared to love more of me, 'cause that's not *all* I found."

"Oh?"

"Found a bunch of deleted e-mails coming from . . . and going *to* . . . the same address—Plasticgirl@nev.isp."

"Which is who?" Warrick asked.

Nuñez shrugged. "And now love fades—afraid I can't find that out until morning. Get me a court order, and I'll talk to the internet service provider and find out."

Greg asked, "*Where* were the deleted e-mails?"

"In unallocated space on the hard drive," Nuñez said. "When you delete something on your computer, it's not really gone forever."

Warrick said, "I knew that."

Greg said, "Me too," but seemed to be covering.

Nuñez ignored both of them and explained anyway: "Deleted things go to unallocated space on the hard drive until that space is used by some other file."

Nodding, Warrick said, "And how many e-mails did you uncover?"

"Couple hundred."

"Whoa," Warrick said, his mouth dropping open like a trapdoor. "*How* many?"

"A couple hundred," Nuñez repeated, "at least."

Warrick, shaking his head, said, "How is that even *possible*?"

Stroking his mustache, Nuñez asked, "How much memory on your first computer—a meg maybe?"

Warrick shrugged. "Yeah, I think."

Nuñez gestured to the computer tower on the counter. "This puppy has an eighty *gigabyte* hard drive. Takes a lot longer, these days, to start reusing hard drive space . . . unless you're downloading movies or something."

"So," Greg said. "What exactly is in these hundreds of e-mails?"

"Pretty much everything you would want for a motive," Nuñez said. "Both of them saying, 'I love you,' both complaining about Kelly, what an obstacle she is to them, and one from this morning where Charlie said, 'We're not going to have to worry about her anymore.'"

The computer expert had a folder of printed-out e-mails, with significant ones marked with Post-its. This he handed to Warrick, who perused them.

"One more question," Warrick said, sitting forward. "If I didn't want to wait until morning and get a court order . . . how might someone go about finding out who Plasticgirl@nev.isp is?"

Nuñez eyeballed him. "Are you going to use this knowledge before you get a court order?"

Warrick waved that off. "I'm not going to use it in court. Just looking to move forward faster."

"Nothing else?"

Serving up a nasty chuckle, Warrick said, "Well . . . I thought I might whisper it in Charlie Ames's ear. Like a sweet nothing?"

Nuñez seemed to like the sound of that. "Okay, then. . . . If you're not going to mention how you obtained the info, you might just ask me."

"*Ask* you?"

Nuñez grinned again. "I have an old friend at nev.isp who I spoke to just a short time ago. . . . You know—just trying to move forward faster?"

Warrick grinned slowly. "I see . . . and what did your old friend have to say?"

"That things have been going really well at work and she got a promotion."

"That's nice."

"Yeah. Oh, and she also mentioned that Plasticgirl is the user ID of a certain Henderson woman named Paula Ferguson."

"Tomas," Warrick said, "has anyone ever told you you're a genius?"

"First time tonight," Nuñez admitted. "One other little detail you might care to know."

"What's that?"

"Plasticgirl, Paula Ferguson? She works at Cactus Plastics."

Warrick's eyebrows rose. "Tomas—you . . . are . . . the . . . *man.*"

"Second time tonight," Nuñez said with a toothy grin, "for that one. . . ."

Forty minutes later, Warrick and Greg met up with Brass out in front of the Ames house; a black-and-white rolled in seconds later. Throughout the neighborhood, lights were off, the Ames house shrouded in darkness. The only sound was a lone dog squawking at them from down the street, behind a fence.

Brass signaled the uniformed officer from the black-and-white to go around behind the house, and for Greg to back him up.

Warrick and Brass went up to the front door and spread out on either side. The detective's look silently asked Warrick if he was ready, and the CSI nodded.

Then Brass hit the doorbell.

Both men had their pistols unholstered and at their sides. They waited, the night air cool, but not enough to keep sweat from running down Warrick's back beneath the navy blue CSI windbreaker.

Nothing happened.

Brass rang the bell again.

This time a light clicked on inside and they heard someone moving around. Finally, the outside light came on and Charlie Ames peered at them through one of the door's tiny windows.

Shaking his head, Kelly Ames's husband threw open the door, wearing navy blue boxers and nothing else. His chest was pasty white with very little hair, and he had skinny arms and spindly knobkneed white legs. And yet at least two women had loved this prize specimen.

Ames's voice was a whisper so harsh and loud that the idea behind whispering was nullified. "What the hell do you people want at this hour?"

Several other dogs in the neighborhood picked up the chorus of the first.

"You might want to ask us in," Brass said, "so we can tell you."

"And maybe I might not. Maybe you have something official to show me, like a warrant, if you're gonna bother me again, after what I been through."

Warrick stepped forward and his eyes locked with the husband's. "It has been a rough night, hasn't it, Mr. Ames?"

Brass's sigh was beyond world-weary, though his smile was perfunctory. "We're going to talk, Mr. Ames—out here, in there, it doesn't matter to us. But we *are* going to talk about you and . . . what's her name?"

Warrick said, "Paula Ferguson."

Brass said, "Thanks . . . you and Paula Ferguson, Mr. Ames. And we're going to talk about you and her *right now.*"

Ames's face went whiter than his chest; then another color, a yellowish green, began to spread across his features, and Warrick wondered if the guy might not throw up on the porch.

"Inside," Brass said, and gently nudged Ames back into the house. Ames did not protest. Warrick followed them.

"What do you people think you know, anyway?" the husband asked.

Brass did not answer, and neither did Warrick, as Ames turned on a light and led them into the living room, a tiny area with ratty olive-green carpeting, a sofa, a chair, a cheap coffee table, and a good-sized TV with a DVD player and a game system hooked up to it; no books in the room, only a few magazines (*People, TV Guide, Sports Illustrated*), and a newspaper opened to the sports section.

Their host sat in the chair and gestured to the sofa, but neither Brass nor Warrick took his invitation.

Into his walkie-talkie, Brass said, "We've got him."

"*Ten-four,*" came the uniform's voice through the radio.

"What do you mean," Ames said, ever more alarmed, sitting forward, "'got' me?"

"Before we go any further," Brass said, "I need to tell you something."

Ames was getting testy now. "About time you explained yourselves!"

"You have the right to remain silent . . ."

"What . . . ?"

Brass shook his head. "Don't interrupt, Mr. Ames, and this will go faster. You have the right to an attorney. . . ."

The detective went on a while, finally saying, "Do you understand the rights I have just explained to you?"

Ames nodded numbly.

"Out loud, please."

"I understand."

Warrick sat next to the man on the sofa and Brass hovered over them.

The CSI asked, "You want to tell us why you did it?"

"Did what?"

"Murdered your wife."

The three words seemed to hit Ames like physical blows, and he said nothing for several long moments.

Finally, he managed, "It's an absurd accusation. I loved her. We hit a rough patch. She committed suicide. End of story."

"Not even close to the whole story, Mr. Ames," Warrick said. "We knew this evening this wasn't a suicide."

Ames glared at Warrick as if the CSI were insane.

Warrick said, "Mr. Ames, carbon monoxide will turn your skin red. Kelly's wasn't. She had no carbon monoxide in her lungs and she had cotton fibers in her nose and lungs, indicating she'd been smothered, probably with a pillow. She was murdered. End of story."

"I don't see it," Ames said, obviously stalling for something, anything.

Greg and the uniformed officer came in through the front door to join the party.

Warrick signaled to the hall with a head bob, and Greg headed down toward the bedroom, pulling a roll of large garbage bags out of his jacket pocket as he went. When he returned, Greg had the pillows from the Ames's bedroom in four plastic bags.

"Mr. Ames," Warrick said, "fibers from one of those pillows are going to match the fibers from Kelly's nose, aren't they?"

"I . . . I don't see how."

Brass said, "Let's talk about six months' worth of hot e-mails between you and Paula Ferguson."

Ames's face fell into his hands.

"Charlie," Warrick said, shaking his head, getting familiar for the first time. "Where did you think all those e-mails went when you deleted them? Outer space? Blew off into the ether, maybe? And you certainly couldn't think we wouldn't catch that the 'suicide note' was written well after Kelly died. You may think you know your way around computers, but our guy can make them talk and sing and bark on their hind legs."

Ames did not respond.

"You had a nothing plan, Charlie," Warrick said, "and you carried it out badly, to boot. Let me refresh your memory."

You've finally had enough of Kelly and her bitching and plan to trade her in for a new model—Paula, but you don't want to give up the house or any of your stuff. You've got a nice little nest egg in the bank, too, right? So you catch Kelly while she's still sleeping. You press the pillow over her head and push down. She thrashes as she fights, but she's not strong enough to keep you from smothering the life out of her. It's relatively quick and not that hard on either of you. . . .

You dress her, but you're so jacked up about the whole thing and how smooth it's going, how smart you are, that you don't pay any attention to the colors or the fact that you're putting her shirt on inside out. You place her in the car, then go back in and type the suicide note, change the computer clock so it looks like Kelly wrote it before she died, then you put that in the vehicle, too. Then you turn the key on and leave while clouds of carbon monoxide form.

Never dawns on you that her friend will miss her soon enough to cause trouble, and it never even occurs to you that she won't have carbon monoxide in her lungs. Dead people don't breathe, after all. . . . That's what makes them dead.

Warrick finished with, "My only question is . . . did Paula know? Was she in on this, maybe even this was *her* idea . . . ?"

Ames's head shot up, his gaze burning into Warrick. "Paula had *no* idea—you have *got* to believe me."

"Yeah," Brass said affably, "because you're so well known for your honesty, right, Mr. Ames?" He signaled to the uniformed officer, who got Ames up. "Get him dressed, cuff him, and take him in."

"*Really,*" Ames pleaded, his distraught look bouncing from Warrick to Brass and back again. "Paula had *nothing* to do with it. She's innocent!"

Warrick thought, *Innocent isn't the word for those steamy e-mails,* but he said nothing. Besides, the e-mails did not indicate a murder plan, just a motive.

"About . . . about Kelly's clothes," Ames said, hesitating to look back at Warrick.

"Yeah?"

"That . . . that wasn't my fault."

"Oh?"

"I'm . . . I'm color-blind."

Warrick grunted. "Not your *only* blind spot, huh, Charlie?"

He said nothing, head hanging now, and the uniformed guys hustled him away.

With their suspect gone, Brass asked the CSI, "Do you believe him about the girlfriend?"

Warrick shrugged. "Kind of. But we'll check her out just the same. We've already got Kelly Ames's killer, though. Between the evidence and what he gave up even after he'd been Mirandized . . . he's nailed."

"At least we got him quick," Brass said.

"Let's hope quick's the way Kelly died," Warrick said. "Because there's nothing more we can do for her."

They walked outside and, before they'd reached their cars, their cell phones started ringing.

"Brown," Warrick said. He heard Brass answer his as well.

Greg loaded the bagged pillows into the back of the Denali and came around just as Warrick's call ended.

"What is it?" Greg asked.

"Another case. We'll head to the new crime scene from here."

"Where?"

"An apartment house on Paradise Road," Warrick said, "over by the convention center. . . . You drive."

Brass came up. "You get the call for the apartment on Paradise, by any chance?"

Warrick nodded.

"See you there," Brass said, and climbed into his Taurus.

Driving more confidently now, Greg turned off Sweeney, going south on Tenth Street to St. Louis Avenue, then back west to Paradise Road and south again. After crossing Sahara, he passed the Hilton on their left, then the convention center. On the other side of Paradise, the monorail tracks followed the road and beyond that the night sky was spiked with the silhouette of V—Shawn Victor's latest billion-dollar hotel.

Immediately south of the convention center, across Terry Drive, squatted a two-story white stucco apartment house that looked more like a cheap motel. Instead of the usual orange-tile roof, this one bore a grimy green number, guaranteed to hold the heat. Tiny air conditioners stuck through the walls below small picture windows whose only view was the convention center and its parking lot. Cars were parked nose-in toward a building in which only a few lights were on.

Their call was on the second floor, toward the east end of the building.

Not like a motel, Warrick thought, reassessing. *More a minimum security prison. . . . Missing only the fence.*

They went through a central first-floor door and climbed dark stairs to the second floor, where the dimly lit corridor was lined with wood-frame doors on either side. White paint, perhaps intended to make the place seem homey, gave instead an institutional feel.

Halfway to the east end, they found a door ajar, revealing a uniformed officer inside talking to a young woman.

The officer was a tall, slender African-American with a very short-trimmed Afro and wide brown eyes. A thin black mustache trailed across his upper lip and his name plate read CHARLES.

He nodded to them as they came in; Brass trailed by Warrick and Greg.

"This is Tara Donnelly," Charles said.

The young woman, maybe twenty-eight, sat on a large brown sofa. Her hair was long and red, her eyes brown and red-rimmed from tears, her skin pale white. Warrick estimated she weighed maybe one-eighty, and she had a certain well-fed farm-girl attractiveness, wearing a long shiny blue skirt and a black Clash T-shirt while she clutched a tissue. At the mention of her name, she looked up and tried to smile politely, but it didn't come off.

Brass introduced himself, Warrick, and Greg.

"Ms. Donnelly," Brass began, "would you care to tell us what happened?"

She blew her nose into the tissue, took a deep breath, and said, "I went out tonight . . . with a couple of girlfriends?"

Warrick knew Brass wanted to know the girlfriends' names, but that could wait. They let her talk.

"We've been wanting to go to Drizzle. You know, the club?"

The trendy, expensive nightclub inside Las Palmeras Hotel and Casino was the vision of the Mateo brothers, Julio and Enrique, who had grown up in Vegas with the dream of owning the coolest, hippest casino in the city; and now they had it.

Warrick and Brass both nodded for her to continue.

"We'd been there for an hour or so . . . when I met this guy?"

She was an up-talker, Warrick thought, a Valley Girl malady with which CSI Sara Sidle was mildly infected; but this woman seemed terminally afflicted.

"Guy have a name?" Brass asked.

"He said 'Rick.' He was medium tall, with dark hair? Receding hairline, I guess you'd say, brown eyes, and he hardly ever smiled. I thought he was way serious and smart and stuff? Turns out he was psychotic."

"Did your girlfriends see him?" Brass asked.

She thought about that. "No, actually, they'd hooked up with their own guys by then. Jamie had left already with some hunk. And Natalie, she was dancing with this dude, but they were on the other side of the club. With his friends? So I could barely see her."

Brass asked, "What happened next?"

"I told Rick I had to get home. Because I had to work tomorrow. He must have followed me, because the next thing I know, he's in the staircase with me, offering to walk me to my door? I tried to say no, but he just kept, I don't know, easing me toward my apartment. Then we were here, and I unlocked the door and he pushed me inside."

"Did you scream?" Brass asked.

She shook her head. "I was going to, but from out of nowhere, he had this little gun, and he pointed it at me! He said that if I made a sound? He'd shoot me and whoever else came through the door."

Brass nodded. "Then?"

Looking down at her lap now, Tara said, "Then . . . he raped me."

That, Warrick noted, she did *not* phrase as a question.

"Did he hurt you?" Warrick asked.

She gave up another half shrug. "He was rough, but . . . he didn't really hurt me. Not . . . not physically, anyway."

"Did you fight him?" Brass asked.

Shaking her head, she said, "I scratched him once, but he slapped me . . . and I stopped."

"May we scrape under your fingernails?" Warrick asked.

"If you think it will help?"

Greg did the honors, scraping the skin from under her nails into a small cellophane bag that he sealed.

Brass asked, "Would you recognize your attacker if you saw him again?"

"In a heartbeat," Tara said, her jaw set. "I don't drink, Officer—I was dead sober when this happened."

"Did he take anything?"

She thought about that. "No—he just . . . *did* me . . . and then he left."

"Did he wear a condom?"

"Yes! Thank God for small favors. And latex gloves, too."

Warrick frowned. "Really?"

"Yeah! It was weird. It was like he was afraid he'd leave fingerprints on me?"

Brass gestured to Warrick and Greg. "Do you mind if our CSIs have a look around while you and I chat a little more?"

"That's fine," she said. "Anything you want, anything you think'll help."

Warrick and Greg went to work, Greg starting in the kitchen, Warrick in the bedroom. The room was small, a queen-sized bed taking up most of the space. A dresser sat on the wall to Warrick's left, a chest of drawers on the same wall as the door, a small television on top.

The bedspread had been disturbed—obviously where the attack had occurred—but using his alternate light source, Warrick could find no sign that the pair had sex on the bed. He did discover a couple of dark hairs, presumably the attacker's; nothing else.

Greg came in from the kitchen. "Nothing," he reported.

"Not much more in here," Warrick said, showing Greg the bag with the hair. "Let's try the bathroom."

The bathroom was barely big enough for one, let alone both investigators. While Greg fingerprinted the faucets and the sink, Warrick got down on his hands and knees around the toilet.

They found nothing.

They talked to Tara Donnelly a short while longer, then worked on convincing her to go to the hospital with Charles to have a rape kit done.

"Listen," she said, "I'm okay. And he used a condom?"

"Please," Warrick said. "It might not show anything, but better to have it than not. Might really be a help in getting this guy before he date-rapes some other young woman."

Soon, out in front of the apartment complex, when they'd watched a squad car take the victim away, Warrick tapped Greg on the shoulder and said, "Let's go for a walk."

At the far end of the building, set back at the end of the parking lot, barely visible in the dim wash of streetlights, was a Dumpster.

Greg turned up his nose even as his flashlight played over the large metal container. "Oh no. I *hate* this sport. . . ."

Dumpster diving.

"I'll do my part," Warrick said.

"Yeah—what?"

"I'll spot you . . . hold the light."

Shaking his head, Greg said, "Dude, this is so not right. Why do I *always* have to be the one—"

"Rank has its privileges."

"Rank is right!"

Warrick held up a finger for silence. "Neighbors are trying to sleep. Get inside . . . your bitching will have a nice resonance in there."

"Very funny."

Greg took the time to slip a white Tyvek suit over his clothes before he climbed into the Dumpster. He came out less than two minutes later, grinning, a pair of latex gloves in a plastic evidence bag.

"Nice going, Speedy Gonzales," Warrick said, looking at the bag under the beam of his flash.

"Right on top," Greg said, pleased with himself. "Guy must have just pitched them in, then split."

Warrick laughed once. "Why is it that the bad guys always think we're lazy, stupid, or both?"

"They're the lazy, stupid ones, not taking their gloves somewhere else to dispose of."

"Yeah—and not just throw them in the nearest Dumpster, like we won't think of *looking* for 'em there!"

Greg held up a finger before his lips, and Warrick stopped his rant.

Greg said, "Neighbors are trying to sleep. . . ."

6

NICK STOKES ALWAYS DID HIS BEST NOT to make snap judgments about witnesses and suspects; but something about this character Keith Draper rubbed the CSI raw—a little too slick, a little too smarmy in that Mr. Monopoly tuxedo and Wal-Mart cologne, his black hair cut just so (probably had to drive to Vegas to a mall salon), and, finally, the guy's emotions-on-his-sleeve mentality. . . .

As Nick, Grissom, and Catherine sat in the security office of the Four Kings with Draper, Chief Lopez, and casino rep Henry Cippolina, Draper was fidgeting in his chair, first sniffling, then worrying a tissue in his hands into shreds.

Not surprisingly, the Boot Hill crime lab was not exactly the biggest, best-outfitted in the nation; but they had a water tank and a microscope, which meant Sara could do firearms comparisons.

Problem was, the bullet they needed to compare it to was not in the town morgue because Boot Hill didn't have one: instead it resided in the local mortuary, inside the body of Nick Valpo.

And the probable difference between some small-town mortician cutting a bullet out of a murder victim and Clark County Chief Medical Examiner Dr. Albert Robbins doing his version of that procedure was . . . troubling. Robbins, of course, could be counted on to get the slug out without tarnishing or abrading any of the markings. A local mortician would be more adept at running a business than preserving evidence.

Nevertheless, as soon as the Draper interview was over, Nick would be on his way to the mortuary to fetch the bullet (whatever shape it might be in) for Sara to compare to a bullet from Draper's confiscated .22.

The gun-toting pit boss sat in a straight-back chair in front of a metal desk. Chief Lopez had deposited himself behind that desk, properly projecting authority, with floor manager Cippolina standing behind him. The seated CSIs were fanned out behind Draper.

"So, Keith," Lopez said with a smile that wasn't cheerful. "Tell us what happened."

"Pretty busy for that time of day," Draper answered. "Maybe a hundred people scattered through the casino. . . . Generally, that late in the afternoon, traffic should be about *half* that."

"Where were you, exactly?"

"Pit six," Draper said, shredding his third tissue. "I was just, you know, making my rounds—no big whoop."

"Then what?"

Draper's face tightened, as if he'd awoken from a bad dream and was compelled to try to recall it. "Then those slimy bastards came."

"The Predators."

"Predators. Valpo leading his entourage, swaggering around like he owned the goddamn place."

"You knew Valpo?"

"Not well. Not particularly. But I knew him and his type, all right."

Lopez remained conversational in tone, not at all threatening. "A type you hate, Keith?"

"I *do* hate that type, and I hated Valpo, as much as you can hate somebody you hardly know."

"If you hardly knew him, then—"

"Valpo and his breed, they barge into a decent town and people are supposed to bend over and kiss their asses just for *being* here, bringing in a little 'business.' We all lose when their type comes to town. When they aren't scaring off regular law-abiding people, then they're wrecking our machines or trying to get something for nothing, out of sheer . . . intimidation."

Nick glanced at Grissom, who was taking all this in with a deceptively bland expression. Draper was growing more heated with each word.

"You know as well as I do, Chief—there are good, decent people here just trying to make a living . . . and this trash rolls in here like God on wheels and tries to take over . . . like we were only put on this earth for their amusement."

As Draper finally paused for breath, Lopez cut in. "All right, Keith—I believe we've established that you don't like the Predators—"

"Not just them! . . . I can't stand the sight or smell of *any* of those maniacs."

Lopez shrugged a little. "Point taken—all bikers are on your bad side. Okay? Okay. Now, Keith—what happened next?"

"Those bastard Spokes barged in and . . ." He shuddered, and Nick couldn't tell if it was real or theatrics. ". . . all *hell* broke loose."

Like a traffic cop, the chief held up a hand: *stop*. "Slow 'er down, Keith—one thing at a time. I'm not looking for a general take on this—one look at the casino and the general idea becomes pretty clear. Be specific. The Spokes came in, and then . . ."

Draper sighed, tried to settle down. "Then I saw Buck Finch."

Lopez glanced past Draper to the CSIs and explained, "Buck Finch is head honcho of the Rusty Spokes."

Catherine nodded, and so did Nick. Grissom remained motionless and might have been in a catatonic state, although those who knew him well could spot the intensity in his eyes.

The chief was saying, "What happened next, Keith?"

"Spokes started pulling guns outta everywhere, pockets, coats, from in back of their belts, even their boots. I kinda took it all in, in slow motion, like one of those old Westerns? . . . Seemed like it took me a million years to react, but it was probably only two or three seconds. But that was two or three seconds too late. When I reached to hit the panic button, it was already all over but the shooting—literally."

The panic button, Nick knew, was something all

casinos had: when a pit boss hit it, all the security men in the place would swarm to that area.

"With so much gunfire blazing," Draper was saying, "I hit the floor. Then I got my own gun out and tried to return fire, only by then the Predators were firing back . . . so many *guns*! So many *bullets* flying everywhere!"

Grissom asked, "Mr. Draper, how many rounds would you say you fired?"

"I can say exactly—I emptied the clip. Eight rounds."

"All in the same direction?"

Draper sighed heavily and hung his head. "I'd like to say I only shot at the Spokes . . . but the truth is, I freaked . . . panicked. Just started pulling the trigger as fast as I could. I . . . I hope to hell I didn't hurt anybody who didn't deserve it."

Grissom asked, "Did you move your position?"

A little embarrassed, Draper said, "No. I stayed in the pit behind a table. That seemed about as close to 'safe' as I could get."

Lopez took over the interview again, and Catherine gave a sign to Grissom and Nick, who followed her out. They huddled against a concrete wall, the empty hallway affording them privacy.

"What do we think, so far?" Catherine asked.

Grissom said, "If Mr. Draper didn't move from pit six, he *couldn't* have shot Valpo from close range."

Eyes tight, Catherine said, "That's my thinking, too—but the security video should show us the shooter, once Sofia and Archie get through it all."

Nick said, "We're not takin' that clown's story at face value, are we?"

Catherine shook her head. "Still, if Draper's lying, be nice to have the bullet from Valpo's head, to catch him in the act."

With a nod, Nick said, "I'm all over that. I'll get one of the cops to drive me over to the mortuary."

"I'm going to work some more here," Catherine said, indicating the casino.

Grissom's head tilted to one side. "I think Chief Lopez is planning to visit the two gangs. . . . How about I go with him, Catherine?"

"Good idea," Catherine said. Her tiny smile told Nick she appreciated Grissom's unobsequious deference to her supervisor role.

The officer who drove Nick across town was a big, strapping concrete block of a kid in a uniform who didn't seem quite old enough to be carrying that sidearm. He'd introduced himself as Dean Montaine and had a firm but not overbearing handshake. Red-haired with pale skin, the young officer didn't seem to have pulled a lot of traffic duty on sunny days.

When they'd been in the car for a few minutes, Nick asked, "Ever play any ball?"

Montaine nodded. "High school. You?"

Briefly Nick told him about Texas A&M and his knee. They talked football and were properly bonded by the time they reached the darkened mortuary.

"Nobody home?" Nick asked. "Nobody who's still breathing, anyway?"

Montaine said, "Mr. Erickson must be 'round back."

After pulling the car into the parking lot, Montaine circled around to the rear of the dark-brick

two-story with the discreet BOOT HILL MORTUARY sign.
They found a dim light shining through an open
door and, under a weak parking-lot light, a blue
minivan, parked.

"That's Mr. Erickson's," Montaine said, indicating
the van as he pulled up next to it.

They got out and approached the building, feet
scuffing the gravel of the lot; but as they grew closer
to the open door, something got the hair prickling
on Nick's neck.

Nick glanced sideways at the young cop. "Would
Mr. Erickson leave the back door open like that?"

"If he's inside," Montaine said with a shrug, "why
not?"

"You guys ever have *any* crime before today?"

"Yeah, a little. But what's to steal in a stiff hotel?"

Nick could think of something, but said, "You
think it's reasonable a Boot Hill businessman would
have the back door of his business wide open . . . in
the middle of the night?"

Montaine's hand dropped to the nine millimeter
on his hip.

Holding out a hand to keep the young man where
he was, Nick eased forward, hand on his own gun's
butt, the strap of the holster undone.

Nick went in first.

A garage awaited, with a hearse and a limousine
both sitting under a naked hundred-watt bulb in the
center of the ceiling.

"Mr. Erickson?" Nick called.

Only half an echo off cement answered the CSI.

Nick took in the surroundings: garage walls clut-
tered with tools, a lawn mower, a workbench, and

other things blocked by the parked vehicles. Easing his gun from its holster, but keeping the pistol at his side, Nick called out again. *"Mr. Erickson?"*

Still no answer but the echo.

Nick glanced back to see Officer Montaine, all business now, pistol out.

Beyond the workbench, a door stood ajar—to the interior of the mortuary, Nick assumed. He brought his gun up and kept it trained on that door. Behind him, he hoped Montaine had his pistol set to cover them if someone popped up from behind a vehicle.

Though that door was open, Nick could see no light beyond. He got out his mini-flash, turned it on, and used his left wrist to brace the pistol so the light and gun were both pointed into the darkness. With a head motion he summoned the young local cop to follow.

The door opened into a small hallway. To Nick's right, in a corner, were two expandable carts that the coffins sat on during transportation from room to room, or to the back of the hearse. The hall in front of him was lined with doors. To his left, at the other end of the short hallway, was a door on the right. He could see no light coming from beneath. Nodding toward that door, Nick kept his pistol on the main hall while Montaine tried the door.

Locked.

The young officer caught up to Nick and they moved slowly down the corridor to a closed door on the left, where Nick signaled for Montaine to cover the hallway. No light escaped from beneath this door, either; but this one was *not* locked . . .

. . . and swung easily open when Nick turned the knob with the heel of his flashlight hand.

An office.

A quick sweep of the flash told Nick that he was in here alone. Closing the door as he came out, Nick nodded for them to move on.

Montaine went through an open doorway to the right. Nick could see a table and chairs under the beam of the young man's flash, but nothing else. The officer came out and shook his head—safe to move to the next door.

Nick did not like mortuaries. He'd had a bad experience at night in another one, not long ago; and while he did not like to think he was easily creeped out, this excursion was making him progressively edgier. He hoped it didn't show, because the last thing they needed was for the young officer to get spooked. . . .

Nick took a breath, and—with the flashlight hand—tried the next door.

His initial sweep of the light joined with pungent chemical odors to tell him he was in the body preparation chamber.

A metal table, not unlike the one back in Robbins's morgue, sat centrally, and counters and sinks and cupboards lined the walls. An embalming machine sat conspicuously on a counter in the corner. At first, Nick thought he had entered another empty room . . .

. . . then he heard the moan.

Turning the beam toward the sound, the CSI saw a man sprawled on the floor beyond the metal table.

"Montaine!" Nick said. "In here."

Without waiting, Nick went to the man, who was groggy but very much alive.

Montaine entered the room and flicked the light switch.

"Oh hell," the young officer said. "Mr. Erickson, are you all right?"

Erickson was struggling to all fours now, his head toward Nick, a bloody wound in the back of his skull.

"Ambulance," Nick said, "now."

Montaine was on the radio immediately.

"Lay back, Mr. Erickson," Nick said.

The mortician peered up unsteadily through glassy gray eyes—a tall, broad, balding man of perhaps fifty. His glasses had been knocked off and lay askew on the floor nearby.

"Who . . . who are you?" Erickson managed.

"Nick Stokes, sir—Las Vegas Crime Lab."

"Oh. Oh, yes . . . the CSI coming about the dead biker. . . ."

"Yes, sir. Lay back now; rest easy. You've probably got a concussion."

"Damnit!" Erickson snapped, suddenly angry. "I never even saw him."

"Who would that be?" Nick asked, holstering his weapon and flicking off the flashlight. Possibly he should have just told the mortician to remain quiet; but this was a crime scene, and Erickson's words were evidence.

"The SOB that hit me—never even saw him. One moment I was leaning over the body, next you and Dean were here . . . and all I've got to show is . . . ahhhh . . ." Erickson winced in pain.

Nick didn't want to ask the next question—he already had a really bad feeling about the answer. He grabbed a towel off a rack by a sink, ran it under cold water, wrung it out, then knelt next to the mortician and pressed it to his wound. "Mr. Erickson . . ."

"Stan . . . call me . . . call me Stan."

"Stan," Nick said. "Do you know where the body is now?"

Erickson glanced forlornly at the metal table. "Oh, hell. Bloody goddamn hell. They stole it!"

"Valpo didn't walk away," Nick said.

"What's the matter?" Montaine asked.

Nick glanced at the young cop. "Whoever assaulted Mr. Erickson did so in order to steal Valpo's corpse."

Montaine looked at the table. "No way."

"Way," Nick said. "And incidentally, we're standing in the middle of a crime scene. So keep that in mind."

The officer looked around quickly, as if he'd just stepped into a room slithering with snakes.

"I'm sorry, so sorry," the mortician was saying.

"Please, sir," Nick said. "Just take it easy till help comes."

"It's my . . . my first bodysnatching."

Nick almost said *Not mine*, but let the man have his special if humiliating moment.

Hauling his cell phone off his belt, Nick could find solace only in knowing breaking this news to Catherine would be marginally better than doing so to his previous supervisor.

After all, Gris could get cranky when evidence got tampered with. And how could you tamper with murder evidence more than by stealing the victim's body itself?

*   *   *

As Chief Lopez's Blazer rolled down the highway out of town, Gil Grissom, in the passenger seat, stared out his window, taking in the beauty of the night sky. He found it pleasant to be away from the constant glare of the Las Vegas lights, and commented, "Pretty out here."

"Yeah," Lopez agreed. He was wearing a white Stetson now, perhaps to announce his status as head good guy. "I never get tired of it. Not exactly the big city, is it?"

"Provides a whole new point of reference for 'big,'" Grissom said, gazing deep into the black sky, searching for the farthest star. "Lived here your whole life, Chief?"

"Nah, started in LA. My folks moved the family out here when I was a sophomore in high school."

"Tough time to change," Grissom said.

"Wasn't that tough," Lopez said. "I was all-state in three sports—didn't have to take as much crap as most new kids."

Grissom turned to look at his new ally; small talk was not his forte, but he knew finding common ground with new colleagues was important. "Sounds like you were quite an athlete—why'd you give it up? Get hurt?"

Lopez shook his head. "Nope. I always wanted to be a cop."

"Why?"

"Putting things right appeals to me."

"We do what we can in a chaotic universe."

"Is it really chaotic?"

Grissom smiled thinly. "As long as people are in it, it is. . . . How far?"

"Six, seven miles. The Predators stay at a camp-ground, out in the middle of nowhere."

"Little early in the morning for a visit. Or is that a little late at night?"

Lopez chuckled. "Either way, Doc, these type of people don't sleep by any regular clock, and with what happened today? Won't be in any mood to sleep."

They had already passed the roadblock on the way out of town—two Highway Patrol cars making sure that no one, especially the Predators, entered Boot Hill without authorization. As yet the governor had not called out the depleted National Guard or instituted martial law; but this was the next best thing. The Highway Patrol had the town pretty well locked down.

Lopez had not enforced a curfew but had already told the CSIs that in the case of more trouble, virtually anything this side of jaywalking, he would not hesitate to impose one. Grissom agreed with this attitude. Various chamber of commerce members, however, had contacted the chief to beg him not to enforce a curfew. The Gold Vault, with its captive audience of Rusty Spokes under house arrest, was doing fairly brisk business, and with the Four Kings down, the smaller Boot Hill establishments were doing okay, considering the only potential customers were locals and the few tourists who hadn't bailed after the gun battle.

The Highway Patrol had informed these bikers that none of them could leave; the state's investigation division would question them when the Rusty Spokes back at the Gold Vault had all been interviewed.

Long before the Blazer got to the campground, the glow of the Predators' bonfires lit the dark sky in a blush of orange, like an early threat of dawn. As Lopez and Grissom neared the camp's entrance, they were greeted by the flashing lights of more Highway Patrol cars and a Highway Patrolman held up a hand for them to stop.

The chief lowered his window and offered half a smile to the middle-aged Patrolman.

"Jorge," the officer said, offering up another half. "How're you doing, now that Armageddon's come to Nevada?"

"Hey, Bill, good as can be expected. We're still sorting things out in town, at the casino."

"I heard it was one righteous mess."

"Oh yeah. . . . Still, it could have been worse—by all rights, we should've had a dozen dead bodies littering the place." Lopez pushed his Stetson back farther, dragged a hand across a sweaty brow. "What's the mood out here?"

The Patrolman turned from the Blazer and looked toward the camp. "They're pissed, obviously . . . but so far, at least, they haven't gone completely nuts."

"Well, Bill, we'll see if we can calm them down a little. Doc Grissom here is from Vegas—a crime scene expert."

"Nice to meet you, Doc."

Grissom nodded hello.

"Here's hoping," the Patrolman said to Grissom, "this whole damn campground doesn't become a crime scene. . . . Good luck, fellas."

The Patrolman waved them through the gate.

The campground's main building was a one-story concrete bunker at right. At left was a bivouac of RVs, pickup trucks, tents, pull-along trailers, and thirty-some small campfires aside from the huge bonfires that burned every hundred yards or so. Motorcycles were scattered everywhere, and men and women, most of them in black leather, were—despite the lateness of the hour—still walking around and talking and partying.

"You weren't kidding," Grissom said. "They *don't* sleep."

Lopez tugged his Stetson back down. "Probably more meth per capita in this camp than anywhere else in Nevada, about now."

Grissom eyed the chief, asking a question without saying anything.

"And," Lopez said, answering that question, "now would not be the best time to bust 'em for it."

Grissom had no argument with that.

Two leather-clad bikers, each carrying a shotgun, approached the Blazer on either side. As the one on the driver's side got closer, he racked the slide, pumping a round into the chamber.

"Help you, girls?" he asked, his accent soft and southern.

Lopez lifted his badge on its necklace, the star catching light from a nearby bonfire and winking. "You have a permit for that weapon, son?"

The biker grinned crookedly. "Yeah—but not on me."

Waving a dismissive hand and smiling back, Lopez said, "Just checkin'. Jake around?"

The biker snorted. "Who should I say is calling?"

"Chief of Police Jorge Lopez and Dr. Gil Grissom from Vegas."

Looking past Lopez at Grissom, the biker frowned nastily. "Nobody called for a doctor."

"Nobody called for a chief of police, either," Lopez said, neither threatening nor loud, keeping his eyes on the biker. "Does this have to turn into something, son?"

Grissom watched as the biker and the police chief sized each other up. The CSI could not get a real fix on the biker's eyes as they kept darting from the chief to the entrance where the Highway Patrol sat, to Grissom, then back to Lopez and around and around.

His tone genial but with the faintest edge, Lopez said, "You've got a lot of questions floating in your head, don't you?"

The biker stayed silent, his grip tightening on the shotgun. Working carefully, Grissom unsnapped his holster, hoping no one had noticed his tiny movements.

"You're trying to figure out if you can get away with killing us," the chief was saying. "You're wondering if the good doctor can do anything before you cap him, too. You're wondering what the Highway Patrol will do when you fire that shotgun. You're wondering if Jake will give you a promotion for knocking off a cop, or maybe tear you a new asshole. All these things you wonder, and more."

The biker's knuckles were turning white on the gun and to Grissom, the guy seemed about to make a move. Grissom gripped the butt of his holstered weapon.

"What you didn't consider, son," Lopez continued,

"was where my gun was while your mind was runnin' through all the other possibilities."

Tensing, the biker got the shotgun maybe a half inch higher when Lopez's pistol seemed to blossom from nowhere, his right hand going through the open window, pressing his pistol's snout to the man's forehead.

Grissom's gun came out and the biker on the other side, whose shotgun nose had stayed down throughout the prior exchange, shook his head as if to say *I'm not part of this* and lowered his weapon to the ground and left it there.

"Why don't you stop trying to think about anything," Lopez advised the belligerent biker, whose eyes tried to look up at the gun barrel pressing into his forehead, "and just go get Jake."

The biker's eyes were wide and his mouth hung open. He managed to nod his head with the barest minimum of movement. He drew away from Lopez's gun, a circle in the flesh of his forehead.

Lopez stopped him with, "Leave the shotgun."

Obeying, the biker eased the gun to the ground and took off to get his boss, his pal falling in with him, looking irritated with what the other sentry had nearly initiated.

Holstering his weapon, Grissom said, "By the way, I hate guns."

Lopez grinned. "Me too. That was kinda hairy, for Boot Hill, anyway."

"That would have been 'hairy' in Vegas, too," Grissom said with a relieved smile. "Chief, you handled it well."

"Thanks, Doc," the chief said, almost embarrassed

by the praise. "But that's what the paycheck's for."

Jake Hanson materialized out of the darkness, a group of half a dozen pissed-off Predators moving up behind him, like a posse. Backlit by the firelight, the tall, handsome Hanson—brown hair parted on the left, blue eyes gleaming with anger, chest bare under a Predators leather vest, abs hard and lean—looked almost like a rock star, but the persona worked fine for a leader of men and motorcycles. To Grissom, Hanson's theatrical appearance did not bode well, considering that this man might be the only thing standing between peace and an all-out biker gang war in a tiny desert community.

"Chief Lopez," Hanson called out as he approached. "I hope you're here with news that you've caught Val's killer. . . ."

A series of whoops and shouts went up behind him, the group growing to a dozen, then doubling almost instantaneously.

"The Predators demand *justice*," Hanson said, his voice carrying over the crowd, and he wasn't even shouting.

Lopez jumped out of the Blazer and, fearless, marched toward Hanson. Grissom questioned the strategy of leaving the vehicle in favor of being afoot, but followed, getting out and coming around the Blazer fast, to provide a united front, even though the pair were outnumbered about fifty to two.

"We haven't arrested *anyone* yet!" Lopez announced to the crowd.

Boos cascaded and shouted epithets and calls for the Predators to "burn the whole fucking town down!" burst from the back of the crowd.

Addressing them, but close enough to Hanson to knock heads, Lopez said, "We're doing everything we can, and we will bring the killer to justice."

The response was more boos and shouts of "Kill the pigs," which struck Grissom as a nostalgic but nonetheless sinister touch.

Hanson's upper lip curled back in what was, technically at least, a smile; but the biker chief also held both hands up over his head, not in a surrender fashion, but to silence the crowd.

"We're not animals!" Hanson yelled to his people, his eyes still burning into Lopez. "We'll trust the police to do their job. We are law-abiding citizens who were attacked in a public establishment—we did nothing wrong. We'll give the police a chance to do the right thing."

Some in the crowd muttered, but mostly there was just a sort of stunned silence.

"We need to talk," Lopez said quietly.

Hanson shrugged elaborately. "Feel free."

"Without an audience, Jake."

Signaling for the group to remain behind, Hanson accompanied Lopez and Grissom into the darkness to a spot behind the bunker building. The soil here was sandy, giving slightly under the pressure of their steps, sparse vegetation springing up here and there. A breeze, far warmer than it probably should have been for this hour, swept over them, bringing with it the promise of an impossibly hot day to come.

"Talk about what?" Hanson asked when the crowd was far behind them.

"If you continue inciting your people like that," Lopez said, "a tragic incident will escalate into full-scale tragedy."

Shrugging, Hanson said, "You say inciting—I say I'm consolidating my position."

"Why? Aren't you in line to succeed Valpo?"

"I'm at the head of the line, yeah," Hanson said, still walking slowly, aimlessly. "But there's others behind me, and none of them have my restraint. If I weren't standing here, it'd be a free-for-all."

"Expecting a coup?" Lopez asked.

"If you don't expect that," the biker said with a fatalistic shrug, "you're not ready, if it comes."

This seemed a perfectly reasonable position to Grissom.

Lopez asked, "Did you see who shot Val?"

The abrupt change of subject caused Hanson to stop. "No. Hell no." He sighed, shook his head. "One minute he was there, next he was down."

"And you didn't see—"

"Hey—Chief. It was a little hectic in there."

Grissom asked, "Mr. Hanson, where were you when it started?"

Hanson frowned at Grissom, seemingly assessing him for the first time. "You're Vegas?"

"Yes. Crime lab."

That seemed to satisfy the biker. "I was sitting at a table next to Val, playing blackjack."

"Then you have a problem," Grissom said with a raise of the eyebrows. "You see that, don't you, Mr. Hanson?"

Hanson sneered. "You think *I* capped him? What

are you, high? Val and me were tight! What kinda crap—"

Unfazed, Grissom said, "You had opportunity, means, motive—"

"*I* had motive?" Hanson exploded.

"Who's leading the Predators now?"

The biker's eyes and nostrils flared. "Screw you, man! Nick Valpo was like a father to me."

"Duncan was like a father to MacBeth," Grissom said.

"Maybe," Hanson said, with a dangerous smile, "but I've got no Lady MacBeth pushing me into doing stupid shit."

Grissom smiled, pleased that his instinct was right: Hanson was a literate, intelligent person.

"Anyway," Hanson was saying dismissively, "I told you, man—I loved Val. And I didn't go into that casino looking to kill anybody."

The crackle of bonfires provided percussive punctuation to their conversation, but the partying seemed to have died down to a rumbling murmur.

Grissom said, "But you *were* armed—and you did shoot back, didn't you?"

Hanson didn't reply—he wasn't anxious to cop to anything in front of the Boot Hill chief of police, even on Predator turf.

"Confirm it or not, Mr. Hanson," Grissom said. "We've got video of the whole shoot-out."

Hanson's laughter was a short, mean burst, like machine-gun fire. "Then you haven't seen it, or you'd already know I *didn't* kill Nick." His eyes narrowed, and he lowered his voice. "But if you have that footage . . . you have pictures of whoever did this thing. Why aren't you going after *them*?"

"We're still looking," Grissom said.

A nasty edge undercut Hanson's attempt to sound matter of fact. "Do you know who you're looking for?"

Grissom did not play games with the man. "We have stacks of security cam tapes to review. We do *not* know who we're looking for . . . yet."

Abruptly, Hanson started strolling again and they fell in with him as he changed subjects. "Look, I can keep the lid on this camp, but I need something from you boys."

Lopez asked, "What's that?"

Just as abruptly, Hanson stopped and turned his gaze on the chief. "The Predators want Val's body."

"You can't be serious," Lopez said.

"I'm as serious as a heart attack."

"You can't have it, not yet," Grissom said. "It's still part of a criminal investigation. His body is evidence."

"His body," Hanson said, "deserves a Viking funeral. And some of these Predators think that oughtta be sooner than later."

"When we can release the body," Lopez said, "we will release it to the next of kin or whatever rightful claimant—but in the meantime, you have to calm your people down, Jake."

"Don't know if I can," Hanson said. "Between them wanting their funeral and champin' at the bit to rip the lungs and guts outta every one of those Spokes, well . . . this party's about to turn real ugly."

"'Heavy lies the head that wears the crown,' Jake," Grissom said.

Hanson's features contorted. "What the hell's that supposed to mean?"

Grissom found that amusing, but Lopez seemed singularly unamused, saying, "Doc here's the one telling you, in his own unique way, that you're the *leader* of this outfit . . . so you better start leading, Jake. Somebody's got to talk them down."

The biker spat. "What, for the sake of your two-horse town?"

"Not entirely for the town's sake, no." Lopez leaned toward the biker. "Truth is, Jake, more cops are coming here by the hour, and if the Predators and Rusty Spokes go head to head, plenty will die on both sides. You survived a skirmish in that casino, but a war? The governor is not about to let two motorcycle gangs annihilate one of his towns."

They were all considering that when Grissom heard an unmistakable whirring: a rattlesnake warning them they'd chosen a bad spot to stop and chat.

The other two heard it, too—Hanson froze and Lopez slowly reached for his pistol. Grissom could barely make out the coiled snake, but there it was, under a bush . . . less than a foot from Hanson's left leg.

For the first time in memory, Gil Grissom found himself drawing his weapon for the second time in one night, firing once, next to the snake, kicking up sand . . .

. . . and convincing the reptile to slither off into the night to search for a quieter, friendlier spot.

Hanson let out a nervous chuckle and he grinned wolfishly. "Looks like you missed, Doc."

"Did I?"

Hanson's smile disappeared as Predators came running from every direction, their guns out, dozens of metal fingers pointing accusingly at Grissom and Lopez.

Hanson held up his hands. "It's all right, it's all right! He shot at a rattler—probably saved my sorry ass."

The crowd did not want to buy this answer and milled there, looking surlier than ever.

"No harm, no foul," Hanson insisted. "Go back to your parties. Grab some booze, grab a snooze. . . . Go on, get outta here! These guys won't cause any trouble . . . and they're just about to go, anyway."

Many in the crowd were still eyeballing the two intruders even as the bikers slowly dispersed, seeming to vaporize back into the night.

When the three were alone again, Hanson said to the CSI, "You mean you *deliberately* didn't kill the snake."

"Tell me, Mr. Hanson," Grissom said, his tone light, "what was to be gained by killing that snake?"

"Plenty—would've stopped the threat of us getting fanged and poisoned, and there'd be one less snake in the world. I *hate* snakes!"

Grissom's eyebrows frowned; his lips smiled. "Hate? Certainly that's uncalled for. That creature has an important place in the ecosystem. Just as we *all* have our place, Mr. Hanson."

"Well, when a snake's in *my* place, I kill its scaly ass. Find a place in your ecosystem for *that*, Doc."

Moving a step closer, locking eyes with the biker, Grissom said evenly, "Let me put it another way— just because my presence makes a predator feel threatened, that doesn't mean I have to destroy it."

Hanson was chewing on that when Grissom's cell phone chirped.

Reholstering his pistol first, he yanked the device off his belt. "Grissom," he said.

"It's me," Catherine's voice said.

"How are things?" he asked.

"Weird. Not good."

"Oh?"

A sigh. "Nicky just called—Valpo's body has been stolen from the mortuary."

Grissom shot a look toward Lopez, whose own cell phone was ringing. "It's evidence. We need to find it."

"Tell me about it," she said. "We're working on it. Bullet's still in the body, by the way. Nicky's working the mortuary crime scene, and Sara and I are still here at the Four Kings; but this is not a fun development."

"I concur," Grissom said. "Where do you want me?"

"Can you check on Nick?"

"Yes." He signed off, then turned to see Lopez looking at him and rolling his eyes. Obviously the chief had just gotten the same news that Grissom had.

"What's the matter?" Hanson asked.

Lopez blew out a deep breath. "As long as it's just the three of us out here, I'll tell you. Jake, this is a show of good faith, a vote of confidence in your leadership if I tell you this."

"Tell me *what*?"

Lopez looked to Grissom, who nodded; then the chief told the biker honcho, "Your friend Valpo's body's been stolen from the mortuary."

Grissom had thought Hanson might explode, but instead the guy seemed to sag a little, a hand going to the bridge of his nose. "Aw, hell . . . how does *that* happen?"

"Don't know yet," Lopez said.

"But," Grissom said, "we will."

"My guys find out about this," Hanson said, nodding toward the bonfires, "don't look at *me* to control 'em."

Lopez stepped very near the biker. "That's why, Jake, you have to make sure they don't find out."

His eyes went wild. "How the hell am I going to do *that*? Why did you even *tell* me?"

"Because," Lopez said. "You're the leader, and leaders need to be informed and respected. I could have kept it from you, but it's not that big a town and you'd probably've found out by lunch and figured I kept it from you. Like I said, this is an act of good faith, Jake. I'm trying to make things right . . . for everybody."

Hanson nodded; Lopez seemed to have gotten through to him. "Chief, I'll do what I can."

"I've got your word," Lopez said.

"If the Spokes did this . . ."

"Hey!" Lopez said. "That's just what we *don't* need."

Hanson gave Lopez a sly smile. "Chief—that was for me . . . get it out of my system."

"You're sure that's all it is?"

"Yeah. Yeah." He grunted a sort of laugh, but the biker's eyes were somber. "I heard what you said before, Chief. . . ."

"Just for the record," Grissom said, "what would be the motive for the Spokes to steal Valpo's body?"

"They hated his ass!"

Grissom shook his head. "If they killed him, no need to take the body."

Grasping at straws now, Hanson said, "Maybe to destroy the evidence."

"What evidence?" Grissom asked. "The bullets that killed him? Why not just pitch the gun?"

Hanson had no answer for that, but he did say, "Look, man, they know damn well we'd want Val's body for a Viking funeral, a real blowout to honor his memory. That's reason enough to snatch him."

"Maybe," Grissom admitted. "But we will find your friend's killer—that I promise."

"You're pretty goddamn sure of yourself."

"Thank you. Mind another question?"

"Go."

"How did you Predators know you could get guns into that casino, past the metal detectors?"

Without hesitation, Hanson said, "Val told us the fix was in—those detectors would be off or dead or something."

"How was it managed?"

"Some friend of Val's, on the inside—that's all he ever told us."

Lopez looked unconvinced. "Come on, Jake— you were the number two guy. That's all you knew?"

Hanson shrugged. "You see anybody but me talking to you right now, Chief? Top guy knows things nobody else does. All I know is, Val had somebody inside the casino. He wouldn't tell me, or anybody else, who that was."

The conversation was over. Nods of goodbye were

followed by Grissom and Lopez returning to the Blazer.

The two of them rode back to town, still in the early-morning darkness.

"Why was the body stolen?" Lopez wondered aloud.

"Maybe whoever stole the body," Grissom said, "doesn't want to give up the gun."

"Murder bullet vanishes, then the gun doesn't have to? . . . Well, if that's the case, we better figure out who stole that goddamn corpse, 'cause this town's a powder keg, and I just handed a lit match to the leader of the biggest gang of bikers in the southwest."

Grissom pondered that. "I think you did the right thing, Jorge. If there's an official inquiry, and this comes up, I'll back you all the way."

Lopez glanced sideways at Grissom, wondering if the CSI was kidding. But Grissom's expression gave no clue.

7

THE MICROWAVE PINGED and Warrick Brown withdrew the bowl of soup like a lab sample whose processing was complete, carted it over to a break-room table, and sat. He was waiting for Mia Dickerson to finish the DNA testing on the sample he'd given her from the scraping under Tara Donnelly's fingernails.

An attractive African-American of around thirty, Mia possessed straight black hair, large brown eyes, and a formidable IQ. He smiled at the thought of her as he dipped a spoon into his steaming tomato soup. The CSI and the lab technician had flirted from time to time, and she'd alternated ignoring him with giving him a hard time, which he chose to interpret as a sure sign that she dug him.

A buoyant Greg strolled in, removed a bottle of juice from the fridge, shook it up, then joined Warrick. This was Greg's normal shift, so the graveyard hours weren't fazing him. Warrick—who had been on the swing shift for a while now—was feeling the hands of his inner clock spinning in confusion.

"Are you tired?" Greg asked, with an impish grin. "Or just laid back?"

"Don't mistake 'cool' for 'beat,' Greg—I'm here for the long haul."

"Don't feel bad. I'm starting to drag, too."

If the young CSI had looked any fresher, Warrick would've had to dump his remaining soup on him.

Warrick asked, "How'd you do with the glove?"

Greg swigged and swallowed, then said, "I did what you told me—turned it inside out, then hung it in the super-glue chamber."

"Raise a print?"

Greg grinned in satisfaction. "Oh yeah—two clear ones: middle finger and index."

Often criminals made their biggest mistakes when thinking they were at their most clever. To avoid leaving fingerprints, a perp would wear gloves—not realizing that cotton gloves had fibers that could be matched, or that leather gloves showed wear in a particular fashion on a particular person and were, therefore, as good as fingerprints.

When criminal masterminds graduated to latex gloves—and once more considered themselves bulletproof (or anyway fingerprint-proof)—they were again proved wrong.

Lawbreaking has a natural tendency to make even the coolest criminal nervous. Sweating, a criminal might wipe his or her brow—then, if touching something at the crime scene, leave a print behind just as if he were wearing no glove at all. The same thing occurs on the inside of the glove; most criminals didn't realize that the inner latex surface is a perfect place for the energetic crime scene investigator to search.

Warrick asked, "How'd you get those prints?"

Greg worked at seeming matter-of-fact, though Warrick could tell the young CSI was proud of himself. "I filled the fingers of the glove with one-inch PVC pipe, then rolled each finger over a black gel lifter. I got clean prints from those two fingers, and various smears from the thumb and other fingers."

"Nice," Warrick said. "Now we've got reverse prints from the inside of the gloves."

"That's pretty slick procedure, 'Rick," Greg said. "Where'd you learn *that* one?"

"Velders and Zonjee—two Dutchmen I saw at the IAI conference last year."

"Who are they, anyway?"

"Theo Velders is a cop from the Netherlands and Jan Zonjee is the research chemist who helped him. They kept trying to find a way to lift prints out of latex gloves, and they came up with this—God bless 'em."

"I'm impressed," Greg said, bright-eyed. "What's next?"

"Go back and photograph the prints you lifted, then reverse them so they're not backward, and run them through AFIS."

Greg chugged the rest of his juice. "What are *you* up to, now?"

"Gonna catch up with you . . . soon as I check on the DNA testing on that skin you got from under Tara's fingernails."

"Oh, really?" Greg said with a smile. "That may take a while."

"What?"

"Nothing." Greg got to the door, dropping his empty juice bottle in the recycling tub on his way by, before saying, "Just, somehow, you seem to spend more time going over DNA evidence with Mia than *I* ever rated."

Greg fired off a grin and was gone before Warrick could throw his soup spoon at him.

Shaking his head but smiling, Warrick cleaned up after himself, then headed for the DNA lab.

Mia, in a neat ponytail, was leaning over a microscope, studying a slide as Warrick sauntered in.

"Hey," he said good-naturedly.

She glanced up at him, eyebrows tense. "Did I call you? Funny, I don't *remember* calling you."

He managed a smile. "People work as well and closely as we do, you can anticipate the other guy."

"You figured just because it was you," she said, giving him a smile that was all sass and challenge, "I'd drop everything and put you at the head of the line?"

"Well . . . yeah. Kinda."

She returned her attention to the slide.

Warrick, who'd felt himself on fairly solid footing when he came in, noticed a shift beneath him and wondered if he was hovering on a precipice. Of a deep hole. "So . . . I should come back later . . . ?"

Mia glanced up from the slide. "Are you still here?"

Warrick could see no way of winning this round, and no way of exiting with even a modicum of grace. "Okay. I'm at your beck and call—lemme know when you have something."

He was halfway out when she said, "You are

gonna have to sharpen up your game, Slugger, if you're gonna play in the big leagues."

She was looking up at him with just a hint of a smile.

He regarded her with suspicion. "I'll keep that in mind."

"Now get out of my lab."

"I can take a hint."

"Oh, and . . . take this with you."

She held out a folder.

He came back and took it, responding like a kid on Christmas morning getting that big gift he'd given up on. "My test results?"

"Was about to call you," she admitted.

Risking no snappy comeback, Warrick merely thanked her and scooted.

In his office, Warrick plopped onto a chair and read the results of the DNA profile; then he punched them into CODIS. The COmbined DNA Index System stored DNA samples from criminals and crime scenes in all fifty states, Puerto Rico, the FBI, and the U.S. Army.

Warrick did not expect much. CODIS worked, sometimes; but nowhere near always. Many offenders were not in the system, and the odds of his getting a match were against him.

Which was why he jumped a little when the ping from the computer went off.

The name staring at him from the screen was Matt David, a convicted sex offender paroled by the state of Nevada less than six months ago.

If convicted of Tara Donnelly's rape, David would be a three-time loser and would go into the system for good and ever. Warrick slow-scanned the material again as he printed the file. If Greg's fingerprints brought up the same name, they were *really* in business.

On his way past the DNA lab, he stuck his head in, acknowledging Mia with "Paydirt—thank you," winning a sincere smile for his trouble.

Greg was staring wide-eyed at the AFIS computer when Warrick rolled in.

"Don't tell me," Warrick said. "A match."

"What are you, a witch? I thought Grissom was the only warlock around this place. . . ."

Warrick leaned over Greg's shoulder. "Didn't take a magician to read the look on your face—anyway, I got a hit, too—on CODIS."

"Matt David," Greg said with a nod toward the screen.

"Matt David," Warrick agreed. "You find an address—I'll call Brass."

"Deal."

Getting the address was not as easy as either CSI had hoped: the CODIS address was a downtown flophouse that had closed over a year ago, and the AFIS address was a house in North Las Vegas that had burned down while David was in prison.

They only had one idea left when Brass joined them.

"Need you to make a phone call," Warrick said to the captain.

"Hey, nice to see you, too," Brass said.

Warrick said, "No, seriously. Our suspect, Matt David—you gotta call his PO."

"His parole officer?" Brass said with a frown, and looked at his watch. "You know, real people are asleep right now. Only criminals and damn fool cops are up."

"Tell me about it. Look, this guy's a serial rapist, Jim, and we need to get him off the street."

Warrick held out a piece of paper with the PO's number; Brass took it and made the call.

"Mr. Tinsley? Sorry about the hour—Captain Jim Brass, LVPD."

A short pause followed, during which Brass shot Warrick a thanks-for-*this*-dirty-job look.

"Yes, sir, I do know what time it is. That's why I said I was sorry about the hour. . . . It *is* 'goddamned important'—about one of your parolees, Matt David."

Another pause.

"We don't know for sure that he's done anything, sir—but evidence in a rape that went down earlier tonight indicates we need to talk to him. May I have his address?"

Another pause, this one longer. Brass cradled the phone against his neck as he got his notepad and pen out, and soon he was scribbling.

"Thanks, Mr. Tinsley, uh, yes—Joe. Yeah, I've got it, thanks."

One last pause.

Brass ended the call and gave Warrick a grin. "Officer Tinsley reminds us to respect the parolee's rights. And *citizen* Joe Tinsley suggests that should Mr. David be guilty of the crime we're investigating him for, one of us might put a foot in Mr. David's ass, with Mr. Tinsley's compliments."

"Always willing to pay reciprocal service to our brothers in law enforcement," Warrick said. "I see you have an address on our sex offender."

"Gold Avenue—not far from MLK Boulevard."

Greg raised an eyebrow. "Always a fun part of town to visit after midnight."

But midnight was a memory, the sun rising over the eastern horizon, when they pulled up in front of the dilapidated one-story stucco house on Gold Avenue, just east of Martin Luther King Boulevard. An old blue Ford in the driveway was the only sign of life as Brass, Warrick, Greg, and two uniformed officers approached.

Brass waved the uniforms around back while Warrick pulled his pistol—Brass already had—and the detective and lead CSI went up to the front door, Greg hanging back near the Denali.

Ringing the doorbell did no good. Nothing happened the second time, either, or the third. But when Brass pounded on the door and yelled, "*LVPD, open up,*" he got a reaction, all right.

Three bullets blasted through the front door . . .

. . . and everybody hit the deck, Greg practically hurling himself under the SUV.

Then, silence.

Silence in which, despite the ear-ringing noise of the gun, Warrick could hear his heart trip-hammering as he struggled to discern the slightest sound from inside the structure.

After a long moment, he heard sounds that were anything but slight—two more gunshots, ripping through the back door, and the uniformed officers returning fire.

On his haunches now, Warrick was just thinking about peeking in a window when the front door swung open and a wild-eyed Matt David burst out wearing nothing but a pair of ragged cutoff jeans and waving a big handgun.

The suspect started to sprint across the yard, apparently having not seen Warrick or Brass, his target clearly Greg and the SUV. Before David was halfway across the dirt yard, Warrick ran and tackled him, the two men rolling to the ground, David's gun seeming to fling itself from the suspect's fingers and skimming across the hard-packed earth.

David scuttled after it, Warrick hanging on to the man's legs as the suspect alternately tried to kick the CSI and pull himself closer to the gun. The guy had just gotten his fingertips on the butt when Brass almost nonchalantly placed the barrel of his pistol against David's temple.

"Pick that up," Brass advised, quiet, confident. "See what happens."

David growled, but his hand drew back from the weapon as if it were white hot.

"Probably a good choice," Brass said, kicking the gun away and handing a hard-breathing Warrick a pair of handcuffs.

"What are you *doing*, harassing me?" David screeched. "I *did* my time! I *paid* for what I did! This is discrim-i-*nation*!"

Shaking his head, Brass said, "Matt, we do apologize for dropping by so early, and we know we probably woke you . . . but even so, it's darn rude of you to fire five rounds at Las Vegas police officers."

"How the hell should *I* know you was cops!" David insisted, twisting his head but stopping when he felt the barrel of Brass's pistol again.

"Well," Brass said reasonably, "out front, we

announced ourselves—and out back, we were in uniform. But we won't sweat that charge, really—it's kinda, you know . . . frosting on the cake."

David's brow knit in confusion. "What are you talking about?"

"The rape charge, Matt. The rape charge."

"What? I didn't *rape* that bitch!" David said, struggling against the cuffs now. "Just 'cause I was inside, that don't mean I can't have normal, consenuating sex, does it?"

Brass lowered his weapon and leaned in close enough to kiss the suspect, though that seemed unlikely to Warrick. "Matt, does the 'bitch' you had 'consenuating sex' with happen to live over on Paradise Road?"

"So what if? It was just a *date*!"

Warrick said, "A date, Matt? A date where you left your hair in her bed, your skin under her nails, and your gloves in her Dumpster?"

David quit talking; he also quit struggling. Something died in his eyes.

Warrick said, "Your 'date' is no bitch, Matt—she's a nice young woman named Tara Donnelly and, thanks to her, you're going back inside for the rest of your unnatural life."

Brass said, "You should feel at home there. And you'll be in the company of your peers. No shortage of rapists in jail, I hear."

The uniformed cops came sprinting around the house and took custody of the prisoner, dragging him off as if his legs and feet had gone limp.

"Well," Warrick said. "Don't you meet the most charming people on graveyard."

Greg had crawled out from under the Denali some time ago; he approached Brass and Warrick with an embarrassed expression.

"Sorry," he said, holstering his sidearm.

Brass patted him on the back. "Nice job, Greg."

"Is that sarcasm?"

"No."

"I mean, damn—I was scared. Nobody shoots at you in the lab."

Warrick grinned slowly and said, "I considered it a couple times."

Grinning himself, Brass said, "Greg—you didn't kill anybody, and you didn't get yourself killed. That's a good day, when we have a crazy trigger-happy asshole like that to bring in."

Greg sighed, but in relief, his chagrin fading. Warrick was pleased with his charge—this kid was going to make it, no problem.

Wiping dirt off his pants, watching the perp being loaded into the squad car, Warrick said, "I got a waffle jones that needs feeding. Anybody up for that? My treat."

Brass shrugged as if to say *Why not?*, while Greg nodded his head eagerly. They had all taken exactly one step toward their vehicles when their cell phones rang—at once.

"Damn," Warrick said. "A man could starve to death in this job."

Brass smirked, patted his stomach, and said, "I don't seem to be," and they answered their phones.

Two minutes later, they were racing up I-15 toward the Speedway Boulevard exit, red lights flashing on both vehicles, Warrick driving the SUV this time, following Brass's Taurus as the detective wove in and out of traffic.

"I don't get this," Greg said, frowning, bracing himself against the dashboard with one hand. "Why are we being called to a traffic accident?"

Warrick glanced at the young CSI. "Didn't you get the same call I did? Who called you?"

Greg shrugged. "Dispatcher. She said she was calling me in case no one got through to you."

Eyes back on the interstate, Warrick said, "Didn't she mention shots were fired?"

"No! . . . She must have figured the other dispatcher got through to you."

"Not good," Warrick said, shaking his head, hands tight on the wheel. "If we weren't in the same car, you wouldn't know what you were getting into. We'll have to tell Gris and Catherine about that."

Greg nodded, but his discomfort was clear, though whether it was over the high speed of their vehicle or that dispatcher screwup remained unclear.

The accident scene was in the northbound lane of I-15 just past the Speedway Boulevard exit. Traffic had slowed to a crawl before Craig Road, with uniformed officers diverting vehicles off the interstate at both Craig and farther north at Speedway. After that exit, the SUV and Taurus were the only traffic as they sped north the last mile to where a squad car sat on the shoulder, its lights flashing, a late-model four-door Cadillac angled crossways in the road.

The driver's door and both passenger doors

yawned open. Two uniformed officers, the only people visible, stood on the far side of the car.

Brass pulled to an abrupt stop on the left shoulder, while Warrick parked the Denali right in the
middle of the road.

The detective and the two CSIs got out of their vehicles simultaneously. While Warrick and Greg
fetched their crime scene kits from the back of the
SUV, Brass was calling to the officers. "What's this
about gunshots?"

The two officers came around the car. One—
short, with a shaved head, light blue eyes, and a
wrestler's build—wore a nameplate identifying him
as KRAMER. His partner's nameplate labeled the
blonde female officer as WHITFORD. Her hair in a bun,
Whitford wore sunglasses, which was appropriate,
because the "night shift" was officially a bright
morning now.

As Warrick and Greg trotted up to the small
group, Officer Kramer was saying, "This is the weird-
est goddamn car accident I ever saw."

"Looks like an abandoned car," Greg said with an
openhanded gesture.

"On this side it does," Officer Whitford agreed.
"Walk your crime-lab eyeballs around the other side
of this bad boy. . . ."

Warrick shared Greg's opinion—from the driver's
side, this looked exactly like a hastily abandoned car,
with three of the four doors left open—but as the
senior CSI crossed in front of the vehicle, his outlook
changed.

Something scarlet had been splashed across the
bumper and up onto the hood.

Looked like blood.

And Warrick at once wondered if it was human; an animal wandering the highway was a possibility—and a human, say a drunk, might have meandered in front of a moving car . . . not likely but certainly not impossible.

The bumper had been dented, the grill caved in slightly—plus a small dent in the hood, near the blood spot there.

Warrick said, "Most likely, the car had hit an animal . . ."

"And the driver lost control?" Greg offered.

Warrick nodded, as he swabbed the bumper. The lab would tell them if it was human or animal.

Greg continued: "Okay, then—why did the driver abandon his wheels?"

"Stolen, maybe."

Walking on, Warrick spotted something and called to Greg, who was behind him several paces.

"*There's* why," Warrick said.

Well past the vehicle, on the road's shoulder, the view previously blocked by the abandoned Caddy and the squad car, lay Warrick's least favorite form of roadkill: a human body.

From this distance, it appeared to be a male—on his stomach, pants and underwear pulled down around his ankles.

"Oh God," Greg said. "Dead?"

"Looks that way."

Brass shook his head as he approached the apparent corpse. "What have we here?"

Warrick thought he knew, and the closer he got, the more sure he was. The CSI looked back toward the car: the passenger-side door's window had a bullet hole through it.

Now he knew for sure.

The bald officer, Kramer, was just behind the CSI. "Ever see anything like this before?"

"Yeah," Warrick said, and heaved a sigh. "At a forensics convention. Similar case happened on the east coast."

The blonde officer, Whitford, asked, "Is this some sort of . . . gay thing?"

Warrick—who had a clear view of the bare behind of the kid on the ground, baggy jeans gathered around his ankles—shook his head.

"Gang thing," Warrick said at last.

The vic, his face turned toward Warrick, was an African-American no more than twenty, probably closer to seventeen. Kid wore a white T-shirt with a hole in the back, blood leaking around the wound, and two more in the head. Eyes closed, gaping exit wound in his forehead. Someone had dropped him from a distance, probably explaining the bullet hole in the passenger window, then made it personal with a double tap to the back of the skull.

"Damn," the CSI said to no one.

Brass was the only one who did not seem surprised.

"This young man screwed up," Warrick explained. "He offended somebody in his gang, or maybe a rival gang. . . . They weren't just going to kill him—they were going to make an example of him."

"That why his pants are down?" Kramer asked.

"No. His pants are down as a form of restraint."

Whitford blinked. *"Restraint?"*

"It's common among some gangs," Warrick said. "They can't afford handcuffs, and they don't want their prisoners running off whenever they want, so they make them drop trou. Not only makes it harder to run, it's humiliating."

Now Whitford nodded, getting it. "The prisoner becomes more compliant."

"That's the idea. Doesn't always work, of course. Especially if you hit something in the road and lose control of the car—that might make your prisoner think he can roll out and run for it . . . even with his lowriders riding way low. . . ."

Officer Kramer's eyes narrowed. "And that's what you think happened here?"

"That's my first take," Warrick said. "Let's not get ahead of ourselves. . . . Check around for animal roadkill, would you?"

The officers went off to look.

While Greg worked the car, Warrick investigated the scene outside the vehicle, starting with the body. Standing over the corpse—the vic's head at left, body sprawled out perpendicular—Warrick began snapping photos of the three wounds: two in the head—one in the middle of the vic's skull, the next down a little and slightly left—another in the lower back near the left kidney. The scarlet line of bullet holes looked like the jagged line of a falling stock.

The bullet holes were all of pretty good size— probably a nine mil. Uppermost head shot had been a through-and-through that exited centrally in the kid's forehead. The lower one had exited over the right ear, the two wounds turning the victim's skull into a pulpy mess. The torso shot had entered but not exited, meaning the bullet was still in the body somewhere.

After taking pictures of the corpse from various angles, Warrick walked the shoulder of the road, looking for footprints. He found several sneaker prints, which he cast in dental stone. Most appeared to be the victim's, but four more had been made by other shoes—two pairs, as near as Warrick could tell. Both uniformed officers wore rubber-soled police shoes whose tire-tread soles looked like no sneakers in the world and could be ruled out; these prints belonged to the perps.

With the footprint impressions and pictures out of the way, Warrick processed the body, starting by scraping under the victim's fingernails—the left index fingernail was broken off—and ending by scraping something oily off the soles of the vic's expensive tennis shoes.

Officer Whitford trotted up and said, "You want to see something weird?"

Warrick stood. "Do I?"

"I found your roadkill."

She led him across the highway and into the adjacent field where a big shape that could almost be a man lay in tall grass, where it had lumbered off to die.

"Tell me," the blond officer said, her eyes large in a face gone pale, "if that's what I think it is."

"That," Warrick said, "would be a lion. . . ."

A dead lion, with a full mane clotted with darkening blood, two limbs broken, rib cage crushed, a magnificent if not-breathing and somewhat bony specimen right out of a circus or a movie.

Soon everyone had gathered around and had circled the dead beast, as if this were a burial service and someone was going to say a few words.

So Warrick did. "Circus Circus, or any of the other casinos with elaborate animal-act shows, report a missing animal?"

"No," Brass said, dumbfounded. "Or a local zoo, or anybody else."

Greg said, "I think I know where this came from."

All eyes went from the king of the jungle to the prince of CSIs.

"Remember when a certain heavyweight champ lived here in Vegas? Wasn't that long ago. He collected exotic pets. A few were rumored to've gotten away. I think this beauty was prowling at night—there's no people around here to speak of, up north. I bet he's been keeping a low profile in these foothills."

Brass said, "Well, he didn't keep much of a low profile when he got in front of those headlights."

Warrick found himself chuckling. "Brother, would I like to've seen the look on the faces of those kids in that car. . . ."

Before long, as Warrick loaded his evidence into the back of the SUV, Greg came over. They didn't speak for a moment as the coroner's wagon pulled up and the two-man crew climbed down and took out their gurney.

"You guys done?" one asked Warrick.

"Yeah—all yours."

The CSIs watched in silence as the coroner's men loaded the body onto the gurney, wheeled it to their van, and soon were swinging across the median for the trip back to the city. When they were gone, the only signs a body had been lying on the side of the road were a few blood drops and two short wheel tracks where the gurney had momentarily slipped onto the dusty shoulder.

"God, he was young," Greg said.

"Get anything?" Warrick asked.

"Load of fingerprints," Greg said. "Mostly off the steering wheel and gear shift, few off the dashboard and door handle on the passenger side. Two ciggie butts in the ashtray. Possible DNA."

Warrick asked, "What about the car?"

"I got a sample of the blood off the hood. That's the outside. Inside, registration was in the glove box. I gave it to Brass to run. My guess is—"

"Stolen," Brass chimed in, coming over from his car to join them. "Registered to a Clark County couple who reported it missing from the parking lot of the Platinum King."

Warrick asked, "When was it taken?"

"Early last night. Our perps probably grabbed it before they snatched our John Doe."

Greg asked, "Did you happen to ask if either of the owners smokes?"

"Yeah, I asked," Brass said. "I saw those cigarette butts, too. And they're both nonsmokers."

Greg grinned tightly. "Good. Cigarette butts came from our perps then. I'll get those right to the DNA lab."

"Good," Warrick said.

"What about our John Doe?" Brass asked.

"We'll catch up to him in the morgue," Warrick said. "Maybe his prints will turn up in AFIS. He was a kid, but probably a gangbanger. Might be in the system."

"We've got the prints from the car to run, too," Greg reminded them.

"And if none of those match anything?" Brass asked.

Warrick shrugged elaborately. "Then we've pretty much got jack squat."

Greg shook his head. "We've really been rackin' 'em up tonight. We'll crack this one, too."

"Yeah," Warrick said, not having the heart to rain on the young CSI's parade. "Tow truck coming for the car?"

Brass nodded. "Should be here any minute. You want it taken to the lab?"

"You know it. Maybe there's something in or on it we haven't found yet."

"How about the lion carcass?"

"We should collect that, too."

Brass smirked. "You gonna ask Doc Robbins to do an autopsy?"

"I don't think so. Poor creature."

"Oh," Greg said, "something *else* was in that car. . . ." He got out an evidence bag from his crime-scene kit. Within the bag was another bag, a fast- food sack that looked to've been used as a trash receptacle.

"If that belongs to the couple who own the car," Warrick said, "it's nothing."

Brass examined the bag in the early-morning sun. "And if it belongs to the perps?"

Warrick nearly smiled. "Then it might just be a break. And Greg gets another gold star."

"I'm up for that," Greg said cheerfully.

* * *

Back in the lab, while Greg loaded the various fingerprints into AFIS, Warrick went through that bag of garbage the young CSI had scored. He picked the items out one at a time: cup from a large orange soda; smaller cup from a strawberry shake; four double cheeseburger wrappers; two large fry boxes; and—at the very bottom, wadded into a tiny ball—the receipt from Bob's Round-Up Grill on Tropicana.

The computerized receipt offered up more information than Warrick could possibly have hoped for: the exact time of the transaction, just after midnight—less than an hour after the couple had reported their car stolen; the register used; the drive-through; and "Sandy," the name of the employee who had taken the order.

After slipping the receipt into a smaller evidence bag, as well as individually bagging each straw for DNA testing, Warrick took them all with him. He stopped to check on Greg's progress on his way out.

"How you doin'?" Warrick asked.

Greg shrugged. "Blood on the car belonged to that lion. Otherwise, slow going."

"Stick with it. Give Animal Control a call about our lion corpse—they should be informed about this incident, and anyway, they're the ones who can properly dispose of the remains."

"Sure thing."

Warrick handed Greg the bags containing the two straws. "And do me a favor—get these to the DNA lab, too."

"Okay." Realizing this was from the garbage he'd

found, Greg asked, "How's it looking for that gold star?"

"You may get *two*. . . . You find anything, give me a call on my cell."

"Why," Greg said, frowning, "where are you headed?"

Warrick said, "I'm gonna take Brass for a break-fast burrito."

"Damn," Greg said. "Forget the gold star. Bring me one of those, will ya?"

Warrick held up the receipt and Greg's eyes widened. "You may get breakfast *and* a gold star, if this pans out. . . ."

Twenty minutes later, Warrick and Captain Brass sat in Bob's Round-Up Grill with Mark Christopher, the day-shift manager—a rail-thin, fiftyish guy with butch salt-and-pepper hair and a slightly saltier mustache.

"Yeah, sure," Christopher said, pressing the evidence bag to better read the slight piece of paper within. "This is one of ours. And Sandy? That's Sandy Worthington, our overnight manager."

Brass said, "Looking at your drive-through before we came inside, we noticed you folks have video surveillance."

"You bet," Christopher said. "Two inside, one for the lot, one for the drive-through. Keeps vandalism to a minimum, plus which we've only been robbed once since we put those babies in. We used to get robbed two or three times a month."

Brass nodded. "Please tell me it's not for show, that those cameras are live, and there's tape in your video recorders."

"Live and recording, absotively."

"Cool," Brass said. "We'd like to see the drive-through security tapes from last night."

"And the parking lot one, too," Warrick added.

Christopher hesitated.

"This is a homicide investigation," Brass said.

"It's the right thing to do, Mr. Christopher," Warrick said. "Might make for some nice publicity, too."

"All right." He rose. "I'll get 'em for you."

When they had the tapes and had given the day manager a receipt, Brass and Warrick got to their feet.

Brass said, "Thank you for your cooperation, Mr. Christopher. Just one more thing—could we have the home address of Sandy Worthington? We'll need to talk to her, too."

"She's probably sleeping," he said. "Night shift, you know."

Warrick grinned. "We know. We're on it."

Brass smiled, too. "*Still* on it, actually."

"I been there," Christopher said with a nod, and wrote the info on a napkin and handed it to Brass. "Glad to help," he said. "Anything else?"

"Actually, yes," Warrick said.

"What?"

"Breakfast burrito to go?"

8

AT A TABLE IN THE FOUR KINGS SNACK BAR, Catherine sat nursing a cup of coffee—enjoying her first lull since taking on the biker/casino shoot-out crime scene.

The last of the witnesses had been cleared out. Two local investigators, Bell and Hamilton, had left for the police station; she'd lost track of the lead investigator, Cody Jacks. For now, she had the place to herself, not counting the two waitresses in a booth near the kitchen door, anyway.

She hadn't pulled a shift this long for some time. At least she didn't have to worry about her daughter, with her mom taking care of Lindsey. Comforting as that was, there remained the aches in her neck and back, the weariness in her legs, and the general exhaustion that came with being up for over twenty-four hours. She was doing all right, she'd make it through fine; but when this case wrapped up, she'd need a day off to collapse and recharge.

Sara ambled up, coffee cup in hand, plopping into

the chair opposite. The younger woman didn't look any more peppy than her supervisor. "Are you as tired as I am?"

"At least."

Sara allowed herself a yawn, covering with a hand. "Long haul. And I was in the laundry room, at my apartment house, when the call came in—just put in a load."

"Washer or dryer?"

"Washer. Had to pull everything out and throw it in the sink in my kitchen." Sara grinned in her appealing way. "Always nice to have a mess waiting, huh?"

Catherine smirked and shook her head in commiseration. "Nature of the job, though."

"Yeah, and I'm not ready to buy a house yet. I've been in an apartment for a long time now, and that's bad enough. Don't know if I could handle all the hassle that comes with a house."

"There is a lot of stuff," Catherine admitted. "But at least you can leave your laundry in the washer when you get called in to clean up somebody *else's* mess." Her cell rang and she picked it up on the second ring. "Catherine Willows."

"Sofia, Catherine. How are things in the wild west?"

"Wild is right. Got something from the home front?"

"The CSI mantra, I'm afraid—good news, bad news."

"I can use the good," Catherine said.

"We're making progress with the videotapes. We've picked out several of the Spokes who opened fire, so we should be able to sort out the perps from the self-defense crowd. . . . We've just been unable to identify them all yet."

"That last part—was that the bad news?"

A long pause was finally broken by, "Sorry. Not really."

Catherine swore silently to herself. "Okay— lemme have the bad."

How bad could the news be? All Sofia was doing was checking security tape. . . .

Sofia said, "We haven't found any footage of Valpo's murder."

That *bad*. . . .

"Impossible," Catherine said. "You obviously haven't gotten through all the tapes yet."

"But we have. And the Valpo murder isn't any-where."

"Damn."

"We got footage of the shoulder wound taking him down . . . but he falls out of frame and we can't see him after that. And that's when the execution happened. We don't see it, so we can't pinpoint the shooter."

Catherine allowed herself a sigh. "When can we expect you back at Boot Hill?"

Sofia considered that for a moment. "I'm not sure. Archie and I are going through tapes again and again, trying to identify shooters based on file and database photos of Spokes and Predators. And the labs are going all out on the other evidence." She let out her own sigh. "Cath, I'd like to go through the tapes one more time myself. Let's say . . . late afternoon?"

"See you then," Catherine said, and rang off.

"What's the problem?" Sara asked.

Catherine filled Sara in.

"Will they be bringing in the riot wagon," Sara asked, "now that Sofia's getting the shooters I.D.'d?"

"Probably by the end of the day, yeah."

Sara frowned over her coffee. "That could get nasty."

"Yeah—sure be a pity if this turned nasty, huh?"

Sara sipped and swallowed; her grin was MIA. "What are we supposed to do in the meantime?"

Catherine rose. "Keep at it. We can start by finding out one thing."

"Yeah?" Sara asked, getting up.

"Let's talk to casino security and find out why those tapes don't show everything they should."

They asked directions from the waitresses and, on the second floor, found Henry Cippolina in the security suite, a less high-tech affair than just about any comparable Vegas casino setup, taking Catherine back, in fact, to the kind of gear she ran into when she first became a CSI.

A bank of videotape players occupied one wall to the right; three uniformed guards sat at different stations watching monitors, even though there was little to see with the casino closed down for business. One guard was keeping an eye on the hotel screens, since that side of the operation was up and running, on a limited basis, anyway.

Three offices lined the left wall and Cippolina was in the middle one, door open. The floor manager sat behind a massive wooden rectangle of a desk, with an equally large workstation to his left laden with computer equipment. The walls blazed with posters touting getaways to, and performers appearing at, the Four Kings Casino. The office otherwise was a joyless affair, medium-sized, Cippolina's desk and workstation taking up much of the space, a few filing cabinets between posters taking up the rest.

Two visitor's chairs were opposite the fortyish security chief, his receding black hair parted on the left and well-oiled, his mouth a thin, straight, colorless line, his skin tone flat-out cadaverous. On one chair was the security chief's jacket, wrinkled, underarm sweat stains visible, tossed haphazardly there.

Though the air-conditioning was working overtime, Cippolina's shirt looked at least as wrinkled and sweaty as the jacket, and the casino man had rolled the shirt's sleeves up to the elbow. He had dark circles under his eyes that seemed to suggest more than simple exhaustion, rather full-time malaise.

Entering without knocking, Sara on her heels, Catherine said, "We need to talk."

Cippolina started to rise, but Catherine held up a hand for him to remain seated as she and Sara came in and ignored the visitor's chairs, taking a position just inside the door.

"Make yourself at home," he said, with just a hint of sarcasm. "Need to talk about what?"

"For starters, about how your cameras don't cover the whole casino floor."

Cippolina held his hands out. "Why, is that illegal? Look, Ms. Willets—"

"Willows."

"Willows—sorry." He got up, removed his coat from the visitor's chair, and gestured for them to sit.

Sara glanced at Catherine, who nodded, and they

took the chairs while Cippolina got back behind the desk, draping his suit coat over his own chair, and sat.

The security chief did his best to affect a genial expression. "Look—you folks up Vegas way get more visitors to the Strip in one *day* than we get down here in Boot Hill all year. We simply don't have as much money for security as we would like." He spread his hands. "Good God, people—everything in this joint is at least twenty years old. You think *I* don't know our security's subpar?"

The speech had no effect on Catherine. She folded her arms and looked daggers at the man. "Mr. Cippolina, we've been going over your security tapes, searching for a needle in a haystack for hours . . . and now I find out there's no damn haystack. Your cameras didn't catch Valpo's killer."

"What can I say? Nobody's perfect."

She ignored his remark. "If there was a flaw in your system, you had a responsibility to point it out at the start of this inquiry. An investigation this size, with violence all around us ready to erupt any instant . . . I expect *full* cooperation."

"I *have* been cooperating. You people waltz in, take over, and—"

Catherine held up a palm. Then, almost gently, she said, "Just please tell me why and how it happened."

Cippolina leaned on an elbow and his expression was almost painfully earnest. "Look, Ms. Willows . . . Ms. Simon was it?"

"Sidle."

"Ms. Sidle. Like I said, I haven't had enough

money to do proper security in this place since I got here, what . . . eight years ago. So, I do the best I can with a . . . not a bad situation, exactly—a limited one." He shifted in his chair. "That means utilizing my assets to cover the most territory. There are, accordingly, blind spots on the floor."

Catherine felt her temper rising again but curtailed it. "How *many* 'blind spots' in that casino?"

"We operate on the principle that the very presence of the video cameras discourages misconduct."

Sara said, "Like a security company sticker on a homeowner's window . . . when the homeowner doesn't even have a security system."

"Well . . . not quite that bad, Ms. Sidle, but—"

Catherine tried again: "How many blind spots?"

"Four."

"Four?" Catherine asked, appalled.

He shrugged; he had the expression of a schoolkid in the principal's office trying to explain after getting caught cheating. "We cover as much space as we can."

"Just how big *are* these blind spots?"

Cippolina toyed with a paper clip on his desk. "Three of them . . . maybe a bit bigger than the size of this desk . . . the fourth one is about twice that. There are no slots or poker machines in any of those areas, although they're all busy traffic sections of the casino."

Catherine and Sara exchanged glances; each knew what the other was thinking.

They had been swimming upstream all day against this crime scene and now they were being jerked around again, this time by the economics of

trying to secure a casino this size with a conven-
ience-store surveillance system budget.

Sara asked, "Mr. Cippolina—how many people in
this casino know about these security-cam blind
spots?"

Another embarrassed shrug. "Everyone in upper
management—the security department, of course,
even some of the floor employees."

Catherine raised an eyebrow. "Who in the casino
doesn't know about the blind spots?"

Cippolina swallowed. "The customers."

Shaking her head, Catherine said, "Are you sure
about that?"

That took Cippolina by surprise. "What do you
mean, Ms. Willows?"

"This is a small town—you're a big employer
here, and even the lower-echelon staff seems to
know about these security limitations."

"So?"

"Well . . . loose lips sink ships."

He shifted heavily in his chair. "Uh—I suppose
you make a valid point. . . ."

"So," Catherine said, quietly seething, "it's con-
ceivable that the only people who *didn't* know about
your faulty security would be . . . us?"

Cippolina's head lowered again. "I'd like to be
able to say that remark is unfair. But . . . frankly . . .
I can't."

The security chief had taken enough of a beating. Catherine shifted gears and asked, "Have you
had any luck locating your missing employee—Tom
Price?"

"No. He's not on the premises anywhere."

Sara smiled and said, "You might check and see if he's standing in a blind spot."

Catherine gave her a look and Sara backed off. "Well, I do appreciate your frankness and cooperation in this meeting."

"It's the least I can do."

On that, Catherine agreed with him. "I need a picture of Tom Price. Can you provide one? Soon would be good. Now would be better."

Cippolina, as if anticipating the request, had one in a manila folder on his desk. He handed it over. "Thought you might want this."

She studied the face of a bespectacled man bearing wide-set eyes, short brown hair with bangs, and a countenance that appeared not to have smiled since sometime early in childhood.

"Can you e-mail one of these as an attached file?"

"Yeah, we do have the internet here," Cippolina said a little defensively.

Catherine gave him Sofia's e-mail address.

He said, "I'll do it right away," got up, and left them alone in his office.

Catherine punched a number into her cell phone and connected with Sofia.

"This Tom Price character," Catherine told her, "who seems to have made himself scarce—his photo should be showing up in your e-mail any time."

"Okay. I'll check right now. . . ."

"See if you can find this guy in any of the videotape."

"Will do," Sofia said. A short pause followed. Then: "Yeah, it's here . . . I've got the photo just fine. Get back to you when I have something."

Cippolina came back into the office as Catherine returned the cell to her belt.

"That was fast," she said, and gave the security chief a smile and a nod. "Nice job."

"We're not incompetent," he said wearily, "just poorly funded." He resumed his seat behind the desk.

"Thank you, Mr. Cippolina," Catherine said, rising, Sara following suit. "We'll keep that in mind."

Catherine took the manila folder with the picture of Tom Price with her.

Once the two CSIs were in the stairwell, heading back down, Sara said, "He seemed embarrassed by their security shortcomings, but not really, uh . . . broken up about any of this."

"What do you mean?"

"Well, when your workplace gets shot up and your fellow employees get wounded or even killed, doesn't a normal person *feel* it?"

Catherine's father, Sam Braun, was a casino mogul in Vegas. She thought back to her relationship with him, and said, "Casinos are a lot more about making money than friends—it's a guarded world that doesn't usually put strong interpersonal relationships first."

"How odd. And sad."

Catherine nodded. "Our friend Mr. Cippolina's biggest concern might just be that a customer named Valpo died with unbet money in his pocket."

At the bottom of the stairwell, Catherine opened the door and led the way back onto the casino floor. Even hours after the firefight, she could still detect the odor of cordite in the air.

"So," Sara asked, "what's next?"

"Everything with this crime scene has worked against us so far. I'd just like one thing to go our way."

"Maybe one thing has," Sara said.

Catherine shot Sara a curious frown. "Spill."

Sara's half smile held a hint of apology. "That 3D scan of the crime scene Nicky and I did? We got so busy collecting evidence after that, we never got a chance to really study it."

"Well, why don't you, then?"

"Why don't I. Why don't *we*?"

On the way back, Sara picked up her laptop from the cashier's cage that had become a de facto HQ for the team and storage site for their equipment. In the café, she took a seat at a table in the middle of the room and rested the computer on the formica surface before her.

While Sara booted up, Catherine pulled a chair around so she could sit next to her colleague and view the screen easily, rather than hover over Sara's shoulder.

Once Sara had logged on and launched the Delta-Sphere's software, only a second or so passed before they were staring at a 3D rendering of the crime scene as it had appeared hours ago, the wounded already gone but the two deceased victims still in place, the detritus of the firefight not yet collected and bagged and marked.

As they maneuvered through the scene on the screen, Catherine had a feeling similar to when she took Lindsey to the IMAX theater to see James Cameron's documentary on the *Titanic*. Watching his drone cameras, Jake and Elwood, motor around the corridors of the world's most famous ghost ship, she had felt a combination of enormous curiosity and a weird voyeuristic guilt about sifting through someone else's life so long after death—as if somehow she were violating someone's privacy in the extreme.

This odd combination of sharp curiosity and near guilt flowed over her again now, even though she'd felt no compunction when surveying every inch of the real scene as she took this 3D tour via Sara's laptop.

The odd sensation almost instantly vanished as Sara manipulated them through the scene, Catherine now feeling wrapped up in some hyperreal video game.

These graphics were far better than she'd expected, and she found herself studying the monitor as if the crime scene on the screen were the real deal and not the digital reproduction.

Fingers flying, Sara put them in position to study Valpo's body from one side.

The Predator leader lay on his stomach, his shoulder showing signs of what Catherine now knew for sure was an exit wound. Though she could see blood on Valpo's head, she had from this angle no clear view of the base-of-the-skull entrance wound.

As if reading Catherine's mind, Sara swivelled the view until they were above and behind Valpo, standing over the biker, so to speak, and looking down into the bloody wound in the Predator's skull.

"Shooter got up close and personal," Sara said, even though they both knew that already.

"Yeah," Catherine agreed. "Plenty of GSR on his neck."

The gunshot residue gave Valpo's neck the appearance that a ghoulish waiter had hand-milled pepper over him after he died, the black pinpoints readily apparent around the wound.

"Let's try something," Sara said, eyes slitted, swivelling the view yet again.

They were still above Valpo's corpse—Catherine was sure they had not moved—but now their view was toward the blackjack table, where the young dealer had died.

From here, the dealer was in plain view, her corpse on the floor, maybe six feet away. The distance between the bodies had seemed greater in the casino; either that, or Catherine had not noticed how close together they were. But she noticed now, all right, from this new vantage point, and had a new thought about this entire matter.

Entire *murder* . . .

"One killer could have shot them both," she said.

Sara nodded. "Grissom speculated that the young woman may have witnessed the 'execution' and been killed for it."

"If so," Catherine said, "she should have had time to scramble out of the way . . . even in that firefight. Why didn't she?"

Everywhere they turned on this case, they got more questions . . . and precious few answers, rolling one snake eyes after another.

Catherine hoped that the other CSIs were having better luck.

When Grissom showed up with Police Chief Jorge Lopez, Nick had been working the mortuary crime scene for the better part of two hours.

The two men climbed out of the Blazer and came over to where Nick was using an electrostatic print-lifter to collect footprints and tire tracks from the mortuary's rear parking lot.

Keeping a proper distance from the evidence-gathering, Grissom called, "Nick—how's it coming?"

"Not bad," Nick said. "Almost done here."

Lopez asked, "How's Mr. Erickson?"

Nick removed his eyes from his work and met the chief's worried gaze. "Paramedics made him get in the ambulance and ride over to Laughlin . . . but I'm guessing it was just a concussion. He seemed less than thrilled about having to walk away—or get *rolled* away—from his business, with it wide open and us poking around."

Lopez chuckled. "Sounds like Erickson. But just the same, you'll get all the help you need from him."

Nick nodded. "Mostly he seemed upset somebody got the drop on him."

"Most of his customers don't sneak up on him," Lopez said dryly. "Where's Officer Montaine?"

Montaine's squad car was still parked at the mortuary.

Nick said, "He had this idea he should go canvassing the neighborhood."

Lopez frowned, shook his head. "Who's to canvass this early on a Saturday in this neighborhood? It's all businesses."

Nick shrugged. "He's been gone over an hour. Can't tell you."

Grissom asked Nick, "What have you got so far?"

"Just that Valpo's body was stolen, still in the body bag. No real trail to follow."

"Fingerprints?"

"On all the doorknobs in the joint, but I'm guessing that once we print Mr. Erickson, that'll be the
only match."

The chief asked, "Anything else taken?"

"Not that Mr. Erickson could see," Nick said. "But,
then, he was shuffled out of here pretty much right
away. He did take a look around the preparation
chamber and said everything seemed to be right
where it should be. Just that one missing item: the
body."

"What about these footprints?" Grissom asked, indicating Nick's current efforts.

Nick said, "That's why I'd like Officer Montaine to
get back here. This footprint looks like a Rocky to
me."

Lopez frowned again. "Rocky *police* boots?"

"Yeah. What's it look like to you?" He turned over
the mylar sheet he had just charged and showed
them the electrostatic footprint of a boot tread.

Grissom nodded. "Looks like a Rocky, all right."

"Hell," Lopez said, and turned up the sole of his
shoe so the CSIs could see it. "Looks like *my* Rocky."

"On the surface," Grissom said, bending for a
look, "it's a match. But you've been doing this long
enough to know that every individual boot wears
differently. Your wear is up on the toes—you walk
on the balls of your feet."

"These boots," Nick said, picking up Grissom's
thread, "show more wear along the sides and on the
heel. These shoes, whoever's wearing 'em? Uncomfortable."

"So," Lopez said, eyes narrowing. "You think a

cop stole the body . . . or did Officer Montaine happen to step here?"

"Either is a possibility," Nick said.

"Just two of *many* possibilities," Grissom said, obviously trying to prevent anyone from taking a premature path. "A lot of bikers wear Rocky boots these days. So we have any number of potential boots in Boot Hill—only one we seem to have ruled out so far, Chief, is you."

"I better go find Montaine," Lopez said.

"Nick," Grissom said, "how much longer do you think you'll need here?"

"Just finishing up, really. Chief, can you get me to your lab?"

"Sure," Lopez said. "Not much by your standards, but I can provide a computer and some basic lab equipment."

"I'd appreciate that."

The three loaded Nick's gear into the Blazer and drove off to find Officer Montaine, which proved a short search: the young deputy was just around the block, walking out of a café with a Styrofoam cup of coffee.

When they rolled up to him, Montaine smiled and waved.

Lopez, leaning out the window, was in no mood. "Are you canvassing the neighborhood," he exploded, "or on goddamn doughnut duty?"

"What . . . this is just coffee."

"Oh, you're drinking coffee, then? Weren't you supposed to be off canvassing the neighborhood?"

"Chief, I'm really sorry," the kid said, "but Mr. Ross . . . the breakfast cook back there at Racheal's?"

He pointed toward the café, barely twenty feet away. "He insisted I take the coffee. And it wasn't such a bad idea to canvass, 'cause he told me he came in a little after five, to start everything up at the café, and he saw some of those bikers riding by—toward the mortuary."

Grissom's eyes tightened. "I thought all the bikers were quarantined—either at the campground or that other hotel."

Lopez nodded. "Yeah. . . . Dean, did Mr. Ross recognize the bikers?"

"He said there were only three bikers, but that the one nearest the café? When they went roaring by? Had on a vest with 'Rusty Spokes' on the back."

"All right," Lopez said. He worked up a smile. "Sorry I jumped on you, Dean. That's good work you did. Damn good work."

The kid beamed. "Thanks, Chief. . . . Okay if I drink this coffee, then?"

"Go right ahead," Lopez said with a chuckle. "Say, do you know where Sergeant Jacks is? . . . Haven't seen him all night."

Montaine nodded. "Cody said he was heading out to the Price place, to see if he was there. That's the last I heard."

"Hell," Lopez muttered.

Grissom asked, "Why is that a bad thing? Don't we need to talk to Price, and isn't Cody Jacks your top investigator?"

"He is that, Doc," Lopez said. "But we've got more important things to be worried about than Tom Price, who lives way the hell southeast of Cal Nev Ari—almost an hour from here."

"I see."

Lopez glanced in the rearview mirror to catch Nick's eye. "Mr. Stokes, I'm going to drop you off at the station so you can get your lab work going."

"Great."

"I can reach Cody from there," Lopez said, "after which, Doc, you and me, we can go talk with the Rusty Spokes about breaking house arrest."

"Sounds like fun," Grissom said.

Nick asked from the back, "Why don't you just call Detective Jacks on the radio?"

"Cody'll be in the Newberry Mountains, which play hell with cell phone and radio traffic. Never reach him from my car, but the transmitter at the station should do the trick."

The police station was just down Allen Street from the two hotels, a one-story brick-and-glass building smaller than the garage back at CSI. A sign out front proudly proclaimed:

BOOT HILL POLICE DEPARTMENT

and in smaller letters

CHIEF JORGE G. LOPEZ

As he parked, Lopez said, "Doc, you can come in or not—should only take a couple of minutes. I'll set Nick up with his chemistry set, call Cody, then you and me can walk up to the Gold Vault."

"I'll stay out here," Grissom said. "I could use the fresh air. Mind if I start up the street?"

Lopez said, "Sure—I'll catch up. If I'm not right

there, wait in the lobby. Don't take on the Spokes without me, Doc."

"I think you can rest assured of that."

Lopez grinned. "Okay, Nick, come on—I'll get ya set up on the cutting edge of forensics circa 1975. . . ."

Grissom watched as the chief escorted Nick—carting his crime scene kit and evidence—inside the modest station. Part of Grissom wanted to stay with his guy and give him a hand—possibly the senior CSI would have a better handle on using the limited materials at hand—but Nick was a first-rate analyst now and didn't need Grissom looking over his shoulder. Better to stay outside and accompany the chief.

The hotel was two blocks away. Grissom started off at a leisurely pace, enjoying the gentle desert breeze. For a guy who lived in labs, Gil Grissom loved the outdoors. The sun was up but not hot yet, and only a handful of people were out moving around. Whether this was normal Boot Hill Saturday activity or a severe curtailment after the gunplay in the casino, Grissom did not know.

He passed a video rental store, a drugstore, and two restaurants. None were open, not even the restaurant, despite its promise of an all-you-can-eat breakfast and twenty-four-hour service.

A block away from the two casino hotels now, Grissom noticed activity out front of the Four Kings.

As he drew closer, Grissom could see that a makeshift memorial to Nick Valpo had sprung up on a chain-link fence that bordered a casino parking lot. Several Predators were huddling around the area, though Grissom had no idea whether they'd stayed at the Four Kings (the Predators did have some rooms there) or had somehow broken containment from the campground.

Crossing the street, Grissom took a bench opposite and was able to watch without intruding as bikers set down flowers and other mementos under a large elaborate colored-pencil drawing on poster board (leaned against the fence and secured with duct tape) of the fallen Predator leader. Some flowers and other items were wired or otherwise attached to the chain-link. A certain melancholy sweetness was undercut by dark black letters over the somewhat idealized portrait of the dead biker captain: MURDERED IN BOOT HILL!!!

On Grissom's side of the street, light traffic passed in and out of the Gold Vault Casino. From his bench near the curb, the CSI had a clear view as a young woman—maybe twenty, maybe not—wearing a flowered hippie-ish dress, her long blonde hair tied back in a bow, approached the chain-link memorial and carefully positioned a bouquet of twelve red roses, bright as blood amid otherwise pastel flowers.

When she turned away and walked toward Grissom's side of the street, her big light-brown eyes brimmed with tears that caught sunlight and glimmered. She moved with an easy, sensuous grace, passed Grissom, and kept going.

Grissom stopped a brunette, fortyish woman walking by wearing a Gold Vault casino employee vest and asked if she knew the young woman.

Without looking at the receding figure, she said, "No," and moved on.

Then he asked a man about his own age who was

carrying a drugstore sack, just as the young woman was turning a corner and disappearing.

"Yeah, I know who that is," the man said, catching her just in time. "Wendy Sierra's her name."

And he kept on walking.

Grissom glanced toward the police station: still no sign of Chief Lopez.

Crossing the street again, Grissom entered the Four Kings, gave his eyes a moment to adjust to the lighting change, then took a step through the metal detectors, which promptly started screaming.

Uniformed and nonuniformed personnel descended on him, Catherine and Sara rushing up, right in the middle. He flashed his ID, which got the security people to back off, and a guard turned off the metal-detector alarm with a key.

"Sorry, sir," the guard said, recognizing the CSI. "We've got these babies active again."

"Good," Grissom said.

He and Catherine brought each other up to speed on what they had learned.

Then Grissom turned to Sara. "There's a name I want you to run—Wendy Sierra. Local girl. That's all I know."

Sara went off to call Vegas. Grissom figured he could get better information that way than trying to get anything out of anyone in this taciturn town.

"Wendy Sierra?" Catherine asked.

"Just a hunch," he said. "There's a memorial out on the sidewalk. This girl left a dozen roses. And tears."

Catherine said, "That's not a hunch. That's just you being sensitive."

That seemed to puzzle him. "Really? . . . Anyway,

I've got to go—Chief Lopez is meeting me to talk to the Spokes."

Catherine's face turned steely and she said, "Then I'm coming, too. Sofia e-mailed us a partial list of shooters; we can start making arrests."

"Oh?" Grissom asked. "Where are we going to put them? Presidential suites of these hotels?"

"In jail is a start," Catherine said. "The list is the first four shooters—*all* Spokes. We can at least get those four on ice."

"Good. That *is* a start."

They had crossed the street to the Gold Vault lobby when Lopez came in quickly and joined them. Highway Patrolmen, a visible presence outside the building, were in greater number in the lobby.

Business continued here, the slots still open, gambling going on for those guests not unnerved by the possibility of another gunfight breaking out. So much post-9/11 chatter had been in the air about Vegas as a possible terrorist target that many casino players were now simply immune to such fears and went back to playing as they always had. Life itself was a gamble, after all.

The chief's worried expression told Grissom something had not gone well at the station. The CSI decided not to bring up the Sierra girl until later; right now he wanted to know what was troubling Lopez. So he asked him.

Lopez craned his neck around to make sure no one was within earshot besides the two CSIs. "I talked to Cody, and he's out at Tom Price's. Price is dead."

"How?" Grissom asked.

"Suicide. Hanged himself in his house. Cody found ten thousand dollars on the kitchen table . . . and a note."

"Which said?" Grissom asked.

"That he was sorry. He didn't mean for anyone to get hurt. And he left the money to the Delware woman's infant daughter."

Catherine said, "You don't sound very sympathetic."

"At least three people are dead, including that single mother, all because this greedy bastard took a bribe to turn off those metal detectors . . . and now I don't even get the goddamn satisfaction of putting him away for it. Far as I'm concerned, son of a bitch got off easy."

Grissom said, "Is Jacks maintaining the crime scene?"

"No—he's on his way back here. Can't waste one of my few detectives on one dead body with so many live threats. I sent Montaine."

Grissom would have preferred to go straight out there, but with so much crime in this one case, he was feeling as much like an air traffic controller as a CSI.

Catherine was handing Lopez the list Sofia had e-mailed to the security room at the Four Kings. She explained what it was.

Lopez quickly scanned the sheet. "Yeah, I know all these guys—Buck Finch is the Spokes leader . . . he'll be the tricky one. We can get the other three without a lot of trouble; but collaring Finch—the Spokes won't love that."

They huddled with the Highway Patrolmen and, when they broke to get back in the game, the uniforms went straight for the other three Spokes and hustled them out of the hotel. Another larger group of bikers began to gather around Catherine, Grissom, and Lopez. Only two uniformed Patrolmen were left to back them up, but Lopez had already made sure that help was on the way.

But right now the reality was this: the Spokes were closing around them, outnumbering the law thirty or maybe even forty to five, and for the second time in twelve hours, Gil Grissom found himself staring down a massive group that seemed only a heartbeat away from tearing him and his compatriots apart.

With the group growing restless, the Red Sea of Rusty Spokes suddenly parted and a tall, leanly muscular man of forty or so strolled up and took a position in front of Lopez.

Wearing a black T-shirt and black jeans, his blond hair receding slightly, worn just long enough to curl up at the collar, Buck Finch might have been a successful businessman on a weekend getaway.

The only giveaway that something more dangerous might lurk within this rugged, handsome figure was a thick, darker-blond Fu Manchu mustache, large white teeth that appeared and disappeared like those of a growling dog, and cold, hard, dark eyes carrying not the faintest flicker of sympathetic human emotion.

The rival gang might be *called* the Predators, Grissom thought, but standing in front of him now was the real thing. . . .

Lopez didn't beat around the bush. "Why, Buck? Why fire off the first round of a war in a casino filled with civilians?"

Finch merely stared at Lopez.

"You may have gotten the metal detectors shut off," the chief said, "but you didn't stop the video. It's all there—reality TV starring you, Buck."

A tiny, mirthless smile flicked across Finch's face. "Since you haven't read me my rights, Chief, I'll just say—strictly for your benefit—that *if* we were the ones who started the fight, it just might be because those so-called Predators disrespected us for too long, too many times."

Grissom asked, "What did the other casino patrons do to you, Mr. Finch?"

Finch ignored the CSI, keeping his dead eyes on the chief. "Those hot-shit Predators think just because some of us choose to live a straight life, when we're not on the road, that we're only *weekend* warriors—wannabes."

"So," Lopez said. "You were just making a point."

The biker's eyebrows rose, his eyes widening till the whites showed all around. "They don't think we're wannabes *now*, do they? . . . But that's just the opinion, the insight of one concerned citizen, you might say. The Predators could just as easily be the ones that started shooting. You say you have evidence, but this is a casino—lots of bluffing goes on in this place." He grinned, the huge white animal teeth gleaming. "Besides, Chief—to arrest me, you'd still have to get me the hell out of here. And how do you propose doing that?"

Catherine stepped up and said, "The Predators weren't the ones who fired first—you were. You personally, Mr. Finch. Not the, uh, 'weekend warriors' surrounding you . . . who may not be anxious to back you up and trade in their 'straight' lives so they can become accessories after the fact—to murder."

The smile remained, turning slightly glazed. But Finch said, "You know, Chiefie—I like her. She's got balls."

"She's from Vegas," Lopez said. "Crime lab—people who are gonna put your ass away for a long, long time."

"*This* fine little lady?" Finch asked, his eyes wandering over her, inspecting her lasciviously.

She held out her hand and gave him her sexiest smile.

"Catherine Willows," she said.

He laughed and took her hand to shake it, but before he could, she twisted his wrist, spun under his arm, and came up behind him, his right arm in a hammerlock, and snapped on a cuff.

Finch reached for her with his left hand and she got his thumb and bent it back until he howled, and she had control of him. This convinced him to put the other hand behind him, and she put on the second cuff.

The crowd surged but didn't do anything about it, possibly taking Catherine's accessory speech to heart; and anyway, Lopez and the two uniforms had their guns out now.

Everyone froze, Lopez and the Patrolmen each aiming at the nearest of the Spokes, none of whom went for their guns, assuming they had any.

"Just because you've got me cuffed, bitch," Finch snarled, something childish and pathetic about it, "doesn't mean you're gettin' me out of here!"

Catherine had her pistol out now, and spun Finch so he was looking her in the eyes again, his arms locked behind him.

She smiled again—not that sexy this time.

"You might be right, Buck," she said. "But here's the game, and the odds: we don't get out of here, you don't either. You are first in line. Look in my eyes, and tell me you get my drift."

He grinned insolently.

Her voice cold, calm, and low, she said, "Look in my eyes, Buck . . . and *tell* me."

Finch's grin immediately disappeared. He swallowed. "Back off, boys . . . I'm goin' to jail with my new girlfriend here."

But before they hauled Finch out, Grissom saw the man exchange a very meaningful look with one of his cronies.

As if to say *You know what to do. . . .*

9

WARRICK BROWN HAD JOINED Dr. Albert Robbins in the autopsy room when Greg Sanders hurried in. Neither CSI was in scrubs, though Robbins was. The body of their lion-roadkill John Doe lay naked on the metal table, a sheet drawn up to his waist. Under the harsh fluorescent lighting, the corpse looked even younger.

As he crossed the room, Greg announced, "That's *not* John Doe, gentlemen. . . ."

The young CSI took a position beside Warrick, with Dr. Robbins gazing patiently at them from the other side of the table.

"What *is* his name?" Warrick asked.

"DeMarcus Hankins," Greg said, without reading from the piece of paper he held. "Snagged him in AFIS, despite his youth."

"Nice," Warrick said.

Greg beamed. "I ran the vic's prints while you and Brass were making that fast-food run—and thanks for the burrito, by the way. Not exactly delicious, but without it I mighta passed out."

"Two-seventy-five you owe me," Warrick said.

Some of the air went out of Greg, and he started scrounging in his pockets.

With a grin, Warrick said, "You can catch mine next time. Eyes back on the ball."

Greg's smile couldn't have looked more relieved had he just received a presidential pardon.

"Oh-kaay," Warrick said to Greg, then nodded at the corpse. "What do we know about our new best friend DeMarcus Hankins?"

"Member of the Mechas." Greg's eyebrows lifted. "Former member, now. . . ."

The Mechas or Mecha Boys or Mecha Street Boys—sometimes even MSB—was a gang that started (not surprisingly) on Mecha Street in a neighborhood that might best be described as low income, the residents "financially struggling," to quote bureaucrat-speak. Not a happy place for a kid to grow up, with role models including crack dealers, crack whores . . . and members of MSB.

"If he's in AFIS," Warrick said, "he earned his listing."

Greg shrugged. "Only seventeen, so this stuff is all juvie—assault, possession. Even implicated in a couple of B & E's, but never charged."

"Not on his way to becoming a model citizen," Dr. Robbins said evenly. "But you never know—he might've straightened out; certainly didn't have to die like this."

"He'd probably still be alive," Warrick said, "if it hadn't been for that lion on the loose. My take is, he was just being taken out for a dressing down."

"If you define 'dressing down,'" Greg said, "as having your trousers around your ankles."

Robbins said, "By the way, I spoke to Animal Control. I'll know more later, but the king of beasts seems to've been somewhat malnourished."

Warrick said, "Who knows how long it was surviving out in those scrubby hills."

"We could have him brought in for an autopsy," Robbins said, a tightness around his eyes betraying a desire to do anything *but* a procedure on a dead lion. "If you suspect he was drugged and purposely sent out into the highway to spook some motorist as a practical joke, or—"

"I don't see it," Warrick said. "That cat is strictly roadkill—unusual roadkill. That former heavyweight champ *did* lose track of some of his exotic pets."

"If you change your mind," Robbins said, quietly relieved, "let me know."

Warrick asked, "Anything we don't know about our *human* subject?"

Robbins shrugged. "He was fleeing when he got shot in the back. That alone would likely have killed him, given the proximity of decent medical care; but he didn't have to wait to bleed out, did he?"

"You're saying either of the head shots would have been instantly fatal."

"I'm saying that, yes."

"Anything else?"

Robbins held up Hankins's left hand. "Note the index finger."

"Already did, Doc—noticed that when I scraped."

The coroner nodded, gestured to the digit. "Severity

of this tear means the nail was torn off—violently. My guess is, while he was scratching an assailant."

Greg's eyebrows rose. "You think he left a piece of himself in his attacker?"

"Possible," Robbins said.

Their next stop was the DNA lab to see Mia, who was alternating between loading more specimens into the DNA analyzer and poring over reports.

"Just can't stay away, can you?" she asked as they entered, Warrick in the lead.

He risked a grin. "Kinda hoping that you could tell us something about those straws and cigarette butts."

Her smile was wide, but her eyes were tight. "Once again, you assumed I would push Warrick Brown to the front of the line. You figured I'd rush it right through, just so I could see you again, I suppose? You thought that I would just drop everything else and—"

"Actually, we're just on kind of a fast track. No pressure, Mia, just checking. . . ."

"I don't remember calling you."

"Well, you, uh, didn't."

"Actually, if memory serves, I said I'd call you when I had something."

Warrick tasted his words as he said, "Your memory serves you just fine," and didn't much care for the flavor.

Without looking at him, she pointed to the door like the Ghost of Christmas Yet to Come showing Scrooge his gravestone. "Then get your bony butt out of my lab until I call you. Ask your friend, the newbie CSI, there, *he'll* tell you—DNA analysis takes time. In the real world, this would take you a month; you're lucky we've got this kick-ass lab."

"I was just telling Greg that," Warrick said, and eased back into the hall, blowing out air as if narrowly ducking a dire fate.

As they headed down the corridor, Greg glanced back at his old DNA haunts. Admiringly, he said, "Wow—now *that's* attitude. I should've stood up to you like that, back when you used to ride *me* for results!"

"If you had," Warrick said, "you'd still be picking yourself up."

Greg nodded. "Good point."

They went back to their individual tasks, Greg working prints in AFIS, Warrick settling in to watch the Bob's Round-Up Grill security-tape film festival.

The first tape was the parking lot angle. After cruising to three minutes before the time on the receipt, Warrick began looking for the late-model Cadillac (which currently resided in the CSI garage). He didn't spot it at first; then the Caddy rolled through the frame.

Warrick stopped the tape, wound it back, then started the car into the frame again and froze it. Soon he was loading that section of video into his computer, digitizing the material to enable him to enhance it. Even after his best computer tricks, however, all he knew for sure was: A) the car was the correct Cadillac, and B) two men were inside . . . who might, or might not, be African-American.

This did not improve his post-Mia mood.

Back to the tape deck and video monitor, Warrick

loaded the second security-cam vid, an angle courtesy of the underside of a beam that held up a small
roof protecting drive-through customers from the
dominant desert sun and occasional rain. High
enough to avoid the glare of headlights, the camera
gave Warrick a direct view down through the wind-
shields of approaching customers. After sunset,
though, car interiors were fairly dark, making those
inside hard or impossible to make out.

The CSI watched three cars glide through the
frame. In two, he could tell a man was driving;
third vehicle, he had no idea. In one he could tell
the customer was white. In the other two, he
couldn't tell whether the customer was black,
Latino, or simply a well-tanned Cauc. Fourth car in
line was his Caddy, and he strained to see something, anything . . . but the car was too far away,
dashboard light too faint. As the car inched closer
to the camera . . . *there!*

What was that?

Warrick rewound the tape and played it again.

A burst of light on the driver's side, then it was
gone. *What had it been?* He rewound the tape and
watched again, this time slowing it way down.

A cigarette lighter.

The driver sparked a lighter, then put his hand
over the smoke to light up. *Could he see the guy's face?*
Certainly not after the driver's hand came up and
obliterated the light source; but in that split second
before, could Warrick make him?

The CSI returned to his computer, digitized about
ninety seconds of key video, and returned to the
frame where the lighter sparked to life. He thought

maybe he could distinguish a face, but the distance was so great.

He enhanced the picture, zoomed in, and enhanced some more.

Illuminated for a frozen split second sat one of the kidnappers, lighting a cig. Didn't the guy know smoking was bad for you? Whoever the smoker was, Warrick didn't recognize him, and Warrick had a pretty good handle on the gang scene, for a CSI, having worked dozens of gang-related cases.

Greg rushed in. "AFIS coughed up another name."

"You need to buy a lottery ticket on the way home."

"No, I won't get luckier than this," he said, waving a sheet of paper. "The passenger-side fingerprints belong to Jalon Winsor, a member of the Hoods."

"Where's their territory?"

"Between Lake Mead Boulevard on the north," Greg said, referring to his notes, "and Vegas Drive on the south . . . from MLK west to maybe Simmons Street."

"If they have so much territory," Warrick said, eyes slitting, "why the hell haven't I heard of them?"

"Guess they've been flying under the radar, mostly. Haven't been caught up in anything big . . ."

"Until a lion ran out in front of their stolen car," Warrick said.

"Until then," Greg agreed. The young CSI's eyes locked with his mentor's. "Grissom and I had a crime scene on Beatty a couple weeks ago, 'Rick—right in the middle of Hoods territory. Which is how they got on *my* radar. I even met a couple, watching us work. Lookouts, probably."

"You know *this* guy?" Warrick asked, pointing to the monitor.

Greg glanced at the screen. "Whoa—maybe I will buy a lottery ticket. *That's* one of the guys Grissom and I talked to! Is he involved in this?"

"Seems to be. What's his name?"

"His buddy called him Fleety. Yeah, that's him, lighting the cigarette. I remember that kid smoking like a house on fire."

"Run the nickname," Warrick said, "and see if anything comes up."

"You got it."

"Then we'll call Brass and see if he can get someone to sit on the kid's lookout spot, case he turns up."

"Right away."

"And, Greg?"

"Yeah?"

"Nice memory."

"Thanks."

Twenty minutes later, Warrick found Greg hunkered down at a computer monitor, nose practically pressed to the screen. Warrick pulled up a chair and sat to Greg's right. He ran a hand over his face and wondered when, or if, this shift would ever end.

Not only were Grissom, Catherine, and the others still dealing with the battle aftermath in Boot Hill, day shift had troubles of their own—two CSIs in court and three more working a massive Desert Shores drug bust on the far northwest side. This was one day nobody upstairs would be bitching about overtime.

"Talked to Brass," Warrick told Greg.

"Yeah?" Greg answered, only half interested as he examined the screen.

"No extra *anything* today. If we wanna find a way to track down Fleety, we're on our own."

Greg frowned doubtfully. "Well, is that a CSI's job, really? Is it . . . evidence?"

"It's the best lead, and we're still in the early hours of this murder investigation. And there's nobody else available."

"Okay, then—how about we start with that name you wanted?" Greg said, obviously a little pleased with himself.

Warrick perked. "Got something?"

"Isaiah A. Fleetwood, a.k.a. 'Fleety'—seventeen, Hoods member, small-time brushes with the system . . . but nothing serious enough to ever get him printed. Not violent like some of the other members, at least nothing violent turns up."

"Strictly a lookout, you think?" Warrick asked.

"Could well be . . . but a mouthy one."

"Oh?"

Greg nodded. "Three uniformed officers've had run-ins with him—big talk, but the kid always backed down. Least, that's how the reports are written."

"Anything else?"

"Yeah—lives with his grandmother. Apparently a pretty good kid till his mom died two years ago. Since then, he's a ticking bomb, looking for a place to go off."

"Address on the grandmother?"

Greg held up a slip of paper with something already scrawled on it.

"Good. Then let's go have a talk with Fleety."

"Or Grandma. And we can check out his hangout

corner on the way." Greg slipped the piece of paper into his shirt pocket.

Warrick drove this time, window down, air rushing in, helping him stay alert (and awake).

Warrick cruised the corner of Beatty and Ludwig where Greg had met Fleety before. As they rolled by, Greg thought he saw a surreptitious figure slip hastily into the shadows of a vacant house.

"I think that was him!" Greg said.

"Thought I saw someone, too. Sure it's Fleety?"

"Not sure. But . . . pretty sure."

"Looked nervous . . . We'll go around the block and stop back a ways, then go up on foot. You do have your sidearm, right?"

An acid rumble burned in Greg's stomach. "Yeah. Never without it."

Warrick took four rights and parked the SUV on the same street as the empty house, but at the other end of the block.

"Let's go," the older CSI said.

Though noon neared, the temperature wasn't high for Vegas and a nice cool breeze whispered pleasantly at them. Nonetheless, Greg felt every pore of his body oozing sweat, and some invisible motor had turned over within him, causing every limb to vibrate.

"Stick close," Warrick said.

Instead of walking up the front walk, Warrick led the way around the side, pressing his body against the exterior wall of the house; Greg copied him, trying to control his breathing. As they edged forward, Warrick unholstered his pistol, signaling Greg to do the same.

It took only all of his strength and half an eternity before the younger man could get the damn strap unsnapped and withdraw his Glock nine-millimeter automatic. The pistol seemed unnaturally heavy, a handful of power and terror. His mind raced through every firearms procedure he'd ever learned. His sweaty back pressed against the wall, Greg moved his left hand up, Glock in both hands—surprisingly, the weapon felt even heavier.

Warrick peeked around the corner, then ducked back and shook his head. "Nobody back there," he whispered.

Greg thought, *Good.*

Warrick was saying, "Back door's open, though—we've got to go in."

Greg nodded and felt sweat droplets bounce off his forehead.

Warrick whispered, "You okay?"

Again Greg nodded and with his chin indicated that Warrick should go ahead.

The rear door had no screen and the flimsy wooden thing hung like a loose tooth from one valiant rusty hinge. The house gave off an awful smell—a mingling of must, dust, and urine. Vacant building perhaps, but someone had been using it for something—squatting possibly, or maybe just a look-out for a drug dealer doing business out of a nearby house.

Warrick—his pistol in front of him—stepped through the doorway into the kitchen.

Greg followed him in, ears perked for the slightest sound, vibration, tremor, anything that might signal the presence of others. In the tiny kitchen—cramped even minus any refrigerator or stove—a patina of dust covered the counters and sinks. The dusty floor had so many footprints, however, they might have been made a minute ago or a month or a year. An angry amber light filtered through yellowed, ripped and torn pull shades, and the layer of dirt on the windows provided an art-film soft focus to this dreary, dangerous reality.

Greg stayed on Warrick's heels as he eased through a doorway into what had once been a dining room. The younger CSI, still consciously thinking of his handgun training, wheeled his pistol left, not lowering the barrel until he had cleared his partner.

No furniture in the room, but a couple of sleeping bags snugged flat against the far left wall beneath a row of windows.

The two CSIs moved through a living room with a shaded picture window, under which a boom box and a pile of CDs sat near a card table filled with empty malt-liquor forties and an ashtray overflowing with butts; at the table, two opposing folding chairs (another two leaned against a wall). In here, the same nasty aroma of the kitchen was spiced with the stale sweat smell.

Warrick withdrew his pocket flashlight and, using his left hand, shone it down the hall, his left wrist becoming a brace for his pistol. Greg kept his Glock pointed toward the ceiling in the narrow hallway, where ancient floral wallpaper was peeling itself off. On the left, a closet, then either a bedroom or a bathroom beyond; across the corridor, another open door, and at the end of the hall, another—probably the master bedroom, a term that seemed arcane in this hovel.

Problem was, the closet door would open *toward* the living room—if Warrick passed the door, then came back to open it, the wood would be between Greg and Warrick. If they both passed the door and turned back, they'd have three unchecked rooms at their back.

Sweet, Greg thought bitterly.

They could go down the hallway, back to back; but one would have the closet to cover while the other tried to watch three doors that might hide Fleety or God knew how many of his homies.

Warrick fell back into the living room and, in a barely audible whisper, said, "If we go back and call for backup . . ." and shrugged.

This conveyed to Greg that if the CSIs called for backup from the SUV, any Hoods currently in the house would be gone before anybody got here.

Greg nodded grimly.

Warrick's eyes locked Greg's, and rarely in Greg's experience had anyone looked at him with such intensity. In that same barely audible whisper, Warrick asked, "Up for this?"

Greg wanted to yell, *Hell, no! Let's go call for backup, maybe get SWAT out here, and if they're gone when we get back, well then . . . we'll get 'em next time.* He might even have actually said that if his mouth and tongue had been working and weren't drier than a desert.

Instead, he nodded.

"Stay close," Warrick whispered, and proceeded back to the mouth of the hallway.

Keeping his pistol trained on the closet door, Warrick moved past it. Greg was right on his heels, but before he could pass, the closet door was thrown open, knocking Greg back, and the gun from Warrick's grasp.

When he regained his balance, the door swung lazily shut and Greg found himself staring into the wild brown eyes of a bare-chested, very angry black kid in red sweatpants and a white nylon do-rag with a gun in his left fist.

The young man was trying desperately to find a way to pull the trigger, but Warrick had him by the arms, and the two men wrestled to the end of the hall, where Warrick got the guy down on the floor, the guy's gun hand extended to the left.

Taking one quick step, Greg kicked the gun out of the gang kid's hand and found himself squatting down and pressing his pistol into the kid's skull as Warrick pulled out handcuffs. On the kid's neck were three jagged scratches.

"Freeze!" Greg shouted. "Just hold still!"

The kid's eyes blazed at Greg. "Fuck y'self! Fuck y'self!"

Warrick locked the cuffs and rose off the young man's back. When someone came out of the bedroom in a blur, sweeping up Warrick's gun off the floor, Warrick never saw it coming, his back to the attacker; in half a second, Warrick's own gun was pressed against his temple.

Rising slowly and taking a step back away from the cuffed guy on the floor, Greg leveled his pistol at half the baby face of Isaiah "Fleety" Fleetwood. The other half of the young man's face remained hidden behind Warrick.

Fleety yelled, "Drop the motherfuckin' gun, you five-oh prick!"

Greg felt the gun shaking in his hand as he pointed it at Warrick and the shorter man hiding behind him.

"Can't do that," Greg said.

"Drop the gun or I drop your bud!"

"Make him let me go," the kid in cuffs whined from below.

"Jalon, man," Fleety said, "I *got* this."

So, the guy on the floor was Jalon Winsor—the scratches on Jalon's neck should have told him that. That meant they had both the guys they had come for: now all they had to do was defuse this little situation and walk them out.

"Isaiah," Greg said, amazed at how steady his voice sounded, "you need to put the gun down."

"How you know my name, blondie?" Fleety asked, obviously agitated.

"Let's keep to what's important, Isaiah," Greg said, outwardly calm. "You need to put the gun down."

From the floor, Jalon yelled, "Just *smoke* his white ass, Fleety!"

Fleetwood thumbed back the hammer on Warrick's Glock; the click was a tiny sound that registered to Greg as the loudest he'd ever heard.

Fleety was yelling, "*You* put the gun down, *you* put the gun down!"

Greg suddenly had an intense urge to urinate, but fought it. Slowly, he lowered the barrel of his pistol.

Warrick gave Greg a look that said, *Greg, you put that gun down, we're both dead. . . .*

And Greg gave Warrick a look that said, *Trust me*.

Warrick's eyes closed and Greg couldn't tell if that meant his fellow CSI understood his unspoken message and accepted it, or was making peace within himself before he died.

Fleety's eyes remained wild, but he seemed more scared than angry as he held the gun to Warrick's head. Greg lowered his pistol to his side.

Instantly, Fleety calmed, his eyes narrowing, his breathing slowing.

"Now," Fleety said, his voice still loud but less strident. "Let my man Jalon go."

Greg shook his head. "Can't do it."

"*Your* man's about to get—"

Greg cut him off. "What *happened* to you, Isaiah?"

"What?" Fleety asked, taken aback.

"What happened to you? Until your mom died—"

Fleety snarled, "Hell *d'you* know about my moms!"

"I know she loved you," Greg said, the gun a thousand-pound weight at the end of his arm. "You pulled a B average when she was alive."

"Yeah, well, she gone."

Jalon butted in again. "Fleety, just *smoke* them, and let's get the hell outta here!"

Fleety twitched . . . but didn't pull the trigger.

Greg looked down at Jalon. "You need to be quiet," he said firmly, not believing how calm his voice sounded. He wondered if at any moment a bullet would explode through him and that would be the end.

"*Fuck* you!" Jalon screamed.

"You kill us," Greg said, somehow keeping his

voice matter of fact, "you 'smoke' us five-ohs, this place'll be crawling with blue uniforms. Then SWAT will swarm in here. Twenty-four hours, Hoods'll be history. Every Hood in town will be in jail or dead. Want *that* on your head, Isaiah?"

Jalon's eyes danced with fear.

Was Fleety wavering?

"Isaiah, you have a chance here to do the right thing. Let my partner go, and we'll talk you through this trouble you're in."

"No trouble *I'm* in," Fleety blurted. "*I* got the gun."

Greg could feel the situation slipping away. "Your mother gave you a name that meant something— Isaiah. Very biblical."

"Think I don't know that?" Fleety said, defensive, and shoved the snout of the gun against Warrick's temple. Warrick's eyes widened.

Fleety was staring at Greg now, and Jalon had the good sense to keep a low profile—especially since whenever he looked up, he now stared into the barrel of Greg's gun.

Fleety said nothing.

Greg asked, "What are you doing with the Hoods, anyway? That's the life your mother worked so hard for you to have?"

The gun inched away from Warrick's head.

Greg said, "Maybe that was divine intervention last night . . . maybe that lion *meant* something. . . ."

Fleety, startled by this—eyes flaring as he likely relived that lion leaping in front of their stolen car last night—flinched.

Not waiting for Greg to talk the kid down further, Warrick dropped a shoulder, spun, and punched the gun out of Fleety's hand. Surprised, the kid took a quick step back and slipped, then Warrick had a hold of him and was twisting one hand behind his back.

Then Isaiah was on his knees, as if praying.

Greg yanked out his handcuffs and passed them to Warrick, who bound Fleety up.

"Isaiah Fleetwood and Jalon Winsor," Warrick said, "you are under arrest for the murder of DeMarcus Hankins. You have the right to remain silent . . ."

He went on, but Greg stopped listening. God, he had to pee. . . .

"We didn't do *shit*," Jalon was whining.

Warrick gave him a little smile. "Those scratches on your neck tell a different story—like, the skin we got from under DeMarcus's fingernails is going to match your DNA."

"Hell you say," Jalon said.

"If I'm lyin'," Warrick said through his nastiest grin, "I'm dyin'."

Standing in that cramped hallway, the crisis over, his guts churning, his bladder about to burst, Greg felt an urge to barf, thanks to the smell of stale sweat and fresh fear. The tongue-on-a-battery metallic taste of terror that still clung to his mouth only served to heighten his nausea.

Outside, they called for a squad car and, while they waited with the two young black men, Greg said, "You got this, 'Rick, for a minute?"

"Yeah. Sure."

Greg paused, nodded toward the house. "Is that a crime scene in there?"

"Well . . . not exactly. Sort of."

"I mean . . . can I take a leak in there? I got in trouble for that one time."

Warrick laughed. "Yeah. . . . Yeah. I wouldn't touch anything, though."

"Evidence?"

"Germs."

Greg felt much better when he came back out, but then something inside him sent him running to the farthest back corner of the property, where he threw up.

When he returned to Warrick's side, a squad car was out front, lights flashing, as two uniforms loaded the Hoods in. A small crowd was gathering, some there to bitch, some to demonize the police; most just came to watch.

"If this *is* a crime scene," a pale Greg said to Warrick, with a head bob toward the side of the house, "I hope *we* don't process it."

Innocently, Warrick asked, "You know what Bob's Round-Up Grill's slogan is, don't you?"

"No, I don't."

"One breakfast burrito, comin' right up."

"Oh man. *Please*. . . ."

They climbed into the Denali, Warrick again getting behind the wheel. Warrick turned the key, slipped the SUV into drive, and rolled slowly away from the curb.

"Remind me to thank you, sometime," Warrick said.

Greg was looking out the window.

"That was a hell of a thing, Greg. That may be the single bravest thing I've ever seen."

Smiling, Greg said, "Or the dumbest."

Warrick shrugged. "Right up there for that, too."

"You know me," Greg said, his hands shaking in his lap, "sometimes I just can't stop talking."

"You stayed cool and didn't panic. That's what you do in a situation like that. You stay calm and let the rest come naturally."

"Hope so. Hope I'm never *in* a situation like that again. But could you slow down a little, 'Rick? . . . You know how easily I get scared."

Warrick glanced at his partner, laughed gently, and eased off the accelerator.

10

IN THE BOOT HILL POLICE STATION, Gil Grissom and Catherine Willows were as much prisoners, in a way, as the quartet of Spokes the Patrolmen were in the process of locking up.

The CSIs headed not to a cell, however, but to the mostly glass enclosure of Chief Lopez's office that looked out on a small, empty bullpen for detectives and officers, all of whom were out and about, dealing with the biker dilemma.

Grissom wondered idly why these small-town police chief or sheriff offices were always so similar and bereft of personality. A basic rule of crime scene investigation was broken by such offices: a CSI always viewed personal domains (offices, bedrooms, dens, and kitchens) as windows into the character of their inhabitants, whether victim, suspect, or even witness.

His own office back in Vegas—with all its mysteries and treats scattered around, from the two-headed snake to pickled pig parts, various things in jars, all the insects on display—certainly fit that pattern.

On the other hand, perhaps an impersonal office like Lopez's—with its handful of framed diplomas and commendations, its bulletin board of work-oriented snapshots and circulars, even its police association calendar—spoke of the chief's professionalism. Not that Grissom considered himself any less a complete professional simply because he chose to put a few of his obsessions on display. For a man who spent so much of his life at work, Grissom could hardly keep his own character out of his quarters.

"What was that old Western," Lopez said as he positioned himself behind a metal desk, the CSIs taking visitor's chairs opposite, "the one with John Wayne?"

Catherine blinked at their host. "I'm a good investigator, Chief, but you'll have to narrow that down a little."

"*Rio Bravo*," Grissom said.

Now Catherine looked at Grissom; she did not blink.

"What?" Grissom said to her. "It's a classic—lawmen holed up in a little sheriff's office, while the bad guys converge outside in the town they've taken over. Wonderful film. Howard Hawks."

"Let's hope we survive," she said pleasantly, "so we can rent that some time."

"Fine," Grissom said, and smiled.

Catherine squinted at him, as if not quite sure Grissom were really there.

Lopez said, "Well, this thing started out like the OK Corral or maybe Custer's last stand; but *Rio Bravo* is what it feels like it's turning into."

"We have Highway Patrol support," Grissom said.

"Not enough, I'm afraid," Lopez said.

"You need to call the governor now," Catherine said firmly. "We need help here."

Grissom offered an open palm. "We might be able to cool down the Predators."

"How?" the other two asked at once.

"By catching their fallen leader's killer. On the other hand, as long as Finch is in here, the Spokes will remain a threat."

A dispatcher, a short, thin woman of fifty with trim blonde hair, stuck her head in the glass enclosure. "Chief, the Highway Patrol just called—Predators've run the roadblock. . . . They're on their way into town."

Lopez kept his voice calm, even as he rose from his desk. "Get everyone inside *now*, Gloria. Blow the horn."

"Horn?" Catherine asked.

"Emergency horn for foul weather," Lopez explained. "But everybody in Boot Hill knows, they hear that, they get their butts inside."

"Might keep some innocents from getting hurt," Grissom said.

Catherine rolled her eyes. "I won't be offended if the guilty stay indoors, too."

"Where's Cody?" Lopez yelled, but Gloria was gone.

The tall, paunchy, fiftyish detective, in jeans, boots, and a blue short-sleeved shirt with western pocket trim, swung into his chief's office.

"Right here, boss," Jacks said, thumb in a loop of a belt that included his holstered sidearm. "Just got back. What's up?"

Sara seemed to materialize, her hair slightly mussed as if she'd come on the run; perhaps she had. As she entered the small office, her expression grave, she first noticed Jacks.

After a beat, she said to her fellow CSIs, "Guys, can we talk a sec?"

Sara gestured with her head, arcs of hair swinging, that she wanted to do so in private.

Catherine frowned, but Grissom said, "Sure."

And they joined her in a hallway just off the bullpen.

The trio gathered in a tight little circle, Sara's voice as soft as her expression was grave.

She said, "Sofia just called. Grissom, you gave me a name to run earlier . . . a local girl."

"Right," he said. "Wendy Sierra. What about her?"

"She's that cop's daughter."

Catherine, startled, said, "Lopez?"

But Grissom, who'd seen the girl in question and now put a faint family resemblance together, said, "Jacks. Cody Jacks."

Catherine turned to Grissom. "Remind me why you wanted her name checked?"

Grissom did so, painting a quick picture of the makeshift memorial at the chain-link fence of the Four Kings, and Wendy Sierra's tearful delivery of roses in memory of Nick Valpo.

"So Wendy is Cody's daughter," Catherine said. "It's a small town. Does this tell us anything?"

Nobody seemed to know for sure. Nick came down the hall from the modest crime lab and fell in with his colleagues.

"The Rocky boots from the mortuary are *not* Officer Montaine's," he said.

Sara asked, "Did we suspect him?"

"Not really," Nick said. "But he's eliminated as far as this line of evidence goes."

A piercing electronic scream made the CSIs jump—
the emergency horn . . . three long blasts.

Lopez appeared at the mouth of the hall and said,
"Would you folks step back in my office for a moment?"

They did, standing with their backs to the window-
wall on the bullpen. Jacks was seated behind Lopez's
desk.

"We clearly have a situation here," the chief said, approaching the CSIs. "I know you're all pros, but I don't
want you on the front lines. With my own people, and
the Highway Patrol, I think we can hold on."

"You need to call the governor," Catherine said.

"I have. He says he'll do what he can."

"Specifically . . . ?"

"He wasn't specific. He's getting back to me, ASAP."

Catherine shook her head. "What the hell kind
of—"

"I don't mean to be rude, Ms. Willows, but I do have
to get out there."

"Which leaves us where?" Catherine asked.

Lopez pointed a finger at the floor. "Right here.
Cody'll stay with you guys."

"Chief," Grissom said, "we're all proficient in
firearms. It's part of the job."

"I'm aware of that, Doc—and have full confidence in
your abilities. Remember *Rio Bravo*?"

Nick and Sara exchanged looks: *what the . . . ?*

The chief was saying, "I need you here to keep an
eye on these locked-up Spokes. We may have a mob—
hell, two mobs—on our doorstep any time. One'll want
to spring and save the prisoners; the other'll want them
made dead, in a hurry. At least in the old days, they

took time to find a tree and string up a rope; it'll be quicker now, and probably even uglier."

The CSIs passed glances around; they were being kept off the front line only to guard a beleaguered fort.

Lopez nodded to Jacks, then returned his gaze to his guests. "I need the five of you to make sure that nothing happens to our 'guests,' either way, while I'm out there trying to keep the lid on this sucker. With the exception of Detective Jacks, and the dispatcher down the hall in her cubbyhole, you'll be on your own. Ms. Willows—you're supervisor. You up for this?"

Catherine said, "Yes."

Lopez said, "Thank you, ma'am. Good luck."

He tipped his Stetson and went off to lead his tiny contingent, twenty or twenty-five strong . . . to hold off ten times that many.

Nonetheless, Nick offered Catherine a smile. "Did he just call you *'ma'am'*?"

Catherine said, "Be quiet," through a smile, albeit a troubled one.

Sara said, "I'm pretty sure he called you 'ma'am.'"

"Sara . . ."

Grissom faced Catherine. "We could phone Sheriff Burdick . . ."

"No," she said, with one shake of the head, "this is Lopez's judgment call."

Nick said, "On the other hand, it's *our* butts."

Jacks was up from behind the desk and parting venetian blind blades to look out at the street through one of three windows side by side that formed a sort of picture window, though each had individual blinds.

With his gray sideburns, gray eyes, and vaguely wolfish countenance, Jacks evoked the image of an old

Western sheriff, which was underscored when he drew his sidearm, a Glock, checked the clip, then reholstered the weapon.

"We should be safe enough here," he said, turning his head toward them but maintaining sentry. "But if things gets hairy, you *do* all know the way back to the cells, right?"

Nods all around.

The detective went back to looking out the window, waiting for trouble that seemed ever more inevitable.

Grissom and Catherine took the visitor's chairs, while Nick and Sara kept their own watch out the wall of windows onto the vacant bullpen and on a door that they all hoped would open only when Chief Lopez returned.

"Did you see this coming?" Grissom asked Jacks.

"Damn bikers'll likely do anything," Jacks said. "Normal humans don't shoot up a casino like that and endanger civilians."

"That type might do about any evil thing," Grissom said.

Catherine frowned at him.

Jacks, rather absently, eyes on the street, said, "Might at that."

"Even seduce an innocent girl away from her family," Grissom said.

Now Jacks spun his whole beefy body away from the window. His eyes were hooded, his complexion pale. "What do you know about Wendy?"

Grissom said, "I know she shed tears for Valpo. I know she put a dozen roses under his picture at that improvised memorial."

Lopez's top sergeant heaved a sigh. Then he returned to the window, fingers prying open blinds; but his glazed expression indicated he wasn't looking at the street . . .

. . . perhaps just into his past.

"Her mom, Nancy, and me," he said in that resonant radio announcer's voice, "we got divorced over what happened to that girl."

Jacks's fingers dropped from the blinds, no longer holding them open. Now he stared directly into the metal slats.

"Two years ago," he said, "this bastard Valpo managed to seduce four underage girls into having sex with him . . . four!"

"Roofies?" Catherine asked.

He shrugged. "Some kind of goddamn drugs. Wendy . . . was one of them. In retrospect, we probably sheltered her. Casino trade or not, this is a small town— church and school and family. She was sixteen then, and'd just . . . developed, kind of overnight; went from being a flat-chested little girl to a . . . looked like she was twenty, or even twenty-one . . . and all of sudden, she started to dress like it. Real . . . trampy."

His eyes closed.

"I tried to put my foot down about that slutty crap, but . . . that girl has a way she can look at you and melt you . . . if you're her dad, anyway. Hell, and me, supposed to be so goddamn tough. But her and her mom? I couldn't never say no to them about nothing. Nancy . . . wasn't that upset about how Wendy dressed . . . least, not until the thing with Valpo, and the drugs."

"If it was date rape," Catherine said, "you could have brought him in—"

"It wasn't roofies! It was . . . weed and pills and . . . stuff Wendy *liked* to use. She got into that lifestyle, not every day, but when the bikers rolled in, it was something . . . *rebellious* she could do."

"Sixteen's the age of consent in Nevada," Grissom said. "So a statutory rape charge was out."

"You are unfortunately dead right on that one, Doc . . . and then she started disappearing weekends—going to Vegas and Phoenix and God knows where."

Catherine asked, "Meeting Valpo?"

"I don't know. I don't know. Wherever it was, she got her drugs there—weed mostly, but still. . . . And when I couldn't get our daughter off the stuff and straightened around, my wife took it out on *me*—blamed me for babying the girl, divorced my sorry ass, went back to her maiden name, Sierra. Wendy went with her and took her mom's name, too. My name—they didn't even want *that* no more."

His expression and his tone bland as a glass of cold milk, Grissom asked, "Is that when a daydream started evolving into a plan?"

Jacks's wolfish eyes narrowed and a faint smile formed. "What the hell you talkin' about, Doc?"

"Your plan to execute Nick Valpo."

Jacks grunted a laugh. "Somebody spike your chaw with peyote, Doc?"

"I don't use 'chaw,'" Grissom said softly. "And I don't mind when my friend Chief Lopez calls me 'Doc,' but I'd prefer you didn't."

Thumbs looped in his belt, Jacks said, "If that, before, was some kind of serious accusation, you better have something to back it up."

"Oh, I'll be able to prove it by the end of business

today, if we're not too distracted by another shoot-out. That can provide a real distraction—don't you think, Sergeant Jacks?"

"I think you're on thin ice."

Grissom smiled gently. "Not a terribly apt analogy, in this climate. By sundown, everything will be clear, and you'll be—"

Jacks's lip curled. "On the stage out of town?"

Grissom nodded in the lockup's direction. "No. Behind bars."

Jacks tilted his head toward the street. "You don't think that biker rabble'll have something to say about *that*?"

Shrugging, Grissom said, "I hope not. A lynching in any form I find distasteful."

The eyes of the other CSIs were glued to these two men now as they batted each other the ball. . . .

"And what makes you so sure you've got this figured . . . Doc?"

"Same thing that always convinces me I've got it 'figured,'" Grissom said. "The evidence."

The detective snorted a harsh laugh. "You don't have anything on me."

"I'd say we have plenty."

Jacks frowned. "Like what?"

Grissom shrugged. "Well, there's your boot print at the mortuary, where you stole Valpo's body. You do wear *Rocky* boots, don't you?"

"Who doesn't around here?" Jacks said with a dismissive wave. "Department policy."

"But no two pairs of boots wear the same—they indicate the feet that trod in them . . . kind of like leather and rubber fingerprints. Plus, there's a tire print that Nick lifted. That's going to match your car, too."

The gray eyes grew cold. "What makes you think *I* was at the mortuary?"

"Because you couldn't get rid of the murder weapon without raising suspicion," Grissom answered. "So you had to get rid of the bullet—that meant getting rid of Valpo's body."

Jacks looked as though he were trying to follow a foreign film, minus subtitles. "Back up—*what* murder weapon?"

"Small-caliber pistol," Grissom said. "A twenty-two. You got a hideout piece—maybe on your left ankle?"

Catherine jumped in. "Maybe you wouldn't mind showing us your left ankle, Sergeant?"

Jacks shrugged, said, "Sure, why the hell not?"

And he lifted his right leg up onto the chief's desk, baring his hairy ankle as his pants rode up . . .

. . . showing them an S&W model 2214 automatic pistol.

From behind Grissom, Nick said slowly, "Just like Keith Draper's."

Jacks returned his foot to the floor and said, "So what? It's a typical backup piece. What in hell does that prove?" A wolfish smile bared yellow teeth. "Anyway, my esteemed colleagues from the big-time Vegas crime lab . . . without the bullet, who's to say *what* gun fired the shot that killed that animal?"

Grissom ignored the question. "Just to satisfy my curiosity—why didn't you just pitch the gun? Would've been considerably simpler than body-snatching."

Jacks's lupine grin contained not a hint of humor. "Since I didn't kill him, I don't need to dump *any* gun. . . . Besides, it was a gift—from my wife and daughter." He waved this off, literally. "And, hell—*everybody* in the department knows I have that little gun. I've had it for years!"

"Years?" Grissom asked.

"Wendy's mom bought it for my thirtieth—gave it to me in both their names. Little something extra to make sure Daddy . . . Daddy made it home every night."

Grissom noted the emotion the detective had betrayed and said, "Well, keepsake or not, we'll need to test if it's been fired."

"Why bother? I'll tell you it has—I was out at the range yesterday before work . . . which I can prove, easy. Both my guns were fired there; and so, yes, I'll check positive for GSR—so what?"

Gunshot residue would tell them if Jacks had fired a gun recently and tended to hang around even if the shooter washed his hands; but Jacks's admission was meant to make that go away. In Grissom's view, it didn't, not entirely.

Jacks returned to his window. Easily, not looking at them, as if it were part of his guard duty, Jacks withdrew the Glock from its holster and held it loosely at his side, the barrel pointed toward the floor. "Maybe that pit-boss sleaze Draper took Valpo out. He hates bikers like poison."

The weapon in the suspect's hand stiffened every CSI spine; but no one moved.

"We won't know," Grissom said calmly, "until we match bullets from both guns against the ones that killed Valpo."

Still smiling, Jacks said, "Gonna be kind of tough to match bullets without the body, isn't it?"

Grissom smiled as well. "I don't have the body . . . but I know where it is."

Again Jacks faced them, the venetian blinds at his back. "Really? Well, surprise me—where *are* the earthly remains of that prick?"

"Here's what happened," Grissom said.

You hated Valpo for what he did to your daughter, and whether that wrong was real or imagined, you decided you had to take him out for it—like a diseased branch that had to be pruned from society's tree.

Valpo would come into town, but with you being a cop, he'd be a frustratingly inaccessible target, always surrounded by company—a social breed, bikers. You couldn't get close enough to execute him without some sort of diversion. So you recruited Tom Price. All Price had to do was not change the metal-detector batteries one day during the Biker Blowout . . . and you made sure Finch and the Spokes knew when that would happen.

All they had to do was come in, fire off a few shots, and you would take care of Valpo, making the Spokes' biggest problem disappear. Perhaps Finch knew about the execution you planned, or maybe he just thought you were helping them out in order to get back at Valpo and the Predators for what they'd done to your daughter.

You of course knew where the blind spots were in the Four Kings video security system, and when the shooting started, you waited for your chance . . . and pounced. The safest place to commit a murder, after all, is a battlefield. And when Valpo got wounded, you had the perfect opportunity to finish him off. He was even magnanimous enough to fall into a blind spot for you. In all the commotion, the act was practically invisible—what were a couple more gunshots when there were over a hundred others going off, and where most everyone was ducking for cover?

So you had your revenge . . . and the Spokes had made their "statement" to the Predators, who'd dismissed them as weekend warriors. The perfect solution—almost. You still had that precious gun, with its nostalgic family ties, that you couldn't bring yourself to give up . . . and there was Tom Price to deal with. But as lead investigator in the case (a predictable turn of events) you had the freedom to deal with both those loose ends.

You hit the mortician, Mr. Erickson, over the back of the head and whisked Valpo's body away. Of course, you hadn't thought about the footprints and tire prints you were leaving in a dusty parking lot . . . maybe that was the small-town cop in you.

Under the pretext of searching for the missing Tom Price, you went out to his place in the mountains to clip off your only remaining loose end. You probably got him to stay there by promising to bring the money out as soon as the deed was done. Or perhaps Price had second thoughts—he might not even have known why you wanted the metal detectors tampered with. Price might have wanted more money or perhaps suffered true remorse—maybe that suicide note was a confession he'd already written up, which you utilized for the occasion. At any rate, you went out, dealt with him—that is, killed him—making it look like a suicide.

Price lived in a remote area, far out of town, and you were necessarily gone so long, and out of touch, that nobody would notice the extra time it took for you to bury Nick Valpo's body on Price's property. With the murder victim buried, and the other loose end on the books as a suicide, the only possible problem left for you is Buck Finch. After all, in your eyes, you weren't murdering anyone, just a drug-dealing biker renegade—you were dispensing frontier justice.

"Conjecture," Jacks said.

"When we've had some time at the scene of Price's 'suicide,' we'll see about conjecture," Grissom said. "Anyway, there's some key evidence you didn't consider, which I've already taken steps to secure."

"Such as?"

"The other body."

A harsh laugh tried to dismiss that, but panic in the gray eyes betrayed the suspect's real feelings. "What *other* body?"

"The young woman's. The card dealer. It's under lock and key at the mortuary right now—I quietly took care of that, after I realized the killer had neglected to think through that bullets were in both bodies. And I don't think anybody'll be sneaking up on that particular mortician again."

Jacks's face was as white as the underbelly of a fish. "Young woman . . ."

"The witness you shot. That wasn't part of the plan, was it, Sergeant? A pity—I understand you knew her. Had even been a kind of father figure to her. . . . Horrible irony for you to have to live with . . . and her to die with."

"Shut up, Grissom. . . ."

"You mean to revenge your daughter's honor and, along the way, you have to protect yourself by killing your *other*, surrogate daughter . . . leaving a child motherless. Who's the predator now, Sergeant?"

Silence shrouded the office.

Then Cody Jacks spoke, the rich voice cracking.

"I . . . I thought the world of that girl. Vanessa. Vanessa." Tears glistened in his gray eyes, but his expression remained feral. "But you know how it is for us cops—shit happens."

Grissom shrugged. "Only this isn't police work, is it, Sergeant? By the way—how *do* you plan to keep Buck Finch from ratting you out?"

The gun no longer hung loosely at the suspect's side—Jacks had brought it up, to aim it directly at Grissom's chest.

"Anybody moves, the know-it-all dies first," Jacks said, indicating Grissom. His eyes traveled around the faces of the three other CSIs. "Drop the pistols in that garbage can—*now*. One at a time, ladies first . . . touch only the butt with two fingers or your boss dies."

Slowly, the others did as they were told, their weapons clunking into the garbage can next to Lopez's desk.

"Now *you*, Doc," Jacks said.

Grissom complied and pitched his pistol on top of the others.

Catherine had an amazed smile and was shaking her head. "Sergeant Jacks—you *can't* think you can get away with this."

Jacks laughed once. He gestured with the Glock. "If any of you had been looking outside, you'da seen that the Predators and Spokes have gathered out in the street and're about to go at it full tilt. There's gonna be a hell of a firefight that'll make last night look like a paintball match. Dust clears, a lot of people won't be alive no more . . . including you four fucking busybodies . . . and some lowlife bikers."

"Including Buck Finch," Grissom said.

"Another Kewpie doll to you, Doc—and what a sad goddamn tragedy it'll be, can't you just see it? Be all over cable news. And Chief Lopez will put his best man—me—in charge of the investigation . . . to figure out how this coulda all gone so very, very wrong."

"We were killed during the riot," Grissom said.

"That'd be my best guess," Jacks said. He shook his head. "Helluva story you come up with, Grissom— mostly on the nose. I don't like the way this has gone, entirely—I certainly meant little Vanessa no harm. But you can't imagine what Valpo did to demean and degrade my little girl . . . used her, raped her, got her hooked on drugs. We had her in and out of detox . . . that scumbag ruined my life and my daughter's."

Outside there was a gunshot, and everyone flinched, including Jacks.

"All of you," Jacks said, his voice hard now, "up against the windows." He did not mean the glass walls onto the empty bullpen, rather the three behind the chief's desk, where minutes ago, centuries ago, Jacks had stood watch.

He was saying, "Hate to have a stray shot come through the window here and not get one of you."

They lined up against the windows, facing the closed blinds—all except Grissom. At the end of the CSI lineup, he remained facing Jacks.

"Show me your back, Grissom," Jacks said, waving the Glock irritably. "I'm sick of that face of yours."

Grissom ignored him. "So many people have to die, all to avenge a daughter who's still *alive*?"

"You call that living?" Jacks snorted, eyes and nostrils flaring. "She's a goddamn shell of herself—Valpo destroyed her. She may be breathin', but she hasn't been 'alive' since he got his filthy hands on her."

"What about Price?"

The smile seemed almost inhuman now. "Poor

Tommy—a gambling problem hardly anybody knew of. Worked at the Four Kings, but played in the casino in Cal Nev Ari. Owed some money to some very bad people and needed ten grand real bad . . . I just happened to know where to get it. Buck Finch hated Valpo and the Predators practically as much as I did. Ten thousand was nothing to those assholes, and they had their pride to think about. After all, the Predators thumbed their noses at the Spokes every chance they got."

"Finch knew you intended to kill Valpo."

"He knew. But he wouldn't have talked—couldn't've, without implicating himself. Only now, I think it's better if he goes to that big Biker Blowout in hell."

Another gunshot from outside made everyone flinch again—except Catherine, who stood before blinds only partly shut.

"They're just shooting in the air," Catherine said.

Grissom turned and pried open two venetian blind slats to look out at the crowd of bikers gathered in the street. Local cops and Highway Patrol stood guard, their backs to the police station, others in a line dividing the biker groups; but the lawmen looked edgy—the least little thing might turn this confrontation into a full-fledged melee.

Grissom swivelled to face Jacks again. The suspect did not see the door opening from the street onto the bullpen.

Catherine was saying, over her shoulder, "Is this how you hope to make your daughter proud?"

"Spare me—I been a cop too long."

"Yes," Grissom said, "you have."

Chief Lopez was coming in the outer office, his gun in his hand.

"Have what?" Jacks snarled at Grissom.

"Been a cop too long," the CSI said.

Jacks sneered and raised his weapon, taking a bead on Grissom's head.

Grissom barely flinched when glass broke, carrying the explosion from Lopez's pistol as he fired, the bullet catching Jacks in the back of the head. The detective's eyes widened in surprise in a final instant of consciousness.

The Glock dropped from Jacks's dead fingers to the floor, his body pitching facedown onto the chief's desk. For a split second Grissom thought Jacks's last act had been to spit in the CSI's face; then Grissom realized he had been sprayed with blood and bits of Jacks's skull and brains.

Looking at the body of the man who'd been just about to kill them all, Grissom said, "On the other hand, frontier justice has its merits."

Lopez rushed in, and the CSIs gladly left their spot at the window to gather near the doorway around the chief.

"My God," Lopez said, aghast, "I had to do it—couldn't risk anything but a head shot. I could see he was going to shoot you, Doc! What in God's name . . ."

Grissom took him gently by the arm. "You saved our lives—let's step out into your bullpen. That glass may give way . . ."

Indeed, the large pane of glass in the office wall had spiderwebbed around the bullet hole.

". . . and anyway, that's a crime scene in there now."

The blond fiftyish dispatcher, Gloria, came in, gun in hand. "Chief . . . I heard a shot. Is everything—"

"Get back to your post," Lopez said, patting the air and holstering his weapon.

The woman's eyes were doubtful, particularly as she saw the cracked glass and Cody Jacks's corpse sprawled on the desk.

She said, "That's Cody . . . Sweet Jesus, that's—"

Grissom said, "He was a murderer. You'd have been his next victim, after he took care of us."

The dispatcher, mouth agape, stood frozen.

Lopez said, "Get to your post, Gloria—now."

Finally, moving backward, staggering, her face white with terror, the dispatcher exited the bullpen.

11

WARRICK BROWN LIKED TO THINK he was in tune with his body.

As a musician, melody was important to him, and the tune his exhausted, aching muscles were playing now was a dirge. He and Greg should both have been home and in their own beds by now; but Ecklie had come in, on a Saturday no less, to personally ask them to hang around.

"I don't have to tell you, Brown," Ecklie said, "how shorthanded we are with this Boot Hill shooting."

Plus, two of the day-shift analysts were in the middle of two-week vacations and a third, Bob Halpern, was undergoing yet another round of chemo treatments; Halpern obviously had issues that made Warrick feel guilty about wanting to go home over something as trivial as complete physical exhaustion.

So, now he was bearing down on a full twenty-four-hour shift, as was Greg, with nothing left to do about it but try to hang in there and be ready to be awake and alert when the next call came in. Toward that end, Greg had sacked out on a couch in Catherine's office and Warrick had commandeered one of the holding cells, so he could crash on one of the crappy cots.

Warrick had notified both the dispatcher and Ecklie as to where the pair of CSIs would be, with the hope that they could both catch an hour or two's nap. They were, after all, only here in case of an emergency; and since the Boot Hill shoot-out had already been the biggest emergency in months, how many could there be . . . ?

Don't ask stupid questions, Warrick told himself. *Not even stupid rhetorical ones.*

On his side on the bunk, Warrick closed his eyes and immediately felt a thick, dark curtain sweep over him. Before long he was with his new friend, at home, the two of them on the sofa, she drawing close to him, warm in his arms. . . .

Her hand touched his shoulder, shook it gently.

"Tina," he cooed.

"Tina?" a decidedly male voice asked. "Do I look like a Tina?"

Warrick's eyes flapped open and he found himself staring up at Greg Sanders. "What?"

"Tina who?" Greg asked innocently, though his eyes had a glitter of mischief.

Sitting up, reorienting himself, Warrick wiped a quick hand across his eyes. "Tina None-of-your-damn-business."

Greg kept up the innocent act. "What is that, a German name?"

"I just woke up, bro. Don't push it. . . ."

"Does Mia know?"

"Mia who?"

"Mia Who-you're-always-hitting on, Mia."

Warrick blinked, damn near fully awake. "Uh, no. Anyway, Mia's just a friend."

"Riiiight."

"Tina is . . . I don't know . . . maybe something more."

Now Greg seemed really interested, and the kidding dropped away. "Really? Something more?"

Warrick shook his head. "I don't know, we just met recently. She's a nurse."

"I like a woman in uniform."

"Let it go, Greg. . . . Why did you wake me up, anyway? Did I look too restful?"

"Ecklie," Greg said almost sheepishly. "Got a call."

Rising now, stretching, Warrick asked, "Where's everybody else?"

"No sign of our Boot Hill buddies yet. The day-shift crew caught a bunch of primo stuff—a domestic disturbance turned murder/suicide, two robberies, one burglary, and patrol found a stolen car that Williams is dusting for prints."

"Glad I was asleep. So, what did *we* draw?"

"Bank robbery."

"What about the Feds?"

Greg shrugged. "They've been called and agents are on the scene . . . but they only have one available crime scene analyst, so we got elected to volunteer to help out Uncle Sam."

Warrick admired Greg's enthusiasm, though at the moment he was having a hard time matching it. "Your first bank robbery, right?"

Greg nodded. "Yeah. I won't lie to you—I'm jacked."

Wanting to settle his partner down some, Warrick said, "Don't blame ya, but hey—let the Feds take the lead. Not only is it their case, they're easier to get along with if you let them think they're in charge."

"Roger that."

The Green Valley branch office of the Mountain Creek Bank was a single-story adobe building with a red-tile roof on the outskirts of a mall on Warm Springs Road. Even though the Saturday closing time of noon had come and gone, the parking lot was full.

As they pulled in, Warrick behind the wheel, he saw only a couple of cars out front that looked like they might belong to customers. The rest were a mixture of patrol cars and unmarked Crown Victorias. Toward the back of the lot, on the right, away from the building, sat three cars that probably belonged to bank employees.

Warrick parked and they climbed down. Greg started to open the back door to unload their equipment, but Warrick stopped him. "Let's get the lay of the land first."

They did take a moment to slip into their LVPD Crime Lab windbreakers before approaching the bank.

Crime scene tape had been set up around the front entrance; a uniformed officer stood just behind it with his arms crossed. He was a bruiser with flattop, wide chest, stovepipe arms, and hands the size of frying pans, sausage fingers poking out. His name was Tucker and Warrick knew, fearsome looks or not, the guy was a real softie.

"Hey, Tuck, what's up?"

The big cop gave Warrick a grin as he stepped out of their way and let them step under the tape. "Brand-new day, same old shit."

Warrick nodded. "Who's the Special-Agent-in-Charge?"

"Jamal Reese."

The officer opened one of the double glass doors for the CSIs, and it took a second for Warrick's eyes to adjust to the light in the lobby.

Despite plenty of windows and fluorescent lighting, the bank interior still seemed dark compared to the early-afternoon's brilliant sunshine. With his vision clearing, he glanced around.

To his left, a waiting area was tucked back in the corner next to a counter running down the wall, three teller windows available. A group of people gathered in the waiting area, along with several men in suits who were obviously FBI.

"Looking for Special Agent Jamal Reese?" Warrick called out. One of the agents pointed past Warrick.

Warrick glanced over to his right and saw a slender white man seated behind a desk, talking to a black man seated opposite, his back to them. The African-American had to be Reese.

He walked over to the pair, Greg trailing behind, and came up on Reese's right. Behind the desk, the other man, presumably the branch manager, seemed to be wondering if he should rise as Warrick and Greg approached. Poor guy seemed flummoxed, as would any bank employee after a robbery.

Seeing that, Reese rose himself, his head swivelling toward them.

"Special Agent Jamal Reese," he said, extending a hand.

Warrick shook it. "I'm Warrick Brown; this is Greg Sanders. Las Vegas Crime Lab."

"Thanks for the help," Reese said, offering an easy smile. "We're kinda shorthanded in the CSI department today."

"Tell me about it."

Reese nodded, eyes narrowing. "Ah, that Boot Hill thing—that depleted you but good, I bet."

"Safest bet in Vegas."

Warrick was pleased to see Reese showing none of the arrogance Warrick sometimes encountered in FBI agents.

A couple of inches taller than Warrick, Reese wore a charcoal suit so well-tailored that the armament bulge on his hip barely registered. He had close-cropped hair and a thick, dark mustache with just a pinch of salt, which was also visible at his temples.

"Single armed robber," Reese began, crisply businesslike. "Came in around ten minutes before closing, carrying a large manila envelope. Only a couple customers inside, along with the guard, two tellers . . . and, of course, Mr. Warner, the manager."

Reese nodded toward the man behind the desk, who had stood up by now.

Timidly, Warner nodded to Warrick, who nodded back. The manager wore wire-frame glasses and his sandy hair was combed over in a failed attempt to disguise a sizable bald spot. His suit seemed almost as expensive as Agent Reese's.

Reese said, "Once he's inside, UNSUB jerks a pistol out of the envelope, cold-cocks the guard, yells for the customers to hit the floor, makes the tellers empty the drawers into a bag, then splits."

"Where's the guard?" Greg asked, at Warrick's side now.

"Office in the back. Got an ice bag on a bump on his

head. I suggested he take a ride to the ER, but he doesn't want to leave. Point of pride—more pissed than hurt."

Warrick frowned. "I'd *make* him take that ride."

Reese nodded. "I'll let him hang out a while longer, then I'll see that he goes and gets checked out; but the bump doesn't look like much."

"Who's your crime scene analyst?" Warrick asked.

Reese pointed across the lobby to a man in a business suit; the CSA had the customers and tellers gathered in a small waiting area. The victims sat on sofas and chairs as the analyst talked to them.

"Mark Bynum, one of our best."

"Never met him," Warrick said, "but his name's come up. In a good way."

"You'll be happy with him. Check in with Mark, and he'll tell you what he needs."

Warrick nodded.

He and Greg went over and introduced themselves to Bynum. Tall, thin, wearing a gray suit with a white shirt and red-and-blue striped tie, he was the prototypical Fibbie with the firm handshake and death-glare eyelock issued to all agents with their badges and guns.

"I'm going to print the vics," Bynum said. "We want to be able to eliminate them."

Warrick ignored being told the obvious and asked, "Do we know what he touched while he was here?"

"You guys can dust the whole front counter," Bynum said, with a nod in that direction. "All the vics agree he touched it in several places."

"No gloves?" Greg asked.

"No gloves."

"Nice break."

"Could be," Bynum admitted. Addressing both CSIs,

he said, "You can also collect any physical evidence you can find. I'll probably start by processing the evidence at your lab, just for the sake of speed."

"We're on it," Warrick said.

They retrieved their crime scene kits, and while Warrick dusted the counter, Greg collected evidence.

After printing the victims, Bynum slipped behind the counter and searched for evidence back there. Warrick knew Reese would be talking to the manager, Mr. Warner, about dye packs and marked bills as bait money the robber might have taken. Greg bagged several items from the front side of the counter, then headed to the rear to retrieve the security video with the help of the bank manager.

Meanwhile, Reese and his fellow agents interviewed the vics in separate areas of the lobby so they would not contaminate each other's memories.

When the CSIs were finished, they had scant evidence to go on.

Tons of fingerprints from the counters, but it would take a good while to sort them out. Greg had bagged the manila envelope that had hidden the robber's gun, as well as some hairs he had found, and had photographed the guard's head wound in case there might be a clue about the gunman's pistol.

Along with the security videos, that was pretty much everything.

Bynum told them to take what they had to the lab, adding that he'd catch up as soon as he could.

"Huh. You do all the work, we'll take all the glory," Warrick muttered.

If there *was* any, Warrick reminded himself. Should the evidence lead to a dead end, the FBI would simply move on to the next case, no skin off their collective nose. Warrick and Greg, on the other hand, were working a twenty-four-hour shift . . . and would end it by doing somebody else's dirty work. . . .

"Get anything from the witnesses?" Warrick asked the FBI analyst.

Bynum shrugged. "Not a whole hell of a lot. One customer thought she saw the UNSUB get into a cab in the parking lot. That's about it."

Back at the lab, Warrick told Greg to get the hairs to the trace evidence lab, then use ninhydrin to find fingerprints, which he would then load into AFIS. In the meantime, Warrick would settle in to study the security videos.

He had been at it for over an hour and had seen all the tapes at least once from the time of the robbery, and now he was doing a more in-depth search, since none had given him a good view of the robber.

The problem with banks was the same all over: though they certainly had high-end money, they notoriously tended to buy the lowest-end video security equipment, depending on the well-known fact that they had cameras as a deterrent.

This meant looking through more blurry, scratchy images searching for one frame that might hold a clear shot of the UNSUB's face. . . .

Greg came in carrying the envelope in a metal tray. "In the mood for good news?" he asked.

Warrick looked up, his eyes burning with fatigue. "Always. Anyway, I need a boost to keep me going."

"Took the hairs to trace."

"And?"

"Composed of Dynel and konekolen."

Warrick didn't even have to think. "A synthetic wig, and a cheap one at that."

"And now for the bad news."

Feeling a little deflated, Warrick asked, "You didn't say there was good news *and* bad news."

"Couldn't. You looked too pitiful."

Warrick sighed. "Hit me with it."

"No prints with the ninhydrin."

And sighed again. "Okay. So we have to try something else."

Greg looked perplexed. "What?"

Warrick said nothing, rose, and left his office for the lab. Greg trailed behind.

"You sprayed on the ninhydrin," Warrick said as they walked, "then heated the envelope in the oven, right?"

"Yeah," Greg said as they strode down the hall. "Of course. Mother Sanders raised no idiot pups, y'know."

"Good to hear. And you got nothing?"

"Right."

They turned into the lab, where Warrick tapped the counter for Greg to set down the tray.

"There's this new thing the Canadians have been doing. Hasn't even been in the JFI yet, but they asked Grissom to verify their tests . . . and he did. Gris says it works great, even showed me how to do it."

"So," Greg said, honestly and openly impressed, "you got this process before it was even in *The Journal of Forensic Investigation*?"

Warrick smiled. "Sometimes it's not what you know, but who you know . . . and Grissom? Guy knows everybody. Like Anissa Rawji at the University of Toronto and Alexandre Beaudoin from the Sûreté du Québec."

Greg frowned in interest. "Who are . . . ?"

"The guys who came up with this solution called Red Oil O. It's better on white or thermal paper than this brown stuff, but it's worth a try."

Greg hovered nearby. "How does it work?"

"Instead of all the steps and mess of physical developer, Red Oil O only involves three steps."

Greg squinted. "Uh . . . what is Red Oil O again?"

"A lysochrome used in biology for staining lipoproteins," Warrick said, "recovered after electrophoresis separation. Sometimes it's used in electron microscopy as well. Didn't you ever use it to stain lip prints on a porous surface before?"

Greg shook his head.

"Well, with fingerprints it's the same theory as with lip prints. The ROO stains the lipids, and we're left with a red print on a pink background. That is, if we get anything at all."

Warrick walked Greg through the process; but, when they got through soaking the envelope and drying it, they still had nothing.

"Another dead end," Greg muttered.

Shaking his head, Warrick held the envelope up to the light. "There's just nothing here. . . ."

"At least we tried," Greg said.

"Wait a minute," Warrick said, turning the envelope in the light. "What's that little rectangle at the bottom?"

Greg peeked over his shoulder. "What?"

"Did you look *inside* the envelope?"

"Yeah, of course. There was nothing."

Warrick opened the envelope and, using tweezers, gently withdrew a slim rectangle of thermal paper. "No, there's something—a receipt."

The paper had turned pink; a beautiful red finger-print showed up right in the middle of it.

"Beautiful," Warrick said as he pressed the receipt out flat. "The wig! He bought it at a dollar store at a mall."

"Maybe *they* have security video," Greg said. "A buck's worth, anyway. . . ."

"You contact them, I'll photograph the print and get it into AFIS."

The partners met two hours later in the break room to mainline coffee and compare results, sitting across a table from each other.

"What'd you get?" Warrick asked.

Greg pushed a photo across the table. "Beautiful head shot of our perp from the dollar store's security system. All digital, very cool."

"I'll see your head shot," Warrick said, "and raise you a fingerprint match from AFIS. . . ." He opened a file folder and compared the security photo to the mug shot inside. "Craig Rogers, real piece of crap character."

"Do tell."

"Assault, aggravated assault, robbery, burglary—just got out of the joint two weeks ago."

Greg grunted a little laugh. "Our new best friend Craig also left a nice mark on the guard's head and drew blood. We can probably match the pistol if he's still got it."

Warrick said, "Judging from his rap sheet, Craig's just too damn dumb to dump it. I went back to the bank security tapes and—though I didn't get a better picture of Rogers—I did find a shot through the lobby that showed him climbing into a black-and-yellow striped cab."

"Sunburst Taxi," Greg said. "Easy trace."

"Better tell Reese," Warrick said, getting out his cell phone.

He caught the FBI agent in his office and filled him in.

"Nice work, Mr. Brown," Reese said in a genuine manner. "I'll get back to you."

Warrick ended the call, expecting to never hear the FBI agent's voice again.

But half an hour later, as Warrick finished bagging up the bank robbery evidence, his cell phone chirped. He pulled it off his belt and hit the talk button. "Brown."

"Jamal Reese."

"Special Agent Reese, what can I do for you?"

"We tracked down Rogers. He's at a fleabag hotel downtown. I'm getting ready to go bust down his door and ruin his day . . . thought you and your partner might want the pleasure of joining in. You earned it."

Warrick smiled. "Appreciate the gesture, Special Agent—"

"Jamal," Reese interrupted. "You can call me Jamal."

"I appreciate the gesture, Jamal, and the name is Warrick . . . but to tell you the truth, we're just too tired. We are running on fumes right now, after the shift from hell."

Reese chuckled. "I hear you."

"Anyway, he's your bust—put him away. Shut the door on his cell hard enough, maybe we'll hear it over here."

"All right. Give it my best shot."

"Really, thanks. Mention the crime lab if you get a

chance at the press conference—my boss, Ecklie, would like that—but Greg and I were just doing our job."

There was a short pause, then Reese said, "And you do it very well, Warrick. Both of you. Thanks again."

Warrick ended the call and reported the FBI agent's words to Greg, emphasizing the "both of you" part.

Greg obviously liked hearing that.

"Is this shift finally over?" Greg asked.

From the break-room doorway, looking half asleep, Captain Jim Brass said, "No."

Within minutes, Warrick and Brass sat across the table from Isaiah "Fleety" Fleetwood in an interrogation room.

After so many hours on the job, Warrick felt like death warmed over; but Fleety looked like it. The kid was obviously terrified after spending hours in a holding tank, waiting to find out just how screwed he was.

Brass drummed his fingers on the table, adding to the kid's anxiety. "Look, Fleety—here's the deal. Jalon's going down for murder. Right now, you're going with him."

"But, man, I didn't kill nobody!"

Warrick said coldly, "You damn near killed me."

"No, man, I was jus' talkin'—I woulda never—"

"Knock it off, Fleety. Now," Warrick said, and he sent his hardest, iciest gaze across the table to Fleety.

Who ducked those laser beams, hanging his head.

Brass said, "You do have a chance here. You can tell us what happened—how and why Jalon murdered De-Marcus Hankins. That way, you can avoid death row."

The kid's eyes looked everywhere but at Brass and Warrick. "I ain't no rat."

Warrick said, "Fleety, we've got both Jalon's and your footprints at the murder scene. We've got Jalon's gun with his prints on it, *and* his bullets in DeMarcus. We have both your fingerprints in the car. We have both your DNA on the straws from Bob's Round-Up Grill. Jalon's DNA matches the skin under DeMarcus's nails. We even have a dead lion you fellas ran down. Truth is, Fleety, we don't need you. Jalon goes down, or you both go down—you choose."

With the evidence laid out that way, Fleety needed little time to make a decision. "Damn straight Jalon did it! But it wasn't supposed to be no murder. Hell, I didn't even want to go out on that party, anyway. But Jalon, he told me, if I didn't drive? Then I was a punk-ass bitch, and he'd make sure that all the Hoods knew it."

"What was the party *supposed* to be?" Brass asked.

Fleety shook his head. "Jalon jus' wanted to knock this chump down to size. We grabbed him in a parking lot? He been, you know, soldierin' through our neighborhood like he own the damn place. Jalon said, 'Fuck that,' and we grab him. Jalon say we had to teach the MSB a lesson, that we ain't no pushovers whose turf don't need respecting."

Tears streamed now, and Warrick decided that Brass could finish this interview without him.

The CSI had had enough of this gang stuff for one shift. Hell, enough for every future shift, too; enough of watching strong young brothers going down this weak old path that ruined so many lives.

Maybe it was exhaustion from a twenty-four-hour shift, but Warrick felt sick to his stomach. He made his way to the break room, where he grabbed a bottle of juice, dropped into a chair, and held the cold bottle to his forehead.

Greg came bounding in like the shift had just started. "That oily substance on DeMarcus Hankins's shoes was motor oil."

Warrick nodded. "They snatched him in a parking lot. He probably stepped in somebody's oil leak. Puts him in that car, too, though."

Greg sat across from Warrick, leaned forward. "How bad will it go on Fleety?"

"He's cooperating. That'll help. But you don't draw down on cops and not do some major time. Felony murder, too, though his age may help him."

Greg shifted in his chair. "I talked to Paula Ferguson—Charlie Ames's mistress?"

Again, Warrick nodded. His head felt heavy. The Ames case seemed like a thousand years ago. . . .

Greg was saying, "She said she was getting ready to dump Charlie's behind, next time she saw him. She'd already figured out he wasn't playing with a full deck."

"Oh, he was playing with a full deck, all right—all jokers. You believe her story, Greg? Or is she an accessory, backpedaling?"

Greg considered that. "No—it rang true."

"Got any evidence against her?"

Greg shook his head. "No."

"She's probably in the clear, then."

Greg yawned and rested his head on his folded arms, like a kid catching a nap at a school desk.

And it looked so damned restful, Warrick did the same.

12

THE EMOTIONALLY EXHAUSTED CSIs and the stunned Boot Hill police chief took chairs at the empty desks in the bullpen and sat facing each other. Grissom, tired of talking, nodded to Catherine, who filled Lopez in.

When she'd finished—a concise and accurate account that Grissom admired—Lopez, shaking his head, his eyes rather dazed, muttered, "I was . . . I was just coming in to call the governor again and tell him that we were about to be overrun."

And the chief reached for a phone.

Catherine raised a hand. "No—get Finch out of his cell."

"What?" Lopez said, astonished. "Why?"

Her colleagues gazed at her in bewilderment—all but Grissom, that is.

Quietly she said, "What does that mob want?"

"Half of them want Finch free," Lopez said. "Half want his head."

"Get him," she repeated. "And I'll need a bull-horn. . . . Chief, you have to trust me on this."

Lopez looked searchingly at Grissom. "Doc . . . ?"

"Do what she says, Chief," Grissom said. "I think I know where she's going, and it's our best chance."

Less than two minutes later, Chief Lopez and the cuffed prisoner, Finch, emerged onto the front stoop of the station, several steps above the crowd of several hundred agitated faces. Catherine, Grissom, Sara, and Nick came out right behind them.

Before them milled two distinct groups, the Spokes and the Predators, a thin line of Highway Patrolmen and Boot Hill cops between the two groups in riot squad formation; another line of lawmen stood behind some flimsy barricades in front of the station.

The two biker contingents had been shouting each other down, but a hush of surprise fell across both camps at the sight of the cops and the prisoner at the top of the short flight of cement steps.

To Catherine Willows, the bullhorn in her hands felt heavier than any weapon she had ever held. Her stomach was doing a fluttery dance and she knew that if she botched this, if her instincts were wrong, they all might die.

She took a deep breath and raised the bullhorn.

"Everybody please listen," she said.

This prompted the shouting to resume, but now instead of each other, screams and yells and obsceni-ties were directed at the front of the police station, in defiance of Catherine's request.

She pressed on: *"No one has to die here today!"*

These words—she would never quite be sure why—caused the crowd noise to dissipate. They were looking up at her, bikers and cops alike, with the same bewilderment that her colleagues had when she first suggested Buck Finch be brought from his cell.

"We know who killed Nick Valpo."

With the Spokes leader there in custody, on public view, the Predators assumed Catherine meant Finch and began to cheer. And the Spokes roared their disapproval.

Catherine put a quick stop to this: *"The killer was not Buck Finch! Not any of the Rusty Spokes!"*

And now the Spokes whooped and hollered, while the Predators booed and catcalled, the small presence of cops below looking uneasy as hell, and Catherine knew the scene was as close to erupting into violence as it had ever been.

"Sergeant Cody Jacks, a Boot Hill police officer with a grudge, killed Valpo. Minutes ago, Jacks was taken down by Chief Lopez inside the station."

The crowd fell eerily silent as it absorbed these words.

Every face, Predator or Spoke or police, froze; so many wide eyes and gaping mouths—it might have seemed comic to Catherine had she not been so terrified.

"You had to have heard the shot. . . . Valpo's killer is dead. Not a result of your feud, but of Cody Jacks wanting revenge."

Murmuring rippled through the crowd, building, building . . . she hoped it would not build into a full-throttle riot. . . .

Then, in the distance, so far away she didn't know if she really perceived it or if it was just wishful thinking, Catherine heard a familiar electronic wail . . .

. . . the swell of sirens.

The crowd heard it, too, and looked behind them, then back at her as she continued on the bullhorn.

"*The four Spokes now in custody—including Buck Finch—will remain with us to answer for their crimes.*"

On the Spokes side of the police line, the bikers began to shout threats and obscenities again. They seemed about to surge forward. . . .

Lopez leaned in where only the CSIs—and Finch—could hear him and see what he was up to. Easing his pistol out of his holster, behind Finch's back, he pressed the barrel into Finch's spine and said, "You care to defuse this for us, Buck? Because if we have any more fatalities here today, I'd say you're first on the firing line."

Finch craned his neck to look into the dangerously placid face of the police chief.

Catherine held the bullhorn toward the biker honcho. "Anything you'd like to say to the Spokes, Mr. Finch?"

He sighed.

And nodded.

Catherine held the bullhorn up.

"*Enough killing,*" he said in a voice that would have been loud and commanding without the amplification. "*You Spokes—all of you! Back down.*"

Some of Finch's gang appeared confused by this order, and a few seemed outright angry, but scattered booing was cut off by their leader's voice.

"*Goddamnit! I still run the Spokes, and I say back down! Now!*"

Both gangs backed off a little, but they did not disperse. The sirens in the distance seemed very real to Catherine now, growing ever closer.

Lopez, who had holstered his pistol without the crowd ever seeing it, held out his hand for the bull-horn; Finch gave it to him.

The chief asked Finch, "Who's your second in command?"

"Eddy," Finch said. All of the air was out of him. "Eddy Prentice."

Using the bullhorn, Lopez called Prentice of the Spokes and Jake Hanson of the Predators to join the group on the stairs. As they waited for the two to make their way up, Lopez called a uniformed officer over and had him take Finch back inside.

"But just inside—out of sight, in case we need to play this card again."

The two high-ranking reps from either gang came up the short flight of steps simultaneously, never taking their eyes off each other.

Prentice was maybe six feet tall, skinny but muscular, with curly black hair, cool dark eyes, and a black soul patch; he had tattoos on either hand and wore tight black jeans and a faded black T-shirt.

The brown-haired, ripped, rock-star-ish Hanson wore a frayed white Harley T-shirt and blue jeans.

Neither man spoke to his counterpart. Catherine could tell that was fine with Lopez, who had plenty to say.

"First thing," the chief said quietly to the new leaders, "is I want you to both look at the roof of the building across the street."

Lopez waved and—out of view for most of the crowd, but plainly visible from the steps of the police station—a Boot Hill police officer wielding a sniper's rifle waved back.

The chief said, "Any questions?"

Prentice shook his head.

Hanson said, "No."

"Eddy," Lopez said to the Spokes rep, "Buck's being charged with inciting a riot and attempted murder. You try to break him out"—he glanced toward the sniper—"let's just say, we *all* know you're top dog with Finch in jail."

Prentice said, "Spare me the threats, Jorge—Buck says it's done . . . it's done."

Hanson nodded. "Yeah. Done. Hell . . . sometimes, both sides lose."

"Town lost, too," Lopez put in.

"What d'you want from us?" Hanson asked.

"I want you gone," Lopez said. "Now. The state police have names and addresses from all of you; we'll know where to find you. Get your people out of here—both of you. This was the last Biker Blowout in Boot Hill—ever."

The Spokes rep nodded and started down the stairs; but he stopped when Hanson didn't move to go, too.

Hanson's eyes locked with Lopez's. "We'll go. This is done. But Chief—we still want Val's body."

Grissom stepped forward. "We don't have it, but we know where to look. We'll get it back, do what we need to, then you can have the body . . . tomorrow, next day at the latest."

Lopez said, "You can stay in town, Jake—send your crew away, and you can stay and collect your leader. I'll need next-of-kin sanction, understand?"

Hanson considered all that; then he slowly nodded. Finally, they both went down the steps, side by side, parting to lead their respective gangs away. The officers on the street—Boot Hill cops and Highway Patrolmen alike—watched the bikers file away; but none of the officers relaxed their stance an iota.

As the stragglers filtered off and the sirens grew steadily louder, Lopez asked, "Doc, can we really find Valpo's body?"

Grissom said, "We'll need a thermal imager, but yes."

"He's been dead for over a day."

"Disturbed soil from where Jacks buried him will give off a different heat signature than the surrounding ground. We'll find him."

"And what about Tom Price, Doc? That's a murder, not a suicide."

"Another crime scene in a very long day," Grissom said.

"How about I call Sheriff Burdick," Catherine said, "and get a fresh team out for that one?"

Grissom smiled. "You're the boss."

Lopez shook hands all around. "I can't thank you people enough." His eyes lingered on Grissom and then even longer on Catherine. "You saved our town—literally."

"Don't know about that, Chief," Grissom said. "You did a pretty good job of staying on top of this yourself. We'll have Valpo's body sent out as soon as possible."

"Appreciate that." Lopez rubbed his forehead. "I just wish . . . hell, wish it hadn't been one of my own."

"He wasn't," Catherine said.

Lopez looked confused.

Grissom said, "Catherine's right—Cody Jacks stopped

being a police officer the day he decided to seek revenge, not justice . . . frontier or otherwise."

Last thing Warrick Brown knew, he was just resting his head on the break-room table for a second. . . .

Something was banging on that table and he sat up with a start, eyes bleary. He rubbed them and saw Nick, Sara, Grissom, and Catherine standing there, like he was Dorothy woken from Oz to find the farmhands gathered at her bedside.

"Sleeping?" Catherine asked, leaning a hand on the table. She was smiling but, for Catherine Willows anyway, looked terrible. "We work our butts off all night, processing the biggest crime scene ever, in the middle of a biker war—and you three are napping?"

Three? Warrick looked around, and Jim Brass and Greg were both groggily waking up, having fallen asleep at the same break-room table.

"Long night," Warrick said.

"Tell us about it," Nick said with a snort.

"Solved three murders," Brass said, trying out the taste in his mouth and obviously not caring for it.

Nick waved that off. "We spilled more than that."

Greg said helpfully, "We had a lion—king of the jungle?—turn up as roadkill at a gang killing."

"Sure you did," Sara said.

"Caught a bank robber," Greg said, only suddenly it sounded kind of lame.

Unimpressed, Nick said, "All *we* did was stare down a couple hundred drugged-out bikers brandishing tire irons and chains."

Brass's eyebrows rose. " 'Brandishing'?"

Somehow Warrick grinned. "Yeah, but did any of you guys have a gun pointed at your head while another of you talked the perp down? And saved your damn *life*?"

Nick said, "Who did that, 'Rick? Jim?"

"Greg."

Grissom said, "Greg—I'm proud of you."

Greg shrugged and tried not to blush.

Catherine said, "Oh, and Greg? Word to the wise. Tip from a pro?"

"Yes?"

"Careful how you sleep on hair with that much product in it. You look a little like a cactus something nasty happened to."

Greg was still processing that remark as if it were a particularly puzzling piece of evidence, when just about everybody else began to laugh. Exhaustion hysteria made Catherine's comment, and Greg's hair sticking up, seem funnier than they really were, causing tears of laughter to flow at an unusual rate for a crime lab.

The only one not laughing was Grissom, who merely smiled—his eyes on Greg, pleased.

A TIP OF THE
TEST TUBE

MY ASSISTANT, MATTHEW CLEMENS, HELPED me develop the plot of *Snake Eyes* and worked up a lengthy story treatment, which included all of his considerable forensic research, from which I could work. Matthew—an accomplished true-crime writer who has collaborated with me on numerous published short stories—does most of the on-site Vegas research and is largely responsible for any sense of the real city that might be found herein.

On occasion, however, I accompany him on these trips, as when we spent the better part of two days with the real CSIs of Las Vegas, who told us of a case that inspired, loosely, the casino shoot-out in *Snake Eyes*. Doing so, they won the dedication of this novel, and our gratitude. We also note, however, that the inspiration was of a basic nature and the crimes detailed in this book are wholly fictional.

We would once again like to acknowledge criminalist Lieutenant Chris Kauffman CLPE—the Gil Grissom of the Bettendorf, Iowa, Police Department—who provided comments, insights, and information; Chris has been an important member of our

CSI team since the first novel and remains vital to our efforts. Thank you, too, to another major contributor to our research, Lieutenant Paul Van Steenhuyse, Scott County Sheriff's Office; and also Sergeant Jeff Swanson, Scott County Sheriff's Office (for autopsy and crime scene assistance). Thanks also go to Gary L. Johansen, crime lab supervisor, Salt Lake City Police Department, for sharing the anecdote from which the bank robbery chapter was developed.

Books consulted include two works by Vernon J. Geberth: *Practical Homicide Investigation: Checklist and Field Guide* (1996) and *Practical Homicide Investigation: Tactics, Procedures, and Forensic Techniques* (1996). Also helpful were *Crime Scene: The Ultimate Guide to Forensic Science* by Richard Platt; and *Scene of the Crime: A Writer's Guide to Crime-Scene Investigations* (1992) by Anne Wingate, Ph.D. We also cite the *Journal of Forensic Identification*, Volume 56, No. 1, Jan/Feb 2006, and thank Anissa Rawji and Alexandre Beaudoin for their article about Red Oil O. Any inaccuracies, however, are my own.

At Pocket Books, Ed Schlesinger, our gracious editor, provided his usual keen eye and solid support. The producers of *CSI: Crime Scene Investigation* sent along scripts, background material (including show bibles), and episode tapes. As before, we wish to especially thank Corinne Marrinan, coauthor (with Mike Flaherty) of the indispensible Pocket Books publication *CSI: Crime Scene Investigation Companion*.

Anthony E. Zuiker is gratefully acknowledged as the creator of this concept and these characters; and the cast must be applauded for vivid, memorable characterizations. Our thanks, too, to various *CSI* writers for their inventive and well-documented scripts, which we draw upon for backstory.

Finally, thanks to the fans of the show who have extended their enthusiasm into following these novels. We have a fairly specific continuity in this series of prose "episodes," which tends to lag behind that of the show itself, and we thank our readers for grasping and understanding that reality of production (and difference between mediums) as we have attempted to explore these familiar characters from within.

ABOUT THE AUTHOR

MAX ALLAN COLLINS, a Mystery Writers of America Edgar Award nominee in both fiction and nonfiction categories, was hailed in 2004 by *Publishers Weekly* as "a new breed of writer." He has earned an unprecedented fifteen Private Eye Writers of America Shamus nominations for his historical thrillers, winning twice for his Nathan Heller novels *True Detective* (1983) and *Stolen Away* (1991).

His other credits include film criticism, short fiction, songwriting, trading-card sets, and movie/TV tie-in novels, including *Air Force One*, *In the Line of Fire*, and the *New York Times* bestseller *Saving Private Ryan*.

His graphic novel *Road to Perdition* is the basis of the Academy Award–winning DreamWorks 2002 feature film starring Tom Hanks, Paul Newman, and Jude Law, directed by Sam Mendes. His many comics credits include the *Dick Tracy* syndicated strip; his own *Ms. Tree*; *Batman*; and *CSI: Crime Scene Investigation*, based on the hit TV series for which he has also written video games, jigsaw puzzles, and a *USA Today* bestselling series of novels.

An independent filmmaker in his native Iowa, he

wrote and directed *Mommy*, which premiered on Lifetime in 1996, as well as a 1997 sequel, *Mommy's Day*. The screenwriter of *The Expert*, a 1995 HBO world premiere, he also wrote and directed the innovative made-for-DVD feature *Real Time: Siege at Lucas Street Market* (2000). *Shades of Noir* (2004)—an anthology of his short films, including his award-winning documentary *Mike Hammer's Mickey Spillane*—is included in the recent DVD boxed set of Collins's indie films, *The Black Box*. He recently completed a documentary, *Caveman: V.T. Hamlin and Alley Oop*, and another feature, *Eliot Ness: An Untouchable Life*, based on his Edgar-nominated play.

Collins lives in Muscatine, Iowa, with his wife, writer Barbara Collins; their son, Nathan, is a recent graduate in computer science and Japanese at the University of Iowa and is currently pursuing post-grad studies in Japan.

There's more forensic mystery and drama with

CSI:
CRIME SCENE INVESTIGATION™

BINDING TIES

by *New York Times* bestselling author
Max Allan Collins

An original novel based on the critically
acclaimed hit CBS series—available now
wherever books are sold!

Turn the page for an electrifying excerpt . . .

WHEN GRISSOM HAD COMPLETED his initial pass at the body, he withdrew his cell phone and punched the speed dial.

On the second ring, a brusque voice answered: "Jim Brass."

"I've got something you need to see," Grissom said, without identifying himself. "It's not in your jurisdiction, but it's right up your alley."

"Cute, Gil. But haven't you heard? I'm on vacation."

"Really kicking back, are you?"

Silence; no, not silence: Grissom, detective that he was, could detect a sigh.

"You know as well as I do," Brass said. "I'm bored out of my mind."

"You know, people who live for their work should seek other outlets."

"What, like collecting bugs? Gil—what have you got?"

"An oldie but baddie—I wasn't with you on it . . . kind of before our time together."

"What are you *talking* about?"

"The one you never forget—your first case."

The long pause that followed contained no sigh. Not even a breath. Just stony silence.

Then Brass said, "You're not talking about my first case back in Jersey, are you?"

"No. I've got a killing out here in North Las Vegas that shares a distinctive M.O. with your *other* first case."

"Christ. Where are you exactly?"

"Just getting started."

"I mean the address!"

"Oh," Grissom said, and gave it to him.

"Twenty minutes," Brass said and broke the connection.

The homicide captain made it in fifteen.

From the open doorway, Grissom watched Brass's car pull up and the detective get out, and cross the lawn like a man on a mission. Which, Grissom supposed, he was.

The compact, mournful-eyed Brass—always one to wear a jacket and tie, no matter the weather—had showed up in jeans and a blue shirt open at the neck.

The uniformed officer, Logan, went out to catch Brass at the front stoop, thinking a relative or other civilian had arrived. The detective flashed his badge, but Logan seemed unimpressed.

"What brings you to our neck of the woods, Captain?"

Leaning out the doorway, Grissom called, "He's with me, Officer. It's all right."

"I'll show you mine when you show me yours."

Ashley leaned into him and the smell of sunshine and dry heat intensified. "Clever man. I suppose closing time will provide us both the answer I've not yet decided on. Stay if you will."

Spinning on her heel, she strode across the pub and slipped behind the bar.

Gareth stole a look at his watch.

Midnight.

Two hours to kill.

If this woman was his last chance? If she could give him the chance to find even a moment's peace before an eternity of torment? There was nothing he wouldn't do, no sin he wouldn't commit. And he would do any of it, all of it, without batting an eye. After all, he was already damned, a dead man.

There was nothing left to lose, only a warm woman to gain.

THE IMMORTAL'S HUNGER

KELLI IRELAND

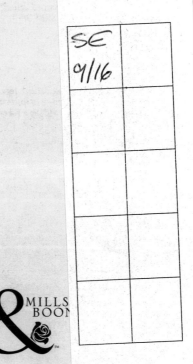

MILLS
BOON

First Published in Great Britain 2016
By Mills & Boon, an imprint of HarperCollins*Publishers*
1 London Bridge Street, London, SE1 9GF

© 2016 Denise Tompkins

ISBN: 978-0-263-92186-1

89-1016

Kelli Ireland spent a decade as a name on a door in corporate America. Unexpectedly liberated by Fate's sense of humor, she chose to carpe the diem and pursue her passion for writing. A fan of happily-ever-afters, she found she loved being the puppet master for the most unlikely couples. Seeing them through the best and worst of each other while helping them survive the joys and disasters of falling in love? Best. Thing. Ever. Visit Kelli's website at www.kelliireland.com.

To all the amazing people who touched my life while I was in Ireland researching this series.

Chapter 1

Gareth Brennan considered the frost-rimed grass, yellowed and made brittle by a persistent cold no summer month in Ireland had ever seen. Toeing the edge of the macabre pattern of cracked earth with his booted foot, a hard shiver raced up his spine. The Old Ones, ancestors lost long before the modern day, held that a man knew when someone passed over his grave. They'd known with certainty what time such events occurred and disbelief at the myth had turned into an old wives' tale, suggesting that the connection between life and death was so thin that the soul rebelled at death's most subtle threat.

Gareth had died here a little more than six months ago. And he'd been resurrected. His connection to this very place had been cemented that day. Whether anyone believed in the old legends, or his reactions, was irrelevant. Gareth knew every time man, animal or...other... crossed this ground.

Clumps of dark, cracked soil broke away as he continued to think. The ground seemed to sigh, exhaustion
bleeding out of the unnatural fissures. It shamed him
that fear, not fury, was his immediate response to that
sound, the sound that called up memories of his death.
The goddess, Cailleach, bound millennia before to the
Shadow Realm, had sought to break her chains and return to this plane. She'd sought to displace the gods and
remake the world to her satisfaction, placing her and her
siblings as rulers over mankind.

Gareth hadn't been of an accord. And he also hadn't
been willing to fight her, not when she'd possessed a
woman who bore no responsibility in the merging of
souls beyond having been born to the wrong bloodline
at the worst possible time. He couldn't condemn her
for something so beyond her control. Well, that and the
fact the Druid's Assassin, Gareth's boss and brother by
choice, loved the woman. That had certainly influenced
him, as well. As Regent to the Assassin and his Arcanum, second in command in all things, he'd made an executive decision. Dylan's happiness trumped the man's
loneliness. So Gareth didn't fight back, instead allowing
the woman to run him through with a sword. A *large*
sword. Bloody bad idea that had been.

He kicked at the earth again, and it did, indeed, sigh.

His fear intensified at the sound, one so familiar to
the breathy voice that haunted him both waking and
asleep.

Death.

Phantoms.

The goddess.

War.

Gareth shuddered and took a step back as he considered the scarred soil.

How much stronger was the connection between life and death if a man experienced death and rebirth in the same spot? How tightly bound would he be to the place if the Goddess of Phantoms and War herself told him she'd see him here again come Beltane?

There wasn't an easy answer. He only knew that each time someone crossed this patch, his entire body shuddered with repulsion. His breath stalled. The goddess breathed into his ear, her voice as chilling as mortals believed it should have been hot.

"Beltane."

Always the same singular word, and always uttered with the same undisguised intent.

She's coming for me.

He fought the urge to run, to get in his car and drive, to get away from Ireland by plane or by sea and never, ever look back. But to what end? History had proven over and over that there was nowhere one could run to that death couldn't find him. The goddess was cagey like that.

Bitch.

He backed away several feet, eyes on the ground as if she'd emerge at his unfavorable thought. When nothing happened, he turned and stalked toward the giant keep.

Mortals, and particularly tourists, who came to the cliffs saw only a decrepit building of tumbling stone and vine. If they came too close, a sense of bowel-loosening foreboding repelled them. And if they persisted? A little magickal push from one of the Assassin's watchmen sent them on their way.

He saw the place, known as the Nest, for what it was. A rather foreboding castle, it had a tower on all four corners. The courtyard had been enclosed to make a huge foyer over two hundred years prior. The garage was a bit archaic seeing as it had, for centuries, housed horses versus horsepower. And Wi-Fi had gone in—thank the gods—four years ago. The place was still a drafty monstrosity, and it always would be. But it was home.

He jogged through the front doors, fighting the compulsion to keep his jacket on. He was cold, was *always* cold, now.

"Yer late," a thunderous voice called out, and he knew for whom that particular boom tolled.

"And you've no cause to announce to the world I've come to drop my trousers for you," Gareth countered.

The burly man grinned as he stepped full out of the doorway to the infirmary. "Ye'll drop yer drawers because I'm the only one who can give ye what ye need."

"Yep, your reputation's toast," an identifiable male voice called from an invisible point and was followed by general male laughter.

"Shut up," Garret called, shaking his head. "Bunch of tools."

He strode into the Druidic version of a physician's office. The eye of newt was missing, but beyond that, it was relatively similar to that which a nonmagickal person would expect. Natural remedies, crushed herbs and preserved root stock shared space with modern medical equipment and, in some cases, drugs. In the midst of it all stood Angus O'Malley, the Druid's version of a physician and owner of the voice that had started the trainee assassins chattering in the hallways.

"Did you have to call out like that, Angus? You know they'll fear coming in here now." Gareth nudged the door shut with his hip and, with reluctance, shed his jacket. The cold that had chilled him became abrasive and he couldn't repress a hard shudder.

Angus looked him over with a critical eye. "No better, then." A statement, not a question.

"No worse," Gareth countered.

"Yer optimism's noted." He jerked his chin to an exam table. "Drop your denims and assume the position."

Scowling, Gareth undid his jeans and braced his palms on the table edge. "You know, I hate this. Just get it over wi—ow! Fecking hell," he said, teeth gritted, hands clenching. The burn of the injection and the subsequent medication was almost as painful as Angus's warm hand laid against the bare skin of his hip. He thought it possible he melted under the incredible heat of the healer's touch, was less than a breath away from calling stop and begging to have the needle removed, when the large man pulled it free of his flesh.

Gareth yanked his jeans up with enough force he doubled over with a grunt. He shot a sharp look at Angus. "What was in that bloody injection? Hydrochloric acid? Perhaps a little potassium sulfate to enhance the burn?" He rubbed his hand over the offended butt cheek. "Gods be damned, but in the course of this…this…*nonsense*, that was the most painful 'treatment' yet!"

"'Nonsense,' is it?" Angus asked as he skewered Gareth with a sharp look. "As Regent, the Assassin's second in both rank and command of the Assassin's Arcanum, and considerin' yer one o' the brighter men I've yet tae meet, I believe I'm safe in saying the problem's no' the mix. The problem centers around yer fear, Gareth, and well ye know it."

Heat, unusual and yet welcome for its rarity if not the cause, burned across Gareth's cheeks. "Tell a soul I'm scared o' needles and it'll mean fists between us, auld man."

Sighing, Gareth tucked the tails of his henley under

his waistband with fierce jabs, retied his combat boots and—more gingerly—situated his pants legs before facing the man who'd treated his every injury since childhood. He propped one hip on the exam table and crossed his arms over his chest, mirroring Angus's posture. "Is there anything you've found in treating me, anything so wrong that himself's a need to know this very minute?"

Besides the fact the phantom goddess marked my soul as hers, sealed the claiming with forced sexual contact and has promised to fetch me home by Beltane? Sure, and there's that.

Thank the gods he'd shared that with no one. "Well?" he pressed Angus.

The healer rolled his shoulders forward, lips thinning. "Nay." He shoved meaty hands into hair that resembled the topknot of a Highland steer. "That doesna mean yer symptoms aren't worsening, though. Only that I doona know best how tae treat ye."

Ignoring his internal voice, the one that latched on to the admission he was worsening with a silent wail of rage, Gareth gave a sharp nod. "Then what do you recommend I tell Dylan? Should I say that I'm…what? Can you definitively prove that I'm…I'm…dying?" He swallowed hard and waited. *What if Angus says yes?*

"I doona ken, but…no." Angus dropped his hands to his sides, his wide shoulders sagging. "Ye've symptoms the likes o' which I've never seen, symptoms as would scare a logical man near tae death. But I cannot predict death any more than you."

Every semblance of attempted humor fell away, and Gareth grew colder than normal. "I assure you, this isn't as remotely scary as experiencing death itself." And Gareth couldn't predict death. He'd been given the date to expect the retrieval of his soul. Only eight days remained. The truth hit him like a sledgehammer to the sternum, and he fought the impulse to clutch his chest, take his pulse and have Angus examine him one more time.

The healer gripped the counter, his gaze locked on some undefined spot to his left. "Ye never speak of it. Of dying, that is."

Because the horrors are too great to relive, and to speak of it could draw the phantom queen's attentions prematurely.

Gareth swallowed, the movement nearly impossible as the muscles in his throat tried to freeze, failed to work and wouldn't respond. Stubborn, he pushed harder, the thought of speaking the goddess of death's name turning his blood to slush, his marrow to ice. He opened his mouth and closed it once…twice…a third time, but he couldn't do it.

The healer paled. "Either you tell Dylan how fast this is progressing, that yer core temperature is dropping and yer symptoms are rapidly growing worse, or…or I will."

Gareth's hands flexed. He'd told Dylan the whole truth and the rest of the Arcanum most of what had transpired, but none knew the extent of his degradation and suffering. He'd kept that to himself on purpose. He wouldn't have them engage the phantom queen and risk their lives unnecessarily. "You've no right."

"Maybe no'," Angus conceded, meeting Gareth's hard stare and then stepping back in the face of that burgeoning fury, "but as he's the Assassin, I've every obligation. Ye've got until the end o' the week."

Gareth shook his head, fighting to speak around emotion's unexpected stranglehold. "I need more time."

"To do what?"

Die. Again. But on my own terms. He would be ending

this before the phantom queen could execute her threat. That pleasure, at least, he could deny her.

His answer, though unvoiced, hung between them as if shouted.

Angus narrowed his eyes. "I'll no' be giving ye time to prove yerself an eejit, man."

Gareth dragged a hand down his face, fighting to shake off the black pall that clung to him like a cloak woven from a spider's web. "If you're worried about me proving myself an eejit, don't. That little fact was proved in roughly 1892 when I slept with the local laird's daughter." He forced a grin but the effort climbed no higher than his lips, leaving his eyes barren. "Her mother discovered us in the haystack...and remembered sleeping with me herself a mere thirty years earlier. Awkward, that, when a man doesn't age as a mortal should."

The healer scowled. "Ye've the heart of a lion, but it's a right jackass ye've become."

"It's a jackass I've always been. And, as always, your kind words come near to sweeping me off my feet—" he reached over and pinched the physician's ruddy cheek "—only to instead dump me on me arse." Pushing off the exam table, Gareth stumbled before regaining his balance and striding across the room where he grabbed his jacket, paused and glanced back. "Be well, Angus." Then he passed through the doorway and headed down the hall.

Ahead, the sound of good-natured taunts and deep male laughter ricocheted off the stone walls. Rounding the corner, he found several senior trainees leading a group of junior trainees out the keep's front door. "Gentlemen," Gareth said, addressing them as a whole.

The young assassins turned toward him, their faces growing serious immediately.

Jacob, the highest ranked individual in the group, stepped forward. "Regent."

Gareth inclined his head, taking in their civilian clothes and the clink of car keys in more than one hand. "You lads out for a bit of sport?"

Jacob lifted his chin, face blank, emotions contained but eyes a bit wary. "Yes, sir. Thought we'd go to the village. There's a group of musicians from Dublin playing at the pub. We're looking for a little *craic* tonight."

Fun and music, maybe a little dancing. He could go in for that.

If they'd have him.

Six months ago, he would have been invited outright, title—and troubles—notwithstanding. The men had enjoyed his company when they got a little rowdy. In return, he'd enjoyed theirs—both their company and the wee bit of hell they'd raised together. But the word *hell* brought about an entirely different meaning now. Once a passing phrase, it had now become a tangible reality not related to fun in any way.

Gareth had been there.

He'd met…her, the Goddess of Phantoms and War whose name he couldn't bring himself to utter, even now. She had changed his perspective on tossing the word *hell* around without a care. She'd forced him to consider what awaited him when this life came to an end, and she assured it would be sooner rather than later. Now he'd grown wary of sleep, fearful she'd exercise her mark on him and take his soul while he lay defenseless.

Conjecture regarding his experience ran wild. The Arcanum and senior assassins had left him be, but the young men, those in training to become assassins, couldn't help but wonder aloud. Speculation regarding his visit to the Well of Souls regularly traveled across darkened rooms, whispered like ghost stories on stormy nights. Conjecture as to what he'd seen ran rampant. But the fear they might die in service to the gods, might see whatever terror it was that had changed Gareth? That ran far more rampant, often followed by brazen boasts that only the darkest of the dark among them should bother to worry about such nonsense. He often interrupted these morbid conversations with simple if hard words. "Train harder, fight smarter and never hesitate to take your enemy down. Then you ladies can finally stop having this conversation. Understood?"

Having died on his own turf, on land where he should have been strongest and had the advantage in any fight, he knew better. The phantom queen could find a man anywhere and would take him without hesitation if he was at all reluctant to strike back. Even if he did…

"Sir?" Jacob's voice said, cutting through Gareth's wildly wandering mind.

His focus shifted to the young assassin. "Apologies. What did you say?"

"Would you care to join us?" The young man's uncertainty was apparent in the tight line of his mouth and the flat tone of his voice.

Gareth considered for a split second before grinning and giving a short nod. He would take tonight to live as he once had, would force himself to get out of the keep and stop looking over his shoulder at every suspicious action, every strange sound, every odd occurrence. His own demise was imminent, by his hand or hers, so tonight he would simply remember. "Who am I to tarnish memories of times gone by? You gents go on ahead and secure a booth near the telly. Ireland's playing Scotland tonight, and I'll want to toast our every goal. I'll be no more than fifteen minutes behind you."

"Fair enough." Jacob winked. "Gives me just long enough to toy with the bartender a bit."

Gareth stopped, brows drawing down. "Is he a new bartender? When did he start?"

"She. The bartender is one hundred percent 'she.' And to a man, we're grateful," one of the group responded, letting out a low, slow whistle and shaping his hands over the invisible hourglass figure of a lush woman while oblivious to Gareth's hesitation. "You being late will let us have a bit of a flirt with her before ye get there and steal her heart, ye careless bastard."

"Good to know." Gareth swallowed hard and waved them on. "Fifteen minutes and we'll see what her type of man is."

Several ribald jests were tossed about then as Gareth historically tended to be *every* woman's type.

Ignoring the men as a whole, he spun on his heel and jogged across the massive entry hall to the wide staircase, taking the steps two at a time. The sudden urge to remain at the keep, to stay inside the protection of the thick walls and the powerful wards that reinforced them, had him reconsidering his offer to go out with the men. But they needed it. Truly. They needed the support of the Assassin's Arcanum, that elite group of five warriors, in all things, from the most difficult of their training all the way to burning off a little excess energy. So he would suck it up, stop his whining and let go of this ridiculous obsession of waiting on the queen's calling card. Gareth was going to the bar. He could check out the new bartender while he was there, perhaps find a way to have a bit of sport as part of his last hurrah. That would also allow him to ensure she wasn't a threat to the assassins here. Shaking his head at his paranoia, his smile felt brittle. He needed to stop seeing everything, and everyone, unknown as a threat. That she'd happened to show up while he was fighting his own demons didn't make her one of them.

Besides, in spite of his hardships over the last six months, Gareth's three life truths still held true. First, nothing got a man's mind off his troubles like a well-built Guinness.

Second, an equally well-built woman was balm to the soul.

Third? Well, third was his favorite. A mutually pleasurable one-night stand could make a man forget his woes.

And all Gareth wanted to do was forget.

Ashley Clement hoisted the tray of drinks above her head, turned and began winding her way through the ever-expanding Friday night crowd. Setting down pints and baskets of bar food as she went, she also retrieved empties and took new orders. An hour ago she'd called in an additional waitress. Ashley would only work the floor as a barmaid until the girl arrived, and the sooner, the better. Seeing to the bar satisfied her far more than running to and fro, fending off wandering hands and keeping her volatile temper in check. The latter had cost her all she was willing to pay in every lifetime she'd claimed as her own. And as a phoenix? That number was vast.

There'd be live music tonight from the traveling group, The King's Footmen. They would play everything from contemporary hits to old favorites and traditional Irish ballads, pulling in a more diverse crowd as the band had a sound both young and old could appreciate. Tonight's festivities alone ensured she would more than double her average take.

Fergus, the bar's owner and short-order cook, emerged

from the small kitchen. The man was huge, his white apron appearing more like a dainty dishtowel banded round his waist. His gaze roved over the patrons, searching.

Ashley knew he was looking for her, but something made her hesitate to raise a hand and wave. His behavior had been odd of late. Odd enough, actually, that she was considering moving on.

He finally found her watching him, and his face darkened. "Stop yer lollygagging. Orders up!"

She offered a jaunty salute. "Soon as these fine men are served, I'll retrieve as commanded." He ducked back into the kitchen and she added softly, "Jackass."

Laughter wove through the crowd nearest her.

"He'll have yer head should he hear ye," said a regular who'd overheard her.

"And a fine trophy it would be to join the others," his tablemate answered.

Others. It had to be a coincidence. Neither mortal man knew what she was.

Ashley shifted her tray as she turned her attention to the table of attractive men who'd shoved into the largest booth nearest the telly. Distributing their drink order with care, she watched them under lowered lashes. To a body, they were larger than most Irishmen in both height and muscle, and instead of harboring the general spirit of goodwill inherent to the Irish, they seemed to blend with the shadows even as they appeared weighed down by some invisible onus. Their auras ranged from the palest shade of early morning fog to a gray so dark it appeared inky. Then there was the way their gazes continually roamed the room, all but announcing that, even in their cups, these men never found their ease. All in all, it had been a lot for Ashley to pick up on in the fifteen minutes they'd been here, but she could relate. And that she'd taken it all in was proof that living the last four centuries on the run had helped her develop a *few* survival skills. Nondeadly ones, anyway. The deadly stuff? Well, that part of her couldn't be turned off any more than the sun could be commanded to rise in the west come morning. So she'd watch the men as she pulled taps, built Guinness after Guinness and poured the hard liquor with flourish. Should push come to shove and she discovered they represented a threat she hadn't yet sniffed out, she'd be out the back door in seconds and with nothing more than the backpack she always kept within reach.

Flipping her hair over her shoulder, she smiled at the group as she set the last of the drinks down. "You gents fancy some crisps or chicken gujons tonight? Clearly I'm headed to the kitchen and would be happy to deliver your order."

One of the men lifted his pint and tipped his chin toward her before taking his first sip. "We've an ear for the music tonight, love, but thanks. Another man's joining the party shortly. He might be of a different mind."

She glanced at the band setting up in the corner. No electric instruments. This would be what the Americans called a jam session. Foot tapping as the fiddle player loosed a rapid flurry of notes, Ashley turned back to the men. "Enjoy yourselves, then, and I'll check with your man when he's here and settled."

Behind her, the vestibule door opened with its characteristic creak followed by a short burst of crisp, cool ocean air. The chill wind whispered a silent benediction over the thin sheen of sweat that graced her skin.

That same breeze lifted her hair and whipped the long curls around her. Small crackles and pops, not unlike strong static, sparked between the strands and against her skin, and the sheen of sweat crept into her nape, dotted her upper lip and further dampened her lower back. Heat pinked her skin and arousal settled deep in her core.

A wave of alarm swept through her as the warning signs settled into place.

No. It can't be time. Not yet. Please, not yet. I should have at least five more weeks.

Every unmated or unclaimed female phoenix dreaded the initial symptoms of her impending epithicas, the triennial fertility cycle that ruled her body for one full week. Every third May, she endured seven days of sheer physical misery. Seven days of hellish sexual cravings. Seven days during which she had to take a lover and hide herself so well no clan member could find her. By their race's laws, any clansman who discovered her could take her without repercussion. She'd be hunted. Actively. And if found, she'd be willing enough during that seven days because the only relief she would find was in sexual contact. But once that week passed? She'd regret every action when her mind cleared and her body became her own again. Humiliation would threaten to drag her into the depths of despair while fear of pregnancy would have her terrified to look in the mirror every morning. Phoenix law held that whichever male had impregnated her could legally claim her as his chattel, tattoo the skin on her arms with his lineage and call her wife…no matter how many other wives he possessed.

After fleeing clan lands at only thirty-seven years old, she'd had three close calls—twice by poor luck, once by poor choice. The first two times had both scared and scarred her. The third time had cost her every dime of emotional currency she possessed and had left her not broken, exactly—unless she considered her heart. It had been shattered. Never, ever did she want a man to hold that much dominion over her again, be it by law or professed affection. Reason was irrelevant and emotions even more so. She would never willingly go there, or be that woman, in this or any other lifetime she claimed as her own.

So now she took precautions, kept a particular incubus-friend-with-benefits on call. He was a nonphoenix with no more interest in a relationship than she. Even the idea of a long-term affair was enough to make them both cringe. The problem? He wasn't due to arrive for almost four more weeks. If her epithicas truly did arrive early? She was, in more ways than one, screwed.

Scowling, Ashley tucked the tray under one arm, spun on her heel and started toward the bar. She had to figure this out, had to determine whether she stayed through the end of her shift and then quietly disappeared or threw caution aside, grabbed her backpack and walked out now. She didn't think there was a male phoenix in the room—she should have been aware of him. If he'd somehow evaded her and she discovered him? The decision was made. She wouldn't walk out of the room. She'd leave at a dead run.

Of course, she could also hunker down here, lost in the little Irish village in County Clare, and find a bed partner to see her through the worst of things. If she could, she might just be able to keep the worst of the pheromones in check. The man would have to be willing to stay with her for the full week, able-bodied in defense should a male phoenix threaten and…well…there was that willing thing.

Lost in thought as she calculated her options, she nearly missed the man who'd swept in on the ocean breeze. Then he moved, crossing her path as he wound his way toward the same table of men she'd just left.

Standing several inches above her own six feet, his hair was the color of her favorite clover honey. Lighter and darker strands wove through the cut to make his hair appear multidimensional, even in the pub's low light. Though he had the body of a warrior, it was his face that demanded her attention. He had a strong jaw, full lips and chiseled features, all of which gave him a near impossible appeal the fashion runways of Milan and Paris would worship. But his eyes were what commanded her complete attention. They were a light, bright blue. Faint creases at the corners said he smiled a lot and, sure enough, he did just that as several men hailed him in greeting.

Something about the man pleased her phoenix, making that part of her heat up until she was sweltering. Now wasn't the time, though. She couldn't afford the distraction—though a man like that would be ideal to see her through this. The problem? She could seduce the stranger for a night, maybe two, but convincing him to give up a week of his life for her as an unknown wasn't realistic.

She slipped behind the bar and toed her backpack for reassurance before grabbing a glass, pulling a lager and then slamming it back. She dropped her chin with the last swallow and found the stranger's gaze boring into hers. Undiluted desire slammed into her without warning, burning her from the inside out and incinerating every ounce of air in her lungs. The taste of ash on her tongue made her pull a second drink and slam it down even faster. Still, grit coated her mouth. She fought the urge to go straight up to the man and demand who, and *what*, he was, because he wasn't a run-of-the-mill human. Oh, no. Too much power rolled off him for that. He also wasn't a phoenix. If he had been, he would have arrowed straight toward her when her hair began the preliminary mating dance that was, as always, out of her control.

Thank the gods he's not one of us. Otherwise he'd have me flat on my back in the middle of the bar, fighting for my life. She shuddered. *At least until the madness claimed me.*

When she shuddered a second time, her empty pint glass slipped from her fingers.

The sound of shattering glass against the stone floor had a wave of attention shifting toward her. Several men laughed and whistled, calling her out—*her*—out over the broken glass. She, who tossed bottles and slid drinks and juggled empties—and had never broke a one. Yet experiencing a polite, if solitary, glance from a stranger had her falling apart.

Damn hormones.

She refused to blush, instead offering the crowd a wicked grin and one-fingered salute.

Grabbing the broom and pan, she cleaned up without comment, never acknowledging the jests. She'd work, simply work, and if the man became a problem, she'd deal with him. Until that point, she wouldn't allow herself to worry. More importantly, she'd keep her temper in check. Good rule of thumb, not killing while on the clock. So far she'd held to that little rule.

So far.

Chapter 2

"Fifteen minutes, as promised," Gareth announced to the men gathered around the large corner table. "I trust you didn't drink the house dry."

His teasing was met with laughter and jests. Several men rearranged their chairs or scooted deeper along the lone bench to make room for Gareth. Instead of slipping in among the men, though, he tossed his jacket down before retrieving a vacant chair from a neighboring table. Flipping the battered and aged oak seat around, he straddled it loosely, rested his forearms along the square back and leaned forward. "Who's buying the first round?"

"Age before beauty," Jacob announced.

Gareth grinned. "Like that is it? Need I remind you to respect your elders lest you find yourself on indefinite kitchen duty?"

"You've resorted to pulling rank. That means I managed to back you into a corner in moments," Jacob said,

grinning. "That's worth peeling potatoes for a week…
hell, a *month*, and without a word of complaint—mostly
because I'd no idea it would be so *easy*."

The men laughed, Gareth included, though he was
obliged to reach over and cuff the young man on the
back of the head. "Mind your manners. I'm older than
you, but I'm far from old. I'll kick yer arse to the Aran
Islands and see you come summertime when it's warm
enough for you to swim home." A flash of color and the
tinny sound of a cheering crowd drew Gareth's attention
to the wall-mounted television where Ireland's national
soccer team played Scotland. "So, what's the score?"

"Two minutes into the second half. Ireland's up by
one."

The woman's voice was as smoky as a two-finger
shot of single barrel whiskey and as smooth as the waters of Loch Mor.

A jolt of pure, sensual pleasure arrowed through Gareth and settled a solid eight inches below his navel. He
closed his eyes and took a bracing breath. "Care to repeat that?" *Please.*

Instead of answering, she chuckled. "Sure and if anything changes, I'll gladly shout it out for you. In the
meantime, what may I get you from the bar? Guinness?
Whiskey? Murphy's?" She must have shifted because
the air moved and carried with it her scent—campfire
smoke, warm flannel and the faintest hint of something
spicy, like cloves. "The kitchen's only open for another
half hour, so you'd best get your order in if you're hungry."

Gareth fought the compulsion to look at her, the pull
that urged him to face her where she stood and pair the
voice with the rest of her, head to toe. "Order of chips
and an Irish coffee. Be generous with the Irish."

"I'll see that you're not cheated a drop," she replied, the smile in her voice an audible caress.

Again, air moved, but this time with her departure.

Gareth spun in his seat, his narrowed eyes homing in on the seductive sway of the tall woman's hips. Narrow waist. Long, long legs clad in skintight denim and knee-high boots. A simple white T-shirt. Skin on her arms bordering on pale. And her hair... It was a red so brilliant, so vibrant, that every strand seemed to come alive as the mass tumbled to her waist. Large, soft curls swayed back and forth as she walked, and the dense mass crackled with static.

He swiveled in his seat to face the men he'd come out to celebrate with. "She's a new face."

Jacob snorted. "And I told ye so earlier. 'She' is the new bartender as of several months ago."

Gareth leaned his heavy forearms on the worn tabletop. Once, he'd have been the man to pursue her, the man to charm her right out of her tight jeans and onto a smooth-sheeted bed for a night of unparalleled pleasure. Now?

He shivered, his near hand drifting to the persistent ache at his side.

Now, not so much. If at all.

So much for finding a means to forget.

The men bantered back and forth, the sound mixing into the mishmash of noise in the crowded pub until all Gareth heard were random words, shouts of encouragement at the telly and, below it all, the faint vibrations of both fiddle and bodhran from the corner where the musicians had begun to prepare for the show.

A fiver slid into his view, followed by Jared's voice. "So what of it, Gareth? You in?"

Slipping the euro back into the middle of the table,

he looked up and forced an approximation of a smile. "My mind's been wandering about. I'd be a poor Regent and even poorer assassin to take a blind wager, don't you think?"

Jacob's smile fell a bit, and the other men went still.

Gareth wanted to yank at his hair, wanted to shout at them to just behave normally, but he knew it had taken months of his withdrawing from them to get the men to this place where he was now unfamiliar. He didn't want them to remember him this way after he was gone, but rather they should remember him as he had been. Might as well attempt to set things to rights.

With an air of feigned casualness, he retrieved his wallet from his back pocket and pulled out a hundred note, sliding it across the table with the general irreverence he'd been known for over his lifetime. "But it's not to say I can't sweeten the pot for the man about to dive into the seedy Shadow Realm of bloody taunts and bodily wagers."

The men leaned in as if he was their puppeteer, the money their master.

"Go on, then," Jacob said, eyes bright.

"I've a hundred that says not a one of you can get the redhead to take you home tonight."

"That was the wager—that you could talk her out of the bar and back to her place," Jacob said, smirking.

"I'm not favored in this one, gents. It's not fair for me to use my gods-given charms—*plural*—against the lot of you." He leaned back, hands gripping the chair back, and kicked his feet out in front of him. "Too much like taking candy from babes. So, you care to play or is it all talk with the lot of ye?"

There was a great deal of shifting in seats and casual glances left and then right to see who would be the first to man up or bow out. Finally, a lad named Alex, slapped a ten-euro note on the scarred table and grinned. "I'll take that wager."

Gareth chuckled. "You're barely out of short pants, Alex. What could you possibly know about seducing a woman?"

"Far more than you think, you gobshite," he responded, his broad shoulders squaring. "I'll have the lass eating out of me palm before sunrise."

Gareth grinned. "And that, right there, is why you'll lose."

Alex's brow furrowed.

Leaning forward with an air of absolute seriousness, Gareth clasped the younger man's shoulder. "The goal in spending the night with a woman has nothing to do with feeding them like a wee bird."

The men all laughed. Several more bills were added to the pile as their group grew more boisterous.

Gareth chanced a quick glance over his shoulder at the woman in question. If he was honest, what he really wanted was another look.

She'd nearly reached the bar. From somewhere deep in the group of men she passed through, a brawny hand snaked out and grabbed her backside hard enough he imagined she'd bruise.

He was out of his chair before his mind registered that he'd responded. It turned out his intervention wasn't at all necessary.

In what appeared to be a single move, the bartender grabbed the offending man's hand at the same time she whipped the tray out from under her arm and swung it down, edge first, on the tender spot between wrist and hand. Before the man could properly yelp, the woman spun the tray in her hand and smacked the man over the head with it. The tray splintered and the man slumped forward. Issuing rapid apologies, two of the patron's companions eased him to the floor.

Gareth hardly spared the downed man a look. No, he was too fascinated by the woman standing over the proverbial body and holding nothing but the metal ring of what had been a wooden serving tray. She wielded it like a weapon. And standing over the man like she was, Gareth could imagine her gladly wrapping the ring around the offender's neck should he offer anything other than an apology following his physical set-down.

But something about the woman, something he knew he had overlooked, forced him to focus on her with more intensity.

With her shoulders thrown back, her breasts appeared fuller, her body leaner, her waist thinner and her legs impossibly longer. Her hair seemed to crackle with life. And her eyes? They conveyed competence and fury in equal measure.

The man at her feet stirred and Gareth took a step forward, intent on aiding her whether she needed it or not.

As if she'd singled out his movement among the bar crowd, her eyes met his. Fists clenched, she tossed her hair and turned back to the man at her feet. A firm nudge of her toe had his head lolling back. A partial beer she claimed from another table roused him…when she tossed it in his face.

The bar quieted so much so that the commentary from the soccer game's announcers seemed to skate across the tension strung person to person—tension that centered wholly on the redheaded woman.

It was sexy as hell.

Behind him, Jacob stood and sighed dramatically, propping his forearm on Gareth's shoulder for mock support. "I'd love to be trapped between those thighs, gents. I've an inkling she'd hurt me in the best possible way."

Gareth knocked the young man's arm aside with only partially feigned irritation. "Sit down, Jacob. You're no match for the likes of her."

He continued to watch the woman. Something about her wasn't quite right, but damn if he could put a finger on the vibe she emitted. It was nothing he'd ever encountered before. But before any of his trainees engaged her, be it in a bit of fun or…something else, he'd know who, and what, she was.

Ashley tossed the drink tray's metal ring over the antlers of a large Irish sika deer with the misfortune to have found itself mounted on the wall in the name of art. She'd never understand men's minds, no matter the effort she put into it. But if her epithicas was about to occur, she would indeed spend a great deal of time considering ways to harness one of them into giving up a week of his life for bed sport. A night? Oh, that was fine. But for her to be safe, to ensure her fertility remained suppressed and as undetectable as possible, she had to have a beck-and-call lover on hand for the hormonal surges. Only regular sex would satisfy that need. It had humiliated her for years until she'd come to realize it was either take a lover or risk end up a branded wife. There was always some part of her that wondered what it would be like to stay with a man by choice versus need, to wake up to him in the morning out of love and not compulsion. The epithicas had always destroyed that, though. Until she'd met Geoffrey the Swedish incubus, befriended him and set up a routine over the last several cycles. That this one might be early? She could call him…

Stepping behind the bar, she dropped the pass-through. It landed with a loud *whump*. The sound re-animated the crowd. Men and women alike began to chatter. More than one looked at her with open curiosity, and she knew that wouldn't bode well. Strangers in Ireland never stayed strangers long. People were too friendly. And curious. No, not "curious"—*wicked* curious. A good Irishman or Irishwoman would have your life story from you before you'd finished your first cup of tea and your hopes, dreams and heartaches before you were halfway through your second. It was part of the reason she loved the obscurity of tending bar. Patrons came in looking to talk to her or with her, not about her. Until now. She'd botched that up with a fair hand.

Toeing her backpack not unlike a child affirming her security blanket's location, Ashley couldn't stop her shoulders from sagging in relief when her foot made contact with the worn canvas. It was there. She had choices, and choices, no matter how limited, were always better than the alternative.

She glanced up and searched out the table of men she'd just served, the antithesis of the smaller traditional Irishmen yet Irish through and through. They tried for inconspicuous as they stared at her with a strange, almost ravenous look. It wasn't too disconcerting. However, the man who sat at the head of the table set her back a step.

His eyes were such an intense blue, heavy-lidded but not with lust. If she read him right from this far, and she prided herself on such things, he was sizing her up more as potential trouble than potential bedmate. *That* she wasn't accustomed to. At all.

Calloused hands curled in on themselves, and he gave a short nod and three-fingered swiping gesture low and to his side. Acknowledgment, then. That single move said he'd recognized her as Other, and he'd just given her the same confirmation. Whatever brotherhood that group belonged to, it wasn't the local farmers' collective.

She knew he wasn't phoenix. None of her kind was built with such a thick, muscular overlay. No, they were far leaner, faster. Potentially meaner.

A second glance at him and those blue eyes narrowed. Okay. Maybe not meaner.

Heat pulsed through her veins, hotter than molten rock. Her knees buckled. The only thing to save her arse meeting the floor was dumb luck and fast hands as she grabbed the counter. Smells intensified—the weight of the Guinness she'd pulled, the pungent yet sweet smoke from the pipe of the old man sitting closest to the taps, the hot oil in the kitchen.

Her sex ached, and she issued a small, quiet curse. *Definitely the epithicas, then, and damned early at that.* It had never been early. Sure, it fluctuated a couple of days either way, but it was never weeks early. *Ever.*

Only one choice made sense, and that was to try to talk Geoffrey into leaving Sweden now. If he'd hole up with her in her small garage apartment, he could see her through the worst of the cravings.

A quick dip below the counter and she had her cell in hand. Geoffrey was buried deep in her contacts, but she found him without trouble and placed the call.

Three rings. Four. Then a breathless, "Ashley."

"Tell me you're free, Geoffrey." The slightly manic edge to her voice irritated her. She wasn't that person, wasn't the woman to panic in a crisis, and she'd be damned if she'd start now.

"I'm not on your rotation for five more weeks." He groaned and, in the background, a woman gasped.

Ashley shoved a hand through her hair, little static pops pricking her skin. *Oh, yeah. It was time.* "Things seem to be a bit early this cycle." And there it was again—the wobble in her voice that brought her fear into the open.

"How soon?"

She bit her bottom lip and let herself simply be aware of her body. The vibration in her blood became a steady hum, the need a constant presence, and she knew it was as bad as she feared. *Worse*, her subconscious whispered. She swallowed and pinched the bridge of her nose with trembling fingers. "I'm guessing, since this is the first time this has happened, but based on the way things have happened in the past? I'm thinking I have two, maybe three days at best. Tomorrow at worst. Then it's here."

"I can't get there, my love. It's simply not possible. Prior commitments and all that." He paused. "You could join us here."

"I'm not one of the merry harem," she said quietly. "You know the only reason I do this at all is necessity."

"Sure. Admit it, though. It's been good for both of us."

True, damn him. But she wasn't feeding his ego. "If things change, let me know. Otherwise, I'll manage."

"Be safe, Ashley."

Hanging up, she assessed the bar again. She had to do *something*. If it meant finding a lover among the locals, she would. But he'd have to be strong—strong enough to ensure neither of them would be at risk if one of her clan or kind came after her. Sex would diffuse the call of her epithicas to the men of her kind, but they could still find her if she didn't handle this right.

That could never happen.

Never.

The vehemence of her denial echoed through her so loudly she instinctively shook her head in response.

"Problem, Red?" The question was delivered with quiet indifference.

Her gaze shot across the bar where the largest man from the corner table now stood. The blond Adonis with the air of wicked sin made her heart race, but his aura winked around him for a split second, an aura so dark it shrouded him like a fathomless black hole. Worrisome, but not so much as the fact she hadn't seen him cross the room.

"Oy! Guinness down the way!"

"On the way," she called back without looking at the patron. She couldn't take her gaze off the man across from her. She blindly retrieved a pint glass and began to expertly build the requested stout, managing the building head without trouble.

At her silence, the stranger's eyes darkened, and he slipped onto the only vacant barstool.

Instinct had her backing up a step at his predatory, assessing look. She reclaimed her ground, but with caution, and fumbled with the Guinness tap. At more than four centuries old, she'd spent three and a half of those defending herself from men she'd never loved and never would. Over three centuries she'd been pursued, her freedom dependent on evading her clansmen with every epithicas. All of the time factors and stresses added up to harden her heart where men were concerned, no matter how pretty the man in question might be.

Like this one.

"Problem?" she asked, repeating his question as she slid the Guinness down the slick bar top. Without taking her eyes off the man across from her, she grabbed a cherry from the setup tray and popped the little fruit in her mouth. "The problem is that you're far too pretty for my tastes yet you keep popping up in my line of sight."

He grinned, slow and wicked. "And here I thought a woman like you would have refined 'tastes.' While it's good to know, I'm not a menu item. Play with the boys in the corner if you're looking for some flirtation."

The hairs on her arms stood up. "I don't play with boys, darling. And 'flirtation' is the last thing I'm about." She pulled the cherry stem out of her mouth and held it up for him to witness the double knot she'd tied it into with just her tongue. "I'm very selective when it comes to choosing the man I take to my bed."

"In the interest of seriousness, I'll ask you for your name and a promise."

"Ashley. No promises. Now run along before I change my mind and decide you're my type."

"Good enough. For now." He nodded and moved away from her before she realized she hadn't obtained his name in kind.

Foolish woman.

She watched as he settled into his seat at the table amid the jests and teasing from the younger men. They ended up huddled close together over the table, each of them pretending to watch the game on the screen.

Ashley knew better.

The problem she now faced was greater than the enigma of the man, though. She had limited time to find a bed partner. Having engaged the blond, she couldn't seem to dredge up interest in anyone else. But she'd have to. Her mouth tightened and turned down at the corners in a righteous scowl.

Good luck with that, Ashley.

Chapter 3

Gareth sat quietly, the young assassins teasing him mercilessly over their perception he'd failed to convince the bartender to play bedroom Twister with him despite his assertions he wasn't interested in the bet. He even tossed another fifty euro into the kitty and bought a round of drinks in an attempt to get one of them to make a move on the woman. He wanted to see her reaction, take her measure and determine exactly what he was dealing with. Moreover, he wanted to take the focus off him and the change in his behaviors. Time passed and the woman, Ashley, avoided the table, leaving glasses empty as she kept well away from Gareth.

Deep in their cups and wrapped up in questionable boasts and a few outright lies regarding their virility, his men hardly paid him any mind as he gathered his belongings. Nothing could have changed his sudden intent to return to the keep. The interaction with the woman had left Gareth off-center and slightly nauseous, like something moved inside him without his permission. As he worked his way to the front door, he asked familiar faces about her and was surprised to find no one knew much beyond her name with any certainty. Several had crude nicknames for her based on some of the same physical attributes he'd admired, but he wouldn't ever address her by such. Then, on the literal threshold of leaving the pub, he ran into a bit of luck. The young barmaid, a lass who had a bit of a thing for him, pushed on the vestibule door at the same time he pulled it open. She stumbled inside leaving Gareth the choice to let her fall or catch her. Grabbing her by the shirt-clad arms, he set her on her feet and smiled with as much charm as he could muster.

She fluffed her hair, arched her back to present her breasts like twin trophies and attempted to offer a pretty pout.

Gareth offered her a small smile. "Siobhan, how are you tonight?"

"Right as rain, love." Reaching forward, she attempted to lay a hand against his chest. "What has you in a hurry to step into the squall tonight? It's much warmer—more welcoming—inside. I assure you."

The smell of secondhand smoke laced through her hair and clothes was overbearing. "Nothing worth fretting over, but I'll thank you for your concern." Dropping her arm, he stepped out of reach. "I've a favor if you don't mind."

Her dark eyes brightened. "Anything."

"What do you know of the bartender?"

The interest in her eyes extinguished. "What's it to you?"

Ah, jealousy. Such a pain in the arse. "She's running a tab for me for the boys tonight. I'd like to pay her square come tomorrow, but I need to know she'll be fair about it." It was an outright lie, but he had no hope of ever reaching the fertile, peaceful lands of Tir na nÓg. He was bound for the Shadow Realm and the Well of Souls, and he knew it. One lie would neither suspend nor hasten his arrival.

"You must think I'm thick. Father Francis will have you doing penance for lyin', and rightly so seeing as your tab is with the bar and not the bartender." Siobhan outright scowled at him. "You know I've fancied you, and where I'd have been good to you, Ashley's a right terror of a woman. Runs the bar front and the floor like a dictator, she does. Thinks she's got the right to—"

Ashley.

So she'd given him her real name.

He glanced at the bar and caught her flipping a bottle through the air, catching it and pouring a generous shot for a young man who looked as if his heart had been broken. Ashley talked to him, apparently teasing and flirting in equal measures. The lad slid a coin across the bar, she tucked it in the till and grabbed another glass to join him in a drink. By the time the lad lifted the shot glass to his lips, she'd charmed a smile out of the man. She toasted him, and Gareth read to the words *to freedom* on her lips.

Lucky bloke.

"Ashley what? What's her last name?" Gareth asked, still staring at the woman in question. Siobhan stopped her little tirade long enough he was forced to turn his attention back to her.

Siobhan sighed. "Her last name's Clement." She brushed passed him, her elbow grazing his bare wrist.

Gareth jerked away with a hiss at the burning contact,

and Siobhan glared at him. "Would it cost you so much you can't afford to offer me the courtesy of at least pretending you're not repulsed by me?"

"You're a fine lass," he started, but she waved him off.

"Save it for Ashley. Where I'd have been good to you, charming that frigid bitch will take all the skill you allegedly possess." She stormed away, wrestled into her little apron and shot him a final scathing look before slipping into the raucous crowd to take orders and clear empties.

The first table she hit was that of his boys.

The musicians tuned up and, with a shouted four count, began to play "Rocky Road to Dublin." Boots stomping and hands clapping in time, patrons began to sing along, near raising the roof with their off-key help for The King's Footmen. The musicians took it all in stride. If Guinness flowed like water, then Jameson's created every tributary. The entire village would be sodding drunk before half past eleven tonight and hung over as hell come sunup.

Gareth turned in time to watch Ashley pour all but a drop from a liquor bottle, slide the shot to the customer and then tip the bottle back to her lips. He swore he felt the burn in his throat and the fine fumes that rose in his nose as he watched her throat work to swallow. It was all nonsense, of course. Bottom line, he was craving the solitude of home, and he intended to get there fast as possible.

Catching himself lingering over the sultry sight of her, he forced his feet to carry him to the door, demanded his hands to relax. The words he intended to utter hung in his throat, fighting his desire to squash any interest in the woman at all.

Ashley. Seeing as you work with bottles, I'll be think-

ing of you as my personal genie, love. I intend to bring us to an agreement that affords me my three wishes— your species, your intention and your departure date from our fine village.

He licked his lips, experiencing the last of the imagined liquor and the faint tang of salt-tinged sweat. "Ridiculous," he muttered, shoving his hands in his pockets before shouldering the door open against the wind's near gale force. He'd had to use the car park around the corner, and that meant a sobering walk straight into a frigid wind.

"Let it be," he admonished himself, hands shaking wildly as he dug out the key fob for his Porsche 911. Thank both gods and goddesses alike that technology meant he only had to have the key in range for the car to start. If he'd had one more task, even had it only been to feed the key into the ignition? He'd have found himself standing in the same spot come morning.

Settled inside the driver's seat, he flicked the vented air away from his skin and then cranked up the heater. Hands numb, he cupped his palms and, without a second thought, whispered the one word of comfort he'd managed to retain. *"Ignis."* Fire.

The fingers on both hands cracked and blistered where the flame touched. Blood ran frigid but free. His focus fractured. All he could manage was to stare through the rain-splattered windshield into the unforgiving darkness. He coveted warmth the way an addict craved their next fix. It wasn't lost on him that, as the keeper of the element of fire, the flame he'd called should have come to him as it always had. Before his death, heat had always been to him something as familiar as a lover's caress, words whispered across the darkness, promises made, opportunities taken. Now it was a stranger to him, and he felt its absence more acutely than a sailor unable to find the North Star on a clear night.

A powerful gust of wind slammed into the car's ultralow profile, striking metal and fiberglass hard enough to have the wide-bodied machine rock on its shocks. Shifting his attention to the dash's muted glow, Gareth rested his least abused fingertips on the wheel. Whether he thought to steady the car or himself, he didn't know. Both needed something he didn't feel qualified to give. Not anymore. But to give up was to accept death with open arms, and that—the ultimate end man simply labeled *death* because he didn't know the truth of its horrors—would be here for him soon enough.

Sitting there protected from the ragged downpour but still blinded by sheet after sheet of rain, the truth became the only thing he could see with any clarity at all.

The goddess queen would come for him and would find him simply by waiting for his soul's collection, not unlike an egg in a hen's nest.

"I've nothing left." He closed his eyes. "No fight. Not anymore."

A leaden blanket of shame settled around his shoulders.

The oppressive darkness grew heavier by the second. His breath was just warm enough to fog the car's windows and block his view. He panicked. Failing to truly call his element had wrecked him. It had barely flickered to life, damaging his hands for the first time, his skin too cold to handle the tail of the flame.

Memories rushed him, memories he hadn't been able to shake since he'd returned to life in October.

She came at him on the cliff side, blade raised, a goddess bent on the possession of a fine woman—a woman his brother by choice would call his own. To fight back

*would be to kill her. It would cost his brother every-
thing he'd never thought to find let alone to possess,
namely love.*

So there would be—could be—no fight.

*He braced and took the blade. With force and fury
greater than any torment he'd suffered, the goddess-
wielded blade ran him through, piercing and shredding
and ripping. Darkness webbed across his vision. Sight
fractured.*

*A coppery tang coated his mouth, his throat, and he
choked.*

*He tried to scream. Pain like he'd never known, could
never have imagined, rendered him mute.*

*Not within his head, though. Gods, not within his
head. His scream ripped through his skull as his heart
rate slowed, his blood cooling. He knew it was the end,
heard the waves crashing against the cliffs, felt their
fading reverberation through limbs grown lethargic.*

*Startling in its suddenness, sunlight winked out and
darkness pulled at him with such force his bones shattered like fine crystal hurled against a stone wall.*

Pain burned along every nerve.

*His scream echoed....and echoed...and echoed. All
in his mind.*

*But there was no one to hear him. This was a solo
trip. The magnitude of his isolation, his desolation,
raked at his soul.*

*Shards of cold shredded his skin until it hung in tat-
ters.*

He didn't bleed.

Dead men don't.

He knew it was the end.

*Pressure gave way to a temporary vacuum, his legs,
his arms, his spine—all broken. Entirely useless.*

Fear choked him, stealing the last of his will. He continued to fall, his body indefensible, his sense of self splintering.

His heart stopped, and the vast depth of the silence inside him created a terror unlike anything he'd ever known.

The darkness began to gain weight, to possess a malicious awareness of him. In the heart of his growing horror, a presence began to form.

His body slammed into the ground. Cold seeped through him and his skin cracked, reformed and cracked again. And again. And again. The cycle sped even as the fissures deepened, skin to muscle to bone.

He opened his mouth and cried out, the horror of his reality skating across his mind on the finest of blades.

A face, both hideous and desirable, parted the mist above him as it moved into view. Macha, the Goddess of Phantoms and War, loomed over him. She didn't bother to hide her vicious delight. "Welcome to the Well of Souls, Gareth Brennan."

She swept low, gripped his hair and canted his head back at an entirely unnatural angle. Cold lips pressed against his, peeling skin away when the contact was broken. Then she produced a metal discus with the Ogham Idad on it. She blew across the face of the piece, smiled down at him and then slammed it into the pad of muscle over his heart.

Skin froze, burned, blackened and flaked off, the metal welding to bone.

Gareth roared with a combination of pain and fury. She'd...branded him?

Bones healed with supernatural speed only to afford the cold the opportunity to break them over and over, as thoroughly as that same cold ravaged his skin, his muscle, his organs.

The goddess gripped him by the throat then and lifted him, holding him at arm's length. "You are forever mine, but your service only begins here. Where my sister failed to release her brethren, I won't. You'll be my tool, my sword arm for eternity. With you as the head of my immortal army, I will release my brothers and sisters and retake every realm."

It turned out the Druidic belief that Tir na nÓg awaited all warriors was a lie.

In the heart of eternity was eternal pain and terror. Nothing more.

A clap of thunder sounded, the sharp sound shocking him out of the memory-induced numbness. He caught the sight of his eyes, wide and panicked, in the rearview mirror. In the ambient dash light, his lips were blue.

Digging through the glove box, he retrieved a pair of driving gloves and sheathed his hands. Then he stumbled from the car and turned toward the pub, the only thought he could grasp was that the woman, the bartender, the woman he'd dubbed "Ash," had generated a warmth that permeated his bones. It suddenly didn't matter what she was, what her intent was. He needed that warmth, needed that affirmation of life in the absence of his own and the damage done to his hands by his element.

He'd never been weak, never been afraid, never been one to avoid a fight. As Regent, he was more likely to seek trouble out, to get to the heart of the matter and eradicate whatever conflict existed by any means necessary. The Druidic race counted on his efficient brutality just as much as his brothers in service counted on him to retain the dregs of who he'd been as a younger man—the fun-loving lad with the sharp wit and quick smile. It had been a balance all these years, one he'd managed. No longer. His control was gone, stolen by the queen's hand.

Dissatisfaction raced through his veins. Every second brought Beltane closer, and what did he do? Sit here waiting. He thumped his head against the headrest. There was more to life than this, more to living than waiting to die.

"Not for me," he whispered, letting his eyes drift shut. "Never again for me."

The music swelled, rallying the patrons. Ashley took orders and slung drinks as fast as she could. Tables were moved aside and an impromptu dance floor was created. Drunken customers spun wildly about the floor in traditional Irish dances, some in pairs and others stepping out alone.

There shouldn't have been time to consider the strange interaction with the unknown man who, for all intents and purposes, appeared to be the leader of the group of young men still collected in the corner booth. For all that, she couldn't get her mind off him. Twice different men from the table had hailed her, but there wasn't time to answer their summons or put down their flirtation as more than juvenile. She'd glanced around, looking for the men's leader as they each retreated, but she couldn't find him. The crowd seemed to have swallowed him. Or he'd left. Dangerous, that absence, given his air of malice as well as his aura's pitch-black, densely saturated depth.

She shivered. A man didn't develop an aura like that from doing good works in life. Not even close. Someone as marked as he was had to have a violent history, a past that would likely keep her—*her*—up at night. His hands, scarred and broad, had been strong and capable, his body even more so. The air of subtle menace that surrounded him, giving depth and substance to his aura, said he had killed before—must have—and wouldn't hesitate to do so again if necessary. That subtlety was far more terrifying than overt aggression. He was a predator who would slit a man's throat between breaths and disappear into the night.

"Don't be a fool," she muttered to herself. "You served him a drink. You watched him across the room. That hardly a killer makes."

But the truth was there in his very presence, his persona, his command of the men at the table. He was Other, had acknowledged her as such and was currently invisible to her searching gaze.

A plan took root, began to form—one that was wild and reckless and measured by levels of desperation. Hers. If the man was as wicked as all that, he could well be the one to see her through her triennial fertility cycle, to keep her safe should the proverbial wolf end up at her door. Would he use that violence to her advantage? Could she convince him to give up a week of his life, maybe a bit more, and commit to staying with her until the worst of it had passed? She could move on then, *would* move on so as to leave no trace of her extended stay here in the village. She took it to extremes to ensure she always stayed two steps ahead of the men of her clan who would seek to call her their own and to hell with her preferences.

She'd get through this cycle and leave not only the *county* but the *country*. Maybe she'd try Wales this time. She could settle in a little village deep in the mountains and make some sort of life until it was time to see Geoffrey and, once again, move on.

But that was years away. This epithicas had to be addressed sooner, not later.

Siobhan, the barmaid, flounced up to the bar's edge and glared at Ashley. "The table in the corner is asking for a round of Jameson's and three pints of Smithwick's."

Ashley ignored the girl's attitude, searching the table again under the pretense of counting out the number of shot glasses needed.

"Eleven," Siobhan snapped. "There are eleven men."

"Seems they're missing the leader of their merry little band," Ashley said with as much indifference as she could summon.

"He left," the girl snapped, flipping her hair over her shoulder. "I'll warn you to keep your hands off that one."

Ashley sighed. "Yeah? And why is that? You involved with him?"

Siobhan narrowed her eyes and Ashley caught her intent before she ducked under the pass-through and tried to use her rounded frame to intimidate Ashley's height. "You know, Ashley, you're a real bitch. I've had my eye on Gareth for more than a year. Keep away from him."

Ashley leaned down and went nose to nose with the girl, ignoring the way her face paled and her toxic breath came in short, panted bursts. "Listen, you gurrier. I'm only going to say this once." *Again.* "You want a man? You claim him. I won't touch him. But if you think you can bop around here like a loose bit, stamping your claim on every good-looking man to pass through the door? You've another think coming, Siobhan." *From me.* "Trust it will be as far from pleasant as East is from West." Rising, she twisted her hair up into a loose knot and stabbed it through with long stir sticks to hold it in place. Then she grabbed the girl's serving tray and loaded it with twelve shot glasses and three pints. She poured the order and, slapping her bar towel down, called to the kitchen. "Fergus! Man the bar, yeah?" Then she focused on Siobhan. "And you? *Tóg go bog é.*" Calm down.

Slamming the pass-through up, she stormed around the bar end. Her epithicas fueled her already volatile temper and heated her blood to the point a flush spread over her skin. She wove through the dancers and approached the table of men. But the man she sought, Gareth, wasn't there.

One of the young men, a tall, perfect specimen of attractiveness with an undertone of violence she had to admire, stood. "Well, and if it isn't our favorite bartender in County Clare."

She let a seductive, suggestive smile spread over her face, forcing it to reach her eyes. "That the best you can do, lad? I'm a bit disappointed. I'd have thought Gareth would've taught you better than to use lame pickup lines on a woman who's in the profession to have heard them all."

He blinked owlishly.

"A bartender," she said on a laugh. "Nothing more, ye bowsie."

He blushed as the other men laughed and poked fun at him.

With deft experience, she slid drinks across the table, found homes for the Smithwick's they'd ordered and picked up the twelfth shot glass. "Gareth?"

A dark-haired young man leaned back, considering her as he ran a fingertip around the rim of his shot glass. "He left a good half hour ago, love."

Her stomach tightened, her breath hanging up in her chest. *Gone.* She'd have to go with an alternate male.

The clinical part of her mind began to assess the men in front of her even as her phoenix rebelled. Loudly.

"Sure and there's one of us as would love to give you a spin…" His grin widened. "Around the floor, of course."

Ashley reached out and slipped his shot from under his fingertip and tossed it back. "The least you can do is buy me a drink before you proposition me." *Who to choose?* Would one of these younger men be willing to defend her if she was found and incapable of defending herself?

The memory of Gareth's hands came back to her, their calloused appearance an indicator of strength. She glanced at the younger man's hands.

Smooth.

Not one of these men would be sufficient. They weren't Gareth, and both her mind and body craved him.

A swift swipe and she picked up the extra shot she'd poured in the hopes of cornering Gareth. Slamming it back, she flipped the glass over and set it top down. "I've a bit of an issue to take up with him. How's the best way to get in touch with him?"

To a man they went still, each doing their best to appear nonchalant and failing so miserably she almost pitied them.

Younger than I thought.

She crossed her arms over her chest and, one by one, gave them a cool stare. "C'mon, boys. How do I reach him?"

"I'll deliver a message," the dark-haired man muttered, his tone laced with disappointment.

"While I appreciate the offer, that's not what I asked for," she countered.

"Repeat the question, would you? I was out of earshot." The chill of his breath skated across the shell of her ear as he leaned down and spoke to her and her alone. Deep and almost mocking, he pressed on. "And now you seem to have taken a shot poured for me. I'll cover the cost out of admiration for your bravado. Once."

Every cell in Ashley's body threatened to divide. Half demanded she take flight and run *from* him; half demanded she turn and run *to* him. The thunderous beat of her heart was like a heavy metal band's kick drum on a fast track. Her pulse hammered savagely at every pulse point. Heat washed through her. She closed her eyes and reveled. No man had ever affected her so physically, rendered her so full of wanting with so few words, and disdainful ones at that. She shouldn't want a man like this, not even in her epithicas. It was the equivalent of losing herself, so similar to falling into a life of obscurity as one of a handful of wives, never cherished, never the one thing a man would give anything for. If she couldn't have that, she didn't want any of it. She'd watched that neglect drive her mother to Final Death when she failed to ever "breed" for her father again. No, that was no life for her.

This couldn't be the man to see her through her epithicas. That half of her that demanded she take flight had her taking her first step away from him.

"I wouldn't," he said below the close of an Irish ballad.

"I..."

"Want to dance," Gareth finished for her.

"No. I—"

He spun her round and pulled her into his body, nostrils flaring on contact. The King's Footmen took up a traditional Irish reel. One hand on her hip, he pulled her closer still and took her hand...within his gloved hand. Eyes tight at the corners, he said nothing.

"New style, leaving your gloves on when you shed your coat?" Trying for flippant, the question emerged far closer to breathless as he spun her across the floor in time with the other dancers. His steps and spins were smooth, polished, as if he'd either been formally taught or had danced a thousand and more jigs and reels in his time.

Gareth didn't answer her, simply spun her faster as the piece took up a more frenetic pace. Holding her hand, he moved to her side and, in time, they began a step dance that had others clearing the floor and cheering them on.

Caught in Gareth's grasp, Ashley did the only thing she could think to do.

She danced.

Chapter 4

Gareth ignored the pain in his damaged, gloved hands as he held on to Ashley. She gripped him tightly in return, having made no more comment than to question him about his new fashion accessory. That suited him just… No. No, it didn't suit him "fine." It didn't suit him at all. He wanted to touch her, skin to skin. How she chased the goddess's chill away defied logic. And he didn't care.

The music sped up, the pace ever faster, and he had to focus to keep up.

As if her body had heard his unspoken request, the point of connection between them heated, seeping through his palm, up his arm and into his shoulder. Sensation trilled through him.

Warmth. True warmth.

Gods, he'd missed it. Having that comfort now, he wanted more. And what he wanted, he typically made sure he got.

Twirling her out and then back, he stepped into the move at the last moment so she didn't have time to adjust her trajectory or stop her forward motion. Their bodies collided. He wrapped an arm around her trim waist and anchored her against him. Despite his heavy sweater and worn denim, the woman's heat all but seared him.

Ashley's chin snapped up and she gasped. Her breath was sweet and sharp on the heels of the whiskey shot she'd taken with the brokenhearted lad. She was a heady mix of alcohol's influence and natural sultriness. The combination speared through him, the sensations so sharp he had to wonder if the gods hadn't shown mercy on him and manipulated the experience to fit his preferences.

He knew better. The gods had abandoned him.

Gareth forced the bitterness away, focusing instead on drinking in Ashley's gift. He fought to keep up with the dance versus simply holding her tight against his body. Reflexively, he tightened his grip. She didn't even flinch. Whatever she was, she could handle at least his rudimentary strength. Or what was left of it.

Good to know.

Crossing their hands, he twisted her around in his embrace under the guise of the dance. He knew better. And from her quick glance over her shoulder when he pulled her against him, her back melding to his front, so did she.

He directed her across the floor, modifying the dance so she was in front of him rather than to his side.

She never missed a beat.

Apparently invasive by nature, her body temperature bled deeper into him, and he missed a step as his element surged toward her. He forced it back. The last thing he needed to do was burn her. Or reveal his gift in front of a roomful of locals who already thought him odd, no matter the respect with which they treated him. It would draw unnecessary attention.

None of the assassins or tyros needed the extra challenge of wiping memories years before it was time. The Elders were the ones to perform that general spell every six years, the spell that made locals forget their faces. It was the only way the Assassin's Arcanum, the assassins and the rotation of trainees could stay in one place across the centuries.

"You're lagging," Ashley called back, reclaiming the whole of his focus. "A man of your stature should be able to dance circles around a common bartender."

He stopped her still in the middle of the floor and leaned forward, his breath against her hair. "Is that so?"

She turned in his arms, the movement slow, almost wary. "So it would seem."

He bent forward, into her space, their noses almost touching. Something elemental sparked in her gaze, something that looked like desire. His heart skipped a beat, and his voice dropped low, emerged gruff. "Let me assure you, *bean álainn*, nothing is what it seems." He'd called her a beautiful woman. And he'd meant it.

Her eyes widened at the endearment. Obviously, she had the Irish. Reaching up, she tucked a strand of hair behind his ear, then cupped his cheek. "Nothing? I'll ask you to prove it."

He grinned. "Oh, I will."

Several wolf whistles sounded, and she startled.

He didn't give her a chance to balk.

Without forecasting his intent, he whipped her out to the end of his grasp, their arms extended. When she would have spun back to him, he twirled her again and landed her at his side. Glancing her way, he was thrilled to find a flush riding high on her cheeks. She was the picture of health, the epitome of beauty, the manifestation of his most vivid dreams. A deep well of craving opened in him, a well he'd believed capped and closed. Not so. Not if the burgeoning hunger he had for her was authentic, not manufactured. The thought irritated him. "Are you a siren, love, because you're doing things to me that defy nature."

She tipped her chin up and laughed. "And have I sung to you then that I don't remember?"

His grin returned, wider than before. "No."

Her eyes met his, the amusement in them clear. "There's your answer, then. A siren I'm not."

"A seductress for sure," he murmured.

Something odd passed through her gaze, but her smile never faltered. "Only under the waxing moon every thirty-sixth month."

"Smart-ass," he teased. She started to respond, but he gave a short shake of his head. "Step dance in three, two, one." Gareth started the traditional dance, setting a rapid pace.

Ashley watched for a moment and then picked up his rhythm, matching him move for move. She followed his lead beautifully, increasing her speed as The King's Footmen sped up the tempo.

Gareth's heart thundered in his chest, and he wondered briefly if the band was trying to kill him. It seemed possible given that they kicked the tempo up a third time.

Ashley laughed again, the sound rich and full.

Sparing her a glance, Gareth found a faint sheen of sweat covering her rosy skin. Her hair seemed to crackle. Her face was more radiant, her lips fuller.

The music stopped abruptly and the crowd's raucous cheer nearly raised the roof. Gareth glanced over to gauge Ash's reaction. For the first time he could re-call, he gaped.

If a being could radiate robustness of, and for, life, she did. Her skin positively glowed. A faint sheen of sweat dotted her nape, and stray short curls stuck to her skin while longer strands that had come loose during their dance hung past her shoulders. Hazel eyes had taken on a burnished bronze shine. Her smile was infectious, particularly when she took a flamboyant bow and then threw her head back and laughed. Her voice was capti-vating. Lyrical. She was, in a word, radiant.

She grinned wider before taking another flamboy-ant bow.

As she rose, Gareth pulled her into his body and, without a thought beyond the need to taste those deca-dent lips, kissed her.

She kissed him back.

It was short and swift, and it wasn't enough. Might not ever *be* enough. Not if the buzz that raced through his veins was an indication of what this woman did to him. No one had ever affected him like this. Never had a woman left him so on edge with wanting, so hungry for her he felt like a starved man given an all-he-could-eat token to the richest buffet in the country. She was vibrant. Spirited. Vivacious. And he wanted her with a desperation he'd never known.

She met his stare and the merriment in her eyes soft-ened. Retrieving her hand, she offered a small curtsy and an almost conscientious smile. "I suppose I should thank you."

"For?" he asked, voice a bit churlish, his heartbeat tattooing a rapid-fire rhythm against his rib cage—and it had nothing to do with exertion. The wound forever frozen on his side burned from the heat rolling off her.

One thin shoulder lifted casually, and she seemed to struggle to hold his gaze. "I didn't realize I needed to let off a little steam."

Gareth stepped into her space. Dancers began to spin around them with the band's next set. She smelled of warm grass, sunshine and fresh earth. Like comfort. A refuge. Like home.

Taking a loose curl between his gloved fingers, he suddenly resented the separation between them. He wanted to feel the silk of her hair. With infinite gentleness, he tucked the curl behind her ear and uttered the only words that came to mind as she gazed up at him in undisguised confusion. "Take me home tonight, Ash."

"Man the bar!"

The words cut through the din and sliced through the music.

Ashley glanced over her shoulder at Fergus, the bar's giant of an owner, before again meeting Gareth's direct stare. "I have to finish my shift."

Blood thrummed through his veins. "That's not a denial."

"Neither is it acquiescence," she retorted.

Gareth reached out and dragged a finger down her neck. "I'll only keep asking until you say yes."

"Persistent." She eyed him carefully. "Care to own your heritage?"

He blinked slowly, surprised at her brazenness. Most Others were far more inclined to pass each other by giving a wide berth and an averted stare, particularly in these parts where the assassins were suspected to reside. But if she wanted to play it straight, he could check off the first of his three wishes—discovering her species. "I'll show you mine when you show me yours."

She leaned into him and the smell of sunshine and

dry heat intensified. "Clever man. I suppose closing time will provide us both the answer I've not yet decided on. Stay if you will."

Spinning on her heel, she strode across the pub, slipped behind the bar and returned to working the sticks and tossing bottles without pause.

Gareth stole a look at his watch.

Midnight.

Two hours to kill.

The common vernacular stung, but he shrugged it off. Killing time wasn't what had earned him his damnation.

Still, it was too much time to waste on a maybe. He might not even be able to touch her without excruciating pain. Except for the warmth she'd infused him with...

One last glance at the bar and his mind was decided. He would stay. Ashley could be the only chance he had for skin-to-skin contact without excruciating pain before he was returned to the Shadow Realm and the Well of Souls. And just once more before the goddess returned for him, Gareth wanted to know warmth. If the woman behind the bar was truly his last chance? If she could give him the chance to find even a moment's peace before an eternity of torment? There was nothing he wouldn't do, no mountain he wouldn't move, no army he wouldn't slay, no sin he wouldn't commit. And he would do any of it, *all* of it, without batting an eye. After all, he was already damned, a dead man.

There was nothing left to lose, only a warm woman to gain.

The clock's hour hand rested well past 2:00 a.m. when Ashley finally closed and locked the bar door. Talented as they were as a whole, each man in The King's Footmen was quite certain he posed a far better catch than any of the others. They'd come on to her individually, each going so far as to offer her the moon and the stars. The lead singer and guitar player had even written her an impromptu little ditty, but she'd been firm. No sex with anyone professionally affiliated with the bar. She didn't fish from the work pool. It complicated things when the affair ended, and, with her, it would always end. Nothing good lasted in her vagabond lifestyle.

The fiddler, with his windswept hair and broad shoulders, that strong jaw and eyes as green as the fields, might have tempted her to break her rule. But the musician's wild appeal couldn't compete with the man who'd ignited her need earlier that evening.

Gareth Brennan.

He'd only offered his first name. It had taken little more than a couple of well-placed questions to discover his surname. Odd that no one knew much about him. He'd seemed a rather amiable fellow, popular with the ladies and well liked by the gents. His reputation at snooker and traditional pool had her itching to pit her skills against his, though it seemed unlikely the opportunity would present itself. Apparently he hadn't been out and about much over the last few months. Shame, that. Her pride could have used the boost of beating him at his own game.

But wasn't that exactly what this was? A game? At least to him. He was intent on seducing her, convincing her to spend the night with him.

As for her? She was intent on convincing him to spend at least the next week with her. So who was beating whom here?

She snorted as she dug out the wide dust mop, broom and dustbin. Her pride would stick this out for the win, willing to take a beating before it bowed out. Always. Such was the curse of most phoenixes. Winning equaled dominance, dominance equaled power and power was everything.

Cleaning the last of the peanut hulls out from under the bar, she repositioned the stools and dumped the pan in the bin. One final polish of the bar and she was finished. The weighted knowledge she'd be back here within hours, stocking the bar and checking kegs and bottles to make sure everything was ready for another go round, had her sighing with exhaustion. She needed to go home, needed to sleep—as much as she could possibly get.

The kitchen door whacked the wall as Fergus shoved his way through. Grease-stained apron hanging loose around his neck, he stomped across the rough-hewn oak floor on feet so large they were more suited to a draft horse than a man.

"For the love of all the gods, Fergus, spare a soul the unnecessary fright of seeing you emerge from your cooking cubby like a raging bull," she snapped, exhaustion making her words sharper than usual. "You take a decade off my life every time you blow through that door and I don't know you're still here."

"You'd have been wise to pay more attention over the last three months," he groused. Stopping at the obscured door tucked around a blind corner, he pulled a set of keys and rifled through them. "Seeing as I live here, it shouldn't shock you so that I come from the kitchen to go upstairs *every night*."

"Smart-ass. It's not that you emerge from the kitchen, it's that you do so like a Pamplonian bull with the gleam of death in his eye. I'm never sure whether to run or... run." She shrugged and grinned.

He grunted, the sound as close to a laugh as he ever issued. "Beyond your impromptu Riverdance, I both saw and heard you toyed with Gareth Brennan tonight."

Her mouth worked like a landed trout's—open, close...open, close—before she finally sputtered, "'Heard?' How in the hell could you have *heard* anything? You never leave the kitchen."

"So you did." He gave a short nod. "It would be humane—" he sneered the word "—to warn you to be wary of that one. Used to be as he was a fun sort, the type that both silly girls and jaded women alike took to like a hummingbird does nectar. Something's changed him, though, and recent-like. But two issues impede my warning. First, I'm no' *humane*. I could give a rat's ass what happens to you that doesna benefit me and mine. Second, it's never wise to get wrapped up with someone else's problems when you've plenty of your own."

Fear skipped down her spine faster than the denial passed through her lips. "I don't know what you're talking—"

"Sure and you don't." He stared over her shoulder, focusing on something so tangible she felt that the "thing" he stared at could only be hovering inches behind her. The sensation intensified until, casting pride aside, she had to turn, to look.

There was nothing—and no one—there.

It took her a moment to work up the nerve to face her boss. Stiff shouldered, tendons corded in his neck, a ruddy flush to his skin, the warning to stay away from the new male... Fergus knew something. His scent shifted, and suddenly she was surrounded by the wildness of the Burren, that alien landscape strewed with dolmen, ocean squalls and scrubby little wildflowers. Sea salt would have glazed her skin had she stood still long enough. Luckily, she never stood still.

Moving a bit farther out of reach under the guise of returning her cleaning supplies to the cupboard, she called over her shoulder, "Where's this oddity coming from, Fergus?"

"It would be none so odd if you'd been paying me the attention I'm due. You and your kind have always had a superiority complex, thinking your ability to resurrect is your right."

She froze. *You and your kind... Resurrect is your right...* He knew what she was. "How?" she wheezed.

"Your scent changed tonight after Brennan arrived."

Studying him in the reflection of the bar mirror, she watched as something not unlike a rolling black-and-white television channel skipped across his appearance. He showed himself as one thing for fourteen of every fifteen seconds, but that one, lone second that rounded out every quarter minute? That one blip? Fergus became something Other.

Hunching forward, he folded in on himself before rising. When he finally stood as straight as he could, he was so tall he had to cant his head to the side to avoid bumping the ceiling rafters. His temple brushed the iron chandelier and set it swinging. He reached to still it with a hand that now sported a palm the size of her dead drink tray.

She couldn't get her mind around what she saw and understood to be true. Both magnificent and terrifying, Fergus had changed. With a sheet of hair as brilliant as a new star and eyes that blazed a myriad of crystalline colors, skin that shone with a diamond hue and hands the size of dinner plates, she couldn't look away. Legend said that the last of the genii—giants who could change their appearance and proportion at will—had faded, passing to the afterlife centuries ago. But that couldn't be true. Not if what Fergus presented was a fleeting image of his true nature. And if that was the case...

Years of education rolled through her mind, flipping faster and faster as she tried to recall what it was the genii wanted with the phoenix. What was it that had rendered them friend or foe? It had all centered around one thing. What had it been? Somehow, it involved dice. Or a card game.

"Confused, little phoenix?" He huffed out a sound of genuine disdain. "I expected better of you. Turns out you're nothing but a stupid bitch in heat. However, your cycle changes my time frame. It saves me having to pay the male I located. They've been looking for you, you know. This saves me having to defend my rights against any of the men of your clan should one or more of them respond to the gods-be-damned scent of you. The timing isn't perfect, but it'll be what it is."

Ashley kept her gaze loosely focused, trying to take in everything around her that she could, certain she needed to find her way out of this mess before she was forced to fight her way out. But... "You called me a bitch. Do it again and I'll be calling you a hearse."

Fight it was.

That's when she remembered the connecting pieces of history.

Their king had made a last stand in the final Tribal Wars, and he'd lost. Desperate, he'd challenged Daghda, the All Father, to a game of dice. Daghda had declined, asserting his right to dissolve the band of giants. The giants' king, with nothing left to barter, wagered the giants' immortality against the god's ability to beat him in the game of Daghda's choosing.

What. An. Idiot.

Daghda chose archery, and the genii's king lost. Badly. In a final stand that had been recorded in the blood of the fallen, the last of the giants had disappeared. Only their legend remained. Those rumored to have survived had been rendered mortal, their lifespans still far greater than a human but shortened all the same. So what could a genii want from a phoenix who had to be less than half his age…

Ashes.

Horror stole over her and her skin felt as if it shrank.

A female phoenix's ashes were the key to immortality if a being knew how to harvest them. To get to the point of harvest typically involved murder and theft—of the phoenix's life and ashes, respectively.

To kill any phoenix was nearly impossible, but the females were far more difficult to dispense than the males. Few knew the secret to forcing a member of the secretive race into irrevocable death. The phoenix had to take her life by removing her own heart. Once that happened, the heart had to be burned to ash. Those ashes could then be harvested. If a mortal tattooed her ashes over his own heart in the constellation symbol for the phoenix? The phoenix's immortality transferred to the mortal and gave him what so many coveted. Immortality.

She had to get out of here. Now.

Ashley shot him a hard, hot look. "Timing?" Her smile was brittle. She'd expected to defend herself from her own tribe, not a damn *genii*. "Your timing sucks. I have a date tonight."

"Whore."

"Screw you and the hearse you're about to ride out on."

He rocked forward on the balls of his feet, arms loose, body ready. "I'll take that which is my due."

"Due? The only ones 'due' anything are the gods, and even their claims are debatable. You? You're not even a minor deity in my handy little Book of Mythologies and Verses, so back the hell off." She raised her hands in front of her, not in fear but to widen the fan of flames that ran from her elbows to her fingertips.

"I've hunted your kind for more than six centuries, aging a fraction every day as I sought to reclaim that which my father lost. I will return to the throne and see the genii recognized as the force they were meant to be."

"Return to *what* throne? And whom do you truly think to rule? Your shadow? There aren't enough of you to reestablish any type of kingdom without serious inbreeding."

He only stared at her.

How the hell had she missed the fact Fergus was Other? She'd been a fool.

Shaking her head, she took one step aside, angling to get a better line on the front door. *Distract him.* "You're sick and sodding mad to boot."

That gave him pause, and he stopped to consider her. "I'll draw together all those left, those Daghda abandoned, and I will see a new reign challenge the way of things."

Ashley arched a brow. "I'm almost sorry about this, Fergus."

The genii's heavy brow furrowed. "Sorry that I'll take your life?"

"No," she said softly, her voice fading behind the wall of flames that erupted around her. "Sorry that I'll be taking yours."

Chapter 5

Gareth sat in his car, having moved it across the road from the pub's front door. The hours passed and, finally, as the last patrons trickled out the front lights were turned off. Ungloving his hands, he found they had generally healed, but the cold persisted, an ache within him that simply refused to give quarter. He fought the need to lash out, to beat against the heavens' doors, to deliver equivalent pain to those who saw fit to punish him in kind. None of it was possible, yet he believed it would happen. It had to.

Shoving free of the low-slung vehicle, his need to control *something* choked him. He rose and stumbled into the wild weather, raised his hands to the sky. *"Ignis, I praecipio vobis!"* Fire, I command you. So close to death and separation from the gods he'd served for centuries, they wouldn't deny him this, surely.

Flames he still possessed, flames as familiar to him

as his reflection, hissed in the torrential downpour, flickering erratically but refusing to wink out. He shook with the effort to control his element. Only the faintest blue of the flame he'd summoned clung to his skin, hovering in the cup of each palm with a tension that superseded the force created by the storm.

Then the tenor of the storm shifted. Rain turned to sleet, pellets of ice sliding down the neck of Gareth's shirt. The flame he'd called winked out in the face of nature's onslaught. Gods, he resented the cold.

Without warning, the pub door flew open. Watery light spilled into the darkness and battled it back.

Wide-eyed and moving at nearly inhuman speed, Ashley followed. Her hair whipped around her, seeming to crackle and writhe. Backlit as she was, a faint nimbus built around her until, magnified by her fury, it brightened and blazed wildly.

For a moment it had appeared she was on fire. Gareth blinked and shook his head to clear his vision.

It was the bar. The *bar* was on fire.

Still looking over her shoulder as she ran, Ashley plowed into him at full speed. Instinct dictated his response. Gareth caught her, hoping to steady the both of them, but her hit was brick-house solid. He grabbed her biceps and down they went, falling into a heap of tangled limbs, shouted curses and pelting rain.

They both hissed at the skin-to-skin contact, and Gareth's first thought was that he'd burned her with his bitterly cold hands. He let her go and rolled to his feet, shocked to see her skin was clear.

Thank the gods.

An unholy roar erupted from within the bar and something enormous moved.

Sirens sounded in the distance.

Gareth grabbed Ash by the hand, ignoring the pain in his own, and yanked her to her feet. "What the hell happened?"

"Genii," she said, breathing hard. "Have to—damn! My backpack!"

She started for the bar and Gareth grabbed her round the waist, hauling her against his side. "If you pissed the genii off that bad and *then* lit his bar on fire? We need to go. *Now.*"

"My life is in that pack! I have to go back!"

Just then, an enormous fist plowed a hole through the side of the bar building.

Ignoring her efforts to fight free, Gareth curled his body around hers to shield her from the plaster and debris falling around them. The genii was pissed, and bad things tended to happen when geniis lost their tempers.

He yanked the passenger door of his car open and dumped her unceremoniously inside with a barked order, "Buckle up!"

Ignoring the odd sensations winding through his system, he raced to the driver's side, jumped in and sped away from the curb, engine roaring.

"What the hell happened?" he shouted, the glow of the fire lighting up his rearview mirror.

"Fergus..." She looked over her shoulder. "Gods, he's not a man."

Gareth's brow furrowed. "You thought—"

"And why wouldn't I?" she demanded. "He's been nothing but a bar owner and fry cook since I've known him. Nothing said he was a..." She snapped her mouth shut, her lips forming a surgically precise line across her lower face.

"A what, Ash?" Gareth pressed. He needed to know how much she knew, how Other she was.

"You ask what Fergus was when you've already referred to what he was." She glanced back once more, gripping the door handle so hard her knuckles appeared skeletal beneath her fine skin. "Is. No, definitely *was*."

The fire had grown to a raging inferno, and the giant had collapsed inside the building. Nothing beyond flames moved inside the bar now. That meant there would be nothing left of him by the time the brigade arrived. No body meant there would be no questions the Arcanum couldn't answer, even if a bit of magickal manipulation was required. Had there been bodies? Or, in this particular case, *a* body? That tended to complicate things.

Gareth quietly considered what little he could be certain of. That certainty was based on that fact that, in all the years the genii had been in County Clare, the creature hadn't behaved rashly or in a manner that would draw unnecessary attention its way. Had he been violent? At times, yes. But the genii had never been reckless in a way that would endanger himself. That meant that, whatever Ashley was, Fergus had wanted her badly enough to give up everything he was to take the woman out.

That decided things.

Retrieving his cell, Gareth dialed the Nest. A young man answered on the second ring. At this point, niceties were obsolete. "This is the Regent. Put the Assassin on."

"Yes, Regent."

Seconds later, Dylan O'Shea's voice came across the line, a trace of humor underlying the man's typically serious nature. "Heard you were finally out for a bit of sport tonight, Gareth. She done with you already?"

"We've got a problem."

Dylan's voice changed in an instant. "Tell me." All

teasing was gone, replaced with a well-earned and accurately described deadly seriousness.

How much to say in front of the woman? Gareth glanced at her and found her staring at him, her slim face paler than a full moon's blaze on a clear night, her eyes wide.

"Assassin?" she asked on a shaky breath.

"You have her with you *and* you're speaking in front of her, Gareth?" Dylan bit out. "There better be a good reason."

No help for it. He'd either have to have this conversation with her in the car or set her on the side of the road. He wanted her warmth more than he wanted privacy, so talk in front of her it was. "Aye. She and Fergus had a wee bit of a mash-up at the pub."

"The genii did what, exactly?" Dylan asked.

"Well, exposed his true nature and apparently threatened her, though I've not got the whole of it out of her yet. But I will," he added harshly, steering with his knee as he raked his fingers through his hair and pushed the wet mass off his face. "End result was that the bar burned down and Fergus with it."

Dylan's silence lasted several heartbeats. "She's Other?"

Gareth glanced at her. "Yes, though I've no more information than that."

The Assassin's curse was long, low and colored the air blue. "You can't bring her here without knowing the danger she poses. Not with Kennedy's lifeline tied to mine. If your woman—"

"I'm aware of that," Gareth said between gritted teeth. "And she's not 'my woman.'"

"She's in your possession, she's yours," Dylan countered.

"And if I'd said the same to you about Kennedy?" he asked so low he hoped Ash didn't hear him.

"I'd have knocked your teeth out," Dylan said, unexpected amusement winding through his words. "But only because I knew they'd grow back."

Gareth huffed out a humorless laugh. "You're a right thicko. I'll hole up tonight and find a way to get her out of the area before I return. We'll need to renegotiate the treaty with the genii as they'll discover I'm the one who drove off with her."

Dylan's silence reined the moment, then he did the unthinkable. "I'm sending Rowan to handle her. If you have to kill the woman—"

"Spare him that." The minimal warmth he'd been able to steal from the brief contact with Ashley fled as if chased by the monsters that haunted him. "I'm already damned, and well you know it."

"I don't accept that."

"I've seen the end, Dylan." The words were barely a breath. "It's inevitable."

"I'm sending Rowan. Until then, keep in mind your limitations," Dylan said quietly. "I won't lose you."

Gareth wordlessly disconnected the call with a swipe of his thumb and dropped the phone in the console. Ash opened her mouth to speak, but he shook his head. "Not right now."

I won't lose you, Dylan had said.

The irony of the statement left Gareth aching with the brutal truth.

He was already lost.

Ashley listened to Gareth's side of the conversation. Most women would have been offended. She'd been thrilled. He had no intent to try to lay claim to her beyond her body. He'd then promised the Assassin—surely not *the* famed Assassin—he'd be spending the night with her tonight.

Bottom line? He was perfect. No commitment issues. No expectations. Strength enough to defend her if her epithicas rendered her unconscious. She didn't think that would be a problem, though. Not if she got sex and, more importantly, orgasm. It would diffuse the hormonal storm building inside her, making her harder to track. And since Gareth had picked her up off the pavement, she'd felt invigorated, her core temperature running hotter than normal. Had to be the thrill of survival. Or adrenaline. Okay, it was the fertility cycle. Whatever. What she knew for certain was that she had more energy than she'd ever had once her cycle began to crash in on her. Odd, but she wasn't one to look a gift horse in the mouth let alone check its teeth. No, she was far more likely to mount the damn thing and spur him forward in order to gain as much ground on life as she could.

There was only one thing left to accomplish. She needed to convince Gareth to remain with her through her entire epithicas versus ditching her in the morning. If he was tied to the Druidic assassins, he was literally *perfect*. But how to convince him to stay? There had to be something in it for him, and she'd lost everything she'd owned when her pack burned in the bar. She couldn't even offer to immediately replace lost wages seeing as she wouldn't be going back for her paycheck. It would take a trip to her bank box, and she doubted he'd carry her across the country for something so mundane as money.

Panic both pushed and pulled her to act and react, respectively. She was effectively homeless, temporarily penniless and left without the few contacts she'd stored in her cell. Worse, though, was that she'd lost the only picture of her mother she'd had. An old and worn etching, it had been the only possession that mattered to her. She wanted to cry, and she *never* cried. It had been rule number one for so long that the urge caught her off guard.

She rubbed her clenched hands against her denim-clad thighs. She'd started over more than once. She'd do it again. And the picture of her mother? The lump in her throat thickened. Her only solace was that nothing and no one could steal her mother's memory from her. It would have to be enough.

Swallowing around the mass of regret that choked her, she forced her hands to relax, forced the heat of her emotions to recede. She shifted onto one hip and faced Gareth. "So, we're headed…"

"Somewhere safe."

"Does this 'somewhere safe' have a name? An address? How about GPS coordinates?"

He slipped her a quick glance. "You're more interested in our trip details than the fact Fergus clearly wanted you dead. Death threats a daily occurrence, then?"

"There are worse things than death," she responded absently, mind on their destination. *Were they headed somewhere they could spend the next week?*

Gareth whipped the car to the side of the road so fast she would have been tossed from her seat had the harness not locked up. "Don't you ever, *ever* tell me there's anything worse than death. *Ever.* Understood?"

She paused her fight to get the safety belts to relax before looking at him. He sat facing forward, his hand gripping the steering wheel so hard the leather creaked. The metallic tang of blood made her look closer. His hands were bleeding. And his eyes… His pupils had eaten up the blue of his irises leaving his face haunted in appearance, his features chiseled and skin taut in the dash light.

"Your hands are bleeding."

He ignored the comment and instead insisted, "Your word, Ashley."

What about death scared him so? The idea he might not be the warrior she'd assumed bothered her, but this was all temporary. If she had to commit to this or worse in order to get him to see her through this, she'd tell him the moon was made of cheese and say it with conviction. "Fine. My word."

He pulled the car back onto the highway, merging onto the M fifteen minutes later.

Ashley watched the scenery pass by through the dark dregs of the storm. "May I ask where we're going?"

"A safe house."

"Who are you that you have a safe house?" she murmured, not looking at him.

"Who are you that you need one?" he countered.

"Fair."

They rode in silence for the next half hour, the only sounds the whispering swish of the windshield wipers, the tires slicing through rainwater on the road and the engine's variable RPMs as Gareth changed gears. He drove like a professional, maneuvering the dark sports car through the sparse traffic like the car was little more than a shadow. His focus never wavered.

The longer Ashley rode, the more convinced she was that he was actually one of the reputed Druidic assassins rumored to exist among the Others. If he hadn't been so cold, she would have been far more certain, but the assassins were reputed to be men. Druids. The chill of his breath was an anomaly, the frigid temperature of his skin one of the strangest things she'd ever encountered.

Just as she worked up the nerve to ask, he exited the M and took the off-ramp at speed. They raced down a narrow two-lane, never slowing.

The sign for the small town of Ennistymon flashed briefly in the headlights. Gareth finally reduced his speed as they passed the cemetery and pulled into the village proper. Not a light shone from a single window of the residences clustered around the town center. They crossed the old stone bridge that spanned the River Inagh and its picturesque falls, all in the continued silence that had begun to weigh on Ashley.

She couldn't help but be grateful when he pulled into a small car park across from an ancient stone building and shut the car down. Still…

"Not to criticize your methods," she said as the engine ticked and cooled, "but if this is a safe house, isn't this car a bit of a beacon to anyone looking to find you?"

"The car will be moved after we're inside."

"By whom?"

Again, he didn't answer but instead unbuckled his harness and unfolded his massive frame from the tight confines of the car.

She followed suit, stretching in the fine mist that continued to fall. The rush of running water cascading over the falls was soothing and she closed her eyes, relishing the calming sound. Had she not, she would have seen Gareth approach her.

Frighteningly cold hands gripped her biceps and she gasped.

"Who are you, Ashley, that you've the ability to warm me, piss off and then *kill* the prince of the genii before burning down his bar all of an evening and without female histrionics?"

Opening her eyes was a slow process as he'd piqued

her temper. "And why would you expect me to be hysterical? I've done nothing wrong." Heat began to gather, flowing through her veins.

The clouds broke and moonlight shimmered in his eyes. "No? You killed a man. Murdered him in his place of business."

Fury thrummed through her, and she tried to pull free of his grasp, but he tightened his hold. Fine. She went nose to nose with him. "I fought back against a man who was trying to kill me! He came up short. That's self-defense, not murder."

"How?" he demanded with a small shake. "*How* did you start the fire?"

"With a flame."

"Smart-ass." He moved into her, backing her against the car and pinning her there with his hips. "How, Ash? Don't play with me."

"But I want to play." Her hands went to his chest. She thrilled as his breath caught and his heart raced beneath her palm. The attraction was mutual, her pulse responding in kind. Heat bloomed between her thighs and she fought the urge to rub against him like a giant cat.

But then the draw to him morphed into something far too close to a requirement. What had been a pleasurable sensation shifted, heating her blood to near boiling. She'd never experienced such a radical shift, never been in a position she not only wanted but *needed* the man she was with. It had to be the epithicas. She'd never accept another explanation, would never subject herself to needing anyone, particularly a male. Species was irrelevant. This was about self-sufficiency, about retaining her freedom, about—

His cool breath swept over her face as he whispered the nickname he'd given her. "Ash."

Desire swamped her, drawing her flame nearer the surface even as it buckled her knees.

Gareth caught her, his brows winging down just before he hissed and whipped his hands away so only his hips held her steady. Even so, he leaned his chest against hers. "Stop playing around."

"Not…playing…" Words eluded her, her mind fuzzy with the sudden combination of the adrenaline crash after the evening's excitement and, of all times, the official bloom of her triennial window of fertility. *Damn Geoffrey for being unavailable.* She had to have Gareth, and soon.

"Tell me how you started the fire," Gareth demanded, shifting against her.

The delicious feel of his erection pressed against her lower belly, and she fought the urge to scale him like a totem pole and wrap her legs around his waist. Instead, she reached up and threaded her fingers through his hair. "Kiss me."

His pupils expanded. "Once you answer me, we'll discuss it."

"Can't wait." She pulled his mouth to hers at the same time he sucked in a breath. Their lips collided. Ashley didn't give him time to think, to consider, to stop. She delved her tongue into his mouth, sipping from him in long draws. He tasted of whiskey and cinnamon. He smelled like fresh snow and leather. He felt as capable of loving her body as he was undoubtedly dangerous to others. Every part of her responded to the elemental force he presented. Her internal flame roared, the sound a rushing wind through her clouded mind. The woman in her craved him. The phoenix in her hungered for him. Combined? She was liable to set a second building on fire tonight, but this time with passion versus intent.

He reached up and gripped a handful of hair, hesitating.

"Don't stop," she said against his lips.

"Ash—"

"Please."

"Damn you," he whispered brokenly. Then he canted her head and took control of the encounter.

Soft kisses followed stinging nips along her jaw. He moved with slow deliberation from jaw to ear then swept her hair away to work his way down the side of her neck.

She let her head fall to the side to give him better access. She'd reached the point her body was going to need him very soon.

Whether he damned her for it again in the morning remained to be seen.

Chapter 6

Gareth's hands ached for a new reason—the heat Ash generated. Even her hair was warm. Intensely so. But unlike all the other sources he'd tried to warm himself with, sources that had burned him horribly, the heat of her body seeped through him. He soaked it up like a dry sponge exposed to a veritable ocean. He wanted to be supersaturated, overloaded, *hot*. And damn if the woman wasn't working him into a right frenzy that centered round another type of heat altogether.

Sexual craving had eluded him since his resurrection. The phantom goddess had taken him against his will in the Well of Souls before he had been pulled back to the mortal plane. The experience had horrified him, breaking something in him he hadn't known had existed when his body responded at her command and against his will. He hadn't been able to shed the memory, hadn't been able to find true desire since. Touch repulsed him.

The idea of intimacy had been reduced to a thing of base nature and brittle resentment. He didn't want to feel. Not anything. But Ash called to something deeper in him, roused physical responses he'd believed had been stripped from him that day.

Now, with her lithe body moving beneath his hands, the apex of her thighs grinding against his cock, he wanted her more than he could recall wanting anyone before. She reacted to him with authentic desire, nothing fabricated, nothing forced. The little sounds she made were maddening in the best possible way. It was clear she wanted him as much as he wanted her.

There was still the matter of the three questions he needed her to answer, most important species and intent. And there was the little issue of the fire she'd started. His brethren's safety came before all else. It had to. So, regardless of his personal preferences, preferences that centered around getting the woman naked and beneath him—or above him, or against the wall, whatever—he needed to obtain answers.

With a nip to her earlobe, he reluctantly parked his hands, warm for the first time since October of last year, on the cold metal of the car. Bone-crushing chills crept up his arms. Those chills inched their way through the heat he'd borrowed and left his arms vibrating with the need to return to her. The brand on his chest hurt all the way through as if his heart had been pierced by a sharp blade. Leaning away from her, he managed to keep their groins in tight contact. He wasn't a complete sexual masochist. "We need to take this inside."

She looked up at him through dark lashes, her burnished eyes assessing. "What's inside?"

"A safe place to spend the night."

"Safe tonight and I appreciate that, but what about tomorrow? The threat you perceive tonight doesn't change because the sun rises."

The threat you perceive tonight. Were there more threats? His mind rebelled at anyone harming this woman. His element stirred in unexpected defense as if it might leap out without his summons and defend her on its own. That was new.

Reaching out, he tucked a strand of hair behind her ear. "Clearly you have enemies. What is it you have, specifically, that Fergus wanted so badly that he was willing to risk exposure and possible censure over?"

Those burnished eyes shuttered before him. "Could have been any number of things."

This time he stepped away from her, breaking all contact. "Evasive nonanswers won't garner you my help."

She crossed her arms under her breasts and stared at an indiscriminate spot on the ground between them. "What will?" she asked so quietly that the force of the wind all but carried her question away.

"Honesty." His answer, sharp and sure, was out before he considered the ramifications. Not at all his usual speed. Hell, he *never* made promises based on less than all the facts, but his craving for this woman was driving him mad. He realized then that he would do whatever necessary, from bodily service to bodily harm, to bask in her warmth. Not good. Not good at all. But the bargain was struck, and on his singular term, so he'd honor it. At least so far as she did.

"Fine. I need your help for seven days."

"Seven days," he repeated somewhat stupidly. "You think you can define a timeline for danger?"

"Yes. Seven days. Beginning now." Her eyes blazed. "Beyond that, I'll take care of myself. I won't need your sword or your...services."

The disdain in her voice chaffed. "You won't 'need' me? And who said anything about my 'services?' I'm no' a bloody stud for hire!"

Her intense gaze snapped to his, unblinking. "You're an assassin. You're damn well for hire. And I've the means to pay."

His heart skipped a beat. She was deep into the Other world to know of the assassins to begin with, but he'd thoroughly screwed up asking for Dylan by title instead of name. The assassins' secrecy was tightly held, and he'd blown that closed door wide-open.

Kill her.

The voice whispered through his mind leaving ice crystals in its wake.

What the hell?

"No," he spat.

Ash parked her hands on her hips. "I can afford your fees, I assure you. It'll take a trip to Dublin to obtain the funds, but I'll see you paid and in cash. You've my word." She hesitated, then added, "And as for the other—"

"No," he said again. "It's…" He hesitated. To admit he was an assassin was to open a dialogue he could never take back. But hadn't he done that already? Had he been clearheaded, had death not hung like a guillotine suspended over his exposed neck, he surely wouldn't have made such amateur mistakes.

Of course, he had tonight and eight more days until Beltane. Beyond that, none of this would matter. He would be dead. Unless he ended it before then, as planned. If he did, he could take with him the secret that he'd fouled up and the woman could do nothing with it. She'd never find the rest of them.

Except he'd been at the bar with a handful of the

tyros, or trainees. She'd seen them, would know their faces and was smart enough to put the pieces together should their paths cross again. Or, worse, she'd know them well enough by sight to go looking for one of them should Gareth reject her.

Hell's bells, he'd screwed this up.

"I'll double your fee."

She thought he was hesitating because of the money? He snorted and shook his head. "You can't afford me, darkling. Trust me."

"Oh, but I assure you, *again*, that I can. My money's just tied up in the city." She pushed off the car and stepped closer. "Seriously, take me to Dublin and we'll settle this."

Her heat was a balm to the brand Macha had left on his chest, overpowering the cold with sultry warmth that spread through him. "Assuming you're right about me, what's so dire you think you need my services?"

She opened her mouth only to snap it shut and look over at the running water, watching it tumble down the rock falls until the river carried it away.

Gareth shoved his hands through his hair and grabbed handfuls, pulling. "You've one shot at this, Ash. One shot at honesty. Lie to me? I'll be leaving you here to sort yourself out, and trust me when I tell you that you won't catch me looking back. Ever."

Arms still crossed, her hands fisted. "Are you always so brutal?"

Months ago, the answer would have been no, no matter who she'd asked about him. But dying had changed him. He had no promise of a better tomorrow, no belief in a beautiful eternity, no hope. He'd spent his life in service to the Druidic race, keeping the peace, defending them against all comers, carrying out the dark side

of assignations so that his brethren could uphold the core
values of their beliefs on nonviolence. *He* had made it
possible for them to live without conflict. *He* had made
it possible for them to shun violence. *He* had operated
under the guidance of the gods. He'd believed the tales
the deities recorded of the afterlife for those who had
served them well. And then he'd died. Everything he'd
ever done, ever believed in, had been destroyed.

Ash snapped her fingers in front of his face, startling him.

"What?" The single word held a vicious bite. That's
what was left of him now—the dark, the ugly, the bitterness. The base truth of who he was. He resented being
reduced to roadkill that had been hit but not killed and
now waited, painfully, to die.

"You need to decide where your head's at, Gareth."
She stepped even closer. "I want you for the week. All
of you. There may be a point where I'll need you at my
six, but I can't know exactly how this will play out until
this week is history."

"Ash, you've got the wrong man."

She shook her head, hair gone dark in the night moving with a susurrus noise against her shirt. "I don't think
I do." A faint shiver stole over her skin and she frowned,
but she didn't mention that he was the source of the cold.

Shrugging out of his jacket, the wound on his side
cracked open. Blood saturated his sweater in time with
the elevated *pump-pump-pump* of his heart, shocking
him. He rarely bled anymore, let alone so profusely.

"When were you wounded?" she demanded, reaching for his sweater's hem.

He gripped her wrist and stepped away to prevent her
from lifting the top. "I'll do." The heat of her skin broke
through the hoarfrost that coated his, melting it so his

grip was slippery. Beyond a reflexive yank of her wrist against his arctic grip, she didn't comment on their differences in temperature.

"That much blood?" Her gaze went from the spreading stain to his face. "I don't think so. I'm a fair hand at field dressings. Let me look."

"I'll deal with it inside. It was foolish of me to stand us out here like ducks at a carnival shooting gallery." Still holding her wrist, he hauled her forward, ignoring her stumble in the name of progress. He'd get her inside, get her settled, tend the bleeding and then do as Dylan suggested, calling for someone else to take over. Yes, the woman needed help. Gareth just wasn't the man for this particular job. Not anymore.

But the kiss they'd shared...

Bloody, lovely, that. There would have been a time not long ago he'd have leaped at the opportunity. But that was then.

This was now.

Ashley fought not to cringe at the temperature of Gareth's skin. How could he be a Druidic assassin, an incredibly long-lived race that pushed the fringes of an immortal lifespan, and have a temperature that stole through her like a bitter January wind? It made no sense, but she wasn't about to ask him now and risk alienating him further than she already had. It seemed she'd made a grave error in offering to pay him. She'd sealed the deal when she refused to answer his direct questions. There had to be a way to rectify her poor judgment.

Honesty.

He'd asked her for the one thing that had been ingrained in her for centuries, the one thing she had to deny when it came to admitting who, and what, she was.

And sharing her state of distress due to the epithicas? Forget it. She'd shared that with Geoffrey and Geoffrey alone after more than a century of friendship. She wasn't going to just open her personal closet and let Gareth pull out the skeleton of his choice and have a good go-round with it. Fergus was now one of those skeletons—animated, aggressive and scary as hell. And Gareth held a peace treaty with the bastard. *Had* held. Past tense. Thanks to her, that was a moot issue, but there would likely be others Gareth and his order, or Arcanum, had peace treaties with—others she'd have to defend herself against. And she would never forego defending herself if she was backed into a corner. Not if she had the means.

She followed silently as he pulled her along, down a dark alleyway, across a street and up another alley. He stopped in front of an ancient stone building with an arched wood-and-iron door, finally letting her go to dig a key ring out of his pocket. Flipping through several options, he settled on a worn skeleton key. He shoved it into the door's decrepit lock. After wiggling it about for several seconds, the locking mechanism clicked loudly and the door swung open. He stepped through and didn't look back, leaving her to follow of her own free will.

The house smelled fresh, clean, but it wasn't the smells of wood wax and lemon oil that struck her dumb as she passed under the stone archway carved in Ogham script. It was the moment Gareth had let go of her wrist. She'd heated in a rush, her phoenix fire consuming her so hard and fast that her hair crackled and sweat bloomed between her breasts. Her heart hammered faster than a semiautomatic with the trigger depressed. The way her legs moved—or refused to—had her stumbling into the foyer. Reaching out, she braced herself against the wall and leaned her forehead against the cool plastered wall.

Too fast. This is hitting me too fast. I have to do something.

Seducing Gareth was the only choice available to her.

Gareth's booted steps, intentionally heavy as he'd previously moved like a wraith, preceded his rounding the corner. His scowl said he intended to chastise her for not following him deeper into the home, but he paused. Taking in her shaking legs and laboring breath, he laid a hand on her near shoulder. His cold was so fierce it bled through her shirt and into her bones, assuaging the worst of the epithicas. "Ash?"

Her skin, too tight only moments before, relaxed. Her sex still ached, but it was manageable. The worst of her condition had returned when Gareth let her go. What if…

She reached for him, gripping his hand.

His brows winged down in a tight V on contact as she sighed with evident relief.

Letting go of him wasn't an option. "Your cool soothes me. Would you just hold on for a moment? Unless it pains you."

"You go from kissing me to insulting me to asking me to hold you?"

Yep. Definite confusion. Add a little irritation and she could probably come fairly close to mimicking his voice.

Squeezing his hand, she put her pride aside and offered him the honesty he'd asked for. "I need the cool to keep me balanced right now. My body is…" She paused, fighting to find the words. "I'm approaching my fertility cycle. Quickly. You seem to afford me some semblance of control."

Brows that had drawn together now winged up. "Your fertility cycle?" He stepped away, but she followed, refusing to let go.

"Yes. Please, just…get me through this. *Please*, Gareth. I can't do it alone. It could cost me. Huge." Actually, it could kill her, causing her to die and resurrect over and over until, at some point, death would be final. Having figured out the key to surviving the epithicas had left her joie de vivre at an all-time high, and she had no interest in turning to ash permanently.

He considered her, weighing her words.

"You asked for truth." Her tone was softer, gentler this time. Persuasive even. She needed him for this, pride be damned, and she'd do what she had to in order to make it work, get him to agree. Anything. Even—she swallowed hard, self-respect leaving a bitter aftertaste—*beg*.

His eyes softened. "I'll give you tonight. It's all I can promise." He rolled shoulders so broad they stretched his sweater's weave. "Tomorrow—"

"Is tomorrow," she quickly interjected. "We'll deal with it then."

His fingers twitched against hers. "Tonight, then."

A wave of relief washed through her, cleansing but somehow not completely satisfying. He was so resistant to anything beyond tonight, and she would need him. Could admit that now, could use that vile word, *need*.

On a sigh, she stepped into him and slid an arm around his waist. "I'd still like to see the wound that has you bleeding."

"It's stopped."

His gruff answer buried the truth so deeply she didn't know if he was lying or not. If he wanted to pretend it hadn't happened? Fine. She simply had to get through tonight. But she'd do what she could to get him to stay longer, her powers of persuasion being historically sufficient. She could only hope that history held and she could convince him a week with her would be worth it.

Wrapping his arm around her, he led her to a small kitchen. "Hungry?" he asked, attempting to let her go as he headed for the fridge.

Ash clutched his hand, stopping him. A glance at the clock confirmed it was almost five in the morning. The knowledge stole the last of her energy, leaving her feeling rather wilted. "I'm exhausted, actually. Will you take me to bed?"

He startled, eyes widening until the whites dominated his paled face. "I can hold your hand tonight, keep contact to keep your breeding heat down, but there won't be sex, darkling. I... There just won't."

It was the second time he'd referred to her as "darkling." As if she was fae. She huffed out a short, unenergetic laugh. Let him think what he would. If he didn't recognize her as a phoenix at this point, he likely wouldn't. They were rare enough, secluded enough, that few of her kind ever ventured into the realm of mortal men. Instead, her race preferred to stay sequestered in the hills of Italy and Greece and the deserts of the Middle East. It was, she remembered, far easier to dispose of the bodies of interlopers in such remote locations. Few came looking, and those who did? More bodies.

She shuddered. It didn't suit her, killing so freely. If cornered, though, her inner phoenix had no trouble defending what was hers, particularly her life.

"Ash?"

"Bed, Gareth, before I fall over. I've been on my feet and running since early this afternoon and then, literally, running. I'm knackered."

He surprised her, pulling her into a comforting hug. "I hadn't considered. Sleep it is."

A burn of tears shocked her. Burying her face in his soft sweater, she simply sagged into the embrace.

"I need to make a call. I need to make a call, but I want to get you settled first. You'll be safe here so long as I'm within shouting distance. No one knows of this place save my brethren, so rest easy," he said softly into her hair.

She looked up and perused the room. "Where's the bedroom?"

"Second floor's the one I want to put you...us...in. If we need to get out, there's a fire ladder we can drop. Or jump. I want the opportunity to get away if someone attempts to break in."

She nodded and yawned. "I can jump."

He considered her carefully. "As can I, but I'm not sure I'm willing to risk breaking something."

"I'd catch you," she offered absently.

One heavy brow arched. "You're that confident you could sustain my weight from a free fall?"

"Sure?" She stepped away, refusing to meet his stare. "If you'll get me settled and then leave, I won't have to worry about traversing the stairs."

"Deal. And I won't leave you long."

"Double deal."

Together, they walked upstairs, Ash's legs noodly still but far closer to al dente than overboiled. She made it, but barely.

The room was rudimentary save for the bed. It was a king-size monstrosity with lush brocade covers, a plethora of pillows and a thick mattress that promised a good night's sleep.

Gareth folded the covers back as she shed her boots, jeans and bra.

She crawled into the plush bed wearing nothing but her shirt and panties.

He tucked her in, his face stark and strained. "Back in ten."

"Make it five. Please." She added the last as her temperature began to rise. Geoffrey had asked her how long she'd had, and she'd guessed days. She'd been wrong. She hadn't had hours. The epithicas had descended, and her only choice was to see it through.

Gareth let her go and stepped back, eyes fixed on her.

Ashley's internal heat surged forward when physical contact with the assassin was lost. If she didn't know better, she'd think her phoenix had reached for him.

But that wasn't possible.

Chapter 7

Gareth paused in the doorway and glanced over his shoulder, watching as Ash began to writhe on the bed, her legs scissoring, her hands wadding up the sheets. Her skin had taken on a flushed, fevered appearance. Whatever this thing was that had hold of her, she seemed miserable. He knew what it was like to lose control of one's choices, to be victim to the body's demands without one's consent.

Dark memories rose and, with a choked curse, he spun away and stalked out of the room, retrieving his cell as he went. He knew what he was doing wasn't entirely fair, asking another assassin to take over here when Gareth had made the choice to get involved in the woman's plight. But fair or not, he was on a limited timeline. He wouldn't spend the days he had left in service but would instead take the time to set the last of his affairs in order and say goodbye to the men who made up his family, the

Assassin's Arcanum, the men he called brothers. A few taps on the screen and the call connected. One ring. Two.

"You tucked in for the night?" Dylan asked by way of greeting.

"I need Rowan here by dawn."

"Where's 'here,' exactly?" Dylan's voice was tighter than stretched barbwire and just as sharp.

"I'm at the safe house in Ennistymon."

"With the woman?"

Gareth nodded as he answered. "Yeah. She's in trouble, but I don't have, or want, details. I'll see her through tonight, but then I need him to take over. She's Other, and she also knows who I am thanks to me running off my big mouth in the car." He sighed and pulled at the neck of his sweater. "I'll have his word that he'll see her to safety before he returns to the Nest."

"Any reason you want Rowan in particular?"

Because he won't touch her. "You suggested him earlier." Dylan didn't respond, and Gareth knew well enough to wait him out. Too bad his mind and mouth weren't of an accord. "Your word, Dylan."

"You know I'll do as you ask. I was only trying to think if it might be better to send Niall or even Kayden. Rowan can be a bit…rough in his demeanor."

He thought of Ash. "She can handle him. And I trust him to deal with anyone who might show up with the intent to harm her. Rowan's canny. He'll get her out of here so she's beyond harm's reach."

"I'll have him there in the morning. Gareth…" Dylan hesitated, the weight of Gareth's name on his lips heavier than censure. "Come back to the Nest. That's an order."

He knew. He knew Gareth was considering ending it. Damn Angus and his bloody big mouth. Whereas Gareth might have slipped away and faced his death on terms he set, he'd now been ordered home where he knew his fellow assassins would demand a fight. How could he tell them he was resigned to his fate? That he had no fight left? What Macha had done to him had changed him on a fundamental level.

"Your word for mine, Gareth," Dylan snapped. "Now."

"You think to manipulate me into what? Finding my peace with this?" Gareth snorted. "You're a smarter man than that."

"And beyond the hurt and fear you carry is the man I've called brother for centuries. I'll have you back here so we face this together."

There was something in Dylan's voice, something Gareth believed sounded suspiciously like guilt.

Gareth shifted in his seat. "Don't press me on this out of some misguided sense of reparation due me, my friend. You owe me nothing more than the promise that you will love your wife to the end of your days."

"Aye, and I will." Dylan's voice was thick with unspoken emotion. "You offered your life so that Kennedy might live." A hard breath hissed over the connection. "I owe you everything, man."

The first part, at least, was true. He'd died to give Kennedy, and Dylan, the chance the gods had afforded them in their godly-but-convoluted way.

As for the second? "I've said it a thousand times if I've said it once, but it seems you've yet to hear me. You owe me nothing." Gareth's dismissal was hoarse, the words laden with something he couldn't hope to explain. Yes, he had allowed Kennedy, the woman who would become Dylan's wife, to run Gareth through with a sword. Yes, it had been the most difficult decision of his life—let the woman possessed by a crazed goddess live or take her out. But Kennedy had been Dylan's one chance at the kind of love that lasted beyond time. It was a poor friend who would allow such an opportunity to go wasted when there was a way to influence the outcome for the good.

When it had all been done, the cost had been his soul for Kennedy's.

Gods but the cost had been high.

Still, he said, "I would do it over a thousand times to see you happy, mate. I don't regret the choices I made."

"Stop acting as if it's a foregone conclusion that you're dead!" Dylan roared. Breathing labored, he blew into the phone with harsh pants. "Home in the morning or I'll be coming for you myself. Your word, Gareth."

"Damn you," he said, voice low and fierce. "You're insistent on making this harder than it has to be."

"And you know that damned goddess wants more from you than your life. With the banished deities who've been tied to the Shadow Realm now rallying, you know there's more at stake than your choice here."

Yes, Gareth knew. But the goddess hadn't been clear, only that his death was the beginning for her. How was he to know what to do?

"Your. Word." Dylan's tone had gone stone cold, affecting the role he was known for. Assassin.

"My word, then."

"Rowan will be there by dawn. Leave the moment he arrives."

"Aye, I—" the phone went silent, Dylan having disconnected before Gareth could finish with "—will."

He slipped his smartphone into his jeans pocket, removed his boots and padded back to the bedroom.

Ash had broken out into a vicious sweat. The sheets were a tangled mess, her hair damp with fever and curling where it stuck to her skin. Her eyes were closed, her lips parted but dry. Heat radiated from her like a furnace.

Slipping into bed beside her, he laid his blue-tinged hand on her forehead and hissed at the contact even as she moaned with evident bliss. Her thrashing slowed and then stopped.

"Gareth."

"I'm here, lass."

"Spoon me."

"Spoon you?" He couldn't help but smile even as she rolled to her side and backed into him. His body curled around hers reflexively, absorbing the warmth she emitted like a plant turning its face to the sun.

"You're cold. It stops the hurting. Please."

Ironic that she needed from him the direct opposite of what he needed from her.

Curling around her, taking in her warmth in exchange for his cold, he fell asleep and, for the first time since October, slept beyond the reach of nightmares and memories.

Gareth woke with a start, whipping his Sig Sauer out from under the pillow and aimed it at the giant of a man who stood over him. One brow raised, the man stripped the gun from Gareth and turned it around so the muzzle pointed at him before Gareth had it sighted. Gareth sagged into the mattress, heart in his throat.

"You know better—" the man began, and Gareth shushed him, gesturing to Ash's sleeping form.

He slipped from the bed with infinite care, punching the man in the shoulder as he passed. It was a "follow me" gesture packed with a little extra in the way of hello. A hard hello.

"You trying to steal the last of my life, Rowan?"

Gareth groused, more irritated with himself that he'd completely allowed the other man to sneak up on him. Putting the teakettle on, Gareth ignited the burner with an absent flick of his fingers. He froze, eyes wide, ignoring whatever it was his fellow Arcanum member said in response. Fire, Gareth's element, had come to call without a thought and with no effort at all. He examined his fingers. No burns. *What in the name of all that was holy had changed?*

His heart surged at the idea Angus might have found a means to return him to normal despite the healer's assertions he had no idea how to help Gareth. Obviously something had helped.

Ash.

But she hadn't done anything. They'd slept, he knew, without waking. She hadn't moved from the position he'd held her in all night—tucked up close to his front, his arm around her waist, his defiant erection settled in the crevice of her ass.

A slap to the back of his head had him rounding on Rowan. "What?"

"I said make your tea to go. Dylan's ordered you back to the Nest as fast as possible. I even had to pull your damn pop can of a car around to save you the time." He scowled. "I'm not a bloody chauffeur *or* a babysitter, and you've turned me into both." The dark-haired warrior pulled the giant sword he carried from the sheath on his back and let it clatter against the tabletop. "What has Dylan frothing at the mouth so?"

Gareth shrugged and turned away, moving to the cabinet to retrieve a travel mug to make his tea. "He's got his knickers in a knot over Beltane."

A heavy hand rested briefly on his shoulder, shocking him. Rowan was a no-touch-ever kind of guy. One squeeze and the other man let go.

"Return to him so you can resolve this."

Great. The entire Arcanum must know. "There's no solution—"

Rowan spun him around and tea flew everywhere, scalding his skin where it hit. He gripped Gareth's shoulder. "I'll handle the woman and return to the Arcanum as soon as I'm able, but in no more than seventy-two hours. We'll fight this together."

Gareth's throat tightened in a rush that made it hard to breathe, hard to swallow, impossible to speak. Nodding and ignoring his blistered skin, he made a second cup of tea before heading for the front door. He paused several steps short. It would be harsh not to say goodbye to Ash. Turning back, he ran smack into Rowan's chest.

"Don't let her make you vulnerable," the larger man said softly. "Only pain will come from it."

And Rowan would know. He was the only Assassin in history to have given up the position versus dying in the line of duty and being replaced. He'd lost his wife and children in an attack over five hundred years ago, and it had left him changed, hardened straight through.

Gareth nodded, regretting that he'd never see Ash again. She had spirit, chose to live free of the confines of fear and, he grinned, had thought to bully him or pay him to "have her six." She hadn't cared which means of currency he'd chosen—murder or money.

Closing the front door behind him, the iron latch settled with an ominous *thunk*, the sound muffled by the dense fog. He stepped toward his car and his ears popped. Shaking his head, he pulled his keys from his jeans pocket. The keys flew out of his hand as if he'd been slapped. Without conscious thought, he reached for his gun. It wasn't there. He cursed softly for not having demanded the weapon back from Rowan. He bent low and slid a lethally sharp dagger from his boot, clutching it tight. Gutting whomever approached was a given.

The fog thickened, swirling about him and clogging his nose. Already chilled, his hands went numb. Horrifying memories of a mist such as this gave terror its every foothold as it clawed its way up his spine. Before the fog began to froth and then part, he knew whom he would find.

The figure emerged at the end of the alleyway and moved toward him with slow, deliberate steps.

The sheer magnitude—the *familiar* magnitude—of her being threatened to drive him to his knees. She was too much for this little village, too much for this world, too much for this entire plane.

Macha, the queen of phantoms and war, appeared, draped in a hooded cloak that flowed around her like a sentient thing as she moved toward him. Her manifested person looked little more than a graceful, feminine outline in the murky morning light.

What. A. *Lie*.

He knew the beauty hidden beneath that cloak, knew it to be an illusion for the horror she truly represented. He'd once misjudged her based on that illusion. He would never do it again.

"Gareth Brennan."

Macha's voice slid through him, a thousand tiny blades that left him as carved up as a tin can under a Ginsu knife, sharp edges and all. His upper lip lifted in an involuntary snarl. "You're not welcome here."

"One man's opinion does not a consensus make." She paused before cocking her head to the side. "It admittedly disappoints me that you do not offer me a more enthusiastic welcome when *you* created for me the path to this realm." Her words were infused with a thousand hissing voices that threatened to stop his heart. "You did such a splendid job that I'm now able to come to you anywhere you are in this world." Her brilliant smile shone from the depths of her hood. "There are no boundaries for me. Not anymore."

"I beg to differ. There are indeed boundaries. Hard ones," he said, jaw tight. "If there weren't, you'd have been here long before now. Tell me otherwise and I'll call you out for the liar you are."

Her grin widened. "Temper, temper, darling. You and I? We have other things, *bigger* things, to conquer than my mere manifestation. You'll be commanding my army of souls upon my return to full goddess status. You'll be a general of sorts, the leader of the damned."

Souls. Those dark, semitransparent, wraithlike creatures that had slithered over the walls. Not wraiths. Phantoms.

Adrenaline hit his system like it had been administered via an IV push. His heart sped up as cold sweat beaded along his hairline. The denial tumbled out before he could stop himself. "I'll slit my own throat before I aid you in anything beyond your own permanent end."

Macha's pale hands slipped from the bell sleeves of her robe, and she pushed her hood back. "Tread lightly, Druid, mine. You are favored, but chattel still. You'll do as I bid you."

"Like hell," he snarled. "I'll never be anyone's 'chattel,' be they a goddess of the heavens or a cast-off demigoddess bound to the Well of Souls and left there to rot."

The screams of the phantoms bound to the goddess began to coalesce around her, a darkening whirlwind of fury fueled by their need for retribution and, more, salvation. They would find neither. Ever.

The cacophony of sound intensified until one of his eardrums ruptured. Blood trickled down the side of his face and dripped off his jaw.

"You came to me at death because I summoned your soul and marked you in the old ways, thus laying claim to you for eternity."

Gareth's knees threatened to give way. He managed to stave off a fall, but his stomach wouldn't be held in check. The little bit of tea he'd consumed came up with violence at the thought she'd destroyed his chance at Tir na nÓg. His own happily-ever-after stolen. Wiping his mouth with the back of his free hand, he stood. "You *bitch*."

"You are mine to rule, Druid. It would seem, however, that you require a reminder."

Macha slashed her hand through the air and the symbol over his left pec froze deep and hard, splitting skin and muscle to the bone.

Gareth grunted in pain, unwilling to give her the satisfaction of a deeper, more visceral response. Coaxing his elemental flame to life, he cupped it in his hands and began to chant, watching the blue light take on a white-hot glow. The goddess wanted to play? He'd play and with everything he could summon. She might control the cold that was killing him, but he controlled at least the rudimentary heat that could, *would*, scar her. Intent on cursing her as he dreamed of burning her to ash where she stood, he tried to coax his flame higher. What had come so easily in the kitchen now defied him. Still, he fought to harness the power of his element. By the gods' own ordination, it was his to command. "I'll never come to you willingly."

"Say my name, darling."

"Never," he ground out.

"Say it," she commanded, those hissing voices screeching at him.

"Never!" he bellowed, raising his hands to release what fire he'd been able to summon.

Macha's face darkened to an inky blackness that revealed the skeletal form of her true countenance. "You smell like a... You took a woman," she screeched, all pretense gone as she rounded on the safe house door. "I need to harvest your soul while you live, but I won't tolerate infidelity. You'll learn to fear me, Gareth," she snarled. "Your actions just cost your whore, and she'll be paying your penance with her life."

Ash woke with the knowledge Gareth had left her alone in bed. Her epithicas burned hotter than ever before. She ached all over as if she had the worst flu, her sex was swollen and she needed him. Only him. She had to get to him, had to find him and admit what was happening. He knew only part of it. Here was hoping the full truth didn't send him running to the hills of Connemara.

Shoving the covers off her overheated body, the phoenix in her screamed its displeasure, and Ash had to fight back the urge to loose the sound on the house. Her enraged call could shatter every glass in a one-block area, crack foundations, push cars off the road and more. Conversely, her unique song could soothe the heart's deepest hurts. It was the most intimate of gestures a phoenix could offer, sharing her song. She'd never done it and had no plans to change her statistics. The song had power, and she didn't share her power. With no one to count on but herself, she needed every ounce of it to survive.

Someone moved downstairs, the smell of brewing

tea and toast winding round her until the temptation, and her stomach's insistence she follow that smell, was too great to ignore. She made her way down the steps expecting to find Gareth. Instead, a huge man stood at the counter, back to her. He spooned sugar into a tea-cup with hands so large they made the utensil look like a condiment spoon. Buttered toast sat to the side. A giant sword lay across the wooden kitchen table.

"Where's Gareth?" Her voice held the hiss of flames laced liberally with fury.

The man rounded on her and Ash swallowed a gasp.

He was beautiful, with dark wavy hair that had grown to brush the neck of his T-shirt, shoulders every bit as broad as Gareth's, muscle stacked on muscle, a trim waist and a good three or four inches on Gareth in height. But his eyes were arresting—a blue so clear it defied labels, his gaze colder than Gareth's handshake.

"Name's Rowan. I'll be seeing you to Shannon Airport." He sipped his tea, grimaced and added another spoon of sugar. "Today."

Gareth had left her? "Where's Gareth? It's him I struck my deal with."

"Gone. You'll deal with me or none at all." He sipped his tea again and added a touch more milk.

"I'll deal with Gareth." Heat suffused her skin, her phoenix rebelling at Gareth's absence as much as it did this man's attempt to dictate her actions. "Where has he gone?"

"Home."

Home? No.

"Who is he to you?" Her hands heated along with her temper, and Ashley began to wonder if she'd actually throw sparks against her will.

"He's a…friend. He asked me to see to your safe passage out of Ireland as he had other, more pressing things to manage. Dress and we'll be on our way."

Turned out sparks were an underestimation of her manifested desire for Gareth. Her hands lit, flames licking at her fingertips before gathering momentum and rolling around her hands. "Tell me when he left and where he went before this gets personal." She didn't bother to couch the demands in a question any more than she attempted to subdue the flames that now danced up to her elbows.

"It *is* personal." Another sip of tea. "So you're a phoenix. It's a testament to his frame of mind that he didn't figure it out himself."

Flames burned hotter, the ends of her hair sparking. "His frame of mind?"

Rowan shrugged one shoulder nonchalantly. "Your eyes always turn gold when you're pissed, Red?" The question held an almost indifferent curiosity.

Before she could show him exactly what else changed when she was furious, the air around them warped, atmospheric pressure pushing in so hard Ashley's ears popped.

The large man hoisted the sword one-handed and started for the door. "Stay here."

"Like hell." She raced past him before he realized what she'd done and, element still hovering over and within her skin, yanked the front door open. Wearing nothing but her T-shirt and panties, she stepped outside and took in the scene at a glance.

Gareth stood, knife gripped, one hand cupping something small but bright as he faced off with a relatively petite, incredibly beautiful woman.

Why would he pull a knife on a woman? Unless—

A skeletal mask flickered behind her stunning face

and bitter cold power that made Gareth seem feverish poured off her in heavy, nauseating waves.

—*she's not a woman.*

Whatever she was, she emitted energy that crawled over Ash like a contagious malignancy.

The woman raised her hands toward Gareth. Mist formed between her palms. The sheer weight of the cold power she wielded made Ash's bones ache.

Without thinking, Ash raced from the house and tackled Gareth to the ground, rolling him away from his car in time to see the machine he'd been standing in front of freeze, its glass shattering, tires shrinking, leather cracking.

But it wasn't the effect the woman's efforts had on Gareth's car that shook the buildings around them. It was what happened when Ashley and Gareth collided that threatened to bring down ancient structures, tumbled the cobblestone road and destroyed the light post they'd come to rest against, glass raining around them.

Ash's flame arced out, connecting with Gareth's palm and weaving intimately through his fingers before winding its way up his arms and around his neck. She fought to draw the flame home, but what came to her call was a foreign entity. Starved heat that fought to survive surged into her. The phoenix within her shuddered, shocked at the cool, weak power that left an aftertaste not unlike the smell of a struck match. It coated her tongue and throat. She coughed and tried to retrieve her hands from Gareth's arms, but they were stuck there as if they'd been welded.

His eyes were wide and his back arched at an unnatural angle. His whole body stiffened. And then he screamed.

Gods, the sound. Ash was caught up in a whirlwind

of confusion as whatever had Gareth suppressed tried to control her phoenix, but her nature rebelled at the stifling attempt. She threw off the invisible chains that bound her to Gareth, refusing to succumb to the pressure on her body, pressure so fierce it threatened to break bones.

"Oh, little phoenix, I'm so glad you've come out to play."

The cloaked woman slashed her hands through the air and a wall of heart-stopping cold slammed into Ash, and her pulse rate became sluggish for several seconds.

What the hell?

"Do not think you can take what is mine." The woman raised her hands again, mist coalescing into an opaque ball that spun fast and then faster still.

"Screw...you..." Ash panted, forcing herself to crawl away from Gareth's writhing body. The man was being tortured, and the cloaked woman was responsible. Ash might be pissed he'd left, but she was *livid* that this bitch thought she could command her, pulling Ashley's strings like a puppet master. "He's his own man."

"Oh, you naive child. It's pretty to think so, isn't it, child?"

Ashley lumbered to her feet and saw Rowan raise his sword.

"Back off, Conan," she spat. "You want in on this, watch Gareth."

Rowan arched a brow at her but moved to place himself between the downed man and the cloaked woman.

Ashley moved to the middle of the alleyway and, without forecasting her intent, flung herself at the woman, igniting every ounce of phoenix fire she possessed as she moved. This creature thought to take the man her phoenix needed to see her through this epithicas? No. No one took what was hers. No one.

Cold hit her seconds before she struck the blonde, but the effort was hardly enough to temper the flames that swallowed her whole. Ash threw a hard right on impact, snapping the woman's entire head to the side and throwing her off balance.

The woman's form shimmered before solidifying again.

Ashley grabbed the stranger as they went down, her phoenix flame raging with fury.

The woman's cloak combusted as her hair curled and shriveled beneath the onslaught of fire. Screaming, the woman beat at her and the flames that refused to die as Ash funneled more and more of her fury into them. Porcelain skin charred and cracked, and then the skeletal face emerged with a screech. Black mist swirled around them as an innumerable number of tortured voices joined the horrid sound.

"You don't threaten me or mine," Ash shouted, her own clothes going up in flames. "Think to touch him again and I'll burn you to the ground and scatter your ashes in three different rivers."

The woman disappeared in a flash but left a sculpted ice form behind, one that resembled her false beauty. Ashley ended up embracing the sculpture, her fire quickly melting the ice and leaving little more than a puddle behind.

She fought to shut down her fury, to rein in the phoenix's desire to raze the town. Her breath came in hard gasps as, shaking with residual rage, she stood and rounded on the men.

"Easy, Red," Rowan said quietly, pulling off his T-shirt and slowly handing it to her to cover herself.

"This would be the 'friend zone.' No need to go barbe-cuing anyone else's ass this morning."

"Friend." The word emerged dull, lifeless. She pulled the shirt over her head, the hem hitting her lower than midthigh.

Then she saw Gareth.

He lay in the gutter, clothes charred and soaked, the bloodstain on his sweater lightened by the pool of water he lay in. His breathing was far too rapid, his eyes too wide. Trembling hands raised, he stared at them with a combination of horror and wonder. "What did you do to me?" he croaked as blue-and-orange flames danced from his fingertips.

She held up her hands and found her flame's color had changed, as well. No longer bright red and orange, it held a hint of blue at the base. Suppressing it, she called it again with the same results.

Gareth fought his way to his hands and knees and lifted his chin to stare at her with blue eyes gone cold. "Ash, what did you do?" he roared.

Her heartbeat paused and, for a moment, she won-dered if it would start again. It did—running triple-time. *What had she done?* he asked. The answer was simple. "I saved your ass from the skeleton queen."

"She flashed out of this realm, but she'll be back. So, no. You didn't *save* me. You only postponed the inevi-table." He shook his head hard and fast as if to clear it. "And that's not what I meant. I'm referring to this." He held up one hand and watched as flames danced mer-rily around his fingers.

Oh. That.

"She called you phoenix. The phantom queen called you phoenix." He gasped, the flames extinguishing, and he cradled his hand to his chest. "What. Did. You. Do!"

"Phantom queen? As in, Macha? You can't be serious."

"You just threw down with a goddess, woman." This from the ever-helpful Rowan. "Even though you likely just signed your own death warrant, you fought well. I'm impressed."

The Goddess of Phantoms and War. "I suppose it would be immature to say she started it." Her response was as dry as her mouth. So she'd saved Gareth, but that seemed secondary when she considered what might have just happened between them. She had to know. "Tell me true, Gareth." She swallowed hard, the taste of ash coating her tongue. "How are you affiliated with fire?"

"It is…was…my element to call." He stared at her, unblinking. "As an assassin."

She nodded, a single, shallow dip of the chin. Honesty for honesty, then.

His eyes narrowed as he struggled to his feet with Rowan's help. "Why?"

She closed her eyes and focused. There, in the heart of her where her phoenix fire had always been, rested a kernel of something different, something she could touch, manipulate and mold to her will, but it wasn't her phoenix flame.

Legend had it that this could happen, that elements could be attracted to one another, but she'd never heard of it happening with the same elements. Perhaps wind and fire, but…fire and fire? No. Because like a glass of red wine poured into a glass of white and shaken, two flames merged could never be separated again. The danger wasn't in the mix, though. It was that neither body was meant to harness the flavor, or power, of the other.

"Answer me, Ash," Gareth said, the warning clear in his voice.

She opened her eyes and met his shocked gaze. "Our elements just merged." Raising her hands, she let the flames lick at her skin. "I've never had the blue base, and I'd guess you've never burned red."

"What have you done to him?" Violence wove through Rowan's question, his face thunderous.

"If the legends are true, I either just saved his life," she said, "or I killed us both."

Chapter 8

Gareth lumbered to his feet, his hands still flickering with fire. There one moment, gone the next. A sense of foreign warmth had settled in his abdomen, not exactly comfortable given the cold still permeating the rest of his body. He wanted to take his sweater off. He also wanted to go inside and huddle next to the fireplace.

Staring at his hands as the unfamiliar hybrid flames danced around and then disappeared again, he recognized another unfamiliar feeling—sexual desire so strong it had his cock swelling with undeniable urgency. His brows furrowed. What the hell was that about? He usually got a cock stand after a good fight, but he hadn't fought. Ash had saved his ass.

Humiliation chased after the rest of his emotions. He'd been all but defenseless when he'd faced the phantom queen. What's worse, he'd known it. The minimal amount of fire he'd been able to summon would have been extinguished by the goddess before he could have done any damage. It galled him to have been rendered so impotent.

Of course, given the raging erection he was sporting, "impotent" was only relevant to what had been. Not what was.

He glanced at Ashley and considered what he knew. She'd been feverish and needed his touch. More often than not, she avoided answering him directly. She had, for all intents and purposes, propositioned him. Her nature was unarguably volatile, far beyond that which he'd been taught was natural for a phoenix. This desire he was drowning in, had it come from her, too? Only one way to find out. "What else did I inherit, Ash? Beyond combining your element with mine?"

She shifted from foot to foot, her lips thinning.

"Own it, woman." Rowan shifted toward her, his stance changing to that of aggressor as he leveled his sword at her throat.

Gareth stepped between them, staring down the larger man. "Stand down, Rowan." When the other man didn't flinch, Gareth used his sleeved arm to strike the flat of the blade away. "Don't force my hand on this. I'm Regent. You *will* follow my order. Stand. Down."

"I told you true in the bar. About the thirty-six month thing," she started.

Before she could finish and before Rowan completely lowered the sword, a door latch clicked and hinges squawked in the preternaturally still morning fog. Two doors down, a woman stepped out onto her porch. "What's with the racket?" she demanded. Her eyes widened as she took in the state of the alley, the destruction and, finally, Rowan's lowering blade that had clearly been pointed at Ashley. Every ounce of color drained from the stranger's face and she backed into her house, slamming and audibly locking the door.

Gareth sighed. "Excellent. Rowan, put it away. *Now*," he emphasized when the man had lowered the blade point but still held the weapon. "Ash, inside."

"Don't think to order me—" Her knees buckled as she turned toward him, and she crumpled to the ground. "Crap," she muttered, chin to her chest.

Gareth strode forward, his energy level a surprise. He felt better than he had since his death, felt like he could actually *do* something. Anything. He scooped Ashley off the pavement, holding her close to his chest. Need drove through him and made his shaft ache. The heat in his belly began to spread.

Ashley mewled softly.

Gareth tightened his grip, the response to the small sound involuntary. "What's going on between us, Ashley? What's the 'thirty-six month thing?' Is that what's making me want to fight with Rowan and then take you to bed?"

She turned her face into his shoulder. "My epithicas."

He racked his brain for the definition at the same time Rowan cursed. "What?" Gareth asked, looking over his shoulder.

"Her epithicas is her fertility window. Happens something like every three or four years for the race's females. It draws the race's males to her." He scowled. "They'll fight you for her. Won't stop 'til one of you is dead."

Gareth stared at him, dumbfounded, before gathering his wits. "What? Why?"

Rowan rolled his shoulders before sheathing his blade. "Any male who impregnates her has the right to keep her."

"Don't let the clansmen get to me," Ashley murmured. "Please, Gareth. I can't..."

He shifted his gaze to her. "Can't what?"

"I won't be owned." She lifted fever-bright eyes to meet his. "I belong to no one, am no man's possession. I'll never be a sexual subservient, never be one of a handful of wives. Ever."

His skin had grown warmer as he held her, his desire for her blossoming. Her words did little to subdue his hunger. His throat worked as he swallowed, the image of her sexually submitting to him driving him closer to a ledge he hadn't even realized he stood on—one that would drop him into an abyss of craving and skin and sex. The breeze shifted toward him and he caught a whiff of the most enticing scent he'd ever experienced. It was the same he'd caught on meeting her, only magnified.

His grip tightened even as his erection throbbed, and his voice was strained when he finally managed to get himself under control. "What are the odds I also got a touch of this epithicas thing?"

"Zero. Men don't suffer the affliction. They just solve the female's problem." Rowan looked him over with as much interest as the man ever showed. "Why?"

"I'm..." Gareth hesitated. Maybe his arousal was simply a result of having survived battle. He closed his eyes and breathed deep. Again, Ash's scent filled his nose, even stronger this time. And he knew. "I think we've broken the race's gender rules."

Ash blinked owlishly. "You're suffering, too?"

Her word choice, *suffering*, grew more accurate by the second. He gave a sharp nod. "How do I fix it?"

Heat suffused her cheeks but she didn't answer.

Rowan's lips twitched and Gareth nearly dropped

the woman. It was as close as the large man had come to smiling. Ever.

"What?" Gareth demanded.

"Sex."

Rowan's deadpan answer caught Gareth off guard. "Come again?" he sputtered.

"That's your job, mate, not mine." The man started toward the front door. "Seems that, given the baton you're sporting, it won't be an issue."

Sirens sounded, still quite a ways away but fast approaching. "Rowan, get the door. We'll sort this out inside." Even as he said it, he knew he was inching closer to that unexpected ledge. He wanted to drown in Ashley's scent, to bury himself in her and stay there forever. The need to see her to her pleasure caused him to stumble, images of what she'd look like after a proper round between the sheets filling his mind like snapshots, one flung immediately on the heels of the last until there was a pile of explicit photos filling his mind. He couldn't think. Couldn't breathe. Couldn't stand the brush of his boxer briefs against the head of his cock. Fear he'd lose control like a teenaged lad had him hurrying toward the safe house door. "Step it up, man."

Ashley drew a breath, presumably to speak, and her eyes flashed wide. The tip of her tongue traced her upper lip, retreating before her teeth sank into her lush lower lip.

"What?" he snapped at her, his desire creating enough tension between them to shatter even the thickest of sword blades.

"You smell like…" She paused and closed her eyes.

"Like what?" he croaked.

"Ozone after a lightning strike," she whispered. "Like the wildness of the sea in a storm. Like the promise of the storm's power." Lifting a hand, she traced his stubbled jaw. "Gareth…"

He pushed past Rowan and kicked the door shut in the man's face with a shouted, "Mind the door."

Sitting Ashley on the foyer table, he ripped at the button to his pants even as she struggled to get the borrowed T-shirt off. It was so long that she was sitting on the hem. Wiggling and fighting, she yanked at the fabric and rocked the table so hard a vase was knocked off. Ceramic shattered against the aged oak floor.

"Leave the shirt." His erection sprang free, jutting from his groin.

A sound of desperation came from deep in Ashley's chest, a sound that wound him up tighter than a self-winding watch attached to an orchestra conductor's wrist.

Still, he had to know. "Do you want this, Ashley?"

She reached for his length, gripping it in her palm and pulling him toward her. "Need it. Need you," she croaked. "Please, Gareth."

"Do you *want* me?" he demanded, fighting the urge to sink into her. Never had he hungered for a woman so badly, but he'd have her acquiescence first, particularly after she'd voiced her fear that a male would use this as justification to support taking her against her will. For Gareth, there was no argument sufficient to warrant a decision like that. Not now. Not ever. It would be her explicit consent or they stopped this here and now.

"Ashley," he prompted one last time. "Answer me. Do you want me?"

Wide, burnished eyes sought his out. "Ever since I saw you at the bar."

Her words drove every thought of waiting he'd had into the dark recesses of his mind, locking them behind a door he hadn't known existed anywhere in his conscious. He became a well of desire that overflowed, his body moving of its own volition to find the heart of her, to bury himself there, to lose all sense of right and wrong, to give himself over to this raw passion.

With fumbling hands, he dug a condom out of his wallet and slipped it on. Then, without hesitation, he surged forward, driving into her with one hard move and reveling as she cried out with unabashed pleasure.

Her heat surrounded him tighter than a clenched fist. She became his epicenter, blurring every thought he had beyond pleasuring this woman until she could say nothing but his name. He thrust once and then again.

Her long legs wrapped around his waist. She ran her fingers through his hair and gripped, pulling him forward for a searing kiss. The woman dominated the moment, her tongue thrusting against his in time with his forceful thrusts, the table rattling its objections against the wall as it rained decorative flotsam, small and large, to the floor—keys, a stack of books and their bookends, a small lamp.

They ignored it all.

Gareth lost himself in the woman, in the vitality of each second in her embrace. She was fire to his ice, the sun to his moon, the match to his kindling.

Ashley broke the kiss and, clutching Gareth's shoulders, slid her ass to the edge of the table giving him great access, more depth, more control.

He took it.

Driving into her mercilessly, the sound of sex, of skin on skin, echoed through the foyer. Her soft cries grew louder, more demanding, and, gripping her hips, he gave her everything she asked for and more. He craved the sight of her skin, promised himself they'd go slower next time. And there *would* be a next time where he'd make it up to her, show her he was a better lover than this, a better man than to take her the moment the door closed behind them. But that was later. Now all he wanted was to take her to her peak, hear her cry his name again and again, and lose himself in her sensual embrace.

Reaching between them, he found the small bundle of nerves that would have her ceding all control to him, would drive her higher before catapulting her into the abyss. When he went, he wanted, *needed*, her to go with him.

He manipulated her with his thumb, strumming the little bud quickly.

It took only seconds to push her over the edge.

Her hips lurched against his and she took him all the way to the hilt. Digging her fingers into his shoulders, she arched her back and rode him hard, crying out as she tightened around him, spasms rocking her lithe form as her body gripped his so tightly that he lost the last tether to his control.

With three rapid thrusts, he roared out his pleasure and followed her into that indefinable chasm where only they existed.

His orgasm seemed to pull on his very soul, drawing out so long his legs began to shake.

Ashley rode him through to the end, finally, slowly, relaxing, softening her grip on his shoulders as she sagged against the wall. Her eyes fluttered shut. A small smile played at the corners of her mouth. "Damn, Assassin," she said, breathing heavily. "Had I known you were capable of that, you might have saved Fergus's bar."

"How so?" he managed to gasp out.

Eyes that had gone a bronzy gold opened and focused

on his. "I'd have had you in the broom closet before you got your coat off."

Gareth chuckled, dragging a hand through his hair, the other still resting on her bare hip. And for the first time since the phantom queen's assertion she would harvest him before his time, Gareth realized he wholly regretted that his life and longevity had been stolen from him. He wanted this woman again, and that meant one of two things: Gareth could either make the most of the eight days that remained before Beltane, or he could fight to find the will to change his fate. The former would be the easier of the two choices but assured his damnation. The latter? That was a different story altogether. If he chose to fight, it left him only one option. Beat the queen at her own game. The problem with that option?

He knew of no one who had survived such a calling card who might tell him how it was done.

Ashley rested her overheated back against the cool plaster wall and let her head loll. The epithicas was beaten back, at least for a little while, leaving her mind clearer than it had been in a couple of days.

First priority was getting dressed. She'd burned her top and underwear up and, seeing as they'd been all she owned, she was stuck wearing the borrowed shirt. Her jeans and boots were upstairs still, so at least she had those.

Second, she and Gareth needed to get out of here. He'd assuaged the worst of the heat, but it would be back. She just didn't know how soon. They'd need to be somewhere remote, somewhere she—*they*—could fight without mortal interference should the need arise. That was assuming he'd fight to help her retain her freedom. But… If the epithicas had actually been shared when their elements merged, he'd be rendered as helpless to his lust as she. What then?

Man, she hated this. She'd give anything to be able to lock herself in a vault with a nonphoenix lover and just get through the worst of... *Nonphoenix lover.* If Gareth *had* merged elements, and if he was experiencing the epithicas, would he expect her to remain loyal to him for a lifetime based on hormones alone? Worse, would he expect her to give her life up to him, remaining faithful to him and, again, him alone while he "collected" wives? Because she wouldn't settle for being wife number one—only number one and *only*. Wait. She was thinking wife-thoughts?

The last thought had her scrambling off the foyer table.

Pants around his ankles, Gareth stumbled out of her way.

Okay, she shoved him. A little. But panic made her irritable, and this was legitimate grounds for panic.

She wasn't wife material. Sure, she'd gone against conventional clan-focused behavior and lived as a nomad, but she had craved home and hearth most of her life. The problem? She could never be sure a man wanted her for *her*, not just another broodmare, that he truly loved *her* and hadn't been influenced by the hormones emitted during her epithicas. Insecurities ran deep, so she rarely took lovers in between her fertility cycle. Lovers, even one, complicated things when she moved on, and the last thing she wanted was complication. Life on the run was difficult enough. Besides, the fewer lovers she took, the less likely she was to risk falling in love. Love made people stupid. Talk about the ultimate complication compounded by idiotic personal behaviors. Plural.

"We need to get out of here," she called without looking back as she headed for the stairs, coiling the T-shirt and knotting it at her hip so it looked less like a dress. Her plan? Retrieve her jeans and boots from the bedroom and then hit the road. There were caves in Killavullen in County Cork, caves with multiple ingress and egress options that would keep her from being cornered. She, *they*, could hide there. The River Blackwater would help disperse the draw of her epithicas. All she had to do was convince Gareth he needed to stick with her through this, and that shouldn't be hard. He now needed her as much as she needed him.

She was halfway up the stairs when booted footsteps made her pick up the pace. He was coming after her, and she had a feeling it wasn't to discuss how she'd like her postcoital cup of tea. The man was an assassin, he'd want to—

"Damn it, Ash, stop! We have to discuss how we go forward."

—plan.

He grabbed the back of her shirt and she lost her balance, falling into him. Strong arms banded around her, keeping both of them upright.

She pulled away from him and started up the stairs again. "There's not much to discuss. That bitch goddess-queen-whatever tracked you here. I pissed her off, and she's clearly not done with you for whatever reason. We've got to move on."

Gareth took her by the arm and spun her toward him.

She braced one palm against his chest and the other gripped his side.

He hissed and twisted away, all color draining from his face.

"Gareth?"

"It's an old wound." He relaxed his hold on her. "If it's best we get out of here, I'm going to assume sooner is better than later."

She looked up at him, confused. "You're not going to fight me over this?"

His brow furrowed. "Why would I?"

He sounded genuinely confused. "Because I'm…" *A woman.* And in her race, women were only good for breeding and domestic chores. The warriors, the decision-makers, were men.

"The expert? Yes, you are. I know next to nothing about the phoenix as a people." When she didn't move, he reached out and slid a hand around the back of her neck, using his thumb to cant her chin up. "I won't bow to your every directive. We'll discuss how we handle things over the next few days—" His eyes darkened, as he said, "—but in this, you know more than I do. Where do we go?"

Ashley stepped away from him, conflicting emotions ricocheting through her. He defied everything she'd ever known about men. It left her out of sorts.

Yanking on her jeans while considering how to respond, she was in the process of fastening the top button when something hit the downstairs door with incredible force. A second blow and the door sounded as if it had splintered.

Gareth raced to the window as she pulled on her boots. One look and he cursed. "Uninvited guest."

Her breath stalled. "Who?"

"No idea. Given the fact the front door is smoking, I'm going to guess phoenix." He glanced at her. "I'm beginning to think you're a total catastrophe magnet—burning down the bar and its owner, engaging the phantom queen known for warring, seeing my car destroyed and now causing an epic fight in a bloody safe house."

She glared at him as she shoved her feet into her boots. "Your car was *not* my fault. And it's too soon for anyone to have tracked me." *Unless Fergus had actually done as he'd said and notified one of the men of my clan.*

"Obviously not," he said, his voice carrying low and hard. "We're out the front."

"What about a car? As you pointed out, yours isn't exactly a getaway machine anymore."

"We'll take Rowan's."

"What about *him*?"

Gareth's smiled, and the look was colder than his skin had ever been. "I feel sorry for the phoenix. Brother's got some rage issues. Now, let's go."

Sure enough, the sound of creative cursing, fists hitting flesh and things breaking rolled up the stairs.

Ashley went to the window that faced the main street. It was a solid fifteen feet to the sidewalk. She could make it, but she worried for Gareth. If he broke something, he'd be a liability—one she wouldn't in good conscience leave behind. Not when their elements were combined. If the old stories were true, his death could kill her and prevent her resurrection because she didn't hold the total power of regeneration anymore. She couldn't let him be caught, let alone killed.

"Out the window, darkling," he said as he ran the windowpane, wavy with age, up its runners. "Rowan will lose his temper soon and kill your clansman, and I'd rather not be around when the man goes up in flames. Burning to death isn't my idea of postcoital entertainment."

Swinging a leg out over the window ledge, she looked

at him without bothering to disguise her concern. "It's probably fifteen feet down."

"You scared of heights?" he asked absently, glancing at the doorway as the sound of fighting intensified.

"I'm scared you'll hurt yourself," she blurted out.

He rounded on her, eyes blazing. The look of unchecked fury had her leaning farther out the window.

"You don't *ever* consider me the weak link, Ash. I'll handle whatever comes my way. Now, go." And then he pushed her.

She twisted to ensure she landed on her feet. The morning was late enough the sidewalk was populated, and people started and stared. They followed her gaze, looking up as Gareth came out the window after her.

He dropped with far more grace than she had, landing in a crouch. Shooting to his feet, he grabbed her hand and took off down the street with only a slight limp. They dodged a group of tourists wielding cameras. Then there was a moment of suspended silence, the type that made every hair on her body stand up. An earthshaking boom shattered the silence. Heat washed over her, scalding in its intensity. She didn't bother to look back. The male phoenix had gone up in flames just as Gareth had predicted.

The only thing that mattered now was survival.

Chapter 9

The heated blast licked over Gareth's back, the consequence similar to that of a blowtorch turned on a cotton candlewick. The only option it had was to burn. Destruction was inevitable. Shirt fabric curled and smoked. His skin tightened, shrank and split in at least one place on his shoulders. He swallowed an anguished shout, gritting his teeth as he hauled Ash along the cobblestone road. They had to get out of here. Rowan would have utilized the other car park in the small town, leaving his vehicle as close to the entrance as possible.

Thanks to the woman in hand, he hadn't been grievously harmed in the morning's skirmish. He was grateful. And even though he was a feminist and truly adored women of all shapes, sizes and—obviously—races, he was irritated he'd been forced to rely on a woman to save his ass. He'd been so focused on forcing his element to heel that he'd missed the authenticity of…Macha's threat.

If he was going to fight her, he might as well start addressing her by name. Somehow, he'd believed the goddess wouldn't collect his soul until Beltane. Now he was forced to reconsider. She hadn't hesitated to strike at him, and that seriously revised his estimation of the time he had left.

Should've known she was a lying bitch.

He stumbled on the thought, and Ashley crashed into him sending him careening forward and bouncing off a signpost. Gripping his aching shoulder with his free hand, he fought to catch his breath.

The goddess had lied.

And if she'd lied to him about the date she would return for him, had she lied when she said she'd marked his soul? Could any damage she'd done be undone? Or... His heart pounded so loud that he couldn't hear anything but the thunder of his pulse through his ears. Was it possible she'd fabricated the whole thing and her mark on his soul, her stamp of ownership there on his chest, could be reversed?

Worse, had he essentially stopped living, given up on life, because of the word of a banished goddess? How could he not have anticipated she would lie? He was an idiot—a *fecking* idiot who'd thrown in the towel when the threat became too personal. The knowledge made his stomach pitch. He was a better man, a better assassin, than this. Or he'd thought he was. Who just gave up without a fight?

Him, apparently.

"Gareth!"

He whipped around to discern the threat but only found Ashley staring at him. "What?"

"You're going to break my hand if you don't ease up."

She massaged her fingers after he let go. "Where's Conan's car?"

"His name is Rowan."

"Big, muscle-bound man. Carries an egregiously large sword as presumable overcompensation. Speaks in grunts and glares. *Conan*. Discussion over."

Despite their situation, a smile pulled at the corners of Gareth's mouth as he started toward the car park again. "I suggest you don't call him that to his face. He's a little unpredictable."

"Too late." She glanced back the way they'd come as if anticipating more trouble. "And so am I."

"The phoenix—how long will it take him to resurrect?"

"No idea. Could take twelve hours, could take up to forty-eight. Depends on his age and strength and whether or not he met his Final Death. I didn't see him, so I don't know who he is. Was." She pushed her hair off her face with a huff. "Is. Whatever. I don't know, okay?"

"You said 'Final Death.' What is that?"

She cast him the side-eye. "Forget it."

"Spill, Ash." When she hesitated, he didn't wait to make this personal—because it was. Very. "This isn't just your problem anymore. You did something to me…"

This time the look she shot him was one filled with undisguised irritation. "Even a phoenix can die. Don't ask me more. I'm not discussing it." She looked around the car park as they passed through the pay gate. "Which one is Conan's car?"

"Right here." He pointed.

"You guys have serious testosterone issues," she muttered, stalking toward the midnight blue Ferrari 599 GTB Fiorano Coupe F1. "How are you supposed to be inconspicuous in a car like this?"

"It's that old adage about hiding in plain sight." Gareth pulled out his cell, opened an app he'd developed that allowed him to take over any assassin's car via the computer and selected Rowan's from a drop-down list. Some might call it hacking. He called it creative forethought. One tap on the screen unlocked the car, and he opened the door for Ashley. She slipped in quietly, her eyes on the building they'd left. The thatch roof had been nothing but tinder at the phoenix's death, and the entire building now burned.

Slipping into the driver's seat, Gareth selected a second option on the app and started. It was the work of a moment to feel around under the seat and discover what he considered a personal treasure. With a grin, he traced the shape of the first one and then the other of a pair of Sig Sauer P220 handguns. Standard issue for assassins. There would also be extra ammunition stashed in the car as well as knives, garrotes and more. Thank the gods Rowan always brought a variety of weapons to every occasion, be it a dinner party or a street fight.

"So, Conan carries a sword and fights with his fists but drives a Ferrari, and you carry a Sig and are tech-savvy but without a vehicle. How is it possible you're both assassins? One an archaic mothball, the other a bicycle-bound geek." Again, she looked toward the house.

"Your ass is in a Ferrari and I'm behind the wheel. That's hardly bicycle bound." He ignored the rest of her question, instead directing the conversation to her as he paid the box attendant and then pulled out of the parking lot. "Why do you keep looking back?"

"To see what's going to step out of the smoke and debris. The way the day is going it seems prudent to be prepared, you know?"

Sure, the day had generally sucked. But seeing as they'd wrapped up an incredible sexcapade less than twenty minutes ago, the comment stung. Never mind that it was his pride that was wounded. Realization made his response that much sharper. "Ah, and for a second there, I thought your generous mood following a great round of spontaneous sex would stick. Obviously, you're far too mercurial to appreciate postcoital afterglow or conversation. Prefer a shag and fag do you, then?"

She shifted to her hip, facing him. "You're only pissed off because I didn't fawn over your male prowess, taking me on a table like that."

"And *ye're* too proud to admit I had ye yellin' me name within five hard strokes," he groused, brogue thickening as his irritation escalated.

"It's the epithicas," she murmured as she settled back into her seat and stared out the passenger window. "I can't help it."

"And that's a right convenient excuse, do ye no' think? 'I canna help meself.'" He laughed, the sound bitter enough to sour milk. "An' I asked ye if ye were sure. I asked ye if ye wanted me. Ye dinna hesitate, did ye? No."

That was the crux of his wounded pride. She'd said she had wanted him since she first saw him, claimed she would've taken him at the bar had she known how good it could be. Now? Now she was using her fertility cycle as a scapegoat, blaming her every action on hormones and not choices. He wasn't above crying foul. "Ye made yer choices, lass. Ye'll stick by them, and stick by the fact ye chose me, for choose me ye did. Hence the reason I waited for yer shift tae end before ye burned down the bar. Don't be thinkin' tae try tae change the choices ye made—"

"Choice we *both* made," she interceded.

"—that led us tae this moment," he finished without pausing. Breathing hard, he schooled his face and wrangled his temper, controlling both with Herculean effort. "You'll own this, Ashley. You won't be pushing this off on some breeding heat. You chose me, and I've paid the price for that choice."

They left Ennistymon at far greater speed than they'd entered, the luxury car purring quietly as Gareth worked his way through the gears. The winding road was as much a joy to drive as the woman beside him was a pain-in-the-ass enigma. He didn't understand her, and he prided himself on understanding women. At the age of five and ten, a man in times past, he'd taken his first tumble in the hay. Literally. It was then he decided he loved women. All women. This one might be the exception, capricious creature that she was.

His mind shifted direction, considering the other temperamental woman he had to manage.

Macha. Goddess of Phantoms and War.

Things had changed, and he needed to speak to Dylan, update him as Regent to the Assassin. He considered dialing direct from his phone and changed his mind. Using the hands-free option in the car, he said, "Call Dylan."

The car's digital voice responded, "Calling Dylan."

Almost immediately, the phone rang across the speakers.

Dylan answered on the first ring. "Talk to me, Rowan."

"It's Gareth, and I have you on speakerphone." It was an undisguised warning to Dylan to mind his words. "Ashley Clement is in the car with me."

"And what of Rowan?" Dylan's tone gave away nothing save that Gareth knew him better than anyone. Beneath the four-word question was a well of fury the other man not only lived with but drew from in order to hold his position and run the Nest with brutal efficiency.

"Cleaning up what's left of the safe house."

"Casualties?"

Gareth glanced at Ashley. "Nothing likely permanent. Rowan took out a male phoenix who thought to enter without saying the magic word. No idea when, or if, the phoenix will resurrect."

"Explain." Dylan's tone had taken an even sharper turn toward outright irritation.

Ashley continued to stare out the window when she spoke. "Given that both the fire brigade and the Garda were in attendance, his ashes may be spread too thin, washed or tracked out and away from the scene. There's a chance he won't be able to resurrect. It's too soon to tell."

Gareth shot her a hard glance. She'd withheld the specifics from him when he asked about her clansman's possible resurrection. Temper pricked, he carried on. "We're going to ground for a day or two, but I need you to do something for me until I'm able to return. I need..." He blew out a breath. "I need you to trust me on this."

Dylan didn't hesitate. "Name it."

"I need you to go to the Elder's Library and see what you can find out about the old ways of marking a soul and what it would take to break the bond between that soul and its claimant."

"Gareth, I've looked—"

"And I believe the goddess lied," he said softly, not unaware that Ashley had turned toward him, eyes wide, all color leeching from her face. "I believe there's a way to break that bond. She tried to harvest my soul early. And by 'early,' I mean today, Dylan. She claimed Beltane was her window of opportunity. If we can break the bond, stop her from forcing me into service... If I can reclaim my soul..." His throat tightened at the very thought. Coughing, he forced himself to continue. "We can stop her bid to rally an army and return to this plane."

"I'll involve the Elder and the Arcanum in the search." Dylan's father, the Elder and leader of the Druids, knew the seemingly infinite tomes in that library better than any other. Then there was the Assassin's Arcanum. That band of men would move the heavens and descend to the very heart of the Shadow Realm itself to spare him this.

Gareth's chest tightened. He had to disclose everything. "There's more."

Dylan's silence was so weighted it seemed the car should have slowed under the burden.

"When the goddess confronted me this morning, the phoenix, Ashley, interceded." Gareth shot her a glance before refocusing on the road. Her normally lush lips were nothing but a harsh horizontal slash, their fullness suffocated by emotion. *Nerves.* "Our elements seem to have merged. Dylan, I need you—*you alone*—to figure out what this means for me. For her."

In the background, Kennedy's light footsteps preceded her voice. "Is Gareth okay?"

"He's going to be," Dylan responded with hard conviction. "How much does the phoenix know about this?"

She scowled at the nearest car speaker. "'The phoenix' is sitting right here."

Gareth spared Ashley another fleeting look and answered Dylan before he and Ash got into it. "Her comment was she'd either saved my life or killed us both."

Dylan's violent cursing colored the air, and when he finally slowed, his words were as brittle and sharp as shards of untempered glass. "Hear me on this, lass. You harm my man and I *will* come at you with everything I've got and every resource at my disposal. I will kill you a thousand times if that's what it takes to avenge my brother."

Gareth's temper reignited. "Don't threaten her, Dylan. She saved my life."

"Aye, and she may have cost it. Until I'm sure which gesture prevails? Keep her away from the Nest. I'll be in touch." He disconnected the call.

"Well, that went well." Gareth approached the on-ramp to the N18 highway. "Which way?"

"Head south toward Killavullen." Ashley stared straight ahead, shoulders as stiff as her tone. "And if that went 'well,' I'd freaking hate to see something go poorly."

"You have no idea, darkling." Gareth accelerated down the on-ramp. "You have no idea."

The miles passed in relative silence, Ashley lost in her thoughts. So much had happened in such a short amount of time, she wasn't entirely sure which event to process first. Everything clamored for her immediate attention. One event stood out.

Sex.

Her body was already aching again, and she'd caught Gareth adjusting his jeans to better accommodate the return of his nascent erection. They had a solid hour left before they reached Killavullen, and then they had to hide the car and hoof it to the caves. The main entrances had been gated and locked years ago, but there were other ways in, smaller openings most people were unaware of. Provisions would have to be acquired, too. Without access to her accounts, she was left entirely

dependent on Gareth to provide for her needs. Again.
That dependency translated to another type of possession, one where he could provide or withhold as he saw
fit. She didn't like it. At all. Centuries of independence
and self-sufficiency left her fighting the urge to change
their course to Dublin where she could gain access to
her emergency monies. But Dublin wasn't an option.
Last she'd heard, there were three male phoenixes in
residence within the city, and she couldn't afford to be
anywhere near them right now. Chances were good that's
where Fergus had found a male to descend on her so
quickly. And if he'd found one, he certainly could have
found others.

She wanted to cry foul.

Instead, she pointed at the next exit. "We need to
pick up a few provisions. Limerick will be a good place
to blend in to the crowds and find what we need." She
gripped her thighs, fingers digging into muscle hard
enough to bruise. "I'll have to rely on you to pay seeing as my pack was destroyed and you wouldn't take
me to Dublin."

He shifted lanes and headed up the off-ramp. "No
worries."

"I'll see that you're repaid."

He didn't look at her as he entered the roundabout.
"Consider the supplies recompense for saving my life
this morning."

"I don't need to be paid for that." She forced her fingers to relax and rubbed them against her jeans. "It was
the right thing to do."

"Merging elements was a conscious choice?"

"Don't sound so incredulous, and no. It wasn't." She
kept her gaze focused on finding a consolidated market area where they could get the items they'd need in

one stop. Moments later they crossed the bridge over the Shannon Estuary and entered the heart of the city. Shops and markets lined the road offering everything she could have asked for. "Stop here."

Gareth pulled into a vacant spot along Dooradoyle and shut the car off. "Where do we start?"

"Nonperishables first. Groceries last. I saw a sign for Tesco's at Crescent Shopping Center. They'll have everything we need." She opened the door and stood, taking in the heavy crowds. "It should be easy enough to remain unnoticed, as well." The crowds would help diffuse her epithicas while they were indoors. The running water of the estuary at high tide and the ocean breeze would definitely help when they returned to the car. Neither detractor would be enough to keep her safe, though. If she could hide in a crowd, a clansman could, as well. She'd never smell the dry, desert heat of him before he was upon her, and then it would be too late. This would have to be a fast stop.

Gareth moved in beside her as she started down the sidewalk toward the shopping complex, shocking her when he slipped his hand into hers. At her confusion, he shrugged, the action stiff and unnatural. "If we look a bit like a normal couple out to market, we'll be less likely to draw attention."

"Right, because we don't look like we've been through the wringer or anything." She glanced up at him, unable to suppress a smile. "Everyone goes out with charred clothing, bloodstains, road rash, T-shirts that could be dresses and no underwear."

His hand twitched around hers. "First, the charred clothing and bloodstain are hidden by my jacket. Second, the road rash you incurred on your hip and knee when you tackled me are hidden by your jeans. Third, I want you out of Rowan's shirt first thing. And fourth?" He sucked in a breath at the same time he reached down and unashamedly adjusted the bulge behind his jeans zipper for the second time in an hour. "Don't discuss going commando with me unless you want to cause a public spectacle. You don't strike me as an exhibitionist."

She grinned. "Neither do you."

Pulling her to a stop, he faced her, closing the distance between them until her breasts rubbed his chest. "I've apparently had a personality transplant because all I can think of is dragging you down a side street and taking you against the first stretch of exposed wall I find." The tenor of his voice dropped. "Voyeurs be welcome or damned. I don't care."

Ashley closed her eyes and leaned into him, careful to avoid the bloodstained area that had pained him before. Her breasts grew heavy, her nipples hypersensitive. Her sex ached. The need to touch his bare skin had her slipping a hand under the front of his sweater and curling her fingers over the waistband of his jeans. Her knuckles brushed the head of his arousal.

He jerked on contact and drew a sharp breath through clenched teeth. "Unless you want to act out my alleyway fantasy, remove your hand."

She did, albeit slowly, taking every opportunity to caress the silky head with her fingers as she withdrew.

"You're playing with fire," he murmured.

She rose to her tiptoes and, lips almost touching, whispered, "I *am* fire."

"So am I."

Ashley grinned. "I know."

Settling to her feet, she closed her eyes and fought to refocus. The need was growing faster. They had to get in and out of Limerick as fast as they could, and flirting with each other like this was to court disaster seeing as it occupied both of them to the point of total distraction.

Stepping away from him literally hurt, but she did it. "We need to make this a fast stop and get back on the road quickly. We'll need to park a fair distance from Killavullen and hike in to the caves. I'd like to be there by dark."

Gareth dragged a trembling hand down his face. "You're right. I just... The epithicas—it's an all-consuming thing. Is it always like this?"

She didn't hesitate for even a second. "It's usually worse. You're only getting a small part of it."

"Gods," he murmured. "How do you stand it? It's... I feel for you."

"Don't pity me. I've done well for myself over the years and have, above all, managed to keep from being claimed." Pulling farther away, she spun on her heel and started for the mall.

He caught up to her in only a few strides, again taking her hand. "Has it been hard, living like that?"

"Like what?"

"Always looking over your shoulder. Always afraid the next man to approach you will be the one that beats you at your own game?"

Her heart ached at the question. *Had it been hard?* No. It had been worse than that. Inexplicably worse. A far more accurate description would have been to say it had been bloody near impossible. She retrieved her hand from his. "It's not a game."

"I didn't mean—"

She gestured toward the large department store she'd been looking for. "Forget it. We'll stick to shopping here. What they don't have, we'll do without." Moving swiftly and doing her best to keep her mind off the conversation,

Ashley took the elevator to the second level, grabbed a shopping cart and started through the home goods department.

Halfway down the first aisle, she paused, her grip tightening on the cart's handle. She didn't want to ask this, didn't want to need permission, but the money wasn't hers. It galled that she was dependent on someone else to provide for her after so many centuries of self-sufficiency. It smacked too much of his possession of her, and she belonged to no one. Not now; not ever. But her feelings on the matter didn't change the question that had to be asked as a matter of courtesy if nothing else. "What's my budget?"

"I'm a fair hand at field survival, but I'm also... financially secure. Get whatever you believe we'll need."

She gave a sharp nod and pushed the cart on.

Gareth kept up with her, quietly scanning the area around them as she shopped.

Improvisation was required when the store failed to offer sleeping bags. Instead, she grabbed blankets and pillows. The caves would be damp and cool, so sharing a bed and body heat would be more practical. And there was no sense pretending the epithicas would cede to their situation. It would demand satiation, and soon.

She also grabbed candles, matches, a battery-operated lantern and batteries, a single-burner butane cookstove with two bottles of butane, two large duffels, bungee cords and a single cook pot. Then it was downstairs to the canned goods aisles where she rapidly pulled together impromptu menus of high-protein, calorically dense meals and more—crackers, cookies, nuts, trail mix.

She had picked up four large containers of water and

was wiggling them into the cart when Gareth finally spoke. "We can't carry all of this."

"We'll have to carry the stuff from upstairs, but half the food can stay in the trunk." She pushed the laden cart toward the checkout lane, then paused and looked back. "We'll keep the car within walking distance in the event we need to make a run for it."

His face closed up, became an emotional wasteland devoid of anything familiar. "I'm sick of running. I've been doing it since before Samhain. I'm done."

"I've been doing it so long it's second nature. And neither of us is done. Not yet." She pushed the cart up to the checkout line and stood, waiting her turn. "After we've paid, pick out clothes and get changed. I'll watch the cart and take my turn to dress after you're done."

He gave an absent nod, his mind clearly somewhere else.

She stepped up to the register and began to unload their haul, half amused and half irritated at the way the cashier kept fumbling goods as she openly stared at Gareth.

The man was total eye candy, and he was completely oblivious to women's reactions to him.

After the last item was rung up, the cashier called out the total. Ashley cringed but didn't say anything. She'd definitely see to it that Gareth was repaid. It was only right.

He stepped up to the cashier and offered her a kind word and smile as he paid cash for their goods.

The young woman accepted the bills with a blush, and Ashley was impressed the girl managed to return Gareth's change without including her number and panties.

Whereas Ashley had been amused before, she was stunned to find her fingertips shifting to talons and her skin flushing. Her phoenix screamed in her head, the noise defiant in the face of the cashier's flirtation with their man.

No. No, no, no.

Gareth was *not* theirs.

That implied emotional commitment. That translated to relationship. And relationship translated to complication.

No, he couldn't be theirs. *Hers.*

Ever.

Chapter 10

Well aware that Ashley's mood had tanked in the checkout line, Gareth had no idea what the catalyst had been. All he'd done was pay for their items and offer common courtesy to the young woman who'd run the register. Yes, she had flirted with him, but surely that hadn't bothered Ashley. Why would it? He couldn't come up with any legitimate reason. The cashier had been a kindhearted girl, but she couldn't hold even an unlit candle to Ash's desirability. It wasn't possible. Yet, if he was honest, it pleased him on a base level that she might be as affected by him as he was by her. He had been happy to provide for her today. It had stirred a dormant sense of chivalry to meet her needs.

Needs.

Yes, needs. No matter her convictions, she *needed* him. They would certainly have to depend on each other to get through this epithicas, particularly if the body's demands grew any worse. But he didn't want her to simply need him. He wanted her to *want* him, to crave him the way he'd begun to crave her as he fell asleep holding her last night. He shifted his packages in order to tug at the collar of the new shirt he'd bought. Despite the V-neck T-shirt's design, it was stifling. Too tight. Touching him everywhere, and it wasn't cotton he wanted rubbing his oversensitive skin. He wanted Ashley's hands, mouth and body all over his.

It galled that, for the first time, he'd had to demand a woman declare her desire for him. He wasn't arrogant. Not really. It was just… Women had always been so direct with him when it came to their sexual appetite. Not Ashley. He'd had to push her to not only affirm but articulate her choice. It was a first—one he didn't care for at all as it left him wondering at the authenticity of it. Worse, it left him with the realization he might want her more than she wanted him. And even worse than that was the understanding that his wanting her had begun well before their elements had merged, and from that wanting had been born an uncomfortable sensation far too similar to his own brand of need, entirely unfamiliar and not at all comfortable.

The private admission startled him.

It has to be the epithicas.

And if it was? Did that mean he'd taken on the possessive nature, the apparent need to own a woman, or… worse? It couldn't be. He'd know. The feelings he was experiencing had to be his and his alone. And they were, in all likelihood, due to the fact he'd felt so little since his resurrection. That had to be it. Particularly if he looked any harder at the situation. Or the woman.

Following a couple of steps behind Ashley, watching her hips sway back and forth enticingly as they navigated the crowds on their way back to the car, Gareth couldn't help but cringe. The physical reaction to his emotional epiphany had nothing to do with her very fine ass. It was all about the fact that he'd openly mocked her for blaming the epithicas for their having had sex, and here he was doing essentially the same thing where his passion was concerned.

He slowed.

That's it. *Not passion.* Com*passion.*

Struggling as he was with this hormonal influx had left him feeling genuine compassion for the first time in months, and he admittedly felt for Ashley as she suffered this affliction every three years. There wasn't another plausible explanation.

Unbidden images of the men she must have taken—*been forced to take*, his subconscious interjected—flashed through his mind. What type of man did she usually prefer?

The thought of her racing out the doorway this morning assaulted him, hitting his awareness as hard as she had hit him in the flesh. Perhaps she favored someone like Rowan. She'd emerged in nothing but her T-shirt and underwear, after all. And the other man had not only seen her in such revealing wear, he'd also seen her full flesh when she'd incinerated her clothes as she assaulted Macha.

Jealousy raged through him, and he wanted nothing more than to break Rowan's nose *after* he blackened both eyes so thoroughly they swelled shut and assured the man wouldn't see Ash's skin again.

What the hell?

Gareth slowed even more. This *had* to be a result of the epithicas. He was never possessive over a woman. Women. Whatever. Jealousy and possessiveness had never been part of his bag of tricks when it came to the fairer sex. No, this was new. And he didn't like it.

At all.

Guilt wove through him like a dense, decorative thread in the loom of his being. A thread so brightly colored that it didn't match the dark, thick, dull threads that reflected what he was truly made of. He could pull at that brilliant thread, but that would leave a gap in the weave. That gap would ultimately unravel, and thoroughly. He wouldn't have a clue where to begin repairs to the very fiber of who he was. Yet by leaving that thread, that *guilt*, alone, the emotion would only embed itself deeper.

He shifted his focus and tried to envision his life's tapestry without that mismatched emotional thread only to find another—one that added multiple dimensions, visual interest and personal appeal. *Ashley.* She neither matched nor contrasted, but had undeniably been woven into his life. She was part of his present. Time would make her a permanent part of his past. No other outcome made sense.

The woman occupying his thoughts looked over her shoulder, those burnished eyes sparking with irritation. "Keep up."

He arched a brow but stepped up his pace. "Perhaps you should keep pace with me seeing as I'm the one with the key code to the car."

She slowed, turning so she walked backward despite the pedestrian traffic, uneven sidewalk and the burden of her share of the shopping effort that she'd demanded she carry. "Your legs are longer than mine. You're in fine shape. You can either keep up or I'll wait for you at the car."

"I thought you'd hired me to 'cover your six.'" It was an unnecessary verbal jab and he knew it. And reintroducing the bargain and her offer to pay him into their personal equation was a hit below the belt, but the words were out before he could stop himself.

Her eyes flared, hurt flashing through them before they narrowed and a cool smile disguised whatever she'd felt. "Oh, I would have hired you, but I didn't. No money ever changed hands. Besides, you're not."

He slowed a fraction more, silently amused when she followed suit. "Not what?"

Turned out it was only to deliver her proverbial shot across his bow.

"You don't have my six, assassin. You're staring at it."

"You don't know that," he blurted. What in the name of the gods had happened to his finesse?

"If my 'six' is my ass, I most certainly do."

He glared at her, the irritation with himself though she bore the brunt of it. "You have eyes in the back of your head, then?"

"No need." She smirked. "Your defensiveness is answer enough."

He stopped.

So did she.

Gareth took a step toward her.

She took a step back.

"You're playing with fire," he said just loud enough for her to hear.

I know, she mouthed back.

He couldn't contain his bark of laughter.

Her eyes glittered, compelling him forward as if summoned.

Several large strides and he was by her side as she spun and resumed her trek to the car. This time he kept up without comment.

Though he did miss watching her ass.

Canny woman.

* * *

Ashley stood by as Gareth circled the car, looking it over carefully. "Are we expecting bombs? Or are you checking for scratches? Conan seems like the type to get a little pissy over, well, everything."

He looked at her over the low-profile roofline. "He's not pissy. He's both indifferent and angry. Big difference."

"How can he be indifferent *and* angry?"

Gareth pulled his phone and tapped the screen. The trunk popped open with a soft *snick* and he kneed the lid up. "Easy. He's indifferent to everyone except those in the Assassin's Arcanum and angry at the world. He's reclusive yet loyal, willful but obedient and, without exception, wields his blade with a conscience."

She considered the man she'd met and realized it was a pretty good description. "Sounds more like a serial killer with multiple personality disorder than a famed Druidic assassin."

One corner of Gareth's mouth kicked up.

"Wait. Let me guess." She shifted the shopping bags she carried. "You'd suggest I not say that to his face."

The smile bloomed, a deep dimple revealed. "Pretty much."

"I need a notebook of all the things I'm not supposed to say."

"Why?"

She grinned in response. "So I can remember to say them." Her grin slipped as a familiar awareness hit her— an awareness that this time with Gareth, no matter how enjoyable, was temporary. Like everything. "Scratch that," she said woodenly, dumping her bags in the trunk space.

Gareth's own smile waned. "What's wrong? I blinked and you went from smiling to somber."

Noticed, did he? Fair enough. "Keeping up with smart-ass remarks is pointless considering I'll likely never see Conan again." He drew a breath as if to reply, but she held up her hand in a palm-out, stop-motion gesture. "I've been through this with you. Once the epithicas is over, we'll go our separate ways and our paths won't cross again."

"Why?" he demanded.

She sighed. "I can't come back here again and you can't leave."

"Why?"

"Really? What are you, two?"

His eyes darkened. "Answer me, Ash."

"I've been here too long. Coming back would be stupid—like hanging out a shingle and inviting every male phoenix to stop by for a cuppa and a chat. And you can't leave because you're an assassin. Your home is here." She leaned into the tiny trunk and dug through a bag, retrieving a hair tie. Movements short and sharp, she pulled her hair into a loose topknot. "The difficulty will be managing our merged elements."

"What do you mean?"

Clasping her hands behind her neck, she pulled. How to answer? He deserved the truth. Always. And she hated lying. "A phoenix's life, death and ability to resurrect are all tied to her element. I have no idea what this means for me now that I only hold half that ability. I can only hope that, if you die, my element returns to me."

He crossed his arms over his chest, the short sleeve seams on his shirt straining against his biceps. "And what does it mean to me if *you* die?"

She dropped her hands to her sides and met his flat

stare. "The most I can do is offer an educated guess based on the legends and myths I grew up hearing."

Impatience marred his features as he gestured with his hands, indicating she should get on with it.

"If I die, you can hope your element returns to you… or that mine does."

"What if I get both?"

"That much heat would be too much for anyone to master. You'd burn to ash where you stood."

"Not exactly the way I want to go." His shoulders sagged a fraction. "I guess that makes survival your first choice."

"That's nothing new seeing as it always has been." She looked away, unable to meet the unguarded emotion in his eyes, an emotion that looked like diluted hope. "I never meant for this to happen."

"What does it—this *thing* between us—mean, Ashley?"

"We'll always be tied together, aware of each other on some level, but exactly how aware?" She shrugged uneasily. "I don't know. You needn't worry that I'll park myself in your back pocket or anything, though. I'm not built that way."

And she wasn't. Even if her lifeline was tied to his, and even if that meant her odds of surviving this elemental merge had cost her the very immortality she'd fought for centuries to preserve, she harbored no false expectations where they were concerned. He had a life, a home and a family to return to while she had a new life to carve out in a new place. Alone. He would return to the familiar, the comfortable, the known, while she moved on to the next phase of her existence. She didn't know what it would look like, how it would feel or what, if anything, would hold any familiarity. The only given was that what lay before her would be populated by strangers' faces and unfamiliar places.

He shifted away from her and looked down the street, offering her only a partial profile. "This doesn't have to be my home. There are assassins all over the world."

"Arcanum members?" she countered.

Muscle knotted at the back of his jaw. "No."

She couldn't get into this with him, debating what they each *might* do, what sacrifices they each *might* make, in order to stay together. Never had she been the type to hang around for the sake of a maybe or a might be. If that meant being brutally practical? Fine. "So... what? Knowing that I can't stay here, you'd leave the Arcanum and follow me wherever I went? Or would you instead insist I stay here? Would you put your family at risk in the name of protecting me when the clans come calling? Because they will. And they'll fight to claim me as their own."

Gareth shot her a hot, hard look.

"I didn't think so. Point. Set. Argument match." She gave him her back and began removing tags from items and consolidating things in a logical way in the duffels so they could pull a grab-and-go once they reached Killavullen. Standing in the open for long in such a tiny village would be far more conspicuous than doing the same here among the crowded streets.

Heat slipped lazily down her neck, tracing her spine like an invisible lover's caress seconds before the cold Gareth's body harbored chased into the warmth of hers. He pressed along the line of her form, pinning her between him and the rear of the car. Leaning into her that way pushed his hips into her ass. Strong, broad hands parked one on each side of the open trunk. His chest and shoulders bowed over her, covering her back completely, forcing her to brace herself, her hands petite beside his.

"Let me make one thing clear, little phoenix."

Goose bumps decorated the bared skin on her arms.

"You aren't going to just walk away from this. From *me*."

"Are you threatening me?" she asked, dismayed at the husky timbre of her voice.

"No. I'm telling you true."

Fear trilled through her, the sound a wild alarm, raising her heat level so fast they both gasped. She whipped her head back and slammed into his chin before shoving backward, knocking him away once he was off balance. Spinning, she faced him, eyes narrowed. "Don't you ever, *ever* threaten to trap me, Gareth. I'll rebel, fight you to my last breath to protect my freedom. You don't own me. Not now. Not in the future. Not ever." She thumped the heel of her hand over her heart. "I'm my own woman, now and always."

He pinched his split chin together to stem the bleeding, never taking his eyes off her.

Silence stretched between them, as thick and unwieldy as a wad of cooled taffy.

Ashley again gave him her back and resumed loading the duffel bags. She came across the two matching ball caps with *Ireland* embroidered across the face. She'd purchased them with the intent of appearing touristy. The less local they seemed, the more likely it was that those who lived in the Killavullen area would ignore them. Ripping the tags off each cap, she passed one to Gareth without comment. Velcro ripped as he resized it. She did the same, settling hers over her red hair.

Should have purchased hair color. Oh, well. There

really wasn't time or the facilities to deal with the mass of curls she possessed. The cap would have to do.

She slammed the trunk lid closed. With no other option, she faced Gareth. "We need to go."

"I think it's more important that we talk about this."

The look in his eyes was unreadable, and that made her more wary than if his emotion had been there for interpretation. Now she had to guess what he was thinking, what he was feeling or, as it was based on the look on his face, *not* feeling. But no matter what might or might not be running through his mind, talking it out wasn't an option. Admitting her fears to this man, fears held for so long they were part of her emotional DNA, would be the equivalent of handing him a bear trap and encouraging him to set it on a path she was sure to travel. The only things that could come from it would be damage and pain. Both. And they would be hers.

That didn't mean she shouldn't think this through and find a way to handle it, and him, better. She did, after all, have to have him in order to get through the next few days. She'd deal with the fallout afterward. "I don't think there's much to say other than this. We need to get to the cave, and soon."

"Why?"

"What is it with you and the question 'why?'" she asked, forcing a laugh and then raising her brows. "The answer should be easy enough to determine."

"You want…need…" He swallowed, the gesture so unplanned she couldn't help but reach for him.

Taking his hand, she met his gaze. "I'm going to want you again. Soon."

"Need me," he corrected, an odd look of determination dominating his face in the set of his jaw, the firm line of lips, the tightening at the corners of his eyes.

And then there were his eyes themselves. They grew darker, the blue taking on the colors of the waves that pounded the Cliffs of Moher—stormy teal, deep blue and powerful black.

"However you choose to identify it, fine. Bottom line, the epithicas is rising, and if it's affecting me, I'm going to assume it's affecting you."

He hesitated, then placed her palm over his groin.

Ashley's fingers curled around the length of his erection as much as his jeans allowed. He lifted his free hand and cupped her face. "Who taught you that being needed was such a horrible thing?"

Ashley jerked away, breaking all contact. Her heart raced so fast she thought it could have independently qualified for international footrace competitions—on its own. The damn thing seemed to have sprouted legs and taken off, bouncing so hard off her ribs she was certain her shirt fluttered with the impact.

"Ashley? Answer me." He reached for her again, seeking to reestablish contact. "Please."

She evaded his effort. Moving to the passenger door, she looked toward him but kept her focus on a point down the street. "Unlock the door, Gareth."

"We need to sort this out, Ash."

"The door, Gareth." She did look at him then, letting the weight of her stare carry her refusal to bend.

Despite the ball caps and touristy affectation they'd donned, pedestrians stared as they passed by.

Leaning her forearms on the coupe's low-slung roofline, she considered him. "How many people are going to remember the attractive couple arguing over the ridiculously rare and expensive car?" She cut him off when he started to respond. "Easy answer? Even one is too many. Unlock. The door."

Gareth retrieved his phone and worked his magic. The lock disengaged with hardly a sound. He stared at her for a moment, opened his mouth to speak and then snapped it closed. Instead of the argument she'd half expected, he slipped into the car and slammed the door behind him.

She followed suit, slipping into the passenger's seat and making it a point to shut her door gently. Not necessary, but thoroughly satisfying.

Bottom line? The conversation had been shut down, and that's what she'd been after.

She buckled and then waited, as Gareth seemed to gather himself before starting the car.

Odd that the uncomfortable conversation had left her with a hollow feeling in her chest. Odder still that that space seemed to have taken up residence where her heart had been only moments before. Perhaps the organ had indeed broken free.

"Better that it breaks free instead of simply breaking," she murmured.

It didn't slip her notice she'd chosen its freedom over its damage. But there was only one way a man could break her heart, and that was if she allowed herself to care for him.

She stole a sidelong glance at Gareth as he put the car in gear, checked oncoming traffic and then pulled away from the curb.

The truth was there, surfing the surface of her consciousness. She didn't like what she found. At all. Because it all boiled down to one simple truth: Gareth Brennan was the kind of man she could allow herself to care about. What was worse?

She might not be able to stop herself.

Chapter 11

Gareth had Ashley search the Killavullen area on his phone. The local Nano Nagle Center regularly hosted a farmers' market and, as luck would have it, the market was open. Road signs advertised large participation. The Center was where they'd park the car and start their hike. They'd follow the River Blackwater to one of the cave entrances Ash knew of, carrying only the goods they'd need to spend a couple of days inside the cave system as they figured out what to do next.

Ashley had been quiet since they'd left Limerick, only answering questions he posed, never volunteering anything or opening conversation.

Her silence had put Gareth on edge, and he didn't care for the fact any more than he liked that she'd positioned him there. Easily. Never had a woman held the upper hand with him. The thought was disconcerting, particularly that she'd managed it with no apparent effort.

Truth was, he'd spent his three-plus centuries without a relationship with the fairer sex or—and?—the complications such a relationship posed. But this thing with Ashley defied explanation. It felt bigger than a passing fling. He knew it shouldn't, not after having just met her. But the truth was the truth.

Perhaps he'd been too quick to dismiss the power of the epithicas earlier. There was one surefire way to find out. He'd ask about that as well, and not only in regard to the breeding heat but also about what she'd meant when she said she'd either saved him or killed them both. It hadn't been at the forefront of his mind. But if the banished goddess had, indeed, lied... It changed everything.

First, though, he'd need to work up the nerve to eat a little crow if in the event he'd been too disparaging without warrant. Easing into the conversation in a roundabout fashion would likely be easier and, in truth, afford him the chance to save a little face.

Yep. That was, without a doubt, the more appealing route seeing as he knew Ashley well enough to know she'd cut him only enough slack to allow him to snap his neck when he verbally hung himself. And with her? The hanging seemed inevitable. That he actually appreciated this about her made him a sick bastard.

His lips twitched and he fought the urge to smile.

She had, without question, stirred up the personal pity party he'd spent months hosting. Her presence in his life had turned out to be the equivalent of spiked punch and a disco ball.

Shaking his head, he couldn't help but grin.

She glanced at him. "What?"

He didn't take his focus off the road. "Nothing."

"Why are you smiling?" Curiosity hid deep her demand that he answer.

Evasion wasn't exclusive to her, though. "No reason."

"Freak," she said, her own lips curling up.

"It's an elite club." He patted her knee. "Don't be jealous."

A short huff of laughter and she returned to silently watching the scenery pass, leaving him to his thoughts.

Pulling off the N72 highway, he took the two-lane road toward the village, following signs advertising the market. He kept the car at well below the posted speed as he considered how to start the conversation. Irritated with himself in less than two minutes, he threw both caution and calculation to the wind and simply opened the conversation with the first question that came to mind. "How do you know about the other entrances to the cave?"

Her hand tightened on the door handle before she seemed to forcibly relax. "I've had to stay there before."

"When?"

She shot him a short look before focusing on an indiscriminate spot down the road. "My first epithicas after I left the clan."

"When was that?"

She shrugged. "Near the end of the 17th century."

"Wait. That makes you—" He rapidly did the math "—over three hundred sixty years old."

"So?"

He couldn't help himself. He grinned and gently tagged her on the knee. "You're a total cougar."

She shifted to face him. "What?"

"I'm only three hundred thirty years old." He chuckled. "Cradle robber."

"Baby, I'm your Mrs. Robinson."

He burst out laughing, the sound rich and full and foreign to him after so long. The thought was sobering, but this wasn't the time to dip into the dark waters of his emotional well of horrors. Honestly, he didn't think it would ever *be* time. Wiping his eyes, he nodded. "Thanks for that."

"Sure?"

"It's been a long time since I laughed." His grip on the wheel tightened as he navigated the one-lane road that, according to GPS, would lead them to the Center.

Reaching over, she rested her fingertips on his arm, her touch light, even tentative. "That's a shame. Everyone should laugh."

He laid a hand over hers, held her for a moment and then let go. It was all the response he could muster.

Taking the final bend in the road, the Center's parking lot came into view. The market was, as advertised, packed. Shoppers of all ages crowded the narrow parking lanes, loading their finds and chatting with others. Still more made their way to the dense crowds shopping the market's vendor stalls. Pedestrian congestion paired with a full lot to make finding a parking space challenging. He wasn't picky, however. Seeing a vacancy deep in the heart of the lot, he steered the car through the pedestrian crowd.

Ashley gave his arm a quick squeeze before letting go. "Keep your hat on and head down when you get out. The fewer people to pay you—*us*—any mind, the better."

"I passed Assassin 101 with flying colors, darkling." He absently rubbed the spot where her fingers had rested. The loss of her touch left him aching to reach for her, to reclaim her hand and hold on. Something about her company anchored him not in the past or the imminent future, but in the now. Curious, that.

In the process of maneuvering the car into the narrow

parking spot, the truth plowed into him with no warning. He hit the brakes hard.

In his peripheral view, he saw Ashley's head whip forward then back. She rounded on him in evident frustration. "Park much, Druid?"

"Every time I drive," he croaked.

"Smart-ass." She reached for the door handle, oblivious to his epiphany. "I'm getting out before you break my neck. When you've gathered what wits weren't knocked loose with that stomp-to-stop, pop the trunk." She opened the door and crawled out of the low-slung car. She shoved the door, caught it before it latched and then leaned in to meet his gaze. "Seriously, though— keep the brim of your hat down when you get out."

He nodded, only half listening. The truth was too busy ricocheting around his mind. Since the day he'd died in October, the only person who had treated him as if he wasn't some death-stricken pariah was Ashley— a veritable stranger-cum-lover. He knew his fellow assassins and Kennedy meant well, but there was a pall hanging over everyone as if, every time he spoke, they were mentally storing away bits for his eulogy.

Ashley was different. She didn't know much about his situation. Even better, after she'd learned what she did know, she hadn't changed her handling of him. And he wasn't naive. She *was* handling him. Strangest of all, he let her. Had anyone else tried it, tried to direct him as he moved through his final days, he'd have not only balked, he'd have locked down. Not so with her. He'd followed her lead, allowing her to tack his sails in the direction she chose after their run-in with Macha. Essentially, he'd ceded control.

The thought rankled his pride, not because she was a woman but because he'd rolled over and given the goddess his belly when cornered. He was better than that, stronger than that, had been trained to ensure both were true. He'd spent centuries making life-and-death choices, had been trained to handle the horrors that both humanity and Others wrought on each other and had excelled at every bit of it. He'd been a killer with a conscience. Of sorts. His loyalty to the Assassin's Arcanum and the Druidic populace had never waivered. From feast to famine, life to death, he'd been steadfast. And yet a single threat based on a possible lie had brought him to his life's lowest point. Courage had not failed him. It had fled his reach altogether.

Gods, he was ashamed of himself.

If the last twenty-four hours with Ashley had taught him anything, it was that he'd not only forgone any claim he had to bravery, he'd behaved as a coward. She'd rushed into a fight on behalf of a man she'd hardly known and had taken on his greatest enemy—the same enemy that was his greatest fear manifest.

Dying.

A sharp rap on his window made him jump. "What?" he roared.

Open. The trunk, Ashley mouthed.

Son of a bitch, he'd nearly pissed his pants. Enough of this.

A punch of a button popped the trunk, the lid flashing up and blocking her from his view via the rearview mirror. Being unable to see her made him uncomfortable. Opening the door as far as possible in the tiny parking space, he crawled out of the car. He was forced to move as if he was double-jointed. He wasn't. He proved it when he knocked his hat to the ground and then scraped Rowan's car door against the Fiat they'd parked next to. Rowan was going to kill him. He snorted. The man would have to beat the goddess to it.

Gareth froze, stunned. He'd actually joked about who would kill him first. He was losing his damn mind, one moment coming out of his skin at a woman knocking on his window, the next jesting about who would be first in line to take his life.

"I need to be medicated," he muttered, retrieving his hat from the asphalt and then settling the token tourist souvenir firmly on his head.

Rounding the back of the car, his breath caught at the sight of Ashley bent over the trunk. His mind blanked. He didn't need medication. What he needed stood right in front of him. His blood heated, and his breath came short. Whether it was the epithicas, the merging of their elements or simple, undiluted desire, he knew what he wanted.

Her.

Ashley pushed through a vine thicket at the end of the man-made trail that followed the River Blackwater from the Center. The river was high and flowed swifter than normal following heavy late-spring rains but had yet to overflow its banks. Clusters of rock randomly disrupted the water's smooth surface. The natural breaks created deep, lazy eddies. It was there that the crystal waters hosted a congregation of trout that waited on the early evening hatch. She'd fish those spots later. Fresh trout for dinner would be awesome. Maybe even a salmon if she was lucky.

"How much farther?" came the deep voice only steps behind her.

"You really *are* two years old," she muttered, picking her way carefully down a steep section of riverbank. Travel would be faster, and less conspicuous, if they stayed close to the water. It would also keep them below any observer's regular field of view.

"Seriously, Ash. How much farther?"

She glanced back in time to see him waving off a dense halo of gnats. "How the hell did you make it through assassin school or whatever it is with your prissy intolerances?"

"Bug spray." He slapped at the little buggers as they reconvened, thicker than before. "And you can kiss my ass."

Heat raced over her skin as one word flashed through her mind. *Negotiable.*

Clearing her throat, she ducked low to do a fast crab-walk under a scrubby tree whose branches arched from the steep bank to touch the water's surface.

"Ashley," he ground out. "Answer me. How much farther?"

Mind on the man behind her, she forced herself to focus. If she was going to treat him like an authentic asset, she needed to share plans, discuss their options and resolve potential threats together. It defied centuries of survival instinct that screamed at her to lie and then run. With the worst of the epithicas bearing down on her, running wasn't an option anymore. Not with Gareth being the only male around. *The only male I want.* She shrugged off the uncomfortable thought and answered. "In about a thousand yards we'll come to the stone bridge that leads to Killavullen. We'll use it to cross the river. Then we'll continue down the bank for about a quarter of a mile. From there, we'll go to the second bend. The entrance is, or was, hidden by a large fall of rocks." She tucked errant curls up under her cap before tightening the adjustable band across the back.

"Light fades fast once inside, but I don't want to chance anyone seeing us pull supplies prior to disappearing behind the rocks."

"Smart to tuck out of sight and then grab the lanterns. With it being daylight, there won't be any identifying glow." He sounded confident, more so now than he'd been since their acquaintance had begun.

She appreciated the change, but it was a curious one. "True. Once we're inside, it's a bit of a convoluted trek to the spring-fed lake I want to camp at, but the water's consumable."

"No boiling?"

"Not the last time I was there, though, as I said, it's been some time." Recalling their recent conversation, she couldn't help but add, "And that's Mrs. Robinson to you." His choked response compelled her to steal a look at him. "Problem?"

"No." He scrubbed a hand over his face. "Yes."

"Which is it?"

"It's… I… Yes, okay? Yes, I have a problem." He crawled out from under the same low-hanging branch she'd just emerged from and then stood.

She arched a brow and fought the wave of heat that threatened to drag her into the abyss where desire superseded common sense and survival. His "problem" was self-evident. Moreover, it was impressive. "Problem, indeed."

"Gender impossibilities aside, I've obviously taken on part of your epithicas. I need to know more about it."

She'd been waiting for this, waiting for him to ask her about what the fertility cycle meant for him. Truth? She hadn't brought it up because she didn't have answers, not ones he'd want or need to hear. Never had she heard of the epithicas jumping hosts and splitting its impact.

Splitting its impact.

She stopped and Gareth clipped her right side hard enough to send her stumbling forward and into the river. She stood there, shin-deep, and stared at him with her mouth hanging open.

"What is it?" He followed her into the water and gripped her shoulders. "Ashley? Talk to me."

"I…" His palms seared her skin through the thin T-shirt, shocking her out of her stupor. "You're warm. Well, warm*er*."

He whipped his hands away and then stared at them like they were transplants that didn't belong to him. "Warm?" A smile bloomed, slow but brilliant. "I'm warm." Gareth tossed his duffel to the shore before snatching her up in a bear hug, burying his face in her neck and spinning her in a circle. "I'm warm. It snuck up on me, my head being somewhere else entirely," he murmured, lips moving over sensitive skin. "Thank the gods. I never thought to experience independent warmth again."

"It's probably something to do with the epithicas." And what was she supposed to add to that? *Chances are it's actually my phoenix's flame creating the warmth. Seeing as you weren't meant to harness the power it holds, this isn't good. So… I'm glad you feel better and seriously sorry if the side effects kill you?*

Yeah. That would go over well.

"I don't care what the reason is. It's a gift." He relaxed his hold and let her slide down the front of his body. The contact was intimate. His arousal more so. "My center is still cold, but there's warmth in my hands."

"I would imagine the warmth will spread. The epithicas is usually more aggressive. It's usually…" She waved her hands between them, vaguely gesturing to their groins. "It's debilitating, Gareth. I mean, it will render a female phoenix completely incapable of either denying a male sex or defending herself against the clansmen seeking to claim her during the fertility cycle."

His brows drew together and he looked down at her, a bevy of emotions warring across his face. "Wait. I'm confused. Are you saying your consent earlier wasn't legitimate, that it was simply biological need?"

"It *was* biological need."

Before she could collect the rest of her thoughts and try to explain to him that she *had* wanted him in spite of the epithicas, that what he'd experienced so far was minute in comparison to what was to come, his eyes darkened. Then they turned colder than an Alaskan tin roof in February. Every emotional offering that had been there on his face, racing through his eyes, disappeared. He let go of her and stepped away, creating a complement of physical distance. "You think you can simply chalk everything we've experienced up to biology?" He spoke as though his throat was raw. "You think that the epithicas buys you some kind of *pass* where your behavior is concerned? You don't get some mythical card that exempts you from personal liability. No, Ashley." He stared at her, his jaw working as he ground his teeth. "No," he repeated. Shaking his head, he spun away and trudged out of the river's shallows. "I'm not doing this with you."

She lunged forward and grabbed his arm. "Don't act like the wounded party here."

He shot her a cold look. "No? If you treat every lover you take with this much disrespect, it's no wonder you were looking around so desperately last night."

Her brows shot up. "You think I was desperate? I could have had any man in that bar!"

"You offered to *hire me*, Ashley. Like I'm some kind of manwhore!" Grabbing the discarded duffel, he swung it over his shoulder. "We need to get to the cave before dark." He stomped away, the gesture's emotional impact reduced by his squelching boots.

She took a couple of steps through his wake. "And you certainly wouldn't have taken me up on the offer if circumstances didn't involve the epithicas, right? You're so morally superior that you would have turned me down. Or, better yet, you would have seen fit to pass me off to one of your *boys*, let me take one of *them* to bed, right?" He paused and, in profile, she could see the fury that painted his cheeks, but she pressed on. "You're a real gem, assassin. Tell me how exposing a lesser man to this would have been remotely fair."

He rounded on her, fury turning his eyes a brilliant blue. "How is any of this fair?" The deadly whisper carried across the water.

"It's not. It never has been." She swallowed. "But I have to survive."

"And this, this 'survive at any cost' attitude, is all about you?" he pressed. She hesitated, trying to find the right words to explain, to clarify, but he charged on without giving her a chance. "That's what I thought. And for the record? Not one of my men is 'lesser.'"

Defending her decisions seemed imperative. She had to make him see that she'd done what was necessary in the face of the choices her mind could only identify as *worse* or *worst*. "But they're boys to the man you are. Don't you see that?" She parked her hands on her hips to disguise their shaking. "And what of this morning? If you want to talk about 'covering your six,' I had yours when Macha would have killed you."

"That had nothing to do with me. *Me*." He thumped

his chest. "You protected the temporary solution to your ongoing problem. Nothing more."

Words had never been so bitter she could taste them, not from someone else, but his response left her wanting to rinse her mouth with mouthwash. Or chocolate syrup. Or tequila. "You don't get it, Gareth. The epithicas doesn't give me a choice."

"You had every choice!" he shouted. "You just don't want to own the fact that you use men, that you need them." He took a step toward her and stopped. "You can't pass all culpability off under the guise of 'the epithicas made me do it.' *Screw. That.* You were of sound mind when you made your choices. Own them."

"Don't you see?" she began, the words thick. He had to understand.

Gareth cut her off with a swipe of his hand. He stalked toward her with such single-mindedness that water splashed up her thighs with his every step. "What I *see* is that the Goddess of Phantoms and War made decisions that may have cost me my life, and you did the same. You didn't consult me, didn't ask my preferences. You merged our elements and shared this gods-be-damned curse of yours without my consent!" The last was shouted in her face as he went nose to nose with her.

"N-None of this was my choice," she sputtered. Some foreign emotion began to brew in her chest, percolating too quickly like a cheap pot of coffee. "The epithicas is entirely unpredictable. The only given is sexual fever. I didn't mean to…" The developing feeling coated her awareness with a foul aftertaste. Every answer she'd thrown out made her sound callous. That wasn't her, wasn't who she had worked so hard to be over the many years. She wasn't someone who justified decisions she made based on her epithicas. And she'd never be the person who made off-the-cuff choices that affected others on such a fundamental level, choices made without their concurrence or consent.

Shock stole over her, the blood leaving her face in such a rush that black spots danced through her vision like inverted starlight.

She was no better than that which she despised the most.

Chapter 12

Gareth silently fumed as he moved down the river's bank, stepping around stretches of slick rock and muddy patches. He assumed Ashley followed, but he couldn't hear her passage over his own heaving breath. And he wasn't looking back. She'd either keep up or not.

Whatever.

Gods, she'd pissed him off. He couldn't remember the last time he'd been so mad. Had he been a whole man and not the shadow of his former self, he might have found a way to exercise some grace. Not now. Not when he was faced with calling the goddess out and challenging her claim to his soul or, worse, being claimed by her as she'd alleged. He needed every ounce of strength he could possibly harness. This, this epithicas, rendered him as randy as a buck caught in the rut. With that singular physical need dominating his mind, he was doomed. He'd never be able to fight with the focus required to beat the Goddess of Phantoms and War. Ashley had sealed his fate. No matter what options Dylan, as Assassin, might discover, no matter the possibilities the man offered, the phoenix behind him had stolen the choices that could have been open to him. Those choices might have saved him from the Well of Souls and the goddess's dictatorship.

He reached the bridge and trudged up the bank, pausing at the road. There wasn't a car in sight. At least they'd be able to go on without being observed. Killavullen was such a small village that strangers would be memorable, particularly strangers on foot. Should anyone stop them and question their presence or offer them a ride, they could claim they were newlyweds who had rented a small place in the neighboring village of Shonee and had walked to the market.

His mind took off on the tangent involving newlyweds and the activities inherent to them, spearing through him, driving his physical needs—or, if he believed the phoenix, the *epithicas*—to a new level of desperation.

A duffel bag hit the ground near his feet with a clattering *whump*. Ashley crested the steep berm and, recovering the bag, moved past him without comment.

That he was the injured party but she was behaving with apparent self-righteous indignation pissed him off. He started after her, long strides putting him next to her in seconds. "You care to explain why you believe you've the right to take the piss out of me over wrongs done me?"

She ignored him and kept walking.

He sped up and rounded on her, forcing her to a stop. "I'm serious, Ashley."

"And here I thought that, given your tone, you were having a go at me."

She made to go around him, but he moved to intercept. "We'll hash this out. Now."

"I'm under the direct impression you're better with your fists than with vocabulary. Lucky for you I'm not of a mind to kick your ass. Step aside."

He couldn't stop his slack-jawed response. "You think... That is..." Clearing his throat, he fought the smile that tugged at the corners of his lips. "You're asserting you could...what? Take me in a fight?"

"I said so, didn't I?" she snapped, never batting an eye. "Now step aside. Light's fading and I want to—"

"Get to the cave. I know." He let her go around him, mind spinning with possibilities. "If you're so sure you can take me, why'd you offer to hire me to 'cover your six'?" A slight sneer accommodated his air quotes quite nicely.

She slowed, then stopped, not turning when she answered him. "I don't have eyes to cover my back. Seeing as that's historically where people most often try to stab me, I thought you'd suffice as defense."

He jerked as if slapped. "Suffice, is it? Are you bloody mad? I'm an assassin. I'd do far better than suffice."

Ashley did turn then, the movement slow, controlled, even rigid. "Obviously, you hit your head against the curb this morning when I knocked you out of Macha's—"

He winced at her easy use of the goddess's name.

"—line of fire. Or cold, as it were." She raised a single brow, her gaze as flat as Dylan's sense of humor. "You should probably see a physician about that. You know, before it gets worse. Head injuries are dangerous."

"Who's done you so wrong, then?" Gareth asked through gritted teeth.

"Life's a bitch, but I can hardly take her out, now can I?" She spun on her heel and was halfway across the ancient stone bridge before he mustered a reply.

"You'd resurrect."

Ashley whirled and kept walking, only backward. "And how did that—coming back from the dead and all that goes with it—work out for you?" She tapped a forefinger against her chin and then brightened. "Oh! That's right. You've got Macha on your ass."

He stopped, his hands balling into tight fists. "Don't say her name."

"Who? Macha?" Ash tipped her head to the side much like a large, predatory bird. "You're afraid to say her name?"

"You can't just say... She'll hear... Names have power." Much as he would have liked to explain, words failed him entirely.

"She's not undefeatable."

"We—you—didn't beat her this morning." The reality of the statement made his skin tighten. "You ran her off."

"I caused her damage in doing so."

He harrumphed, mind on the earlier fight. The outcome had surprised him, but the reality was the goddess would be back and primed for confrontation. That didn't sit well with him. If she could claim his soul early, provoking her only ensured his order of execution moved up her priority list.

"For a man who demanded I talk to him, you're having a hell of a time, you know, *talking*." She shrugged. "Whatever. I'm not going to cow down to some bitch who can't manifest without shedding the blood of an innocent."

Gareth ran a hand around the back of his neck,

gripped a handful of hair and pulled until his eyes watered. "I'm far from innocent."

"As am I." Ashley smiled, but the appearance rested closer to bitter than happy. She took a deep breath, held it and let it out in a rush. "You asked about the epithicas—about what it means for you."

The change in conversational direction threw him. All he could do was watch her.

"I haven't answered your questions because I don't…" She wrapped her arms around her torso as if to cradle herself.

"You don't what?" he pressed.

She shifted, offering him her profile and looking down the road. Once, then twice, she started to speak and stopped. "I don't know how to do this."

"Do what?" He took a step closer. "Just be honest."

"I always am. Honest, that is," she said with quiet surety. "That's what makes this so hard."

"Let me ask you a question, then, and you respond with the first honest answer you come up with." He closed the distance a bit more. "Fair enough?"

She shot him a sidelong glance. "Ask."

"You said you'd either saved me or killed us both." He was close enough to touch her, but he didn't. Instead, he set his duffel between them and looked down at her. "What have you done, Ashley?"

She worried her bottom lip but didn't answer.

He hated to be a hard-ass, but his survival was spread across so many fine lines a palm reader would have had an impossible time knowing where to start. "First truth you come up with. Answer the question. Now."

"Fine." She looked up at him. "I don't know."

Fecking hell.

The three words he didn't want to hear.

* * *

Ashley's stomach plummeted at Gareth's stunned look of disbelief.

Locking his hands behind his neck, his biceps bulged. "What do you mean you don't know?"

"Exactly that. I'm so sor—"

"Go." Gareth snatched up the two duffel bags, grabbed her by the arm and propelled her across the bridge. He didn't slow when they reached the other side. He simply encouraged her down the embankment with a push—gentle, but a push all the same. Sliding down after her, he slipped under the first archway.

A car passed overhead.

Settling her cap more firmly, she chanced a glance around the pillar and watched the car coast down the hill and then motor away. "I didn't even hear it coming."

"Ironically, it came from behind you." Gareth pulled his hat off and shook out his hair.

"So you covered my six." *Oh, the irony.*

"It appears I did." Gareth moved close and loomed over her. "You still owe me an explanation."

Her stomach resumed its free fall. "I still don't have answers."

"Then guess," he ground out.

She took a deep breath. "The female phoenix's elemental flame burns hotter than any other known fire." Unsure what to add that wouldn't make the situation worse, she started picking her way along the riverbank. "We need to get to the cave. Dusk will settle in before we do if we don't pick up the pace."

His response came from closer than she'd expected. "Then we'll walk and talk. I've seen you carry a loaded drink tray and dodge groping hands, so I assume you can carry a pack, traverse a riverbank and still talk." He was silent for a moment, then tacked on the phrase she couldn't dismiss. "I need to know what I'm up against."

How many times since leaving the clan had she wished she could ask her mother everything she needed to know about mature phoenixes? How many times had she wished she'd had another phoenix to simply talk to? How often had she craved the solace of knowing she wasn't alone, wouldn't die alone...again? Oh, she'd died before. Two of the three close calls she'd experienced had been with males of her species. The third had been with a male fae. She had loved him and believed he had felt the same. Gods save her, she'd been a fool.

Each incident had resulted in a fight to the death. She'd been mortally wounded by each phoenix and outright killed by three vengeful fae after incinerating Aodán. Dying sucked. Her only comfort was that, every time she'd died, she'd taken the male with her. One male phoenix had experienced true death at her hand. The other she hadn't been able to handle seeing as she'd died shortly thereafter. Thank the gods she'd resurrected first and been able to get away. The third time? Well, that had been outright murder. On her part.

"Answer me, Ash."

The command broke her train of thought, saving her from reliving the single time she'd chosen to get involved long-term.

Gareth moved in close enough she could feel his presence behind her. His words were strained, though. Far from easy. "The phoenix flame. How is it possible that it burns hotter than any fire?"

Her desire for him grew, and she knew she had to mend the fence she'd cut between them minutes before. If she failed, they'd be forced to interact with each other far more intimately in the cave, forced to engage in intercourse to assuage the demand laid on them by this impossible circumstance. And she knew he'd end up resenting her as much as she'd resented former lovers taken out of necessity versus conscious choice.

The only thing she knew to do to make things right was to give him information never shared with those outside the clans. "A phoenix's fire is more than part of her elemental nature. It's, well, it's more a part of who she is. It's wedded to the deepest part of her. Her soul, if you will. The fire isn't something she thinks about. That heat is simply hers." Ashley paused, struggling to find an easier explanation. There wasn't one. Man, this was going to ignite Gareth's temper. She just knew it. "Male phoenixes don't burn as hot. They don't typically resurrect as fast because it takes longer to create the scenario for rebirth."

"Scenario?"

She rolled her shoulders, trying to break the tension stretched across her shoulders. "It takes longer to turn him to total ash. A female can accomplish in seconds what it takes a male minutes to do. Sort of like sex, but reversed."

"Funny girl," Gareth said so quietly she was certain he hadn't meant her to hear. "You weren't complaining earlier," he added more loudly.

"Funny guy," she parroted.

"Ears like a freaking elephant," he whispered.

"Better ears than an ass."

Gareth's laughter wrapped around her. The sound did little to relieve the anxiety crushing her chest. She had to offer him the remaining truth before what little momentum she'd created was lost to cowardice.

Onward, she mouthed.

Stopping without warning, she closed her eyes. The

breeze washed over her carrying with it the organic, earthy smells of the river basin and, below that, the more subtle scent of warm cotton and sundrenched skin.

The weight of his hand at her waist startled her.

She turned, breaking his hold, and faced him. "There's more."

He refused to be dissuaded. Reaching forward, he curled his fingers over the narrow waistband of her jeans and held on. "Isn't there always?"

His dry tone proved kindling to her fear. "Seems like it." She took a step back.

He took a step forward and arched a brow, whether in challenge or consternation she wasn't sure.

"Fine." *Get it over quickly.* "Men aren't strong enough to harness the strength and power of a female phoenix's flame." His eyes tightened and the corners of his mouth turned down, but she refused to stop. "The female's flame is necessary to bear a child because the embryo begins the cycle of death and rebirth in the womb." He opened his mouth to presumably ask a question and she cut him off. "I don't know specifics, so don't ask."

"I'm curious."

"You and me both. After losing my mother to Final Death, I didn't exactly hang around to talk genetics and breeding potential with my clan." Mere mention of her mother made the invisible band around her chest tighten even more. She wasn't ready to discuss this, would rather deliver the conversational deathblow and get it over with. "The male of the species is compelled by his very nature to respond to a female's breeding cycle. He's drawn to her. Not out of love, mind you. Out of need. He craves her without reason and will do anything to ensure she's impregnated in that week. Then he officially claims her before the clan Master—" she hated that title "—and the female is forced to submit to being tattooed to identify the male's ownership."

"That sucks," Gareth said, his eyes never leaving hers.

"That's an understatement."

He traced his thumb over the small area of skin he'd revealed when he'd gripped her waistband. "So what does this mean for me, having inherited part of your flame? Why is it potentially life-threatening?"

"Men weren't created to harbor a woman's strength."

His eyes flared and a deep flush spread up his neck. "You're saying…what? That I'm too *weak*?"

She rolled her head shoulder to shoulder, popping her neck.

He gripped her chin and forced her to meet his heated gaze. "Ashley, is that what you're telling me?"

"The tattoos a male places on his wives' arms bind her ability to do him harm. Otherwise? We'd be a matriarchal society and men would be the subservient sex."

"*How* do the tattoos bind a woman's power?"

She shook her head. "Never had it done and don't plan to. I'd end myself before I'd allow…" Biting off the explanation, she clamped her mouth shut.

"End yourself?" His free hand came down on her shoulder, heavy as an unfavorable judgment. "Explain."

The one-word demand pissed her off. "I don't owe you an explanation about decisions that don't affect you. I'm sorry our elements merged. I'm sorry I didn't get to hold a political summit about the pros and cons before I *saved your ass*. Bottom line? There's no undoing it." She wrenched free of his grasp and then backed away. Distance. She needed distance.

Blue eyes narrowed even as they sparked skepticism. "You haven't told me why you may have killed us both."

"Oh, I did," she said softly. "You just weren't listening."

He waved a hand at her to continue.

"The male wasn't created to harness the strength of a female's flame, no more than I was created to harness the weakness of yours. My phoenix fire may well consume your element. If that happens?" She fought the urge to turn, to run and run and never stop. "If that happens," she repeated, softer now, "you'll be consumed but never reborn, and the next time I'm killed?"

He started, but she pressed on.

"The next time I'm killed, it will be true death because there won't be enough of my element to fuel my resurrection."

Chapter 13

Gareth followed Ashley around the fall of rocks she'd described and found not a walk-in tunnel but a tiny, horizontal fissure in the rock wall. Shadows cast across the dark entrance made it impossible to see more than a couple of feet into the Earth's maw, so he leaned closer. Then he scrambled back.

The entrance was crawling with spiders. Different sizes, colors and shapes, the arachnid populace outnumbered those of Killavullen's residents, likely five to one. Possibly more. He self-consciously swiped at his bare arms. The thought of those eight-legged monstrosities crawling over his skin gave him a severe case of the creepy-crawlies.

Ashley must have witnessed his revulsion because she bit her bottom lip even as her nostrils flared with suppressed laugher.

"Kill them." A shudder raced through him. "All of them."

"I will not." The color of amusement rode high on her cheeks even as indignation infused her denial. "But I *will* smoke them out and clear the way for you…assassin."

"I know you're not making fun of me," he groused.

"Only a little." She bent low, balanced on the balls of her feet, and collected a handful of twigs and dry grass. Then she called her internal fire to hand. Bright orange-and-red flames with a deep blue base flashed through her fingertips before settling to a consistent burn. Lighting the tinder she'd collected, she held it to the narrow cave opening. She blew into the little bundle, encouraging the fire to spread. Grasses smoldered but nothing like the rain-dampened wood did. Just as she'd promised, the spiders fled the increasingly dense smoke and created a relatively bug-free zone.

Ashley snuffed out her phoenix flame and, with flourish, waved him toward the cave's entrance. "After you, princess."

"You're a right chancer." He dropped his duffel and went to his knees beside it, digging out his lantern. "We should've bought proper headlamps."

She didn't pause in her smoke-out-the-leggy-bastards campaign nor did she spare him the briefest glance when she answered. "You can do the shopping next time."

"Next time? You're planning to haul me to caves around Ireland, then?"

"No," she barked. "No." Calmer the second time around. "This is a onetime deal."

"So hard to manage, am I?" He *tsked*. "And here I thought women were made of sterner stuff than that."

"I'm smoking out the entrance to keep you from squealing, Your Highness. If it was just me? I'd have crawled through the lot of them and gone on. Risking the smoke being witnessed is for your benefit, not mine."

He blinked slowly. "I'm a bloody assassin, love. I may not care for the unappealing little shites, but I've suffered far worse for far less."

She huffed out a short laugh, her breath dissipating the narrow smoke column. "And which am I—far worse or the payoff?" Her tone was light, even teasing.

Too light and teasing.

"Never mind," she said in the face of his brief hesitation.

"No. You answered my question earlier." He quietly set everything down and closed the finite distance between them. "I'll answer yours now." Taking her elbow in one hand and grasping her opposite shoulder with the other, he spun her and backed her into the ivy-covered rock. Several spiders waddled away.

He ignored them.

He let go of her arm and deftly knocked the miniature smokestack from her hand. Then, gripping her hip, he stepped into her.

Their bodies aligned perfectly, his throbbing arousal settling against her lower belly as his groin pressed against her pubic bone. The intimate contact demanded his absolute control. His mind rebelled, flashing increasingly erotic images at him, each snapshot focused solely on the woman in his arms.

Hazel eyes bright with surprise focused on him. Undisguised desire was seamlessly, wordlessly, conveyed when her full lips parted and the tip of her tongue peaked out to trace only the very top of her Cupid's bow.

Lowering his head, he brushed his lips over hers once, then twice and dipped back for a third sensual caress. Beard stubble scraped over her petal-soft skin.

A short gasp escaped her.

He seized the opportunity and fused their mouths

without hesitation or apology. His tongue delved into her depths, plundering, dancing and claiming. She was his just as he was hers, clan practices and rules of possession be damned now and always. He wanted her. Only her.

Gareth wove his hands through her hair, canting her head to one side to allow better access.

She nipped his lower lip.

A deep rumble rolled up from the depths of his chest. "More."

Ashley grabbed a handful of hair and yanked his head back. She traced her tongue through the hollow at the base of his throat.

The rumble deepened. Heat raced through him and a fine sheen of sweat broke out over his chest. His T-shirt stuck. He wasn't willing to break away from her, to lose the intensity of the moment, to remove the thin barrier between them. Instead, he gripped the neck and yanked. Cotton separated where there was no seam, the distinctive *rrriiippp* a precursor to the remnants pooling at their feet.

Her chest brushed against his. Gareth fought the urge to yank at the button of her jeans, to take her here, now, without consideration for potential consequences— hikers, locals seeing smoke and calling the Garda or, worse, one of their many enemies tracking them to this point where they were cornered. He didn't care. Couldn't care. Sating the inferno that drove him to claim her ruled his thoughts and dictated his actions.

The head of his arousal worked free of his boxer briefs and slipped over the waistband of his denims. Her shirt brushed over that fraction of his arousal. It took every ounce of constraint he possessed not to dispatch her shirt in the same expedient manner he'd handled his own.

Ashley slipped a hand between them. She met his gaze and then thumbed the moist tip of that hypersensitive skin.

At her touch, his head fell back and an unwillingly ragged breath escaped him. If he didn't lose himself in the depths of her heat, and soon, it wouldn't be only his bloody mind that he lost.

Shadows crept over them.

Gareth jerked as the darkness slid over his face and the light that had burned through his closed eyelids was lost. He pulled Ashley closer, intent on putting himself between her and whatever posed the threat.

"Ease up, Gareth," she wheezed.

He relaxed his hold and, without warning, whipped around. One arm out, his goal was to keep her behind him. Fluid and fast, he pulled the Sig Sauer he'd taken from Rowan's car. Leveling the weapon at the perceived danger, he found himself pointing at empty space. The setting sun had fallen behind the tumbled limestone boulders giving birth to shadows his mind had cast as villains.

Tentative fingers wove through the hair at his nape, paused and then began to pet him. "Don't lose yourself, *a chara*. Don't paint fear into every dark corner or every suspicious sound."

"What would you know about fear?" he asked, ashamed at his ragged tenor.

"I know what it is to look over your shoulder every second of every day. I understand what it feels like to fear every unfamiliar face. I know what it is to jump at every unannounced knock at the door. I've walked this mile in my own shoes." Her fingers stilled. "I know what it is to stare down death with the understanding that the face of the man who struck the killing blow may well be the very face that chases me straight to hell."

A hard shiver raced over his skin, talons of the fear she identified leaving bloody tracks in its wake. "It's the face that greets you when you open your eyes *in* hell that you should fear."

She curled her fingers against his scalp and began to hum only to stop short and let him go. "We should get inside." Stepping around him, she caught herself mid-sigh. "Your chest."

He glanced down, expecting to find something like a spider. What she'd seen, though... Turning away, he swept up the remnants of his shirt. "It's nothing."

She moved around him, staying his attempt to turn away and hide his chest. "Gareth, were you *branded*?"

"And if I was?" Shrugging into the shirt, he knotted it in the front, all the while refusing to look at her.

"Who did it?" The question, so quiet, held an edge of steel he didn't understand.

"Does it matter?"

"Answer me." When he hesitated, she moved into him and laid a hand over the bitterly cold brand. "Please."

He swallowed through the tightness in his throat, ashamed at the rush of despair that choked him. "You know who did it."

"Say her name."

"I can't."

Her pupils expanded and Gareth would have sworn flames danced in their depths.

She gave a short, sharp nod and, without further comment, she bent to gather more detritus to create her smoky defense. "The spiders are back."

Gareth laid a hand on her shoulder and encouraged her to stand. "Leave it."

Her brow creased. "If I do, you'll get spiders on you."

He grabbed the gear he'd dropped and bagged the pieces of his shirt. "They don't seem so bad."

Not anymore.

Less than an hour later, Ashley had led them to the small lake, set up the lanterns, laid out the pallet and set water to boil on the single-burner camp stove—just a precaution thanks to Gareth's paranoia. Crouched on the narrow shoreline, she sluiced water over her dusty arms and face. She could take a lot. Being gritty didn't make the list.

The cold water was all the colder thanks to the subterranean temperature. Thermals would be welcome. As would sharing body heat.

Visions of Gareth loving her less than twelve hours ago tripped through her mind. *Burden, indeed.* She touched a finger to her lips and traced their shape as she recalled their most recent kiss outside the cave. Gods, he was magnificent. Longing for more blossomed, her core aching with her wanting.

As if summoned by her thoughts, the man knelt on one knee close beside her. He leaned forward to rinse the silty grit from his shirt. His thigh brushed against hers. She jolted. Scalding sexual hunger flashed through her with the intensity of lightning striking cold steel.

He sucked in a sharp breath. Shifting to rest on both knees, he swiveled to face her.

Ashley watched the riot of wild yearning flash through the most expressive blue eyes she'd ever seen.

When he spoke, his tone was low, almost sonorous. "Does it always build like this?"

"What?"

"The way my body demands action. It's like this

quenchless thirst I can't slake. I can't…" He shoved his hands through his hair, water trickling down one temple.

"What?" she repeated, throatier this time. She longed to hear he wanted her. Only her. It was madness, seeing as he was as driven by unwelcome hormones as she, but hearing him voice his avarice seemed to cement some internal emotional requirement she'd never known she possessed. Or was possessed by.

He dropped his shirt before inching toward her. Taking one of her hands, he laid it against his right pec. "I don't know how to articulate what it is I want. There's this space in me that seems too large to explain, let alone fill." One corner of his mouth turned up. "I know, you'll say it's the epithicas. Maybe it is. I wouldn't know otherwise."

A sharp pang of something seriously akin to regret stabbed at her. She could have said that was ridiculous, that it would be ridiculous to assume the fertility window resulted in emotional voids like he described. The words wouldn't coalesce into coherent thought. Not with her hand resting on the smooth, heavy pad of muscle.

She shifted her gaze from his and focused instead on the brand on his chest. "Does it hurt?"

"I've had worse." He took her hand and ran it down his torso with achingly slow movements, not stopping until her hand rested over a thick, ropy scar.

Easily eight inches long, the flesh was puckered and pale, almost blue. The color made sense seeing as the poorly healed wound was colder than their underworld environment.

"How?"

"Cailleach possessed a woman—the Assassin's heart mate. I couldn't fight her without risking killing the woman she'd chosen as her physical host."

Her wide-eyed stare snapped up. "You *let* someone run you through?" She couldn't temper the incredulity in the question.

He shrugged and looked away. "If you knew Dylan, knew how he felt about the woman, you'd understand."

She focused on her fingers again as she traced the scar. "You're an amazing man."

"He'd have done the same for me."

He flinched when she hit the coldest spot of all, so she moved her hand up his body. Reveling in the crest and valley of his musculature, she continued until she circled his nipple.

He hissed, the sound far from pained.

Shifting her hand, she let it rest over his brand. "This was too great a price to pay for any friend."

Gareth hooked a finger under her chin and lifted. "Love like that only comes along once in a lifetime, and that's if you're lucky. No price was too great."

Emotion rose in her so quickly she couldn't stop the short sob. It echoed in the cavernous space. She closed her eyes and, with infinite gentleness, rested her forehead against the valley between his pecs. Her eyes burned with unshed tears. More than three hundred years had passed since she'd last cried, and that had been over the loss of her mother. Nothing had mattered since then. How he'd reduced her to this so quickly, how he'd fractured the dense walls she'd erected against the threat of authentic compassion, she didn't know.

A large, work-roughened hand slid under the edge of her T-shirt. His other hand slipped under her fall of hair to trace each vertebra, stopping between her shoulder blades only to start up again. The warmth of his breath washed over her scalp as he crooned unintelligible words into her hair.

She relaxed.

A single tear escaped, falling only to be caught between the seam of their bodies.

"Doona cry for me, lass." A gentle kiss to the crown of her head.

"I'm not."

"Okay." He didn't bother to disguise the smile in his voice.

Raising her other hand, she twined her fingers with the hand he rested against her hip. "If the gods allow this, they're neither fair nor blameless."

"Every life has an expiration date, my *a mhuirnín.*"

"This isn't your time." A second tear escaped. "Not now."

"I have days yet." Hard hands framed her face and lifted it to his. He kissed her tenderly. "Help me to forget."

Chapter 14

Ashley watched Gareth stand and then reach for her, pulling her to her feet. She leaned into him, unwilling to let him experience even a moment of disconnect. It was too important to her to give him everything he wanted, give him every experience he craved and honor every sacrifice he'd made, be it out of duty or love. He was an honorable man who hadn't struck at her for the predicament she'd inadvertently put him in. No, he'd stuck by her.

And if the Assassin could find a way to save Gareth?

For the first time, she wouldn't run. She'd stay—be part of the solution.

And if Dylan didn't find a way to save Gareth… That wasn't an option.

Trembling, she went to her toes, pulling him toward her, wanting nothing more than to lay her mouth to his. But she paused with less than a degree of separation, slid her nose against his and breathed in everything that lay between them. Passion, hormones, the intimate knowledge that finally someone truly knew how it felt to be trapped by circumstances beyond their control. She let the moment stretch, watched him.

His eyes searched her face, looking for what she didn't know. Then he spoke. "Ashley." Her name was reverent, an invocation from lips made for sin.

Closing that finite distance, their mouths met. The initial touch was gentle, tender even, despite the epithicas's demand they sate the insatiable.

She sipped from him, savoring him like the finest whiskey. Tongues touched, tentative at first. The exploration grew bolder, more demanding with every inhalation, every caress, every exhalation.

Their breaths melded until he breathed her in, she breathed him out.

Bending his knees, Gareth wrapped his arms around the backs of her thighs and lifted.

Ashley wound her arms around his neck and pulled herself up so her legs went around his lower ribs to avoid pressing on the killing wound. She was tall enough the position forced him to tilt his head back to maintain the kiss.

Starting at his temples, she tunneled her fingers into his thick hair. It was a simple matter to push the mass off his face, to grip handfuls and guide the position of his head. She turned him a fraction, pulling away despite his sound of protest. A little nip at his lips and then she moved to his jaw, working her way from chin to ear with nips and laves.

Gareth let his head fall back farther, his fingers digging into her ass. "Yer a seductress, *bean álainn*."

She'd been called a beautiful woman before, but never

had her lover's opinion been crucial to her sense of self. But what Gareth thought *mattered*. What should have scared her, would have terrified her days ago, failed to hold dominion over her. The man in her arms was all she cared about.

Lips at his ear, she fought to keep her voice from shaking. "Take me to bed, Gareth."

Shifting her weight so he held her balanced with a single forearm, he gripped her hair and pulled, returning the gesture as he forced her head back. He spun with surety and stalked straight to the pallet. Toeing the top covers back, he went to his knees and settled her on the bedding with infinite gentleness. "I would tha' we'd been able tae carry in pillows. It's no' right ye lie on the ground like this. Ye should be laid on a fine bed and surrounded by silks and brocades and an abundance o' pillows." He traced the line of her jaw, down her neck and along her jawbone. "Yer body should be cast in candlelight. I would give ye all o' that if it were within my power."

"It's a lovely thought," she said huskily, "but all I want is you, *fear dathúil*."

He sat beside her and undid his boots, toeing them off. Then, with slow, deliberate movements, he stood and unbuttoned his jeans, shed them and his boxer briefs in a single move. Standing before her, he was glorious. Heavily muscled, but not overly so. Smooth-bodied with only a trace of hair from his belly button to the thatch from which his heavy erection jutted.

Beneath her bra, her nipples created diamond-hard points that ached as the fabric moved over them with her every breath. She reached a shaking hand for her pants, but he laid a hand over hers, staying her movement.

"I'd see ye taken care of by my own hand."

"Gareth." Whereas her name had been smooth on his lips, she answered him with undiluted desperation.

"Aye. I'll hurry, for yer no' the only one tae crave, *a stór*."

He was good to his word, stripping her to bare skin in under a minute, yet not once was he rough with her.

Lying bare before him, Ashley wanted to ask him what he saw, wanted to know if she pleased him. She fought the urge, biting her bottom lip to secure her silence. Pride still intact, she refused to look away from him. She needed to see in his gaze what he had yet to say, words she hadn't ever wanted to hear but now seemed as imperative as her next breath, her next heartbeat. The longer he looked, though, eyes roving over her bare body, the more she realized she couldn't bear his scrutiny.

She laid a hand on his thigh when he went to his knees at her side. "Gareth, do you want…this?"

"I want ye, Ashley. No' because o' the epithicas. I want *you*."

The words she'd craved, that he had asserted it was her—*her*—he wanted undid her. Unleashed her control. She surged toward him, gripping his hair and drawing him down to her.

He planted one forearm next to her head, his upper body curling over her even as he worked a knee between her legs. Opening her to him, he slipped his other hand between her legs.

"Gods, Ash. Ye're sae wet."

She arched her back, her breasts rubbing his chest. "I want you, Gareth. Now."

Lowering himself, their bodies melded together, obliterating any space between them.

Heat bloomed at her core as his turgid arousal pressed into the flat of her belly. She wanted him, craved him, had to have him. This crush of voracious *feelings* threw her off her thinking game, and all she could do was respond. This, *this* was what the epithicas was—a mind-numbing, react-don't-think, have-to-assuage-this-now ache. An undeniable urge. A power she couldn't compel to be anything other than what it was.

Gareth rested on both forearms, one on each side of her head. Then he lowered his chest gently to hers, his mouth following until their lips met.

She'd only thought they were as close as they could be.

This kiss was everything the first had built toward—heat, longing, passion, hunger. It was all that and more. It quickly evolved into an oral duel, the thrust and retreat of their tongues, the pursuit of one into the other's mouth both a precursor and parody of what would, inevitably, come.

He shocked her then, pulling away.

She pushed up on her arms and followed him, unwilling to let the contact end. More. She needed more.

Gareth knelt between her knees and watched her through heavy-lidded blue eyes that blazed with intent. Gripping her under the arms, he pulled her up and settled her on his lap. He rested one hand at the small of her back, one elbow hooked under her armpit.

Ashley rocked against him, the hard ridge of his erection creating the most delicious friction against her clitoris. "Gods," she breathed, letting her head fall back as she increased the tempo.

Gareth spread his legs and bent her back, increasing the friction. Then he dipped his mouth low to suckle first one nipple and then the other.

Her shouted pleasure echoed through the chamber.

His hand at her lower back pressed and released, encouraging her to increase the tempo until she was mad from desire.

Leaning back a fraction, he began to thrust against her. Then, voice raspy and strained, he gripped her ass, forcing her to bear down on him and issued a command that gave no quarter for refusal. "Come for me, *a stór.*"

She did as bid, cresting with a mind-shattering rush even as she came apart in his embrace.

Before she could coalesce, he let go of her ass, slipped his arm under her knee and lifted. He slipped into her in one deft move.

Ashley slid down his length with a gasp, her fingers digging into the heavy trapezius muscles on either side of his neck. Holding on was her only option as he rose halfway, just enough to allow him total control of her body. She was a slave to his every thrust. Never had she thought to be so grateful to cede control, to simply be, to thrive on the experience, to allow her body to be ruled by another with no interest in regaining control.

He worked her up and down his length with increasing fervor.

The last contractions of her orgasm had yet to fade, instead reforming without respect for her need to recover, regroup, breathe. No, he drove her hard and then harder.

Shifting his hips subtly, she was suddenly racing toward the precipice and then throwing herself into the chasm without concern for what lay at the bottom. She fell, blinded by pleasure and unaware of everything but Gareth's shout as he chased her over the edge.

And, for the first time, she truly let go, confident that her lover would be there to catch her.

Two hours later, Gareth lay with Ashley in his arms and what he assumed was a satisfied smile on his face.

The epithicas had been sated after the first hour. As for the second? That had been mutually gratifying. Gods save him, she'd rocked his world...right off its axis. Never had a lover taken him with such intense focus, such heat, such unchecked passion. She'd been focused on him and him alone. When she'd cupped his sack and then taken him in her mouth? They might be more than two hundred feet below the terrain, but he'd seen stars.

His grin widened. Of course he'd been obliged to return the favor.

She was amazing.

Body pressed up against his right side and her head resting in the hollow of his shoulder, she sighed. Her featherlight touch traced the pattern of muscle across his torso. The tattooing rhythm of her heart beat against his side. His heart beat in counter time, just as fast. He wanted to lay here for hours, reveling in her small sounds of contentment, sounds she likely had no idea she made. Moreover, he wanted to tightly clutch the reprieve she'd given him. For the time they'd spent lost in each other, he'd forgotten everything bearing down on him. It was the greatest of gifts.

"Gareth?"

He hooked his free arm behind his head and canted his chin so he could see her.

Long, deep auburn lashes dipped low.

Shifting so he rested on his elbow, her head pillowed on his forearm, he traced a fingertip from her throat to her navel and then spread his hand wide, palm across her stomach. "What is it, *a stór*?" The term of endearment—darling—slipped from him without thought. He stilled, waiting for her to cut him off, issue a fierce denial or physically withdraw. His heart thrilled when she did nothing he'd expected. Instead, she turned to her side and buried her face in the crook of his arm.

"Where do we go from here?" she whispered.

He stared at her, studying her profile. Was she asking where they went physically or emotionally? Not that it mattered. There wasn't an easy answer for either question.

He ran a hand slowly down her arm, ending at her hand.

She laced their fingers together.

Something in him shifted and came to rest, filling an unfamiliar vacancy he'd never known existed. He sucked in a sharp breath as that unfamiliar piece settled into place. No way could he be falling for her. He was a dead man walking. It would be cruel to both of them to allow anything like that to happen. Better to keep this thing between them uncomplicated.

He squeezed her hand. "Ash, I don't know—"

"Hush," she said sharply, slapping a hand over his mouth.

"What?" The question was muffled against her skin but still discernible.

She shot him a hard glare before breathing her one-word answer. "Company."

Gareth grabbed the Sig Sauer he'd rested atop his clothes and silently surged to his feet. He searched the wide cavern. Too many tunnels. Too many options. The threat could come from any direction. Glancing at Ashley, he pointed at the nearest tunnel.

She shook her head and pointed two over. The same one they'd come in.

Damn it. How could anyone have tracked them so quickly? They had to have been seen.

He moved to his duffel and dug out two blades. Heft-

ing them for weight and balance, he passed the better of
the two to Ashley and kept the other for himself, even
as he wished it were a proper long sword. Bullets were
highly efficient for slowing attackers, but beheadings
were just so much more effective at keeping them down.
For good. If he had to hack this son of a bitch's head
off, he'd fill the threat full of lead and then do what he
had to do. Messy job, but it wouldn't be the first time
he'd done it.

Gareth dropped the blade but managed to retain the
gun.

Flames flickered in his palm before spreading to en-
case first one hand and then the other. His skin remained
entirely undamaged. More startling was the desire he
had to let himself flame unchecked and burn the in-
truder to the ground.

What the hell?

He shot Ashley a quick glance. She'd risen from the
pallet and moved to stand near him. Assuming a forty-
five degree angle off his less dominant side, she watched
the tunnel directly across from her for a moment and
then held up a hand indicating two more approached
from her side. The news wasn't what stunned Gareth.
It was *her*. She was as nude as he, but her arms were
encased in flames. Hands loose at her sides, her focus
didn't waver as she waited. Her hair sparked and crackled. Lucent eyes glowed like molten gold. Confidence
radiated off her as thick and visible as a desert mirage.
She was, in a word, resplendent.

Adrenaline swam through Gareth's veins and his
semiflaccid cock flooded with arousal. Gods, a good
fight always gave him a fierce hard-on. That he had his
element back? He wanted to throw down with any chal-
lenger, and in the worst way.

Ashley made a sharp move and a broad stream of fire shot across the cavern.

A man shouted, the curse as colorful as it was fierce. Then the ground shook.

Gareth stumbled toward her but kept his focus on the tunnel before him. He swept low and retrieved his blade. Finger on the Sig's trigger, he began to pull. Whoever came through that narrow opening was about to have a very, *very* bad day. Lead poisoning was only the first of his worries.

A dark head emerged and Gareth got off a single shot before a male voice shouted, "Stand down, Gareth!"

At the same time, a second male voice called out, "Cut it out, Zippo! You're going to hurt someone with that…day-um. Nice body, Red."

Gareth didn't think beyond the fact someone looked at Ashley's naked body and that "someone" was male. Gareth simply spun and pulled the trigger. Rock exploded next to the dark blond's head.

The man ducked behind a wall of dirt and stone that hadn't existed seconds earlier. "What the fuck, Gareth! Did I miss the sign that said this was a reenactment of the bloody scene from *Road to Perdition*?"

Magick hit Gareth and wove around him, thick and viscous. The gun he held softened and warped, lengthening and reshaping into an exceptionally large dinner fork. The knife in his other hand went limp before stiffening and recasting itself as a child's wooden pirate sword. Only one man could do that, control the aether to reconstruct his environment. Spinning, Gareth faced the large man with shoulder-length black hair and luminous green eyes who stood, palms out, casting a dense cloud of the most complex of magicks.

Dylan O'Shea.

The man who had become *the* Assassin to all other assassins, the same man whom Gareth had trusted for centuries, slowly lowered his hands. He didn't, however, retrieve the aether he'd loosed. "Pull that trigger again, brother, and I'll turn your bullets into a ball vice and custom fit it to you myself."

Gareth lowered what had been weapons, calling to Ashley, "It's cool, Ash. These are my men."

Ethan Kemp—American warlock and general pain in the ass who had refused to leave Ireland after his best friend, Kennedy, married Dylan—peered around the earthen wall he'd created and grinned. "Well, well, my band of merry asses. Looks like we weren't needed after all." He waggled his brows at Gareth. "You never call anymore, Irish. You never write. Dylan was wringing his hands in fear that you'd, literally, fallen off the face of the Earth, and all the while you were gettin' a little bow-chick-a-wow-wow."

Gareth's element, his to command once again, flowed down his arms to his hands and simmered at the surface. He created a fireball and flung it across the wide-open space, grinning coldly when the warlock ducked behind his magick-made barricade. "You talk a tough game for someone whose magick relies on a little moonlight chanting and tools."

Ethan stepped out from behind the defensive barrier he'd created and held his arms wide. "Do you see any tools here?"

Raising both brows, Gareth blinked slowly. "I'm looking at it."

The Assassin's Arcanum, the men that formed the elite Druidic assassins—Dylan, Kayden, Niall and Rowan—stepped out of the parallel tunnels they'd traveled.

Mouth twitching, Ethan managed a strong, "Asshole."

All but Rowan chuckled. The largest man stood quietly, eyes averted.

Gareth whirled around to find Ashley struggling to strip a blanket off their makeshift pallet and cover herself.

"Look away," he barked at the men.

They all immediately gave the pair their backs.

Irritated beyond reason, Gareth strode to Ash's duffel and pulled out a change of clothes. "Dress."

She snatched the clothes from him, her eyes narrowing. "You need to tread lightly, 'Irish.'"

He sighed. "Please. I don't want them to see you."

"Little late for that," Ethan called over his shoulder.

"You can forget what you saw, or I'll wipe it from your memory," Gareth bit out. He typically appreciated the warlock's irreverence, but not on this. *Never on this.* "You know I'm fully capable of seeing the task through, so do tread lightly here, witchling."

Ethan cocked his head to the side. "Reduced to name-calling even as you threaten to play in the gray area of magick, are you?"

"If the shoe fits." Gareth retrieved and pulled on his boxer briefs and jeans, and then shoved his feet into his socks and boots. All the while, he kept his gaze averted from Ashley. "And as for the latter, be grateful I didn't simply curse you to an eternity of hellfire. Seeing as I'm already damned, I've nothing to lose."

A burning sensation took up squatter's rights behind his heart, spreading through his chest. He didn't care for the feeling. At all.

Ashley moved to stand beside him, arms wrapped around her middle as if she was cold. "While it's always awkward to enter a kill-or-be-killed situation with complete strangers, it's even more awkward when only half the troops elect to fight in the tradition of medieval Scottish Highlanders. Seems like there should be a memo regarding the rules of engagement so everyone's junk is treated equitably."

Gareth dropped an arm around her shoulders, surprised to find her skin didn't scald him as it had in days past. "I'll have Dylan's secretary get right on that."

"My 'secretary'?" A dark grin colored Dylan's face. "That would be *you*, mate."

"Only because you're illiterate, computer and otherwise. Grunts and snarls don't translate well to written correspondence." Gareth pressed on before Dylan could respond. "Ashley Clement, this is Dylan O'Shea, head of the Assassin's Arcanum. The tool hiding behind his homemade dugout is Ethan Kemp, American warlock and all around pain in the ass."

"I prefer 'mascot,'" the handsome man responded.

"Only if I get to choose your costume, and I'm envisioning something from Victoria's Secret," Gareth countered. "The guy over here posing as our modern-day, dark-haired Rapunzel is Kayden MacNamara. The guy to his right—short brown hair and tattoos—is Niall O'Connor." He nodded at Rowan Brady. "And you know Rowan."

Ashley nodded. "Conan."

Ronan nodded back but didn't speak.

"So." Gareth crossed his arms over his bare chest and watched Dylan carefully. "Why are you crashing my two-person cave party?"

"Your cell fell off the grid. I…" Neither Dylan's stance nor his countenance changed. "I worried."

The history between them, covering each others' backs for so long, meant Gareth couldn't help but grin. "Thanks, Ma."

Dylan considered him, and Gareth knew he was weighing the humor that had been missing since Dylan's wife had run Gareth through. Seeming to come to some internal conclusion, Dylan spoke carefully and quietly, wiping the humor off Gareth's face. "We need you to come home. There's a chance we've found a way to break Macha's claim. It's a long shot but a chance all the same."

"Say that again?" Gareth choked out, dropping his arm from Ashley's shoulders and stepping toward the man who'd had his back across the centuries. Always. "How?" he croaked.

"She's able to manifest in this realm thanks to the tear in the veil." Dylan tipped his chin back and stared at the ceiling for several minutes before lowering his gaze to Gareth. "The Elder believes her physical body has to be bound to this realm in order to destroy her. Tied to the Well of Souls as she is, she'll be forced to return as a revenant spirit."

"A revenant?" Ashley asked, drawing Dylan's attention.

Gareth answered. "A revenant is a dark spirit that has no form, no physical host. It's a spirit that can be…"

"A spirit that can be what, Gareth?" she pressed.

Rowan uncrossed his arms and stepped forward. "A revenant is a spirit that can be cast out and bid never to return."

Dylan gave a terse nod. "We can cast her to the Well of Souls, and there won't be a bloody damn thing she can do about it. She'll be bound to that realm. Unless you enter the Well of Souls, she'll have no dominion over you."

Gareth tried to keep his voice steady. He failed. "And her claim to my soul?"

Dylan looked away. "We're working on that."

The hair on the back of Gareth's neck stood up. "Tell me."

"To break her claim and repair the veil, a blood sacrifice has to be made." Dylan took a menacing step toward Gareth. "It won't be you, brother."

"What type of blood sacrifice?"

"The Elder is trying to figure that out." Dylan worked his jaw. "We'll sort it out once you're home, Gareth. Most important? We'll be breaking Macha's hold on you."

Gareth went to his knees and buried his face in his hands. He'd been resigned to spending the last of his days in the arms of the phoenix who had taught him to live in the moment. Now?

For the first time in more than half a year, he found the courage to hope.

Chapter 15

Ashley pretended not to listen as the Assassin's Arcanum argued about whether or not it was safe to take her back to the Nest. It took her a bit to figure out that "the Nest" was their fabled keep. Part of her wanted to see it desperately. Another part of her was offended they had turned the decision into a subterranean summit. She'd proven she could hold her own. The last thing she needed was to be forced to prove herself all over again to a testosterone-laden group of warriors, the leader of whom was married and an obvious fretter if not totally whipped.

Listening as she heated up every tin of soup she and Gareth had purchased, she did her level best not to resent the gender bias that the female should cook while the male provided and then took it upon himself to solve all of their problems. She kept at it, though. Truth was, the task kept her out of the line of sight and gave her the chance to learn about both the men and Gareth's situation. Knowledge was another source of power, and this particular knowledge would allow her to make smart choices about when and where she'd be the most use. That was, if they "let" her.

She huffed out a short laugh chock-full of disdain. If they thought this was a matter of "letting her" participate in the solution, they had another think coming. She might have always run before, but she'd made a personal—albeit silent—vow to help Gareth find his freedom. Backing out wasn't an option, not if she intended to maintain any level of self-respect. When that was all a girl had, she tended to cling to it. Tightly.

As she stirred, she listened to the men debate what they'd do with her. She made her internal list of allies and "indifferent parties"—she didn't need more enemies—based on each individual's articulated opinion.

What she gathered was that, while Dylan was entirely opposed to having the threat Ashley posed come anywhere near his wife, Kennedy, Rowan was entirely indifferent to what they did with her. Kayden and Niall were united in that whatever gave Gareth the best chance of beating the goddess should happen. And Ethan remained almost entirely silent, waving off their requests to throw his hat in the ring.

For all that the men razzed the warlock, it was clear they respected his opinion. Yet he didn't volunteer anything in the way of planning save for one comment. "This discussion is ridiculous. Whatever chance we have at saving Gareth's soul is where our collective focus should lie. Beyond that? I'm hungry." Then he'd gone silent again.

Ethan's eyes were soft, unfocused even, and his mouth

turned down at the corners as he absently picked at a loose thread on the seam of his jeans. More than once, one of the men asked him another question, rousing the warlock from his thoughts. Bits of conversation had to be repeated before he would comment.

Each assassin watched him, casting covert glances his way as the group debated the issues at hand. It was Rowan, though, who remained entirely focused on the warlock. Ethan avoided Rowan's gaze, even when the larger man directly addressed him. Whatever hovered between them had created tension the others ignored.

Shaking off her curiosity over the warlock's internal battle, Ashley reduced the heat on the cook stove's single burner, stood and then stretched. The weight of intense attention settled between her shoulders and she chanced another look at the group.

Dylan watched Gareth, the scowl on his face speaking volumes.

Because Gareth watched *her*, his focus unwavering.

She offered Gareth a single dip of the chin in acknowledgment before crouching in front of the stove again to stir the soup as it came to a boil. There was a four-pack of plastic bowls, two spoons, six men and her. Easy way to handle distribution? She dished up her serving and moved well out of the way. "Cook gets the first bowl. The rest of you are on your own."

As predicted, conversation was abandoned as the assassins stampeded the stove. Shoving and threats ensued. Rowan and Dylan each emerged with a bowl, but Ethan was the one to emerge with a bowl *and* the other spoon.

He poured a reasonable serving, looked around and then shocked her by crossing to sit beside her. Shooting her a sardonic grin, he spooned up a bite but stopped shy of his mouth. "You ladies can have a bitch-slap fight over who gets to wash my bowl and spoon when I'm done. Until then?" He downed the bite and loosed a dramatic, almost erotic moan. "Best can of soup I've ever had. You're a damn fine cook, Ashley."

Rowan stared at him, deadpan. "I've eaten in far more trying conditions. A spoon isn't necessary."

"That's right." Ethan downed another bite. "You're, what—over five centuries old, right? I suppose you have experience eating with your hands. Or your face."

Tipping the bowl to his mouth, Rowan kept his eyes on Ethan as he swallowed mouthful after mouthful of the scalding soup. He didn't stop until it was gone. Blindly passing the bowl to Kayden, Rowan grinned at the warlock with eyes so devoid of emotion that Ashley shivered. "Don't pretend to understand our history when you're barely out of your nappies, mate."

Ethan obviously wasn't fazed. A brief salute with his spoon and then he shifted his attention to Ashley. "So, you're a phoenix."

"Yes." She was unsure of him, and her inner phoenix was screaming at her to flee all these alpha males. The men were stronger, faster, more capable than she. They could catch her, trap her, steal her freedom.

He snapped his fingers in front of her, regaining her attention. "Sorry. Lost you there for a second. So, what's it like being an immortal bird with a siren's song trapped in a Hooters girl's body?"

"Hot?"

His sharp crack of laughter bounced off the domed limestone ceiling. "No wonder Irish is all about you. He has—or had—a wicked sense of humor."

She jumped to Gareth's defense. "He doesn't have much to laugh about right now."

"Yeah, well, that whole dying thing?" He absently

gestured at Gareth with his coveted spoon. "It changed him." Ethan shot her a shrewd sidelong glance, not bothering to attempt to disguise his purpose. She *felt* him take her measure. He reached his conclusion quickly, leaned toward her and spoke in a hushed voice. "It's good to see him smiling again, even if it's only a little. We've missed him and the man he used to be."

She raised her brows.

"All I'm saying is, you're good for him."

Ashley tucked her legs up under her. "It's complicated."

"Relationships always are."

"We don't have a relationship." The low but vehement answer was supplied by rote.

"Friends with bennies?" Ethan nodded sagely. "That's cool." He set his empty bowl aside, ignoring Niall's subsequent snatch and grab. "Whatever it is you've got with him, don't let it go. If he's going to beat the goddess, he'll need this. Need you."

"Needs what?" *Sex?*

"A reason to live."

Ashley looked over at Gareth, a sense of responsibility she did *not* want settling around her.

The assassin, her lover, caught her watching him. One corner of his mouth feathered up as he stood. "I'll have your bowl when you're done, Dylan." He crossed the floor, his eyes locked on hers even as he addressed Ethan. "Scamper away, witchling, or I'll set your briefs on fire."

"Ouch, Irish. That's a serious violation of the Bro Code, and you don't violate the Code. You just don't." Ethan popped to his feet and, looking down at Ashley, winked. "I don't care how much you like the woman."

It didn't slip Ashley's notice that he'd addressed the

threat issued but not the comment regarding his feelings for her.

What are you doing worrying about feelings anyway?
You know how this will end.

Why it bothered her to acknowledge, even to herself,
that this thing with Gareth would be over soon made no
sense. She shouldn't be so bothered. And she was. Im-
mensely.

"Ash?"

She looked up at Gareth. "Sorry. Mind wandered."

"I get it." He sank to her side, taking the spot Ethan
had vacated. But where the warlock had respected her
personal space, Gareth ensured their legs touched from
hip to knee. Their arms brushed with every breath.

She leaned back on her hands, needing at least a little
separation in order to keep her head clear.

Gareth didn't comment on the move, instead broach-
ing the topic of the Arcanum's discussion. "It'll be best
if we spend the night here and head back to our cars in
the morning. Seems everyone except Dylan parked in
Killavullen in order to get here faster." He shook his
head. "Dylan left his car on the bridge."

"Excellent. Because if everyone here drives cars similar to yours, an abandoned car of *that* caliber won't
draw attention."

"I suggested Dylan leave tonight for that very reason."

"And?"

"Didn't go over well, but the others agreed. He'll head
out after dinner. The rest will sleep deep in the tunnels
they came in through to ensure no one catches us unaware." He bent his knees and parked his feet flat so
only his near hip touched her. Leaning forward, he let
his chin dip to his chest even as he rested his forearms

on his knees. "It'll be safest if we leave in groups of one and two tomorrow."

She couldn't help her choked laugh. "I can't imagine a group of men with your collective size and appearance materializing outside the cave would not cause a stir, even—or *particularly*—in such a tiny village."

"That's why we'll stagger our departure. Rowan will be closest, sleeping in—" he pointed across the room "—that tunnel. He'll stay nearby as we leave in case a male phoenix is in the area. For tonight, though, I'd afford us what little privacy I can." Using only his legs, he stood. The movement was fluid but powerful, the strength in his body undeniably lethal. He held out a hand. "Finished?"

She silently handed over her bowl and spoon.

Before she could ask, Gareth answered her unspoken question. "I drew the short straw. Kitchen duty is mine."

As if that was some secret code, all but one of the men rose and piled their bowls near the lake's edge before slipping into the darkness. Only Dylan remained.

The head of the Arcanum stared at her for a moment, green eyes flaring bright, then shifting to focus on Gareth. "Don't screw around tomorrow. Get your ass back to the Nest."

Gareth glanced down at Ashley and smiled, the look totally irreverent.

She'd never seen him like this, and it made her galloping heart trip in her chest.

He leaned toward her. "I suppose that means stopping for sex under every bridge is out."

"There are a lot of bridges in Ireland," she said, voice a bit breathless.

Gareth nodded slowly. "Shame, that."

"Shame," she echoed.

He shook his head, the smile widening. "I'll eat and then do dishes and bag our trash. You should get some rest."

She spared Dylan a final look, but the man who hadn't wished her well any more than he'd wished her ill had faded into the darkness while she'd been focused on Gareth.

Bloody dangerous, that.

Gareth made a single circuit around the cavern, listening for anything out of the ordinary—including chatter from the Arcanum that would indicate they were too close to what he had of a private life.

Ashley.

She'd lain down as he suggested and, unless she was faking it, had fallen asleep quickly. Her color had been a little off, her face pallid. That thought alone was enough to prompt him to make his security circuit quickly, anxious as he was to return to her.

Walking the edge of the lake, he did an impromptu systems check. He hadn't felt this well since last October. Energy hummed through him, as vibrant as it was electrifying. The awareness of his element had changed, intensified, even as its signature had morphed. That had to be a result of the unplanned merger with Ash's flame. If this, this awareness of life, was the payoff? He couldn't be angry. She'd given him his life back in so many ways, from warmth to humor to hope.

He could never repay her.

The realization that he could finally share body heat with her instead of being the one to constantly take had him resuming his trek. Rounding the far end of the lake, he stepped up the pace even more. He wanted to bury his nose in her hair, smell the signature scent of arid heat that clung to her skin, run his hands over the lush curve of one hip as he settled himself against her ass. Then he'd let things go where they may.

Unadorned lust surged through him. Wanting her now had nothing to do with her fertility cycle and everything to do with the woman she was—funny, edgy, charming, sharp, compassionate. That she'd paid close attention to the Arcanum's discussion tonight hadn't slipped his notice. He knew she'd weighed their words and developed opinions. He wanted to talk to her about them, discuss odds and options for taking Macha on…

He stumbled to a halt.

Macha.

He'd used the goddess's name, but not really. Like every other time, he'd only thought it.

Suddenly, that wasn't enough.

Having lived under the weight of the terror that bitch imposed infuriated him. She had taken so much from his life. None of it had been hers to take. In turn, she'd left him broken. Cold. Hopeless.

No more.

Ashley's words whispered through his mind. *Don't paint fear into every dark corner or every suspicious sound.*

He'd been angry with her for saying it and yet grateful when she went on to define fear, from the threat of every unfamiliar face to the unanticipated knock at the door. Once, shortly after he'd been resurrected, he'd tried to talk to Dylan about his fears. The man had listened, had attempted to understand, but he hadn't been able to. Not really.

Ashley? She'd been hunted so long, had lived with the understanding that her capture, her loss of self and freedom, was always one wrong step away. She understood.

For the first time in months, Gareth hadn't been alone with the weight of his fear. He'd had a partner who understood what it was to live, eat, breathe and sleep in a constant state of terror. He was ashamed he'd so easily ceded control to the goddess who thought to force him into an eternity of indentured, violent service as the sword arm of her immortal army. He would never fight his own brethren in her name, for her purpose. The thought of being her puppet, the idea that she possessed the power to supersede his free will, had terrified him into blindly believing her when she claimed she controlled both his present as well as his ever-after.

"No more," he said softly.

He wasn't going to allow the goddess to dictate his fate or his future.

No. Not "the goddess."

Gareth swallowed around the bitterly familiar fear that surged into his throat and anchored itself.

He drew a deep breath, held it to a count of ten and blew it out through his nose in a hard rush. If this was what it took to reclaim a little more of his own, he could do it. Summoning the dregs of the man he'd been, he spoke.

"You, Goddess of Phantoms and War, have no claim on me." He licked his lips, his mouth and tongue as desiccated as a centuries-old grave. "I renounce you… Macha."

Something shimmered in his peripheral vision. His stomach surged, and he spun toward the mirage only to find Ashley rolling over and pulling the blankets to her chin.

Nothing there.

His heart hammered against his sternum with the speed of a machine gun ripping through an endless ammunition belt, the *rat-tat-tat* ricocheting around inside his chest.

Rubbing a hand between his pecs, he forced himself to breathe. Gods, but he was tired. Even the discomfort of sleeping on the hard-packed earth held appeal if only because it meant he'd get to lie down.

With her.

A second mirage shimmered just out of his regular field of view. This one was closer, though.

Gareth's breath fogged the air…and he knew.

Every movement brutally precise, he squared off with the cloaked goddess who materialized only a few feet away.

His element flared. Sweat bloomed on his skin. He basked in the intent with which the fire he carried came to heel. He reveled in the glut of strength rolling through him on a cellular level and called for more. He savored the fury that rushed in and smothered his fear. Finally, *finally*, he was in control. *He* would master his emotions. *He* would dictate the terms of engagement. *He* held jurisdiction over the outcome.

Fingers stretching, his element drew even closer to the surface, racing across his palm to rest at his fingertips. Loosing that power would be a matter of thought. He encouraged the heat to wash through him like a fiery whirlwind as he focused on the goddess.

No. Again, not "the goddess." That bitch had a name, one that smeared the air when uttered. "Macha."

She slid her hands—wrinkled, charred and cracked—from her cloak's bell sleeves. Moving with care, she slipped her hood back.

Gareth fought not to retch. He'd seen gruesome wounds over his centuries of service, but every memory paled in the face of Macha's physical reality.

Blond hair that had previously hung to her waist was entirely gone, revealing scalp riddled with scar tissue and open wounds. Skin on her face had been burned and now puckered. A raw, ragged wound, the edges of which had failed to seal, ran down the front of her neck and disappeared under the cloak. But it was her eyes that he knew would haunt him. They were wide, the irises no longer pallid but a milky white.

She was a walking, talking horror story. A nightmare manifest. *His* nightmare.

Time to wake up.

"You finally speak my name." Macha steepled her fingers, palms pressed together. "It would seem your little phoenix has fueled your confidence. Rest assured, I'll break it."

He raised his chin and shook out his hands. "Just words. They hold no dominion over me. Not anymore."

The milky film over her eyes took on a gray pallor. She smiled. The gesture wasn't at all reassuring, hedging much closer to a peeling back of lips that revealed the dichotomy of perfect teeth. "I told you in the village that obsequious behavior would carry you further than defiance. You neither listened nor learned. I intend to rectify that. Now. I would have preferred your respect, assassin." She gestured with her hands, palms up, as if to shrug. "Now? I'll settle for your fear." Macha blew across her open hands.

Shards of ice shot across the distance separating them.

It happened so fast that he had no time to defend himself.

Those shards pierced his skin like a thousand poisoned darts and chased his pulse through his veins. Soft tissue hardened as his heart slowed and his blood turned to slush. Pain, shockingly similar to what he'd experienced in the Well of Souls, made his knees buckle. Memories rolled over him, the weight crushing. Only sheer force of will kept him from dropping to the rock-strewn ground.

His legs shook as he forced himself upright and locked his knees. Blood trickled from an impossible number of tiny wounds to stain his chest and faded jeans. He wiped his forehead. His hand came away painted in fine crimson strokes. "That the best you've got?"

An unfamiliar male voice cursed so loud the caustic diatribe reverberated through the still cavern.

Gareth's chin whipped around of its own volition.

"No," Macha purred. "*That* is."

Across the small lake, Ashley shot from their pallet. Whirling to face the man who lurched after her, she caught a vicious backhand. She spun away and went down hard.

Frenzied wrath ripped an involuntary, animalistic sound from Gareth.

Ashley rose on unsteady feet. Her gaze met his and she took a couple of unsteady steps toward him. Then she reached for him.

The long-haired man, easily a head taller than her and half again as wide, stepped in front of her. She refocused on the stranger. Brilliant flames raced down her arms and swallowed her hands. She amassed two fiery orbs and launched them in rapid succession.

The man caught the first strike and cast it aside. Fire skipped across the cave floor and collided with one of the two duffel bags and sent it up in flames. Distracted, he missed the second fireball. It caught him square in the chest and lit him up.

Gareth's chest seized. Then he breathed out a harsh, "No."

The stranger swiped at the flames, shedding them with each pass of his hands. His skin appeared angry and welted, but no serious damage was done.

"How?" Gareth wheezed.

"I won't suffer the harlot to live, assassin mine."

"How?" he roared, rounding on the deceptively diminutive goddess.

"She thought to take what I claimed! You belong to *me!*" Macha screeched. "I will not tolerate disrespect."

Chest heaving, Gareth took an unconscious step forward. "What have you done?"

A slow, wicked grin infused with madness spread over Macha's face. "Delivered her worst nightmare to her door."

Flames erupted from his fingers and spread up his forearms. He drew on the blend of elemental magicks that burned inside him, coaxing the inferno to life. "This ends now."

"You're wrong. This is just the beginning." Macha flung her hand toward the lake, and a massive wall of water rose. It splashed against the ceiling and froze, creating a solid wall between him and Ashley. "What will you do, assassin mine? Will you direct your rage at me as you long to do, or will you ride to the female's rescue and save her from being taken back to her clan? You cannot be in two places at once." Black mist swirled around the hem of her cloak. Shadowy forms with gaping mouths began to take shape. "Choose," she hissed, her voice infused with the screams of the damned.

Flashes of orange and red confirmed the battle raged beyond the ice wall. That meant both phoenixes were engaged. He'd seen Ashley fight. The woman was fierce and could hold her own. She'd had centuries to hone her skills, had survived against the odds based on cunning and would resurrect should she fall. She'd even intimated she hadn't *wanted* help. But this thing with Macha...

Gareth drew a ragged breath. There was no way he was turning his back on the goddess. She wouldn't just let him walk away. No way. He could end this here. Now.

Power coursed through him and he drew deep, his strength fueled by the rage he harbored for the Goddess of Phantoms and War. That rage bordered on madness.

He didn't forecast his intent, didn't afford her any warning. Instead, he flung a hand toward her and shouted, *"Flammis destruunt quod dedignor!"* Flames *destroy that which I despise!*

Macha's phantoms scattered to avoid the brilliant flash of light. The goddess's robe lit up, the flames licking up her legs. She screamed and, with one hand, cast a heavy mist down her body in self-defense. Throwing her other hand out, she curled her fingers toward her body in a summoning gesture. *"Anima Peto, derelinquetis gloriam vestram et exercitum meum ordinesque turbaverat. Praecipere meus es tu!"* Soul I claim, leave *your host and join my ranks. You are mine to command!*

The brand on Gareth's chest split and cracked, and from the depths of his body came the most disconcerting sensation. It was as if the very heart of who he was fought to separate from his consciousness and heed Macha's summons.

He forced himself to ignore the hissing scream of fire rebounding off ice, forced himself to trust that Ashley could take care of herself just one more time.

He slammed a burning hand over his chest and willed the very heart of who he was to stay put. "I choose to end this now, on my terms!"

He rounded on Macha and, drawing on the power coursing through him, lunged at the goddess.

Chapter 16

Ashley had leaned against the man crawling in bed with her only moments before, certain it was Gareth. That assumption had amplified when his bare skin slid over hers, the heavy weight of his erection resting between her ass cheeks. The way he'd slipped his arm around her and then thrust against her had been her first major clue. Then she'd caught his scent. Arid. Hot. Unfamiliar.

That wasn't who Gareth was to her.

She'd rolled over, the movement deceptively sensuous… and then junk-punched the uninvited bed guest in order to escape his tightening grasp. He'd roared as he curled into a fetal position. That was her chance, her *only* chance, to get away, to defend herself from a man whose image had been burned into her mind centuries ago.

Christos Margalos.

The first man who had elected to kill her instead of let her go.

She didn't think she'd be so lucky this time.

He lunged after her before she was steady on her feet and delivered a vicious backhand, the ring he wore, her *clan's* ring, splitting the skin over her cheekbone. The impact spun her like a top. She went with it, using the momentum to create much needed distance between them. How the hell had he found her, and here of all places?

Her gaze shot across the lake to find Gareth facing off with Macha. The goddess was responsible.

That bitch.

Ashley started for Gareth. If things went the way they had in the village, he was in trouble. She couldn't let him face this, the darkest personal demon she knew of, alone.

Christos stepped into her path, forcing her to draw up far short of her intended goal.

"Little Asia Panos. It's been far too long, my little chick."

"I haven't been 'Asia' for centuries." She summoned her phoenix's strength. Twin fireballs flashed into being and spun wildly in her palms.

Christos's eyelids slipped low, and he regarded her through eyes turning more bronze by the moment. "You'll always be Asia to me."

"Bank your lust or you're going to have the worst case of blue balls Ireland's ever seen." She stepped to one side.

He mirrored the movement. "I'll not accept your refusal as graciously this time, Asia."

"You bastard," she spat, her temperature rising. "Last time I checked the advice columns, killing your unwilling lover because *you* failed to impregnate her wasn't considered gracious."

His face darkened. "The epithicas ensured you were

willing, woman. Your failure to accept my seed entitled me to take your life."

"Entitled? No one has any right to my life!" Fury roared through her that this man believed her life was his to do with as he saw fit. This was why she could never belong to a man. She would never be anyone's property, and that was the only value male phoenixes assigned their women. Property. Chattel.

She flung the first handful of fire at him, but he batted it away. Gareth's duffel bag intercepted the orb, the dense nylon smoking furiously as it went up in flames. She threw the second fireball at him. This one stuck.

He stunned her when he wiped the fire off his bare skin as if it was no more than rainwater. "Your powers are weak, Asia. The epithicas cannot be starved or you will suffer. I will satisfy your hunger."

Need bloomed hot between her thighs. *Gods, no.* It had been too long since she'd been with Gareth, too long since she'd been sated. Her nipples pearled. Heat washed over every inch of her. With it came the long-suppressed shame that she had fought to conquer, shame that she couldn't control her body's response. She didn't want Christos. She wanted Gareth.

Desperate, she sought him out at the same time a wall of water rose in the middle of the lake. It froze solid, but that wasn't what had stopped her heart in her chest. Gareth had looked at her, had met her frantic stare. Then he'd turned toward Macha. And turned his back on her.

A vicious smile spread over Christos's face, his eyes having focused on her breasts. "You respond to me still." He held out a hand. "Come to me of your own accord and I will be gentle."

She forced herself to remain in place.

"Do not think you can deny me," he said in a gravelly

whisper. "Pregnant or not, I will kill you when I'm done with you. There will be more epithicai, but your lesson in subservience cannot wait." He took a fractional step closer. "Know this, Asia. I took your heart before. I will not be as swift this time. You will long for death before I deliver the final blow."

Anger fought to the surface and trounced the devastating fear that threatened to pull her under. She clutched that anger tight as she called her phoenix.

Silence met her summons.

Denial coursed through her. She called again. Same result. Like a frayed tether, the connection to her phoenix was weak, but the tie to her phoenix's strength? Her flame? It had somehow been lost. The compounded result was that she found herself free of the epithicas and shockingly clearheaded. The cost? Her best means of defense, her strength and her flame, were gone.

No, not gone.

Taken.

Gareth. He'd taken them in the fight against Macha. Taken them and abandoned her.

Something so much worse than impotent rage consumed her. Devastation. Betrayal. Things she never would have felt if she'd kept the assassin at arm's length as she should have.

He left me to die...

Except no, he hadn't risked her death. That, that she could forgive. But Gareth knew what she faced, knew what she was up against. Another phoenix. A lifetime of sexual servitude. He'd seen her worst fear crawl in bed with her and turned his back.

A sound of unadulterated rage lodged in her throat. Backing up in a rush, she slammed into the rough rock of the wall. Her skin tore. The impact jarred the sound loose. That raw sound ripped through the cavern, knocking stalactites free from the ceiling.

She would not go down without a fight. Christos had no right to her body, and she would die before she allowed him, or anyone, to take her against her will.

She shuddered as reality struck.

Ending her life would result in Final Death. Suicide was the only guaranteed means by which a phoenix could relinquish the ability to resurrect. The intent behind the death made all the difference. Being murdered wasn't a matter of individual will, but suicide? No one purposefully died by her own hand without express intent.

She didn't want to experience true death, but what he threatened wasn't living. It was slavery. And that was what had driven her mother to end her life.

Christos held one hand out to her, curling his fingers into his palm in a come-hither motion. The other he used to grip his arousal and stroke. He clearly thought he was the lesser of the two evils she faced—servitude or death.

He was wrong.

Faced with those two options, there was only one she could accept. Consequences be damned. She would never allow herself to belong to someone, to become a numbered possession instead of a necessary person. If her partner couldn't live without her, she couldn't live with him.

She began to chant in a language lost to mortals and Others alike, a language fiercely guarded by the phoenix clans. Ignoring the shock on Christos's face, she summoned her phoenix to rise against its will. Her hands scaled and claws split the ends of her fingers. She would need them to rip her heart out.

Gods, this was going to suck. She dug one hand into

her chest, claws ripping at skin and grating over bone. She fought the scream charging up her throat.

Christos charged her.

He struck her hand away.

Flesh tore.

Her wrist broke.

With her phoenix so near the surface, her agonized scream emerged as a heavy shriek.

Christos gripped her hair and yanked her away from the wall. "You will not deprive me, Asia."

Pain made her eyes water. Her throat was so raw, her sharp comeback emerged as a strangled rasp. "You have no right to me."

"I'll see you tattooed before the night's out. The clan Master will allow it given your proclivity for self-inflicted harm." He shoved a knee between her legs, forcing them open.

The depth of her denial, something far too close to shock, softened reality. She wouldn't survive this. Couldn't survive this.

The air sang with a high-pitched whine.

Blood arced as a heavy blade separated Christos's head from his neck. His body collapsed on top of her.

She whimpered and shoved at the corpse. The flames required for a phoenix's resurrection burned hotter than any other. If she was pinned beneath him when he lit up, she'd be burned to a crisp. If Christos resurrected before her, he could cause her true death by scattering her ashes. How she died would be one more choice taken from her.

The corpse started to smoke.

A booted foot immediately connected with the dead phoenix's ribs, tossing the body several feet away. There

was a brilliant flash and both body and head were consumed by flame.

Panic rode her, blinded her to reason, stole her senses
and demanded she act. She dug her claws into her chest.
If she didn't finish this—

Her wrist protested the abuse. An anguished cry un-
coiled from deep in her chest and emerged as a hopeless wail.

Heat from the burning body winged out in a brutal
strike against the two living bodies within range.

Ashley.

And Rowan.

The assassin was forced back a step, but his gaze
never left hers. It bored through her. Assessed her claws
buried in her chest and silently demanded answers.

Her decision to die and the phoenix's opposing will to
live crowded her mind, overriding her ability to speak.

Rowan took a step toward her, stopping at the sound
of talons on bone.

Hers.

"Remove the claws, Red."

She didn't move. Couldn't.

His jaw tightened. "I will kill you without batting
an eye if it means stopping this nonsense." When she
still didn't remove her claws, he spoke through clenched
teeth. "Don't make me do this, Ashley."

The use of her name shocked her from her stupor.
Chin to her chest and fingers still embedded in her body,
she tipped sideways and landed in an awkward heap on
the floor.

Rowan closed in on her. He raised his sword and
drove the tip into the earth. Dropping to his knees beside her, he gently removed her clawed fingers one at a

time. "None of this, darling." He pulled his shirt off and pressed it to her chest. "Hold this with your good hand."

When she didn't move, he took her uninjured hand and pressed it to her breast.

She began to shake.

Rowan situated himself beside her. "I won't hurt you."

Then he pulled her into his embrace.

She clutched his shirt to her and curled into his warmth, her damaged wrist resting on his thigh. "Help Gareth. Please."

Ethan emerged from the tunnel he'd occupied, scraped, bruised and bleeding. "Fucking cave passages are *not* meant for running through." He stumbled to a stop, eyes wide with obvious disbelief. "Rowan? When did you start hugging it out, man?"

"Leave it," the assassin bit out.

The deep voice reverberated beneath her ear.

Ethan shook his head and then glanced first at the burning body and then the flashes of magick and fire that could be seen through the ice wall. "What the hell happened?"

"Get over here and help her," Rowan ordered, gently extricating himself.

Ethan sprinted to Ashley and slid to a stop beside her, arms open. "Come here, baby girl. Uncle Ethan's got you."

She was passed with infinite gentleness into Ethan's embrace.

Free of her, Rowan sprinted toward the frozen wall. His physical form flickered seconds before he ghosted through the ice.

Ashley sat up a bit. *Did I just see...?* She clutched the blood-soaked shirt to her chest and blinked rapidly. "What the hell?"

Ethan leaned just far enough back to pull his shirt off and, with brutal efficiency, replaced the assassin's offering with his own. He pressed against the five wounds harder than she had. "I have medical training and no supplies beyond 'bippity-boppity-boo.' Hell of a lot of good I am. Lay back." He wiggled around to rest her bare back to his bare chest. His lips thinned. "If you were attempting to do what I think you were attempting to do, Gareth is going to lose it. I do *not* want to be here, hands on your very lovely chest, when that happens. I may be delicious, but I was never meant to be a s'mores component."

She couldn't stop staring at the point where Rowan had disappeared. "I repeat, what the hell, Ethan?"

Beyond the ice wall, magick raged—flashes of fire, enraged shouts, blurred movement.

"Lay. Back." He pulled at her until, given her weakened condition, she couldn't help but comply. "Rowan doesn't possess a traditional elemental magic."

"You think?" She gasped as he pressed even harder on her chest.

"Not happy with the blood you're losing."

"Don't worry. If I bleed out, I'll resurrect. Just protect my ashes." She rolled her head back and looked up at the handsome blond warlock. "Rowan?"

Ethan snorted. "He has ties to the spirit realm that no one discusses. I think—"

A thunderous explosion rocked the cave and stole whatever he'd been about to say. The unnatural ice wall blew out, pieces raining around them. Ethan twisted them around and shielded her with his body. With his throat next to her ear, she couldn't help but hear his pained grunts as debris pummeled his back.

There one moment, he was ripped away from her the next.

Gareth stood over her, skin flushed, eyes bright as flames danced deep in his irises. He took in her nudity, her ravaged hands and the bloody shirt she clutched to her chest. "Oh, baby." He stepped toward her, hands outstretched.

"Don't." She scooted away and curled her body protectively around her chest.

Confusion stole over his face as he looked her over. "Ash?" She saw the moment understanding dawned. "Tell me you did *not* attempt to…" He waved a hand at her chest and hands, clearly unable to finish his sentence.

"And what would that be?" she said, voice raw. "Spell it out for me."

"Ashley." Gareth's warning was clear.

Forcing herself to sit up, she had to lean against the wall to keep from falling over. Her mouth was dry and her head pounded like she had an angry gorilla trapped between her ears. All that combined wasn't enough to stop what came next. "What do you want from me, Gareth? I won't lie to you any more than I can tell you what you want to hear."

His jaw flexed and his Adam's apple bobbed as he swallowed hard. "Tell me you weren't about to take your own life."

"I just told you I won't lie to you." So many emotions—hurt, pride, rage, betrayal—rolled through her that she didn't know which one to latch on to. She spread the shirt over her in an attempt to hide her nudity but left the shredded skin in view. "Take a good look, Gareth. You know exactly what was about to go down."

"You would do that to me?" he asked, voice low and blade-sharp.

"It wasn't about you!" She forced herself to look up, to meet his tortured gaze. "This was about me. *Me*. You drew on the elemental tie, drained it…drained *me*. You left me with no means to defend myself. It was end up a member of Christos's harem or end myself. I chose the lesser of two evils. You had to choose to face Macha or help me. Obviously, you left my six exposed in order to end your personal demon. I couldn't end mine, so I made the only choice that would spare me from spending the rest of my life as a sexual slave. The epithicas takes me too close to that very edge every three years. Christos intended to claim me, Gareth. That? His claiming me? It would have pushed me over. There would have been no coming back." She was devastated that Christos had exposed her weakness, driven her to that point—that his taunts and physical threats had hit the heart of her. "We all carry the burdens of the choices we make."

The devastation that settled over Gareth's face wrecked her. "The thing is, Ash? You wouldn't have been around to carry any of the burden. You would have left that to me. Only me."

"You might not have survived it."

"And if I'd died?"

She twisted the edge of the shirt around her fingers. "You didn't."

Somehow the fact they had both made it out alive didn't carry the reassurance that everything was going to be okay.

Chapter 17

Gareth stared at Ashley. Her body was bruised, bloody and nearly beaten. So was his. But the physical reality was nothing compared to the horrible pain that strangled his heart and made it near impossible to breathe. He hadn't realized, hadn't been able to see what was happening beyond the wall that separated them. The decision he'd made—to face Macha and trust Ashley to handle her own demons—had almost cost the woman her life.

Macha hadn't held anything back. Neither had he. She'd tried repeatedly to rip his soul from his body even as he'd tried to bind her to this realm. He'd almost done it. If he'd been successful, he would have burned her alive. The craving for the violent end had consumed him. Macha's magick grew wilder as Gareth had pushed his own magick to bring his torment to an end. He intended to incinerate her and scatter whatever might remain.

Then Rowan had ghosted through the wall.

The other assassin's appearance had distracted Gareth just long enough to allow Macha the opportunity to dematerialize. He'd roared his denial at the ceiling.

"Get to Ashley," Rowan had demanded.

So Gareth had.

He hadn't been prepared for what he'd found and had been desperate to hear her deny what he knew to be true.

She'd intended to kill herself.

Truth and understanding drove him toward her again. He needed to touch her, to reassure himself she was whole.

More than seven months he'd wasted, focused on ending his life. Nothing else had mattered. No one else had been enough to sway his determination, change his end game.

Had this been what the friends he called family had suffered with? And did she think so little of him that she truly believed he was making this about him? Because this had nothing to do with him, his choices, his wants or even his needs. This was about her.

Seeing Ashley like this changed everything, from the way Gareth viewed death to the way he honored life. His mind replayed scenarios where he'd hurt the people he loved by rationalizing that the choices he'd made were about his wellbeing, not theirs. In split seconds, he went through what felt like a hundred conversations in which the bottom line never varied. Retrospect made it so easy to see that the choice to end his life had been about him, about terminating his misery, fears and suffering.

He'd been selfish because he'd known these people loved him and he'd chosen not to consider what his death would mean to them. But Ashley? She didn't have the reassurance that she was loved unconditionally.

His chest ached at the thought she'd never known what it was to be loved beyond reason. Rubbing his hand over his heart, he forced himself to slow down. To think. Whatever this thing between them turned out to be, whether it was a few days of pleasure or the start of a long-term affair, he couldn't accept that this...this emotional *torment* was love's foundation. It hurt too much.

Gareth considered Ashley who had paled even further. What could he say to her that would sufficiently explain that he had courted death for months and hadn't cared if he died, but the thought of a world without her in it wrecked him. He choked on a thousand words and issued not one.

A single idea rapid-cycled through his mind. It offered one solution. He had to find a way to make her see that his death meant little in the face of hers. If he died as a consequence of her death, so be it. But the real loss would be in her leaving this world too early. It had nothing to do with him or whether he lived or died.

He shifted toward her, lifted a hand in a stop-start manner, his insecurity translated loudly for everyone to see.

It didn't matter.

All that mattered was setting things right with Ashley.

Rowan intercepted Gareth's gesture. Parking a big hand on Gareth's chest, he pushed Gareth back a step. "You left her alone earlier, you can leave her alone now."

"You ordered me back to her and now want me to leave her alone?" Gareth's temper narrowed his field of view until he saw no one but Rowan. "Back off, man."

"What were you thinking, leaving her to defend herself?" Rowan demanded, his words low and fierce, carrying an acidic undertone so caustic they burned.

Gareth met the other man's stare. "Ash has made it

perfectly clear she's entirely capable of protecting herself and doesn't need anyone else's help." Hands balled into fists, he parked them on Rowan's chest and pushed back. "Ever."

"You're a fecking eejit." Rowan's mouth thinned into a hard line. "And don't push me again."

Of course Gareth did just that. "And what would you have had me do?" he demanded. "I couldn't turn my back on Macha. I trusted Ash to defend herself. And why wouldn't I? She's done a bang-up job so far."

The next shove from his fellow assassin nearly landed Gareth on his ass. Rowan stepped into his personal space. "You're a fool if you think leaving the woman you care for alone to face her personal demons is *ever* the better choice." Voice raw and chest heaving, Rowan leaned even closer. "You protect what's yours or you lose it. Always." He thumped a fist over his heart. "I know. *I fucking* know!"

Gareth paled. Gods, how could he have not realized how this, almost losing Ashley, so closely paralleled the loss that had destroyed the former leader of the Assassin's Arcanum? "Rowan—"

"Don't you dare apologize to me," his friend snapped. "I'm not the one who's due. She is." Gripping Gareth's shoulders, Rowan leaned in, pressed their foreheads together, closed his eyes and spoke in a harsh whisper. "I lost everything because I…" He audibly swallowed and slowly opened eyes that blazed an unearthly crystalline blue. "I lost my heart's pulse, Gareth, and I'll never get her back, never hear her voice, never see her again. *Never.* Don't be a fool and miss what's right in front of you." Shoving Gareth away, the dark-headed warrior spun, scooped up a handful of Christos's ashes and stalked down the cave tunnel he'd been charged to defend. Proud, straight shoulders shook under the burden of ancient memories unleashed.

He forgot his sword. Not that Gareth would be pointing that out. Rowan needed space, needed quiet and darkness and privacy to stitch back the gaping wounds that time had never truly healed. Wounds that current events had ripped open. He was bleeding out but would allow no one to help him.

Gareth would see that his brother in arms got what he needed, no matter what it cost in personal currency.

Shoring himself up in the wake of emotional turmoil, he forced himself to face Ashley. The wounds on her chest screamed at him, accused him of the worst of betrayals.

He couldn't draw a sufficient breath.

How was it that tapping into the element available to him had hurt her?

The barbed accusation she'd flung at him twined around his lungs and begun to burrow. *You drew on the elemental tie, drained it...drained me. You left me with no means to defend myself.*

His legs went weak, and he thought, for a brief second, he'd simply sink to the ground under the sheer weight of what was suddenly clear.

What he'd been drawing on wasn't his. It was *theirs.*

Gods save him, he'd unwittingly taken everything and left her entirely defenseless in pursuit of his own agenda.

He wanted to go to his knees, to plead with her and find absolution in her grace. What came out was, "I'm taking you to the Nest. It'll be a safer, more defensible position."

Her eyes narrowed and her chin jutted. "You turn into a travel agent? Because unless you did, you're not issuing mandates on where I go."

"Ash, please."

She shook her head. "No, Gareth. I listened to your conversations earlier, and Dylan's hesitation at bringing me into the Nest wasn't reassuring. I'm not at all sure it, or the assassins, will be the best choice. Not anymore."

He tunneled his fingers through his hair, pushing the mass away from his face. "If you're uncomfortable at the keep, I give you my word I'll take you to the place of your choosing. I'll go with you. We'll sort this out, Ash."

"You don't get it, Gareth." She wrapped one blood-slicked arm around her middle as her free arm still pinned the destroyed shirt to her chest. The raw ends of her fingers were already healing. "You abandoned the trust I invested in you. Threw it away, really. I agree that we'll have to 'sort this out' seeing as our elements have merged, but once we figure out how to coexist?" She drew in a sharp breath. "That's where this—we— will end."

Gareth fought an inexplicable rise of panic. "I'm sorry, Ashley."

"Seems you probably should have considered open-ing the conversation with that." Her sharp-edged laugh raked down the cave walls. "Even Conan... Rowan... understood the value of 'I'm sorry.'"

He wasn't above groveling if it would help. "Please, Ash."

Ethan had kept out of the conversation but had clearly been listening, his attention shifting back and forth like a tennis chair umpire's focus. He gave Gareth his back as he sank to balance on the balls of his feet. "Listen, my little chick, I know you may not want to hear it, but Irish here has a point. We need to get you somewhere safe where we can address those wounds. The last thing you, or any of us, need to worry about while we're doing that is having another misogynistic asshat show up trying to force you to take and bake his baby batter. The Nest is safe."

She tightened her hold on the shirt she still clutched to her chest and nodded. "Okay."

She'll cede to the warlock's concern but not mine?

"That's my girl." Ethan reached out and rested a hand on her shoulder. "I knew there was a reasonable mind behind the undeniable beauty."

Gareth's hands tightened into fists. Ashley was *not* Ethan's "girl." Not in any sense. And the man needed to stop looking at her. Sooner would be better than later.

Ashley rested her head against the rock wall and rolled her face toward the warlock. "You have to agree to be my personal physician."

"I'd be honored, of course."

Ashley winced as she shifted to lean into Ethan's touch but managed a faint smile. "You realize you had me at 'bippity-boppity-boo,' right?"

Ignoring Gareth's cold stare, Ethan waggled his eyebrows at Ash. "If sweet talk and movie quotes are all you're looking for, I'll be Prince Charming to your Cinderella."

The relieved look Ashley shared with Ethan nearly provoked Gareth to violence. And if she kept looking at the warlock like that, he and the man *were* going to have words...punctuated by fists...wrapped up with a body count of one. *Ethan's.*

Gareth cleared his throat and something in his chest loosened just a little when Ashley looked at him bearing the ghost of the smile she'd aimed at the warlock. "Will you go home with me, Ash, let me offer you the safety and security of the Nest and see you well?"

"The epithicas—"

"We'll deal with it together." No way would he step aside and let someone else see her needs sated. Besides, his own needs would demand a lover and he didn't want another.

Her brow furrowed. "I was going to say it's almost over."

"How?" he demanded and then shook his head. "What I meant is, it hasn't been a week. I was under the impression we had a couple more days at least." And why did he sound hopeful, even to himself?

She lifted a shoulder to shrug and winced. "I think splitting it between us cut the time, and intensity, in half. You know, that whole 'a burden shared is a burden halved' thing."

He opened his mouth to tell her what she'd said made sense. The exception was that he didn't consider her a burden. The words spilled to the tip of his tongue before they evaporated like a sheet of water exposed to the summer sun's intensity.

When the epithicas ended, she'd be gone.

She'd said as much, and more than this once.

The urge to snatch her up and hold her tight was overwhelming. He wanted, *needed*, to convince her that there was more to this thing between them…

Gareth stumbled to the side when the cave appeared to tilt at a hard right angle. Vertigo struck and he collapsed into a near-boneless heap. Understanding hit him square in the chest at the same moment his ass made contact with the rock-strewed cave floor. He didn't know whether to laugh or call Rowan back and ask the giant to knock some sense into him.

Somewhere in this entire mess, between her murmuring the soccer score in his ear at the bar and him finding the courage to face Macha, he'd fallen in love with Ashley.

Leaning forward, he braced his forearms over his bent knees and let his head hang loose. He huffed out a short, sharp breath. This was so screwed up. Why couldn't he have realized this earlier? If he had, he never would have left their pallet. He would have crawled in bed with her and held her close, cherished every minute he had left with her. He would have found a way to love her outside of the epithicas's boundaries. Hell, he might even have found a way to tell her what his heart had obviously known and his mind had just come to understand. The last dregs of the epithicas would provide his only chance to convince her that being wanted *and* needed was neither a death sentence nor damnation. Because she'd been clear from the beginning: the end of the epithicas would be the end of *them*.

"Gareth?"

Her voice. Gods, he would never tire of hearing her say his name. The weight of her stare pulled his chin in her direction. She was his safe harbor in this perfect emotional storm and had been from the first when she'd danced with him. His gaze found hers, and his heartbeat slowed into a sure, steady rhythm.

She looked at him quietly, considering. "What?"

A slight shake of the head was the best he could manage.

He rose and retrieved her duffel, dug out her remaining change of clothes and handed them over. "If you'll dress, we'll get out of here. I'm sure Rowan intends to scatter Christos's ashes in the River Blackwater, but you should have that pleasure. The phoenix won't ever come after you again, Ashley. You have my word."

She accepted the yoga pants and shirt with a soft, "Thank you."

Ethan gave Gareth a hard look before issuing a parting comment. "Get Gareth to help you rinse the wounds with bottled water before you cover them with the clean shirt. I'll have Rowan hold those ashes. If the phoenix resurrects, we'll kill him again." A dark pleasure spread over Ethan's face. "For fun." Then he disappeared down the same tunnel Rowan had taken.

Gareth retrieved the last of their bottled water and silently helped Ashley clean up before she dressed.

The one time he'd started to speak, to try to bridge the chasm of hurt, she'd stopped him. "Don't. Please."

Bagging the last of their supplies, he'd wordlessly followed her slow trek from the cavern.

Her request had gutted him. Things were so broken between them. He had to fix this.

If only he had a clue where to start.

Ashley had been a bit surprised to find herself escorted by two additional men—a very pissed-off Rowan and an unnaturally quiet Ethan.

"I thought we were leaving in ones and twos," she said as she scattered a handful of Christos's ashes in the river.

A few feet ahead of her, Rowan grunted. He moved like a giant panther, slipping silently through underbrush without disturbing a branch while Ashley crashed through every bush, snagging her clothes and hair. She made enough noise to chase off the cows that had come to the riverbank for water.

"The grunt means what, exactly?" Casting another bit of Christos's ashes, she listened—hoped?—for a smile in Rowan's voice when he answered.

He didn't look at her when he answered. "I sent Kayden and Niall back to their cars earlier."

Hope was, apparently, futile. The dark-haired man seemed to have lost the thread of humanity he'd reclaimed earlier. She pressed him. "Where were they?"

"I caught Kayden and Niall on their way into the main cavern following the fight. They'd been stationed closer to the exits so it took them longer to reach us." Rowan held a branch for her. "Could you be any louder?"

She shot him a deadpan stare as she passed under the low-growing tree. "Only if I really tried."

Emerging from the thicket, she slipped to the river's edge, spread the last of Christos's ashes, then knelt and rinsed her hands. She sat back on her heels and stared at the deep night sky. Stars still liberally decorated the heavens even as sunrise stained the horizon. Another half an hour and the starlight would be obscured. A shooting star shot across the sky. She traced the trajectory with a fingertip and considered making a wish. But hanging her hopes on a dying star had always struck her as ill-advised. Even if she'd felt differently, she wouldn't have known what to wish for. There were too many choices and she was too tired to sort them out.

River rocks shifted as one of the men approached, the noise obviously for her benefit. Otherwise, she would have come out of her skin.

Gareth settled beside her. "How's the epithicas?"

"Rising," she said on a sigh.

"Do we need to get a hotel?" He tucked a strand of hair behind her ear. "While I'm not a proper physician, I'm a fair hand at field dressing. I could patch you up and see you through the morning. Then we could finish our trip to the Nest later and have Ethan tend your wounds."

She watched him from the corner of her eye. The

trust between them had been fractured. Badly. Fixing it seemed impossible.

He didn't press, though, letting her work through possible answers. Sorting through rocks near his feet, he settled on a flat stone and then skipped it across the river's smooth surface. Then he began the hunt for the right rock all over again.

Ashley didn't know what course of action would be most prudent. That irritated her. Not as much as the fact she didn't actually know what she *wanted* to do. She'd been clear with Gareth that the end was near. An odd look had passed over his face, but he hadn't argued with her. It hadn't been a compassionate choice on her part to let possible arguments slide. Her silence had been a product of a confusing emotional onslaught. She was so angry with him. Beyond angry, really. She was drowning in fury. But those weren't the only feelings she was slogging through. Betrayal rode a real contender for the right to claim top spot in her emotional derby. All those feelings jockeying for position left her churned up. Unsteady. Scared that whichever sentiment crossed the finish line first would destroy her, particularly if the winner turned out to be the dark horse. *Affection.*

She'd never expected to feel anything for Gareth. The epithicas didn't work that way. Discovering the unexpected reaction to him, from his appearance to his personality to his strength—that and more combined to make his betrayal beyond devastating.

"Ash?" he asked quietly. "If you don't want to grab a hotel, I get it. It's two hours back to the Nest. Can you make it that long?"

Rising, she ignored the pain in her chest and hands. "If you can hold out, it would be best to get to the Nest."

"I agree." He dropped the rock he held and stared

down the river. "We can't know who else Macha sold us out to besides Christos."

She hadn't considered that. "You're right." Hesitating, unsure how to ask what she wanted to know, she shifted from foot to foot.

"What is it?"

Out with it then. "Can you make it two hours?"

He rolled his shoulders as if his skin was too tight. "I intend to break a couple of land speed records getting us back there." He took a deep breath, his shoulders and chest emphasized by the movement. "I need to know…"

She waited, but he didn't continue.

"Step it up," Rowan called from downriver. "We need to make the most of the last of the dark."

"Be right there," she called before turning to Gareth. "Need to know what?"

He gripped handfuls of his hair. Blue eyes met hers, the torment in them so clear her heart ached for him. Dropping his hands to his side, he watched her intently as he spoke. "I want to see you through the epithicas—want you to see *me* through the time we have left." He stepped closer. "Please."

Looking up at him, she had a hard time catching her breath. He was so beautiful cast in the light of the breaking dawn. There were a thousand things she wanted to say, could have said. She could have railed at him for a thousand more. But she didn't. The hope on his face diluted the anger she carried. For all she hated the choices he'd made, he'd been a generous lover. It was more than she'd hoped for going into this epithicas. Denying herself the comforts he afforded her smacked of masochism.

"Through the epithicas, then," she agreed.

He nodded and gestured toward the rudimentary trail they followed. "You first. I've got your back."

She laughed softly and moved past him, her mind pressing her to include a necessary addendum to her logic. Because she made it a point not to lie to herself, she couldn't exclude the other self-evident reason she'd agreed to see the epithicas through with Gareth.

The darkest horse of all had closed in on the frontrunners in her emotional race when she wasn't watching.

Desire.

Chapter 18

"Cliché much?" Ashley muttered under her breath as she and her band of not-so-merry men approached the foreboding Nest's ironbound wooden doors. The arched peaks had to be twelve feet tall. She couldn't help the fact her mouth fell open when Gareth waved a hand and the doors swung open on silent hinges.

A dark-haired beauty rushed down the grand staircase and threw herself into Ethan's arms.

He has a woman?

The warlock spun the woman around and then set her on her feet and gestured Ashley forward. "Red, this is my best friend in the whole world and the woman unlucky enough to have saddled herself with the head ass in this place. Kennedy, meet Ashley. Ashley, Kennedy."

Kennedy held out a hand. "It's nice to meet you. I understand you've met Dylan, my husband."

Dylan was her husband? Poor woman. "I, uh… Yes.

I've met Dylan. It's nice to meet you." Ashley took Kennedy's hand and started at the rush of power that burned along her nerves.

Kennedy pulled her hand back. "Sorry. I'm just getting used to my personal power grid."

"Pardon?"

The beauty blushed. "I'm an amplifier."

"She increases the baseline power a person possesses. It's a new development. Like learning to ride a bike, she's still got training wheels." Gareth stepped in and hugged the woman. "Hello, Mrs. O'Shea."

She laughed, a bright light in a gloomy interior.

Ashley wanted to like her just as much as she wanted to rip the woman out of his hold.

"You look amazing." Kennedy stepped back but still ran her hands up and down Gareth's arms.

Visions of singeing Dylan's bride—just enough to make it clear Gareth wasn't a free-touch zone—flashed through Ashley's mind. No one the wiser, she smiled benignly.

"Might want to shut the flames down, Red," Rowan murmured in her ear. "It's a bit of a tell where your emotions are concerned."

"Shut up, Conan." But she did as bid, repressing her phoenix's flare of temper. No need to tell anyone it hadn't been voluntary.

Rowan slapped the flat of his sword blade against his shoulder and, without another word, slipped down one of a half dozen hallways that opened off the entry hall.

Movement caught Ashley's attention. Her gaze snapped back and forth between the two men descending the staircase in step with one another. She recognized Dylan, *the* Assassin and leader of the Assassin's Arcanum. The man at his side could have been Dylan's older brother. Immense power radiated from him. Dylan stopped two steps shy of the hall floor, but his companion kept coming. The older gentleman went straight to Gareth, drawing him into a fierce hug and murmuring words meant for Gareth alone.

Her lover nodded before breaking contact. Fine lines webbed the corners of his eyes when he sought her out, reached for her and waited.

She closed the distance between them with cautious steps, her stomach churning. Reaching his side, she ignored his proffered hand to instead cross her arms under her breasts in an effort to hide her ragged fingertips.

Gareth dropped his hand to his side but didn't look away from her when he spoke. "I'd like to introduce you to Ashley Clement. Ash, this is Aylish O'Shea, the Druid's Elder and Dylan's father."

She glanced between the men, her gaze finally settling on the Elder. "Given the weight of the introduction, I get the distinct impression I should either curtsy or keep my distance." The stranger's grin was infectious, and she answered in kind.

He surprised the hell out of her when he pulled her into a warm embrace. "Thank you for bringing a man I consider a cherished son home to me. To *us*," he whispered, soft but fierce. "I am in your debt." Breaking contact, he gave her some space before adding for the rest of the group, "You young men know how to pick the beauties."

"You're getting maudlin, auld man."

"Thank you, Aylish." Kennedy glared at her husband. "And you still need to work on your missing manners."

Ethan arced a brow. "He's the King of the Asses, honey. He'll never change. I told you that you should have registered for a saddle as a wedding present. Much more practical with him than, say, utensils."

Dylan glared.

The warlock grinned.

"If he's the king, what does that make me?" Aylish asked drily.

The answer was out before Ashley could stop herself. "The Grand Pooh-bah of Asses?"

Aylish roared with laughter and slapped Gareth on the shoulder. "You were wise to bring her home, cub."

"Seemed sensible."

"Aye, it did." Laughter still marked his face when Aylish addressed Ashley. "We'll see you situated—"

"I'll handle that," Gareth interrupted, but added, "Sir."

Ashley watched the byplay between everyone and had the strangest sense that they were more a family unit than she'd ever witnessed, or been part of, before. Longing for what they had left her moving away, outside the intimate circle. Touching her fingers to her wounded chest was the reminder she needed that she wasn't part of their group.

She could crave belonging all she wanted, but she'd never have it. Family created emotional liabilities, created vulnerabilities, and those together created the ultimate weakness. She would never let herself go there.

Dylan watched her through emotionless eyes.

She met his stare, hers equally as guarded. Empty.

He nodded.

She blinked.

Whatever it was between them, this distrust that made him watch her like a hawk would a field mouse, ignited her indignation. Who was he to judge her? And if he thought her a mouse? Well, he'd never seen her wings. She wouldn't bow to the fear he tried to instill.

A broad hand rested at the small of her back. From the infusion of warmth that spread through her and settled deep between her thighs, she didn't have to ask who touched her. She knew.

Gareth.

What he said caused an immediate evolution, fueling the simmering warmth in her core and turning it into a ravenous inferno.

She leaned into him, and that hand at the small of her back slid under her shirt and around to her belly. Skin to skin. Desire to desire.

He drew a shaky breath.

She laid her hand atop his and pressed. "It's time."

His fingers spasmed. "Yeah."

Glimpsing the tight-knit family environment he came from left her craving more than short-lived intimacies. She wanted more than the finite time they would spend sequestered from the world, lost to touch, taste, tenderness. The latter was what she hungered for. Oddly, she had no doubt that, despite their differences, Gareth would give her what she needed in spades.

At least for the epithicas.

She couldn't afford to need him in any other way. He'd betrayed her, and that negated any other feelings she might fool herself into believing she had.

Need. Feelings.

She rocketed away from him, stumbling to a stop when Ethan stepped in her path.

A large, gentle hand rested on her nearest shoulder as he grasped her chin and lifted it until she couldn't avoid his searching gaze. He took her in with irrefutable authority. "You okay, Red?"

"I... I..." She had to have time, had to reevaluate what she knew about herself. Never had the word *need* been part of her vocabulary. Not after losing her mother. Ashley had needed her, but loving her mother hadn't been enough to anchor the woman whose need for freedom had proven greater than her desire to live for the sake of her only daughter. Swallowing around the devastation lodged in her throat—devastation composed of memories and resentments and regrets—Ashley silently pleaded with Ethan to do something. Anything. To save her from herself, even if he didn't understand why.

He took a deep breath. "Okay."

Gareth stepped closer. "'Okay' what?"

Ethan never looked away from her. "I've got this, Irish."

A low, threatening noise emerged from Gareth's chest. "You do *not* have this. Not where she's concerned."

Ethan tucked her under his arm and pulled her close. "I'll bring her up in thirty minutes."

"Touch her and—"

"End up covered in boils, suffer a lifetime of terror, die a horrible death, blah, blah, blah." He shook his head and turned her toward the staircase. "I'm going to treat her wounds, not ravish her. And if you have half a brain, you'll think before *you* do any ravishing."

Ashley sneaked a sidelong glance at Gareth and found his arms crossed over his chest and his jaw set in a stubborn line. He stared at her unblinking. "You have ten minutes."

"Fifteen," she responded. "Twenty if you argue, and how-about-never if you go caveman on me."

He opened his mouth and snapped it shut, then gave a sharp nod.

"Fifteen it is," Ethan murmured, humor vibrating

through him. "No time for foreplay. We'll have to be quick."

She shot him a sharp look.

"Kidding," he admonished. "I have a small corner of the infirmary at my disposal despite Angus's conviction that I'm a 'useless Yank.'" He steered her toward a set of double doors, chatting all the way. "You're in good hands. I haven't lost a patient since I've been here. Well, if you don't count the last one, but he had an exceptionally difficult ingrown toenail. Best part about this? I get to see you naked." He glanced back at Gareth. "Again."

Ashley jabbed him in the ribs with her elbow. "I realize you're only poking the bear over there to get a response. I'd suggest you don't."

"There are no bears in Ireland, Red."

"Fine. Then don't turn up the heat on the testosterone soup." She fought the unexpected laugh bubbling in her chest. "It's clearly approaching the boiling point. Play with fire—"

"You'll get burned," Gareth said from so close she and Ethan both jumped.

"Damn, Irish," Ethan grumped. "Make a little noise when you move, would you?"

"No."

A warm hand gripped her arm gently and turned her around. Gareth stepped into her space, lifted her chin with one hand as he ran his other through her hair to cup her head. He claimed her mouth in a searing kiss. Tongues tangled, the taste of him flooding her. Their elements pulled at each other and stole a gasp from her. *That was new.*

Breaking the kiss, he kept his focus on her when he spoke. "Let me be clear, warlock. You will be gentle tending her wounds. You will not hurt her, but you *will* be swift about it. When you're done, you'll deliver her safely to my door. And you won't try my patience. Not on this." He traced her kiss-swollen lips with a single finger. "It's not a demand of you, Ash. It's a plea that you return to me."

He didn't give her a chance to answer, spinning on his heel and striding across the entry hall. He reached the staircase and took the steps two at a time.

Ethan waved a hand in her face. "While I would typically laugh off his banter, I don't think he's joking this time."

She rested her fingers over her lips and watched Gareth until he disappeared from sight. A visceral shiver raced through her. "Neither do I."

Gareth moved through his bedroom suite, picking things up and setting them down over and over until he finally ended up at the bar. Whiskey might not be the ultimate answer to every question, but it was a great emotional placeholder. He poured himself a solid two fingers, threw it back and followed that by pouring a more generous allotment. That his hands shook when he lifted the highball glass was an annoyance. Nothing more.

"Tell yourself whatever you need to hear, mate," he murmured, glass to his lips, breath swirling the alcohol's aroma around him.

A knock at the door had him jerking around, movements so sharp he sloshed his drink all over his hand.

All but slamming the drink down on the soapstone counter, he wiped both hands against his thighs as he crossed the room. Hesitating at the door was senseless. He knew who was on the other side. It had to be her. Anyone else ran the risk of being maimed for creating false hope in him. Still, he rested his hand on the iron latch and waited, willing his heart to slow, his chest to stop its rapid rise and fall, his palms to stop sweating. Impatience drove him to act, to lift the latch. The door swung in. And there she stood.

She'd brushed her hair and it shone even in the dim hall light. Eyes downcast, a faint flush colored her cheeks. Her hands were clasped together so tight that her knuckles were skeletal beneath fine skin. She chanced a peek through her lashes. "Hey."

A door slammed somewhere below and she jumped.

"Hey back." He couldn't help but drink her in. "Ethan treat you well?"

"All patched up. I heal quickly, so this should be pretty much gone in a couple of days." She worried her bottom lip. "It'll probably scar."

"Scars are just reminders of what we've survived."

She looked up at him then, eyes wide and pupils dilated.

"Come on in." He stepped aside and breathed deep when she passed, the familiar smells that were all her own soothed his nerves. She was here. That was all that mattered.

Ashley moved straight to the tall windows that overlooked the cliffs and, beyond, the sea. Resting her fingertips against the glass, she let out a deep sigh. "Great view."

"It is." But he was referring to the way the black pants appeared painted on, sculpted over her luscious ass and toned legs. The slight indention he knew marked her waist was hidden under the loose T-shirt she wore. He wanted nothing more than to see it right then, to have her shed the shirt and let him look at her here, in this space. His place. What could be *their* place if she'd only allow herself to feel something for him.

Anxiety returned in full force. It was something he'd never dealt with. Not like this. And he hated it, hated that it nearly reduced him to wringing his hands and fretting like a helpless fool.

No, not a fool. A man in love.

He shook his head. "Like that's any better."

Ashley faced him. "Pardon?"

"Talking to myself." He gestured to the sofa. "Care to sit in front of the fire?"

She glanced at the cold hearth. "Sure."

Rolling his shoulders, he tried to ignore the level of idiocy he'd been reduced to. He flung a hand at the fireplace. Stacked logs lit with a whoosh, and warmth immediately radiated from the giant fireplace.

Ashley sank into the deep leather sofa. Toeing off her sneakers, she tucked her sock-clad feet under her and stared at the flames. "Why is this so awkward?"

"No idea." He gestured to the bar. "Something to drink?"

She watched him then, unblinking. "It's not a drink I need—that either of us need."

His blood went from simmer to boil before she'd finished speaking. "I'll do this right, Ashley."

"Right?" she asked, tone uncertain.

Gareth parked his hands on his hips and studied his boots. There was no easy answer. He couldn't simply tell her that he intended to love her, to *make love* to her. He had to show her what he'd come to understand, what he both feared and cherished above all else was *her*. He had fallen for her. It was irrevocable. She was irreplaceable.

Lifting his chin slowly, he wanted to force his heart

to stop throwing itself around in his chest like a trapped rabid animal. He needed to do this right, to go slow.

She watched him approach, her fingers curling into the sofa's cushion.

Gareth went to his knees in front of her. Her legs were folded underneath her, so he gently retrieved one and then the other, settling one foot on each side of his thighs. He drank in her nearness until her very presence intoxicated him. He was drunk on her and hoped to never be sober again.

Smooth fabric snagged on his rough palms as he skimmed his hands up the outside of her thighs. He paused at the hem of her shirt, his eyes asking what his tongue was too thick to say.

Ashley responded by reaching for the shirt hem.

He stayed her hand, moving it to rest on the sofa. "I've got this."

She opened her mouth only to snap it shut. Again, she worried at her bottom lip.

Gareth reached up and traced a thumb over that tender flesh. "Save a little for me."

Her shallow gasp brushed over his knuckles. It shouldn't have affected him, not like it did. His shaft thickened and lengthened in a painful rush. He paused to straighten himself in his pants.

Ashley focused her attention on his efforts…and didn't look away.

Gods, he wanted her. Now. But he'd sworn he'd do right by her in this.

He gripped her shirt. "Hands over your head."

She complied.

Shirt off, he stared at her small, lush breasts. Her nipples pearled in the cool air and beckoned him forward. He nuzzled one, then the other, ignoring the heavy bandages taped to her chest. Gently cradling a breast in each hand, he suckled one, flicking his tongue over the nipple and eliciting a second small gasp from his woman. He moved to the other breast, lavishing it with small kisses and the most tender nips until Ashley raked her fingers through his hair and brought him infinitely closer.

"Please," she said, dragging the word out over a long exhale.

Gareth drew her nipple into his mouth even as he ran his hand down her bare back, slid under the waistband of her pants and cupped her ass. He slid her forward until the apex of her thighs settled over the hard ridge of his erection. Gods, he wanted to move, to grind, to thrust. But this was about her—*her* pleasure, *her* care, *her* fulfillment. And, ultimately, her understanding of what she meant to him. That didn't stop his small, involuntary thrusts as she snuggled closer. When she wrapped her legs around his waist and her arms around his neck, and followed by arching her back and proffering herself, Gareth was lost. He gave a final tug of lips to breast before letting go, the sound a tiny pop.

"Hold on." Pulling her tight to his chest and slipping an arm around her shoulders, he surged to his feet.

Ashley ran one hand up the back of his head and, gripping a handful of hair, levered herself up to his mouth, his name on her lips.

They came together, passion untempered. She opened to him, tasted him as much as he tasted her, breathed her in just as she did him. He loved her mouth as he intended to love her body—thoroughly, without regret and without holding any part of himself back. Because he loved her as he'd never loved another...and never would again.

Unwilling to break the kiss, he kept her balanced in

his arms as he made his way into the bedroom. The edge of the tall bed hit the back of his thighs and he toppled onto the mattress with her firmly atop him.

Chapter 19

Ashley stared down at a chiseled face framed by heavy walls of wavy hair. Blue eyes burned from within, and a faint smile tugged at lips made for loving.

"Never."

"Never what, love?" Gareth froze at the easy term of endearment—they both did—and then he rolled over on top of her. Wrapping her hair around his fist, he began to kiss his way down her neck. Biting and nipping, he paused to lay tender kisses from the hollow of her throat along her collarbone and out to the edge of her shoulder. Then, with the tenderest of touches, he kissed her bandaged wounds.

Her heart thundered in her chest with a locomotive's fierce, ground-rattling force. Blood hummed under her skin. Nerves began firing faster, yet she didn't struggle to control the situation. No, with Gareth's lips working wonders along some of her most sensitive areas, she found she could only encourage him under her breath. She arched her back, pressing her breasts forward, and was rewarded with his sharp inhale.

Raising her hands over her head, he let his hands drift down the soft undersides of her arms and trace random patterns along her sides, thumbs following the outer swells of her breasts.

"Gareth." His name was a tender plea from her lips.

He lowered his head and sought out her nipples again.

She brought a hand down and wove it through his hair. The most she could do was cup the back of his skull and press him closer. It earned her a deep, appreciative growl. He caught the tight bud gently between his teeth and sucked on it while flicking the tip with his tongue.

Ashley gasped and arched harder. She couldn't think. Not with the sexual hunger rising between them faster than her runaway heart rate. "Keep this up and you'll be the death of me," she murmured at the ceiling.

He didn't comment but smiled against her skin. To her dismay, he let go of her nipple. "No dying." Working his hands under her hips, he paused and looked up. "I'm not here because of the epithicas, Ashley. This is more than satisfying nature's demands."

She hesitated.

He started to pull back, his eyes narrowing.

She tightened the fist she had in his hair. "Don't."

"Ye'll have heard what I just said? This is more than want for me, Ash. Far more."

A sharp pang of hurt hit her somewhere much too close to the heart. "I want you, Gareth. Can you live with that?"

"Can you?" He rubbed his chest, avoiding the brand that was darker than ever before.

She didn't answer, the answer too complicated to articulate.

"I assure you it would be far easier fer me if tha' were all I needed, the wanting." A crease marred the untouched skin between his brows and fine lines of tension radiated from the corners of both his mouth and eyes.

Ashley nodded, the action more solemn than any words she might have offered. She tried to wiggle out of her pants. Warm hands that bordered on hot closed over hers and stopped her efforts. Releasing her waistband, she pulled one hand free. It took all her focus to raise it and lay her thumb against the line between his brows. "We'll sort it out...after."

"I'll have yer word ye willna joost disappear."

She searched his face. "No."

He arched a brow and waited, one hand still trapping hers at her waist.

She twisted her hand in his grip and laced their fingers together.

When it became clear she wouldn't answer, he asked, "No *what*, Ash? No, ye'll be leavin' me, or no, ye'll not run off come dawn?"

She heard the question beneath the question.

"So proud," she murmured, stroking her thumb across the deep crease that formed between his brows at her silence.

He waited, his gaze locked on something over her shoulder.

"I won't leave without saying goodbye. You have my word."

He looked at her then, his eyes focusing on hers even as he drew her pants down her hips. Exposing her sex, he stopped, chest heaving.

Cool air hit her overheated skin. Belated modesty struck her, and she tried to cover herself.

Gareth caught her hands and pulled them away. "Don't be ashamed. Not in front of me, *mo aingeal chothaímid*. Never in front of me."

My cherished angel. Lovers had called her pet names before, but never had she believed they meant it. Not like he did.

Lust bloomed in her, dark and demanding. She struggled to form a single coherent thought as his fingers traced down her belly and over her hips. It was so easy to give in to desire and revel in the feel of his fingers on her bare skin. Staring at him, she licked her lips slowly.

His eyes grew hooded as he watched, and a shiver shook her. "Cold?" A small smile played at the corners of his mouth. Blue eyes saturated with passion rose to meet the yearning echo that no doubt lit her hazel ones.

The heat in his fingertips almost burned. Raising unsteady hands, she encouraged his to cup her breasts. She curled her fingers around the edge of his palm and shivered.

A deep dimple marked one cheek when he grinned. "Can't have that."

"Keep me warm."

Gareth let her go in order to stand, his hand resting on the button on his jeans. The silence between them spoke in ways they couldn't. Not yet. Maybe not ever.

"This thing between us…" She blinked, surprised at the burn in her eyes. Tears had eluded her for three centuries.

He reached up and pulled his hair away from his face. "This 'thing' is about more than tonight, Ashley. It's about more than wanting. Let it be what it is." He took her hand and laid it palm down over the impressive bulge growing beneath his jeans.

Her fingers curled inward of their own volition.

Gareth's hips jerked forward and, when she looked up, his head had fallen back.

His hand slid over hers and pressed down. "Harder."

She complied, watching him for clues. When he finally looked down, all she found was a hunger that equaled her own.

Unzipping his jeans, his erection sprang free. He offered her his profile as he worked to peel the pants down legs corded with tension. Buttocks flexing hard, he balanced first on one foot then the other. It was the work of a moment, and the pants were discarded without a care. He faced her, his engorged shaft brushing his belly button.

She sighed. Heaven and hell had to have come together to create such a tempting creature—part angel, part temptation, all man. The covers were hard to manipulate, but she managed to get them flipped back. Before she could scoot over, he was there.

Strong arms slipped under her and shifted her across the bed so he could climb in beside her. Fingers traced down her belly. "Seems you're still wearing those low-slung pants." He worked the pants free and tossed them aside. Running his hands up the insides of her thighs, he coaxed her legs open. Deft fingers stroked her slick sex and her whole body shuddered. Every caress took her higher.

"Gareth." His name was an unsteady invocation on her lips. "Don't let me go."

She heard herself utter the words, knew there was more to them than the superficial meaning, but damn if she could get her mind to work. With Gareth working her body over like a master, she couldn't get her common sense to withdraw to that clinical place she could always access, the one that let her think clearly. Gareth broke that connection in her.

Thoughts she had no business entertaining crept in and whispered dark promises of what might be if he could beat the goddess. She could explore this thing with him, see what it might become. Fighting the temptation to fall into the possibilities, she lost herself to Gareth as he pushed her body ruthlessly.

His fingers drove her mad, demanded her release on his terms, not hers.

Her neck bowed back and she pushed herself toward his touch. A sob ripped through her as desperation ruled her body.

Gareth draped a leg over one of hers to hold her in place. Shifting his touch, he pinched the small bundle of nerves at the apex of her cleft, thrumming it with his forefinger.

That was all it took.

Ashley came apart in his arms with a keening cry, hips bucking wildly.

Legs tangled, she rolled toward him and reached blindly for his shaft. "I need you, Gareth."

She froze at the admission. *I can't* need *him.*

But the truth wouldn't be denied.

Her heart lurched and she struggled against the urge to push him away, to withdraw, to run as far as she could before she found herself bound to the man she'd come to care for. Gareth was everything she'd ever wanted and more, but the epithicas was ending. They'd be done then, no matter how much he wanted her to stay. Clear of the haze the breeding heat caused, things always looked different. She knew. *She knew.* She'd been there too many times before.

Panting through the clog of emotion in her chest, she tried to regain her ability to reason.

Panic rose in her, a wave that would drag her under before she could reach safety. Only one thing was clear to her as Gareth rose above her.

She'd admitted she needed him, and that admission?

It was only one degree of separation from the ultimate sacrifice.

Love.

Moving over Ashley, Gareth settled between her spread legs.

Wide hazel eyes stared up at him, wild with unspoken desire tempered only by terror.

"Aye, *anamchara*, yer soul calls to mine, and I need you all the more for it." He slid into her slick heat, those feminine walls stretching to accept his girth. The sensation briefly robbed him of speech. Then he began to move, a slow, rolling motion that tested his stamina even as it drove Ashley wild. He gritted his teeth, vowing not to give her the words that would lay him at her feet. Not yet. Those words would give her cause to run. That didn't mean the desire, the *need* wasn't there, though, the words trapped inside him. No, the demands of the waning epithicas were at the forefront of his mind. But parallel to those demands stood something fresh and new, something he'd never thought to hold in his lifetime: love in its most raw, untempered form. He wouldn't look too hard, wouldn't break it down into its fundamental pieces. Not now. This time with her was a gift he'd been given. Ashley Clement was right where she belonged.

Here.

With him.

The pace of their lovemaking became frantic as that articulated need rose to a crescendo, and he sought to push her to crazed heights of passion.

Her hips bucked against his every downstroke and he wondered that he didn't hurt her. Yet when he tried to restrain himself, she demanded more, hooking her leg around him and drawing him deeper.

She pulled his face to hers for a blinding kiss, one that tasted of her—warmth, always warmth, and hearth and home. The scents of flannel and wood smoke descended like a veil across his senses until he wasn't sure he could break free. Didn't want to.

Muscles in her abdomen quivered as she yearned for that elusive pinnacle.

He thrust harder and stole a hand from her grasp to reach between them and, placing his thumb on her clitoris, pressed. Hard.

"Gareth!" Her hips moved of their own volition. She dug her fingers into his arms and used them as anchor points to ride out wave after wave of her pleasure.

He was lost to more than the moment as he fell into the abyss with a roar of unspeakable satisfaction and inarticulate terror. He loved her hard that she might never forget him. Because he knew now what he had to do. Jealousy and vengeance would drive Macha to make an attempt on Ashley's life before the goddess turned on him. He wouldn't stand for it. Eternity in the Well of Souls would be better than knowing he'd let the woman he loved die an unnecessary death—one dealt by a goddess who would ensure Ashley never rose again. While Gareth might not have time to repair the damage he'd caused this woman, he could spare her true death.

He would summon Macha and end this. Tonight.

Before Beltane.

And he'd do it alone.

He wouldn't risk the life of one of his brethren. The blood sacrifice required to repair the tear in the veil between worlds was his responsibility. He would fix this. He would give Ashley the chance to live without looking over her shoulder, without fearing Macha would forever send male phoenixes after this woman.

His woman.

If it took his death to secure her life, so be it. He'd been prepared to die for so long now that the idea shouldn't have hurt. But it did.

Because as Gareth stared down into Ashley's flushed face and saw in her all that might have been had his life taken a different course, he grieved that truth even as his own release racked his body.

Chapter 20

Ashley stretched, her muscles deliciously sore. Gareth had loved her all morning and then had lunch sent up to the room sometime after noon for what he deemed a "naked picnic." She'd been famished but thoroughly confounded when he'd insisted on slipping her little bites of fruit and cheese between her own efforts to eat.

Amused as he had deftly slipped a grape into her mouth in between her protests, she'd chewed the tart fruit as she had watched him watching her. "You don't have to romance me."

His shrug had been lazy, almost indifferent. "And if I want to?"

She hadn't been able to come up with an answer. The last of the epithicas had faded long before their lovemaking ended. Confusion had muddied her thoughts. The center of that melee had been the fact she'd given an open-ended promise that she wouldn't leave *when that's what she did.* There had been no reason for her to assure him she'd stay. Gareth had obviously performed a lobotomy on her, likely during the throes of orgasm when she would have been least likely to notice.

Meal finished, he slid under the covers and reached for her, pulling her against him and draping his body around hers. His warm exhales had ruffled her hair as his breathing slowed. His heartbeat had been sure and steady against her back. His arm and leg that rested over her had grown heavy as sleep drew him under.

She'd followed without a thought, her exhaustion greater than her concerns for the first time in…well… forever.

Now, as the sun settled on the western horizon and cast brilliant colors across the sky, Ashley found herself wide-awake and entirely alone. Gareth had left the bed at some point and she'd never known. Silence afforded her time to think. All of the weighted concerns she'd been able to cast aside in favor of sound sleep churned in her tumultuous mind. She couldn't settle on one problem. Instead, everything crashed one into another until she couldn't sort out the worst of her worries. Everything overwhelmed her.

The need to get out of bed, to move and spur her mind to work drove her to flip the covers back and slide out of the tall bed.

"Gareth?" She gathered her clothes, waiting on his answer. Nothing. Padding into the living room, she found her shirt and boots. Her movements were sharp and jerky as she dressed in front of the fire's embers.

Where is he?

After all, he'd insisted she not leave. Then he'd done just that.

It didn't sit well.

Heart in her throat, Ashley gave in and replayed the part of their conversation she couldn't shake. Feelings she'd never wanted to experience ran unchecked and were accompanied by thoughts she had no business even toying with—thoughts of a life with the only man to have ever filled the empty spaces in her soul.

The very idea of leaving him *hurt*.

Bad.

And that was all the reason she needed to do the very thing she'd promised not to do.

Run.

She fled the living room, taking care to shut the door softly.

The hallway was damp and drafty. It lacked the comforts of Gareth's private suite, the feelings of home and hearth and the man that occupied the space.

"Stop it," she whispered to herself. "Just *stop it*."

Her destination wasn't relevant. All she knew was she had to put distance between her and the assassin in order to figure out what was real and what wasn't. She flew down the steps, her mind a mess. Her trajectory carried her toward the front doors. Freedom lay beyond. She didn't slow. At all.

Had she been paying attention, she would have—probably—seen the glint of the sword in the shadows. At the pace she was moving, though, all she saw was the arm that snaked out to grab her before she reached the doors. A hand settled over her mouth and smothered her scream.

"Easy, Red. I'll let you go when I'm sure you won't toast my ass."

She stopped struggling and, true to his word, Rowan let her go.

Both fear and fury fueled her temper as she rounded on the large warrior. "What the hell, Conan?"

He ignored her question, responding with one of his own even as his attention roamed the massive space. "What are you running from?" Apparently finding no immediate threat, he leaned against the wall and set his sword at his side. "Or would the more appropriate question be, 'Who?'"

"Nothing." A dense mass comprised of too many emotions to name settled behind her heart and made every beat painful as if the space in her chest was suddenly too small. "No one."

"Liar."

The flat accusation pricked her pride. "Pretty bold charge coming from someone who lurks in the shadows and watches others live their lives while he refuses to do the same."

Gripping her chin, he lifted her face to his and waited until she met his cool stare. "Careful. Condemnations are far more effective when the person whose behavior you're damning doesn't mirror your own."

She yanked her chin free and took a step that put her out of reach. "I didn't ask for commentary."

Rowan arched a brow. "I must have missed the part where I did."

With no sufficient retort, she said nothing. She was so focused on the hallway that would take her to Ethan's door that she almost missed the assassin's sobering question.

"Why are you running from him, Ashley?"

The fluttering feeling in her stomach wasn't eased when she pressed a hand against her abdomen. She refused to look at Rowan despite the weight of his stare. "I'm not running."

He snorted. "If that wasn't running, darling, I'm a ladies' man."

She shot him a hard look. "I was heading to the dining room."

Rowan crossed massive arms over an equally massive chest and spread his feet, waiting for her to answer. "When did they move it outside?"

The stance was so similar to Gareth's that Ashley chanced a quick look at her lover's door. *Closed.* Not that she'd hoped to find him there. Not really. Part of her had hoped for another glimpse of him before...what?

Her shoulders sagged.

"You know," Rowan said softly, "I make it a point to keep out of others' business."

"Yeah? Well, you're doing a bang-up job here." The chuffed sound he made so resembled a laugh that she couldn't help but look at him to see if he smiled.

He seemed to understand her surprise and shook his head. "Don't get your hopes up." Rowan took a deep breath, held it and let it out in an entirely controlled manner. "You're irritating me. I don't appreciate it. At all."

Her brows winged up. "It sounds like you expect an apology."

"What I expect is for you to stop fucking *running*."

"Excuse me?" *What was he—a mind reader?*

He sighed, his exhalation decidedly not controlled. "Your chance at happiness is staring you square in the face, and what do you do? You run. Most sane people would grab that chance by the throat and hold on for dear life." He held up a hand. "And before you try to throw that back at me, let me assure you I don't claim 'sane' on my list of personal attributes. Never have."

Panic tickled the bottoms of her feet, and she curled her toes in her boots. The truth poured out before she could censure herself. "I'm not made for happily-ever-afters."

"No?"

She shook her head so hard her hair slithered around her shoulders with a susurrus sound.

"What makes you so sure?" The question held a hard edge, one that demanded honesty.

As if he'd uncorked some well of truth in her, the admission poured out. "I have to take a lover every three years. *Have to.* You have no idea what it's like to never know if the man I take wants *me* or is simply responding to pheromones. And if I take the same man, I expose him to the possibility of death should a male phoenix come across us."

"You've created a situation that gives you an out, Red, and you know it. He isn't responding to pheromones. Never was."

"I won't ever belong to someone, Rowan. Ever."

He tapped one finger against his thigh in a rapid rhythm. "Being loved isn't about possession. You know that, even if you haven't realized it yet. So what's this really about?"

She knew her eyes were wide, felt her chest heave. "My lover has to be able to defend himself, defend *me* should I be incapacitated by the epithicas."

His eyes narrowed and his nostrils flared. "And you don't think Gareth can defend you? Both of you? You don't think the rest of us would have your backs?"

Her answer cracked with accusation. "He didn't. He fought his battle and left me to fight mine. And for what, Rowan? He didn't beat Macha. If I let myself love him, it's going to destroy me when... Macha is going to take him and I don't trust him to beat her." And there it was. The truth. What she'd thought had been pain, what she'd believed had hurt her before, was nothing to this wound ripped open by her very admission.

Then Rowan was in her face, his words whipping against her skin even as they flayed her soul. "You spent every minute of every hour after you met convincing him you didn't need him. I was only there for part of it in Ennistymon, but you did a damn fine job of convincing *me* you wanted to handle your shit on your own, and I wasn't in your bed. Educate me, Ashley. He did exactly as you demanded he do. So tell me where—*how*—has he failed you? For honoring your wishes but failing to interpret that you might not really mean it all the time? And now you berate him for giving up the fight with Macha to go to you? You didn't see what happened to him on the other side of the wall any more than he saw what happened to you." He stood abruptly and grabbed his sword. "Don't you run around casting blame where blame isn't due. He deserves better than that from you. If you're going to leave, leave, but make damn sure you have a valid reason. Otherwise? You and I are going to be at odds, and you don't want to be there with me. Ever."

He shoved past her and started down the nearest hall.

She stared at the front doors—took one step, then another. And stopped.

Could she truly hold him responsible for doing exactly as she'd asked him to do all along—respect her independence and her desire to need no one? Could she hold it against him that he'd let her fight her battles as she'd seen fit, just as she'd demanded of him? Moreover, could she forgive him for doing the very same?

She rested a hand against her throat. "There's nothing to forgive." The admission resonated far deeper than simply through the palm of her hand.

If she was going to do this, going to try, it meant no

more running. She would stay and try to build on the trust that had begun with Gareth from the beginning. She would stand beside him and help him beat Macha. If it could be done, they stood a better chance together than he did alone. And once the goddess was defeated, they could see what might truly exist between them, maybe find a way to carve out a life together.

A disoriented feeling, like something had stirred her insides, had her swaying on her feet. Shaking her head in an attempt to clear it, she stumbled sideways at the same time a deep male voice shouted.

"Shit! Rowan! Niall! Ethan!"

Booted footsteps rushed into the entry, Dylan at the fore. The Assassin brandished a huge sword. Behind him, as if they always hovered somewhere near their leader, were the very men he'd summoned. Each bore a variety of weapons, even Ethan. But...

"Where's Gareth?" she demanded as they headed for the doors.

Other men were coming out of doorways.

"Stay put," Dylan ordered them, ignoring her.

She would do no such thing, and he had to know it.

Taking a step toward the Assassin's Arcanum, a far stronger wave of dizziness hit and sent her staggering aside. She careened into a stone pillar and slid to the floor. Her head ached. Gods, did it ever. And she couldn't have felt more scrambled if someone had taken a hand mixer to her insides. Half-moons of sweat decorated her armpits even as rivulets collected and ran down the hollow of her spine. She might get warm in extreme conditions, but she'd *never* sweat.

Fire erupted and rimmed her skin until, like a wood match turned on its side, a thin sheet of flames encased her. The clothes she wore began to smoke and then burn.

The flames that encased her created a silent wind that whipped her hair about, loose curls sparking and crackling as if the mass was a sentient thing.

Ashley let her head fall back and did the only thing she could do.

She *burned*.

Rowan's voice cut through the erotic rush. "Red?"

With infinite control, she lowered her chin until their eyes met.

"Where's this coming from?" he demanded.

She could only stare.

His face darkened, and he reached for her in apparent anger only to yank his hand away. "You *know* where this is coming from, right?"

It was hard to hear him over the roar of flames in her head.

"Gareth summoned Macha," he snarled even as the front doors flew open behind him and his three companions charged into the moonless night. "He won't drain your element, won't leave you helpless if she's sent someone else for you."

The flames guttered and then flared again as that disconcerting feeling swam through her. Hot on its heels came understanding. Gareth was pushing everything he had at her. That's why her element—and his—burned out of control. And that left him only his skills with blade and gun to defend himself. Against a goddess bent on taking his soul.

Ashley shoved past Rowan, ignoring his bark of pain at contact with her flaming skin. She raced into the night. Her heart had constricted so hard it fluttered like a trapped sparrow in her chest as it tried to beat, tried to push blood to her pumping arms and legs. She couldn't breathe. Gods, the power racing through her.

All because Gareth wouldn't leave her without her element. Unprotected.

If Rowan hadn't kicked her emotional ass earlier, this would have done it.

Her lover wasn't going to die. Not tonight. Not ever if she had her way.

Macha was going back to the Well of Souls as a revenant, no matter the cost.

She couldn't lose the man she...

The man I love.

She went to her knees, skidding across the ground. Curling her fingers into the damp earth, she bent over and lost the contents of her stomach. Gareth... Oh, gods. She loved Gareth. It had been a swift but subtle thing, sneaking into her heart without her awareness let alone her consent.

Rowan was at her side, moving silently as ever. "Get up, Red. He's losing."

Lurching to her feet, she staggered around the edge of the keep.

She couldn't let him die. Couldn't lose him. Couldn't lose the only man she had ever loved...and ever would.

No matter the cost.

Chapter 21

Gareth went to one knee to avoid Macha's attempt to take his head. He bore a dozen wounds large and small, and his strength was fading fast. Blood decorated his arms, chest and thighs, but he'd drawn her blood and stabbed the stained dirk into the deadened earth. She was bound to this realm. He could kill her body and send her back to the Well of Souls as a revenant, never to rise again. That wouldn't spare his life and well he knew it.

The veil would be closed and Macha rebound to the Well of Souls if he could take his last breath on the scarred earth where he'd originally died.

And his death would secure Ashley's life.

He surged to his feet. Sword heavy but surprisingly steady, he swung at Macha. He'd been aiming for her head. She lunged out of the sword's path but not before the tip connected with her collarbone. The sharp *crack* was gratifying. Not so much as her shriek, though. Not by half.

Macha staggered away, her burned hand spread over the gaping wound. "You will pay for drawing blood, assassin mine."

"I'm. Not. *Yours*." Gareth lunged forward on the last word, intent on burying the tip of his sword into the space where her heart should have been. The bitch didn't have one. He was sure of it.

She crossed blades with him, blocking his drive.

The phantoms screamed, their rage palpable. In the dark of night, he couldn't see them and it was disconcerting as hell. He dared not draw on his, or Ashley's, element, though. She might need it, and he wouldn't leave her unable to defend herself again. Ever. Even in death, he'd ensured her safety. The letter he'd left for Dylan guaranteed it. Gareth had asked that the Arcanum treat her as his heart's own blood. It shouldn't be a stretch, seeing as she was the heart of him.

Macha circled him. "You think to control the manner in which you become mine."

He backed toward the broken earth. "I belong to no one."

"Liar," she snarled, the sound slicing his skin. Fine welts rose and split, blood running down the bare skin of his forearms. "You only think you've given your heart to that whore. But I? I shall take it from your dying body as my due."

"Talk, talk, talk. Let's finish this." He pulled his Sig Sauer and shot her. Or shot *at* her.

The goddess shimmered and the bullet passed through her.

His gun hand fell to his side.

"I am the Goddess of Phantoms and War, assassin."

She smiled, baring her teeth. "I assumed you would have understood that every drop of blood I draw from the one who tore the veil, every drop *you* shed, strengthens me. I will be unstoppable when we are finished here." She ghosted forward and struck him a devastating blow on his sword arm. *"Bleed for me."*

Muscles in his hand went lax, and his sword hit the grass with a muffled *whump*. The gun followed, freeing his other hand as instinct had him gripping the bone-deep wound below his shoulder.

"Shit," he spat, furious she'd drawn a reaction from him. He'd been so determined to do this without giving her the satisfaction of his pain. In that, he'd failed.

Dark forms shouldered past him and placed themselves between him and the goddess. He recognized Dylan and Niall. Ethan eased around him, shaking his hands out at his sides.

"Leave," he ground out. "This isn't your fight."

"Shut up," Kennedy said, taking up the vacant position on his other side.

"Kennedy," Dylan roared, never looking away from the goddess. "Back to the keep."

"Fight her now, me later," she returned.

Spots danced through Gareth's vision. *Bleeding out. Again.* He had to get to the broken earth. If he didn't die there, his every effort, his intent to serve as the necessary blood sacrifice to repair the veil, would have been wasted. He took a step forward. The world spun. When he opened his eyes, he was staring at the star-filled night sky.

"Stay down." Rowan's voice slid across the sea-kissed air.

"No." He struggled to roll over, managing only because Rowan allowed it. Gareth could crawl, hell, drag himself if need be. There wasn't much time left.

His elemental power created a bone-deep ache as it fought against the spell he'd cast—the spell that sent his flame to Ashley's keeping. That had been his only option, the only way he could ensure he wouldn't reach for his natural defense in the heart of battle. The only way he could guarantee he didn't draw too much on the shared strength. The only way he could be sure Ashley had access to everything she might need.

He dug the toes of his boots into the loamy earth and pushed with his feet even as he pulled with his one good hand. The defiled ground was so close. *Thirty feet.* He pushed and pulled. *Twenty-nine feet.* Again. *Twenty-eight.*

Brilliant light seared his corneas as it raced by him, a comet splitting the night. Eyes watering and vision fractured, he was reduced to relying on sound instead of sight to tell him what was going on.

A screech of rage he recognized.

A feminine grunt he didn't.

Deep shouts of confusion followed by a heartbeat's silence.

A whistling hiss like a bullwhip splitting the air.

Then a deafening roar.

The night lit up so bright that the people around him cast defined shadows.

Phantoms scattered into the blackness, fleeing the pyre that beat back the darkness.

His friends stood around him, stepping forward only to be driven back by waves of heat.

Rowan's booted foot pressed on his shoulder, harder

this time. "Gareth." That deep voice was saturated with broken emotion.

Gareth hadn't been terrified. Until then.

He struggled to push on his good arm as truth battled denial's stranglehold. And won.

An enraged, wordless howl erupted from deep inside him. Fighting to get up was pointless with Rowan pinning him. That didn't stop him.

Gareth swung at the side of the other assassin's knee, connecting with his stronger arm.

Rowan's knee buckled.

Gareth rolled away and tried to scramble to his knees. *Too weak.*

So he crawled.

Dragging himself forward, tears streaming down his face, he couldn't contain his despair. "No!" The screamed denial was all he could manage as he watched the woman he loved more than his own life wrap herself around the goddess and blaze brighter. Hotter. Irretrievably.

A single flame shot into the sky and split the sky.

Thunder rumbled.

The ground shook.

Gareth blinked rapidly, his good arm reaching for where Ashley had been. Where she had burned.

Only a pile of ash remained.

The denial he'd issued seconds before was nothing to the despair that erupted from him then. He raged, tearing at his hair. His muscles convulsed as his element came rushing home.

And that was when he knew.

It had all been for naught.

She was gone.

His heart was gone.

* * *

Activity surrounded Gareth, but he couldn't think. Couldn't breathe. Didn't want to. He was numb but not numb enough. Never enough.

Hands and voices cataloged his body's wounds.

"Deep laceration to right brachialis. Needs stitches."

Ethan.

"Fetch the field kit."

Dylan.

"You die and her sacrifice means jack shit."

Rowan.

He struck out blindly and was rewarded with a grunt of pain. That hurt, that pain, was nothing—*nothing*—to what he bore. "Feck off."

Rowan's grim face swam into view. "Like no one's ever suggested *that* before."

"Move aside, Conan," Ethan ordered, a syringe in his hand.

Swiveling on the balls of his feet, Rowan gripped Ethan's throat. "You don't call me that."

Gareth let his eyelids slip shut. Blessed darkness. He never wanted to see the light again.

Someone slapped him hard enough it registered.

He ignored it.

So they hit him again. With a fist.

"What?" he demanded in a voice that sounded like it had been a severe case of road rash.

"Open yer feckin' eyes. That's an order."

Dylan, then.

Centuries of training had his body struggling to obey where his mind didn't give a right shit. His body won, and Dylan appeared, their noses inches apart.

The Assassin cradled Gareth's head. "You listen to me, brother. Listen!"

Gareth's head bobbled as Dylan shook him. "Get on wi' it."

"Yer no' thinkin', man. *She's a phoenix.*"

His heart stuttered. "No one comes back from the Well o' Souls."

Dylan's fingers flexed against Gareth's skull. "You did."

Tears traced unapologetically down his temples. "I bound my element to her. The only way to break that is death." He swallowed the emotional gorge choking him. "It returned tae me, Dylan."

Dylan disappeared from view with a suddenness that advertised he'd been physically removed.

"So that's it?"

Rowan. Again.

"You'll just give her up? That easily?" Rowan shook his head. "I had it wrong. It wasn't that she didn't deserve you. *You* didn't deserve *her.*"

Empowered by rage, Gareth gripped Rowan's shirt. But the angry words he reached for, the denial to his brethren's accusation, eluded him. "I love…loved…her."

A suspicious sheen covered the other man's eyes. "Then don't let her go."

Then he was gone, and Gareth was left staring at an infinite number of stars.

What could he do? Kennedy had followed Dylan to the Shadow Realm, but that had taken the entire Arcanum and the Elder's involvement. With Kayden gone, they couldn't secure his soul. Beyond that, Gareth knew he hovered too close to death's maw to even attempt to retrieve her. Even if he was successful and recovered her spirit, she had no physical body to which she could return. There was only ash.

Ash.

He heaved himself up, bracing a hand against the grass to remain upright. "Ash."

Dylan crouched at his side. "I would give anything to spare you this."

"No." Gareth's body fought him as he attempted to stand. His legs collapsed. Struggling like a babe who had yet to walk, he reached for Dylan. "Your hand." Dylan complied without question, and Gareth made it to his knees. "Your shirt." When the Assassin only stared at him, Gareth lost it. "Your fucking shirt!"

Rowan ripped his own shirt off and laid it in Gareth's outstretched hand.

Half crawling, half walking on his knees, Gareth made it to Ashley's ashes. He knelt in front of the pile, protecting what was left of her from the wind and the rain.

Clutching the shirt, it hit him. The earth was no longer cracked, the grass no longer dead. The veil had been repaired.

He almost quit then, would have if it hadn't been for Rowan's understanding.

Ethan appeared, taking the shirt and settling himself beside Gareth before laying the heavy cotton over the ashes. "We'll wait. Together."

"How long did she say… I can't remember… How long until…"

Aylish knelt beside him and laid a hand on his shoulder. "It's different for every phoenix."

Dylan knelt across from him. "We wait."

"We wait." Niall sank to his knees beside Dylan.

And Rowan. He simply fell, chin to his chest, hands on his thighs.

"Do you see her spirit?" Gareth asked through numb lips.

The man's shoulders bowed as if he bore the weight of Gareth's grief. It was the only answer he gave.

And Gareth understood. He would hold his vigil. He wouldn't leave until he knew what he suspected was true.

Ashley was lost.

Chapter 22

Gareth didn't move as Angus silently tended his wounds. He simply waited. The only sound he made was a wordless denial as he refused the lidocaine offered. He wanted to feel something. Anything. Physical pain couldn't touch his ravaged soul.

Odd that he'd been willing to do anything to preserve it before last night, yet now it meant nothing. Less than.

The sun broke the eastern horizon, its radiance washing over him like an unwelcome, unwarranted attempt at benediction. The warmth meant nothing.

He let his eyes drift shut even as he continued to touch the edge of the shirt. Waiting. Willing warmth into the ashes it protected.

She had to come back to him, for if it was true that no man could live without his heart, Gareth was as good as dead.

The hours passed, and no one moved.

Kayden returned sometime after noon. He slipped a small package into Gareth's hand. "It's done." And then he joined the vigil.

Rain clouds rolled in and turned day to dusk. Lightning struck nearby and the crack and subsequent rumble of thunder preceded the skies opening by mere seconds.

Rain slicked his hair to his head and washed away the blood that stained his body. Water dripped from his nose and eyelashes.

He never looked away from the small bump under the shirt.

The rain quit before sunset.

"Brother," Dylan started as the first sliver of moon crested.

"If it were Kennedy?" Gareth shook his head. "Leave me."

Dylan stood and reached for his wife's hand.

One by one, the men followed, disappearing into the depths of the night without a sound.

Gareth wouldn't leave what he had left of Ashley. He would stand watch until there was no hope.

Hope.

A false by-product of the faith the gods demanded.

Frenzied wrath built in him, layer upon violent layer, until, near midnight, he broke.

He leaned back and loosed an animalistic cry that raked bloody runnels into his very being. "Daghda, All Father, I demand an audience!"

There was no dimensional shift, no parting of the heavens. Nothing.

And then the deepest, most resonant voice Gareth had ever heard spoke into his ear. "You think to command me, assassin?"

Gareth ignored the ire in the question as he refocused

on the shirt. "I have served you my entire life and asked for nothing. I would ask now." He fought to control his breathing. "Bring her back to me."

A cloaked and hooded form filled his peripheral vision. "I ask again. You think to command me?"

He gave terse nod. "I would do that and more, worse, if it would compel you to return her to me."

"You are arrogant in your appeal. Tread lightly," Daghda cautioned.

"I will not," Gareth replied, the words nearly lost on the breeze.

Daghda flipped his hood back and stared at Gareth through wintry eyes. "You have served our purpose for you, Gareth Brennan. That does not afford you the right to irreverence."

Gareth lumbered to his feet. "Your purpose for me."

"Macha gained much in her sister's effort to release chaos. If the Goddess of Phantoms and War had not been re-bound to the Well of Souls by a willing blood sacrifice, she would have opened the gates to the Shadow Realm. War would have raged. The loss of life would have been immeasurable."

Blood thundered through Gareth's head. "Do you fear her?"

Daghda straightened. "Your understanding is limited, assassin. The phantoms she commands would have devoured the inhabitants of every realm."

Gareth shoved his good hand through the tangles of his wet hair. "Why me?"

"You were, are, fire to her ice. Heat to her cold. No one else was as well suited to enter the Well and emerge unscathed."

He opened his mouth but nothing came out. Panting, he tried again. "Unscathed?"

Daghda clasped his hands behind his back. "You must understand she had to be stopped, no matter the cost."

No matter the cost. "It cost you nothing. Nothing!" Gareth's muscles vibrated with the need to do violence. "I have served you faithfully for centuries. Not once have I asked for recompense."

Thunder rumbled as clouds moved through the god's sky-bright eyes. "You are *not* implying I owe you."

"I died for you," Gareth shouted, thumping his fist over his chest. "I. Died."

"And yet you live," Daghda mused. "You seem to have emerged from the ordeal fairly well."

"And you, husband, seem to have lost your connection to humanity." Danu stepped out of the night, a nimbus of starlight crowning her head. She turned her fathomless gaze on Gareth. "I would see you well, assassin."

He didn't attempt to repress the pain woven through his very being. He let it go, let it infuse his every cell and flow through his every word. "I am not above pleading, Mother of All Things. I will beg." He fell to his knees and bowed his head. "There is nothing I would not do if you would only…" He touched the cold, wet edge of the shirt. "Please. Return her to me."

"What is she to you?" Danu asked with a gentleness that slowed Gareth's runaway pulse.

"She is the air I breathe, the sun on my skin, the joy in my morning, my reason for being. My lover. My soul mate." He blinked rapidly, unashamed of the tears that broke over his lower lashes. "She is my heart."

Daghda's eyes narrowed. "Would you trade places with her so that she might live?"

"Yes," Gareth blurted.

Danu spared her husband an exasperated glance. "And what good would that do?"

The god shrugged. "I was curious."

"You have been too far removed from your people for far too long, husband mine." She knelt in front of Gareth and took his face in her hands. "You are sincere in that you would do anything to have your heart returned to you? Be sure."

His trembling turned to full-on shaking. "Anything," he breathed.

The goddess waved a hand at Daghda. "Fetch Niall."

Gareth started.

She didn't pause in her instruction. "Have him bring his tattoo machine and black ink."

"I'm not your errand boy," Daghda objected.

"Neither are you compassionate enough to stay with our cherished warrior. You'll go, Daghda." Power infused her command.

She held Gareth then, continuing to cradle his face as her very gaze stripped away everything he'd thought himself to be. He was reduced to his most fundamental self, raw and hurting and broken.

More than one pair of feet pounded the ground as they approached at a flat run.

Danu laid her lips to Gareth's forehead. "Seems you have a loyal following," she murmured.

Niall slid to a stop and went to one knee in front of the goddess. "Mother."

She pressed her forehead to Gareth's and spoke so softly he had to strain to hear. "What happens when a male phoenix claims a wife?"

"She loses her freedom," he responded.

"Think beyond their broken culture, favored child of mine."

Panic shrouded him. He couldn't think beyond what he knew Ashley abhorred.

"Tattoos," she prodded.

"A bond is created," he whispered hoarsely. "She can never harm her spouse."

"And her loss—has it hurt you?"

"I can't…" He shook so hard he thought his muscles would separate from his bones. "The air I breathe isn't breath without her."

"And if *you* were tattooed, you would be bound to her under the same geas. Would you risk that upon her return, the most harm you could do to her would be to hold on to her? Would you risk that she would seek her freedom in order to be happy?" Danu laid a finger over his lips. "Consider your answer. Once done, this cannot be undone. You will be tied to her forever, never able to take another to your bed. You will give up the chance to love any other in your lifetime."

"I would give anything," he choked out.

"Niall. Your machine." She held out a hand.

And then she set to work.

The needle's first bite into his neck was vicious. Gareth only asked her to work faster. He couldn't see the symbols she tattooed into his neck, only knew that the process was slow and that every second he spent waiting was a second Ashley spent in hell.

He lost himself to the buzzing sound and the burn of the process. Never did he flinch. Never did he offer to move. He bore the pain even as he willed his heart to still its insane rhythm. There was a chance Ashley might not want him. If that was the case, he would honor his pledge and let her go. It would be enough to know she lived. It would have to be.

The tattoo machine stopped, and the ensuing silence hit him like a runaway truck. He closed his eyes and curled his fingers around the edge of the shirt he had yet to let go of.

He didn't speak, merely waited. Surrounded as he was by those he called family, he had never been so entirely alone.

"Look at me, warrior."

He forced himself to meet Danu's gaze.

She caressed his face. "Call her home."

Resting his hands on either side of the tiny pile of covered ash, he laid his lips to the shirt and breathed, *"Mo chroí." My heart.*

"Again," Danu ordered.

"Mo chroí."

The goddess removed the shirt, exposing the ashes. She placed one of his hands directly on top of the pile and pressed the other over his heart. "Again," she said, laying her hands over his.

Power pulsed through Gareth. And then he began to burn.

Flames raced up his arms and circled his neck, tightening. He curled his fingers into the ashes and into his own chest, tipped his head to the heavens and shouted, *"Mo chroí!"*

Danu's touch disappeared.

Wild with unchecked panic, he looked around. Gods, had it gone wrong?

"Holy shit," Ethan gasped.

Beneath his hand, the ashes began to smolder. The first flame, tiny and seemingly insignificant, sprang from the edge, then another and another until the flames far exceeded their fuel.

An arm reached from the flames.

And Gareth reached back.

A torso formed. A lean leg. And then he was pulling her from the fires of rebirth.

Ashley fell into his arms, naked and shivering.

He held her as tight as his mangled body allowed.

"Told you...before," she gasped, weakly shoving at him. "Need to...ease...up."

"I canna seem tae let ye go," he said, voice ragged.

"Don't."

His heart stilled. Setting her back, he waved a hand blindly and was met with someone's leather jacket. "Look away," he ordered the Arcanum.

Shrugging into the jacket, she looked up at him and opened mouth to say something. Her mouth hung open as she took in the tattoo around his neck. "What did you do?"

He gripped her hand so hard he felt the bones grind. "Nothing I wouldna do a hundred, a thousand, times." Letting her go was the hardest thing he'd ever done, but he did it.

She wrapped the jacket tighter around her and stood, staring down at him. "You bound yourself to me for eternity. You can do me no harm without suffering debilitating pain."

"I willna ever hurt ye. Nor will I bind ye tae me unwilling, *mo chroí*. I promised Danu ye'd have yer choice and I'd see my word honored." He took a deep breath. "It's yer choice, Ashley Clement. Yer freedom, yer life— they're yers tae claim. As am I, if ye'd have me." He picked up the small package he'd dropped, the one he'd sent Kayden after. Unfolding the delicate paper, he took out a necklace and put it around her neck. "No matter yer choice, this belongs tae ye."

She looked down and stiffened. "How?" The question was so small.

The small locket contained an etching nearly identical to the one she'd lost in the fire—the image of her mother. Gareth had sent Kayden into the clans to retrieve anything he might that had belonged to the woman. His fellow assassin had come through. In spades.

"I'd move the heavens and traverse every realm in hell to see you happy, *a stór*."

Ashley let out a short sob and gripped the locket, pressing it to her chest. She shifted her weight and looked over her shoulder at the open field, tremors racking her. Then she faced him, a look of determination paired with sheer terror coloring her face. "I died for you, you gobshite. If you think you're rid of me with the threat of forever, you have another think coming."

He surged to his feet and, with his good arm, pulled her close.

She wrapped her arms around his neck and pulled his mouth to hers.

Their lips met, and she opened to him.

He kissed her as he'd never kissed another.

The smell of flannel and wood smoke flooded his senses as warmth suffused him, his element settling where it belonged.

Breaking the kiss, she leaned back and traced her fingers over his face. "I never thought to see you again." She traced his cheek with her fingertips. "That was when I truly died."

He pulled her close and said into her hair, "I love you, *mo chroí*."

Wrapping one arm around his waist, she slid her fingertips to the band around his neck. "Flames?"

He grinned. "Seems appropriate."

She laughed.

The sound passed through his chest and kick-started

the heart he thought he'd lost. "Tell me what I need to hear, Red."

She leaned back once more and framed his face with her hands. "I never thought I'd be able to tell you." Her chin quivered then stilled. "I love you, Gareth Brennan."

"By your customs, that would be 'husband' to you."

One corner of her mouth kicked up. "Not until I bear the same tattoo."

A wicked grin spread over his face. "Niall? Bring the ink."

* * * * *

MILLS & BOON®

n o c t u r n e™

AN EXHILARATING UNDERWORLD OF DARK DESIRES

A sneak peek at next month's titles...

In stores from 20th October 2016:

- **A Hunter Under the Mistletoe** – Addison Fox & Karen Whiddon

- **Immortal Billionaire** – Jane Godman

Just can't wait?
Buy our books online a month before they hit the shops!
www.millsandboon.co.uk

Also available as eBooks.